Rebel Skyforce

Book 2 of the Mad Tinker Chronicles

By J.S. Morin

ISBN: 1939233178
ISBN-13: 978-1-939233-17-2

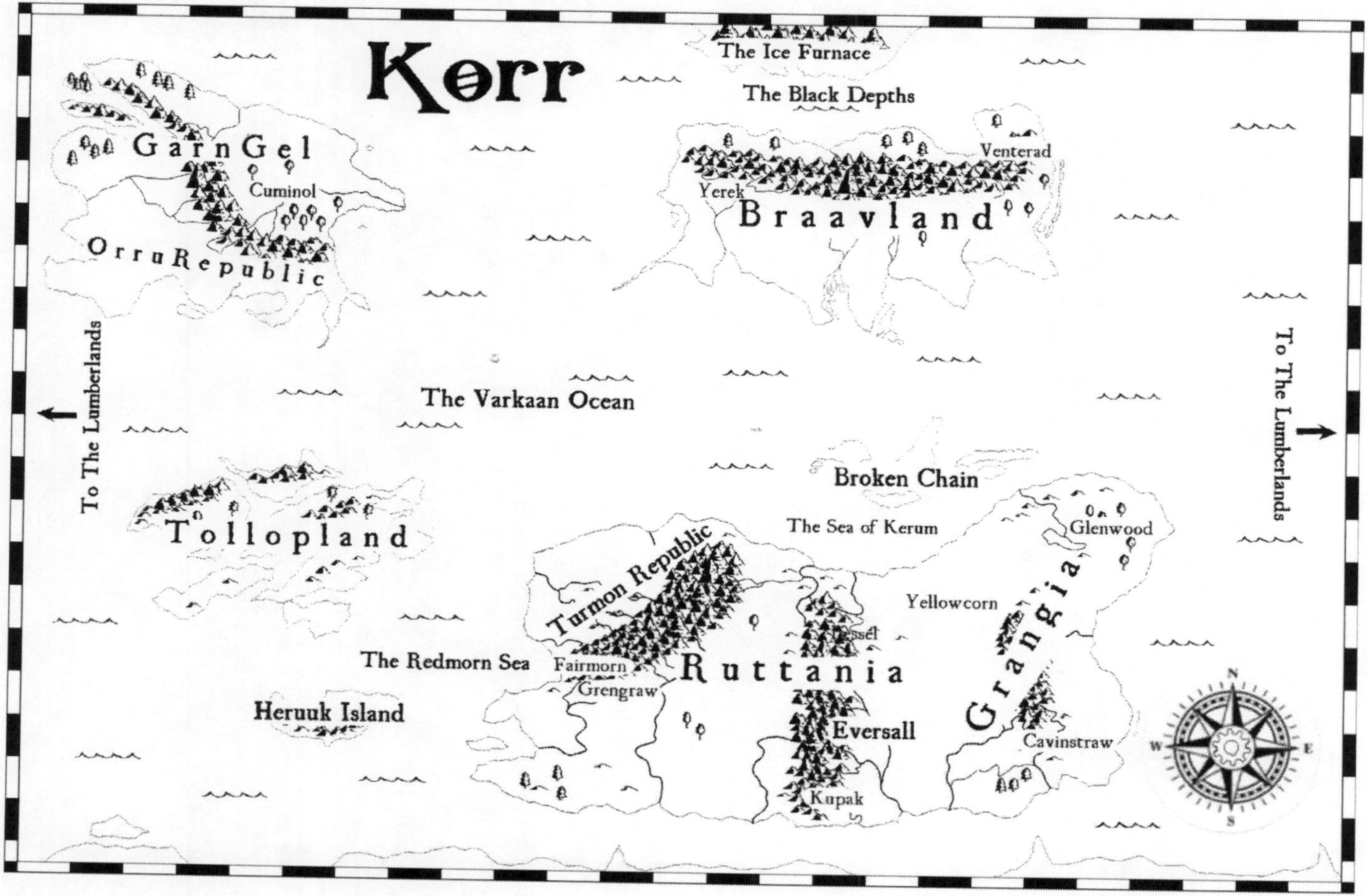
Korr
The Ice Furnace
The Black Depths
GarnGel
Cuminol
OrruRepublic
Yerek
Venterad
Braavland
To The Lumberlands
To The Lumberlands
The Varkaan Ocean
Broken Chain
Tollopland
The Sea of Kerum
Glenwood
Turmon Republic
Yellowcorn
Grangia
The Redmorn Sea
Fairmorn
Grengraw
Ruttania
Heruuk Island
Eversall
Cavinstraw
Kupak
N
E
S
W

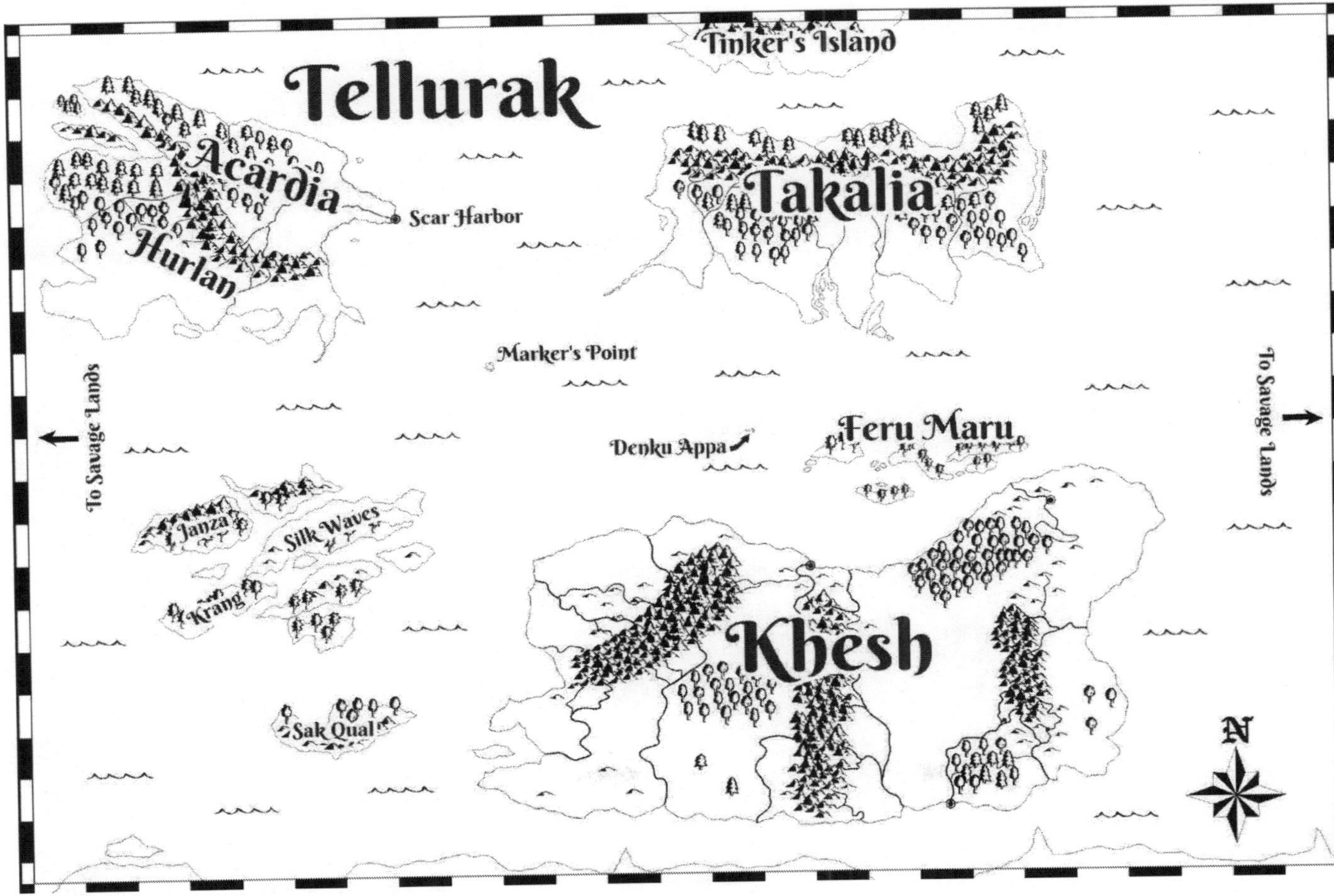
Tellurak
Tinker's Island
Acardia
Hurlan
Scar Harbor
Takalia
Marker's Point
To Savage Lands
To Savage Lands
Denku Appa
Feru Maru
Janza
Silk Waves
Krang
Khesh
Sak Qual
N

Chapter 1

"The second version of anything never looks quite like the first."
–tinkers' proverb

The throaty whirr of the liftwing's engines drowned out every sound but the wind. From a sky speckled with clouds, it descended like a hawk. At the control stick, the airship's human pilot felt his stomach lurch as it tried to remain above. He felt light in his seat, held to the aerial contraption by harness alone as he steered into a dive. A quick glance confirmed that the other liftwing was mirroring his attack, wobbling as its pilot fought to keep a fixed position a few dozen paces to the right and behind.

The ground spread out below like a map enlivened and rendered in miniature. Rectangular patches of discolored land were entire farms. The river appeared no bigger than a trickle of wash-water flowing toward a drain. Even through scratched and smudge-blurred goggles, it was wondrous to see. The thunderail tracks were a pencil sketch, the locomotive and cars too small to be a child's toy. The plume of white smoke that trailed behind was the only hint that the vehicle below was a real, working machine. As the liftwing descended, everything below appeared to grow by the second.

Rennon was one of the lucky few chosen to pilot the rebellion's stolen airships. He'd been a pilot for only a week, and it was his first live mission. He wondered what a little craft such as his could do to the behemoth, but he had his orders: *aim for the boiler.*

There is a common love among small boys for all things large and loud. The thunderail was the holy potentate of those admirable traits, and its disciples watched it in awe and cheered its arrivals and departures. The thought of attacking one was an affront worse than blasphemy. If doubt crept into Rennon's mind, it was shunted aside by a greater love that stays with boys into manhood: the love of destruction. It was not the wanton sort that defiled statues and painted slogans on store windows, but the sort that stared rapt at the dynamiting of a quarry wall, or watched scrap metal melt to slag in the smelters.

Rennon swooped in low, coming at the thunderail from the broadside. Whether the engineer and crew were aware of the danger, he couldn't tell—there was nothing to be done. Hemmed in by tracks and sluggish by comparison to the airships, the locomotive could do nothing but chug onward in the stoic hope that it could weather whatever was to come. Rennon lined up with the locomotive and reached for the gun lever.

The floorboard of the airship shook, numbing Rennon's feet. Out of view under the belly of the craft, a tri-barrel rotogun spun. Though the bullets flew too fast for him to see, he heard the staccato clanging as they riddled the locomotive. The airship approached at a startling speed, and the thunderail began to look the proper size at last. Rennon released the lever and pulled back the control stick just in time to avoid a collision. He burst through the cloud of smoke that trailed in the steam engine's wake, coughing as penance for neglecting to hold his breath.

A glance over his shoulder threatened to lose Rennon his lunch. Delane's airship made its strafing run parallel to Rennon's, as the locomotive had kept on moving. Rennon hoped he was far enough out of the way; those tri-barrel rotoguns were frighteningly powerful. He heard another off-key symphony of bullet strikes from the second airship's pass, the boiler explosion its crescendo. Rennon winced and ducked his head inside the cockpit.

A second glance back revealed a blossom of dust and smoke where the boiler had blown, but the thunderail kept on moving despite missing half its locomotive. Delane's airship wobbled as it cleared the coal cars. It hit the ground awkwardly in a barely controlled crash.

" Delane!" Rennon's shout was devoured by the wind.

He banked hard right, then hard left, coming around in a loop to make a second run at the thunderail. The boiler was gone, but momentum carried it onward. There were mission priorities, and Rennon knew that if the thunderail passed too far beyond the crash site, there might be no help to spare for Delane.

Rennon guided the airship in even lower than his first pass, and kept the locomotive's husk in his line of fire. He pulled the gun lever, and a string of bullets ripped into the locomotive's wheels. Rennon held the lever until the flow of bullets stopped, then jerked back the control stick just as the locomotive crashed to the rails below him.

The thunderail skidded along with a shriek of grating steel. After a few hundred yards, it dug its front end into the dirt and derailed, dragging the coal cars and the first handful of passenger cars along with it. The thunderail stopped.

Rennon looked up. Amid the clouds he saw two giant vacu-dirge airships that had been trailing him along the thunderail tracks. They were descending.

"Put us down halfway between the crash site and the thunderail wreck," Chipmunk ordered. The helmsman of the *Jennai* brought the ship about and turned the crank that let a trickle of air into the vacuum tank above them. The dirigible began to sink toward the earth.

The bridge of the *Jennai* was crowded with twinborn. They were her officers and agents. For weeks they had been rationing food and keeping the one-worlders from both sides working together in a semblance of harmony. For all their efforts at diplomacy, the full bellies promised by the raid would go farther in quelling the bickering and brawls that were growing commonplace on board.

Her father's ship, the *Cloudsmith*, steered toward the vicinity of the locomotive. They spoke largely by megaphone of late, but Erefan had gone along with her plan for a thunderail robbery. It was the fourth that Chipmunk had taken part in, but the first time she had eschewed stealth entirely. It struck her just then how much her circumstances had changed since her days in Eversall Deep, not so long ago. She and her friends had been mosquitoes to the kuduk then; now she was an escaped lioness.

Chipmunk leaned on the airship's railing, looking out the window. "Get me ten men," she said to no one in particular. It was a habit she was developing, since anything she said in a commanding tone of voice got done. As they neared the ground she tried to assess the condition of the downed airship. One of the wings had taken the brunt of the impact with the ground. It certainly would not fly, but looked reparable.

Chipmunk took up her crutch and hobbled to the stairwell. None of the rebels moved to aid her—they had all been chewed out for that offense enough times to have given up trying. At the bottom on the stairs, she encountered the throng of riflemen who would pour down the gangplanks as soon as they touched soil.

A few of the men acknowledged her, and she exchanged perfunctory well wishes. As she waited in the cramped quarters, she put a finger to the iron collar around her neck and poured aether into it without even noticing that she did so. It was among the habits that had crept up on her in the last few months. The one she most despised was her newfound shortness of temper. She couldn't place the reason for it, and like an engine that had a knock but still ran, she was forced to press on without fixing herself.

Thump.

The gentle jarring of the *Jennai's* touchdown made Chipmunk wince. Her swollen foot had been resting on the deck floor and even the light jostle sent a stabbing pain all the way up to her hip.

The side of the airship folded down and allowed the daylight in among the soldiers. They flocked toward it, rushing out to bask in the mild breeze with solid ground beneath their feet. Chipmunk let the crowd clear before she followed the ten men she'd chosen to accompany her to the crashed airship. The clamoring of so many humans had overwhelmed the sounds of the ship. As Chipmunk made her way down the gankplank, she could hear the air valves taking in air to keep the ship on ground as its ballast disembarked. It also let her hear the arrhythmic clopping of her crutch as she made her way down.

Erefan was the first person at the doors of the *Cloudsmith* when they hit the ground. He had his belt of tools at the ready and his mechanics lined up behind him, ready for plunder. It was a disconcerting thought, knowing that he was engaging in piracy of a sort, the kind of thing that his twin from Tellurak despised more than nearly any other crime.

This is different. This is war.

War was the ultimate excuse. It could justify practically anything. Many an old soldier would tell a tale so filled with mayhem and depravity that one would question the sort of monster that could even bear the retelling. Then the soldier would shrug, say "but it was war," and throw a pint of ale down his gullet. As if that made it all fine and good.

I want more. I want better. That's why the pirates do it, isn't it?

When the door in front of him opened, Erefan had a clear view of the locomotive from a hundred paces away. He threw his self-pitying thoughts back in the box where he habitually kept them and set about to get work done.

The locomotive was in a piteous state. The boiler had ruptured and blown most of the cabin away with it. The twisted iron and steel inside was beyond the use of salvage, given that Erefan had no smelter to reclaim it. The floor and what little was left of the wall was spattered and smeared with blood. Two bodies were inside—coalmen, by their uniforms, kuduks, by their beards. There was no sign of the engineer.

Erefan oversaw soldiers from both vacu-dirges as they flushed the passengers from the cars and herded them into clusters. Rifle shots rang out, demonstrating the folly of the few kuduk passengers who tried to run. The humans on board were taken aside, freemen in one group, slaves in another.

"Have them point out their owners. Up to each of them if they want to stay slaves or come with us," Erefan said. The thought that some might go back sickened him, but it was their right to choose their fate, and he would give them that freedom, even if they accepted no other. "The ones that come with us can decide what happens to their owners." There were several more shots fired in the wake of that decision.

With the kuduks and humans sorted out (and no daruu aboard at all), Erefan oversaw the inspection of their haul. Cadmus—his twin from the other world—had grown accustomed to it, but Erefan was still adjusting to the idea of having manpower at his disposal. He didn't have to open a single freight car himself. By the time he had finished his other duties, the cars had already been pried open and inventoried. Many of the men doing the inventorying were crude sorts—uneducated, uncouth, simple thinking—but they meant well. Reports on foodstuffs were both welcome and relatively accurate. Dry goods were catalogued in the most general of terms, and some of the goods were alien to the soldiers who had been plucked from Tellurak and brought to Korr in Erefan's service—he refused to admit that most of them considered his daughter to be in charge.

Erefan was in good spirits, and drew genuine amusement from the reports on the more technical cargoes. "Box o' twirly things" turned out to be a crate of piston springs. "Worst swill I ever done smelled" was over a hundred gallons of turpentine. "Bunch of green metal logs with things out the top" was how one of the men described a shipment of acetylene canisters, complete with the fittings and other paraphernalia required for welding. The last was the "worst moustache wax I ever tried," which was understandable considering the soldier was describing industrial lubricating grease commonly used for printing presses.

It was a strong haul. Other cars contained tools and replacement parts for various types of equipment. None of it was exactly what the airships needed, but there were things that could be adapted to serve, especially once he rigged up the welding equipment. Erefan prioritized what to take and what to leave behind. It hurt to have to leave good steel and parts for the kuduks to recover, but first and foremost, they needed all the food and potables that the thunderail had aboard.

As he swept through the dining car, he picked at platters that hadn't been upset in the derailment. He had enough sense to know which foods contained kuduk ingredients that his stomach couldn't handle—saltpeter, carbon black, iron oxide and the like—and managed to quell his hunger.

In over a decade as a slave, he had never had to go hungry. It wasn't until he became a free man again that he had to worry about keeping fed.

"Get the pilot out of there," Chipmunk ordered. She swallowed back a pang of guilt and hoped that it didn't show in her face. When she saw the crash, her first thought had been the recovery of the liftwing. It hadn't occurred to her that the pilot might have survived and needed attention. Fortunately for Delane, Chipmunk wasn't the only one doing the considering. Though she had been aboard the *Cloudsmith*, Sosha was running toward the crash site with her medical bag.

Chipmunk kept out of the way of the able-bodied men who extracted Delane from the wreck. She turned her attention to the condition of the liftwing itself. One of the propeller blades was half missing, and fabricating a replacement was iffy given their circumstances. There were irregular holes torn in the thin lightsteel outer covering of the craft, evidence that shrapnel from the boiler explosion had punctured it. She rested her crutch against the hull and grabbed the intact wing to swing herself underneath the wreck.

Please let it be intact.

The tri-barrel rotogun was a powder-and-cartridge device she had torn apart and rebuilt with the limited resources available on the *Jennai.* It was ugly and awkward, and she loved it all the more for being that way. It was hers. The one she found under the airship's belly was dinged and dislodged, but just whole enough that she knew she could repair it in time.

"How's it look?" Sosha's voice asked from behind her.

"Looks like I'll be able—"

"He's bleedin' bad and his legs both bent funny when we pulled him out," one of the mechanics answered. Chipmunk felt her face flush. She had forgotten about the pilot again the moment she started examining the ship.

Chipmunk slunk out from beneath the hull and retrieved her crutch. Her ribs hurt after the long trek from the *Jennai*, and her hand was tired from gripping the handle of the steel tubing she had fashioned for herself. She made a note to rebuild the crutch from lightsteel when she found enough of it.

"Get him clear of the wreck, then get moving hauling this back to the *Jennai*," Chipmunk ordered. Giving orders helped clear away the guilt of forgetting the pilot's plight. She had more to worry about than just one man.

"We'll need a stretcher to get him back to the ship," Sosha said, not bothering to look up. Chipmunk glanced at her work as Sosha field bandaged the gashes in the man's legs and torso.

"Can't we just carry him?" Chipmunk asked. She fished in her jacket and pulled out a pocketclock. "We haven't got much time."

"Not with his legs this bad."

"We don't have a stretcher."

"You're the tinker; tinker one up!" Sosha said. "And hurry up about it."

There were few among the crews of either ship that could get away with addressing her like that, but she knew Sosha was right. She couldn't let a small problem like a stretcher's lack of existence stop her from delivering one.

"Tobson, Swails, run to the thunderail, grab up curtains or blankets from the sleeper car—whatever you can find that's sturdy fabric and big enough to hold a grown man. Send another ten men over here, too—Eziel knows we have enough of *those* to spare. The rest of you, set that airship down. I need some of it."

Chipmunk took a hammer to one of the wing struts and bashed at it until one end came loose, then worked it back and forth until the other end broke free. She hobbled around to the far side and repeated it on the wing strut on that side as well. A group of soldiers from the thunderail looters arrived to help haul the airship away when she finished.

Tobson and Swails returned with a set of thick velvet drapes in hand, the brass rings from the curtain rod still jangling from the top end. It was better than Chipmunk had hoped. The two mechanics laid the curtain out flat on the turf.

"Good. Lay Delane on there. Line him up right there," she pointed with the end of her crutch. Chipmunk lowered herself down on the side opposite the brass rings and drew a pocket knife. She slit the velvet at intervals, large enough for the strut to feed through.

"Wrap it up and thread the strut through the whole thing."

She was glad she'd brought mechanics along instead of soldiers. Mechanics got how things worked without having to be beaten over the head. They knew how the stretcher would look in the end: like a trussed pig.

In the distance, she could see the cargo from the thunderail being ferried onto the *Jennai* and the *Cloudsmith*. The wrecked liftwing was already well on its way to the vacu-dirges by the time Delane was ready to be moved. There was little else for the rebels to do except get the wounded pilot and their general back aboard before they left. Chipmunk checked her pocketclock again.

"Damn! They'll have missed the thunderail at the next siding by now. Someone's bound to have sent a cable about it. It's just a matter of time before Ruttania's air force gets here."

Tobson muttered something to Sosha that Chipmunk couldn't make out as she limped along on her crutch, trying to keep pace. Sosha traded places with the burly mechanic and took one end of the stretcher.

"Sorry 'bout this, ma'am," Tobson apologized on his way over to Chipmunk.

"Sorry about what?"

Tobson lowered a shoulder to Chipmunk's midsection and hoisted her over his shoulder in one fluid motion. He took the crutch from her with his free hand. "Ain't got time to pretend you can walk, is all."

Chapter 2

"You may have a man bought and paid for, but you're as good as his once he realizes you can't get by without him." –Kezudkan Graniteson

The lift from the trolley levels opened into an above-ground cavern of steel and glass. Pale light filtered in from the smoggy skies outside, green in hue from chemicals in the air. Gantries and chain hoists spanned the aisles between machines, all whizzing, whirring, clanking, and humming according to their multitudinous functions. Kezudkan had seen such machines before, and judged the ones in this factory to be top of the line.

"Right this way sir," his escort said. The pudgy kuduk with the grease-stained hands toddled off ahead down the main corridor of the factory floor. Kezudkan grunted in reply and ambled along behind him. He carried his cane as a walking stick, tapping it gently on the floor in time with his stride. His joints had been better of late; the petrification of his knee was working itself loose with all the walking he'd done in the past month. He had never attributed his condition to idleness, but suspected otherwise now. He was still none too swift afoot.

"Hold up. I'm not the young daruu I once was," Kezudkan grumbled, not caring whether his escort heard him or not. He needed neither guide nor nanny. He continued at his own pace as the kuduk left him behind.

Kezudkan peered at the workers and their projects as he passed by. They were building valves and pumps, casings and enclosures, sprockets, chains, and gears. It was hard to find good gear-makers, so the latter spoke of a quality operation—but Kezudkan had already known that. He hadn't traveled all the way to Cavinstraw Deep in Grangia on a whim.

Near the center of the factory floor was an eye in the storm of flying metal. Desks and drafting tables clustered together with kuduk mechanics and tinkers toiling away. At the very center was a singular kuduk who looked up in calm anticipation at Kezudkan's arrival.

This kuduk stood to greet him, and Kezudkan got his first look at the "gear-made man." Ganrin Draksgollow stepped around his desk with one leg nothing more than a contraption of piston rods, gears, and springs from just above the knee. Kezudkan considered the troubles he'd had with his own joints and wondered which of them was the worse off. When Draksgollow held out a hand, it was of similar construction, with fine-made brightsteel fingers and sinewy cables threaded through. Kezudkan took the hand gingerly, knowing that the rock-like darru flesh of his own hand was liable to crush the delicate mechanism.

"Please to make your—oof, quite a grip you've got there, Mr. Draksgollow."

"Good of you to come, Mr. Graniteson," Draksgollow replied, a hint of a smile on his face. He was clean-shaven, which was unusual for kuduks, who regarded a lack of facial hair as a human look. Kezudkan suspected the reason when he noticed the irregular pattern of stubble—old burn wounds, he guessed. What marvelous stories the tinker must have had, to warrant such an array of injuries. Decorum alone prevented Kezudkan from asking.

"I hope my message was not too vague. I had no intention of misleading you—I just don't have any great faith in the vaunted discretion of the cable tappers."

Draksgollow shook his head. "Me neither. Bunch of gossiping whoresons, the lot of them. If we come to an arrangement, I'll give you a code book that I use for my business dealings."

Kezudkan raised a hairless brow. "Do all your clients have this code?"

"I have them printed up in pairs. I'll just mark your name on my copy."

"And the printer? What's to say he can't keep a spare copy?"

Draksgollow stared hard a moment. If he meant to cow Kezudkan, he'd need a better glare, for Kezudkan had been glared at quite professionally of late, and by kuduks better inclined to back up those glares. Draksgollow turned slightly and hollered over his shoulder. "Kep, get over here."

A moment later a mechanic arrived, hands stained black with ink, not grease as Kezudkan was tempted to believe at first glance. "Boss?"

"You make more than two of any of my code books?"

"Slugs, no! Who's sayin' I have? This old fossil?" Kep said.

"Mind your tongue, Kep, this is a new client—maybe. He's just being cautious. You can get back to work."

Kep had a better glare than Draksgollow, by Kezudkan's estimation, and used it on the daruu as he departed.

"Satisfied? Have a seat then."

Draksgollow gestured to a steel stool across the desk from him as he resumed his seat. Kezudkan eyed it with skepticism. Few kuduks took proper account of just how much a typical daruu weighed. Though already wider than kuduks by half a measure, their rocky compositions made daruu a good deal denser. Finally deciding that Draksgollow didn't look like the sort who took half measures in his tinkering, he settled his bulk onto the stool, gasping as the pressure was relieved from his old bones.

"So tell me a bit about this place? Why above ground for one? What experience do you have with complicated systems? Have you done work with runes? You must have had skeptics among your clients before; win me over," Kezudkan said.

"I've worked with daruu before, and you're a bit of a clean pump, aren't you?" Draksgollow said. Kezudkan smirked. "Most of them would have bored me halfway to madness with their lineage and titles by now—"

"Oh, if you'd like, I could—"

Draksgollow held up a hand—the fleshy one. "No, no. I'm not complaining. To answer your questions, we built topside for the light. My machines guzzle spark like a human drunkard. We've got gas for night work and bad weather, but any spark I've got goes into the machines."

"Why not purchase another dynamo? It looks like you've got plenty of work; you must be able to afford it." It wasn't always a polite topic, but Kezudkan needed a sense of the kuduk's financial situation. He needed someone who could afford to float a bit of risk.

"If I had another dynamo, I'd use up the spark putting in more machines. More profit in that than in buying spark lights when I've got a perfectly good system running."

"Fair enough. Can't argue with higher profits."

"As for the rest, I've got the best factory for custom jobs you're likely to find. I've built airship parts here, and not just those ridiculous vacu-dirges you Ruttanians seem so fond of."

Kezudkan held up his palms. "Don't look at me. It's a kuduk decision which airships to purchase."

"Anyway, those liftwing airships are finicky. Shape the wing or prop wrong, they fall out of the sky. That's why the Grangian aerial command buys from me: I don't build anything half-arsed. They get what they put on vellum."

"Runes?"

"Didn't I just say I worked on airships? I don't care how light you think you can make one, no liftwing can get airborne with a load of coal on board, or a steamer big enough to get the prop up to speed. So yeah, we do runes here."

"Yes, but do you call in for someone to empower them, or do you have—"

"Eleven humans who can manipulate runes. Mr. Graniteson, I don't mind questions, but you're starting to sound like you don't have confidence in my operation here."

"If you're looking for an apology—"

"I'm simply looking for an explanation, Mr. Graniteson."

"Not here," Kezudkan replied. "Somewhere private."

The lower levels of the factory were more suited to Kezudkan's taste. The walls might have been buttressed with steel beams, but rough cut stone was all around. The tunnels and caverns had been kuduk carved, and appeared passably safe. There were gas lamps throughout, leaving the air with a heavy odor that brought back memories of a youth before the spark had spread like a plague and made the lights all sterile, with an annoying hum.

Draksgollow chased a handful of workers out of a tiny chemical etching room that had tables for Kezudkan to lay out his plans. As Draksgollow tidied up the etching plates and bottles of acids, Kezudkan picked up one of the pieces and examined the runes. They were commonplace workmanship, lacking the style and purposefulness of runework chiseled by hand. His eyes wandered the patterns, following the logic of the designer.

"These getting ready to be rolled flat?" Kezudkan asked, brandishing the piece.

Draksgollow grabbed a work log and scanned it. "How'd you—well, of course one of *your* kind would be able to read them. They're for a new airship. They need the lightsteel to be hair-thin. Runes will get flattened out in the rolling process, then they'll get new ones to strengthen the material after it's formed."

Kezudkan nodded absently and fished inside his coat pockets. He withdrew a folded wad of papers and opened them in the spot Draksgollow had cleared. They were hand drawn in a tidy, efficient script, but what drew Draksgollow's eye were the diagrams. Kezudkan smiled as he watched the kuduk tinker's eyes widen as he browsed the documents.

"What is all this?" Draksgollow asked.

"The key to our fortunes. Unlimited wealth and power."

"Cut the rat-baiting. What does it do?"

Kezudkan leaned in close. "What would you say if I told you there were other worlds besides Korr?" he asked.

The tinker's face twisted into a scowl. "I'd say I've wasted my morning. Good day to you, Mr. Graniteson. Find someone else to buy your bunk."

Draksgollow moved toward the door, but Kezudkan's cane swung up and barred his path. The tinker tried to push past, but the cane barely budged. Old though the daruu was, the strength of the stone still resided in his muscles. He lacked what little grace and agility he had as a younger man, but holding his ground was no trouble at all. Kezudkan stepped in front of Draksgollow, interposing himself between the tinker and the rest of his factory.

"Not so fast, Mr. Draksgollow. Your cable said you'd be willing to hear me out, and you've barely heard the first words I've uttered."

"I've got near to a hundred men—"

"And all I'd need to do would be to grab hold of you and squeeze," Kezudkan countered. "But let this not devolve into childish threats. You said you'd listen and I intend to hold you to that promise. If I don't convince you, then I'll be on my way and waste no more of your time or mine. I came to you because I heard you were the best, not the only."

"So what, you want me to believe that there are other worlds out there among the stars? I've heard the astronomers' guild's nonsense before. Even if there are, I don't see that airships are quite ready to get there yet."

"I've seen them."

"Seen what? Other worlds? What sort of telescopes are those nutters building these days?"

"I've seen another word. Through *this*." Kezudkan jabbed a finger at the papers spread on the desk. There, sketched in pencil, was a rendering of an archway, studded with bulbs and coils, webbed with wires. Draksgollow leaned over and looked to the page, then up to Kezudkan's eyes, as if searching to see whether there was any madness in them.

"You built one?"

"You must have heard the rumors from Eversall. That little debacle was *my* tinker slave! He built the first one and destroyed it. Somehow he must have brought allies from another world, because there were no hidden tunnels to my home, as they claimed. You kuduks just can't understand; I'd have *known* if the stone around my estate was breached."

Kezudkan paused a moment to catch his breath and regain the dignity he had entered with. Draksgollow leafed through the papers on the desk. "This doesn't look like enough to build much of anything. And this writing is nonsense."

"It is, and it isn't. These are copies of copies. I have a whole book that goes into how to build and use it. If you and I come to an agreement, I can supply all that you need, including my notes on the little I have gathered of the text. But let me assure you: there *is* enough there to build one and make it work."

Draksgollow shook his head, as if to clear it. "Wait now. What good is this machine? What's on these other worlds that's worth the trouble? That thing could take weeks to build."

Kezudkan raised a brow. He had expected even longer than that. When he didn't answer immediately, Draksgollow pressed on.

"Your message said a contingent build, so this thing has to earn its keep and then some. How much are the astronomers willing to pay for something like this?"

"Oh, who cares about them?" Kezudkan replied. "There are at least two worlds out there identical to this one, and there are ore veins ripe for the picking with no quibbles over claims and rights, no guessing, no geologists to hire. Gold, silver, platinum, diamonds, rubies, sapphires, all waiting for coordinates and a strong arm with a pick.

"I've seen it. The machine can take us there."

Draksgollow stared for a moment, eyes flitting about. Kezudkan had seen the same from Erefan on occasion when he was puzzling something out in his head. It must have been a tinkers' trait.

"Deal."

Chapter 3

"Some folks like to take shortcuts through other people's hard work. I have no sympathy when they get what's coming to them." -Cadmus Errol

The foothills of central Khesh were always cooler than the lowlands. The Dragon Fang Mountains gave up their winters slowly, and the pervasive chill of the glaciers seeped into the surrounding hills. Even once Madlin Errol and her companions found themselves north of the year-round ice, the rolling hills continued to present a favorable road over venturing into more heavily settled lands.

She had started her journey with a company of fifty men, armed with rifles. She returned from her business in the southern half of Khesh with only five plus her two new companions. Jamile was along as well, of course, but Madlin had ceased counting her some time ago. She had become like a puppy or a younger sibling—though Jamile was two years Madlin's elder, her presence was expected.

Some part of Madlin believed that she was safer with the two Veydran twinborn for her protectors than she had been with fifty one-worlder riflemen. The rest of her worried that the two were a greater danger than anything that might threaten from the road.

Madlin rode with Dan in one of the middle wagons. Throughout the trip they had kept up a mutual pestering of one another. The boy warlock was every bit the brash adolescent when he wasn't reminding her that he could reduce them all to ash if he sneezed too hard.

"I keep telling you, you're not ready."

Madlin gritted her teeth. "You last told me that two days ago, and I've been practicing. I'm ready for more."

Dan put a hand to his forehead and rubbed his eyes. "Let me see if I can explain this better. Imagine I'm a butcher's boy, or a stable-mucker, anything but a tinker."

"A warlock?"

Dan gave her a condescending frown, but continued on. "Fine, a warlock. Imagine I've been tinkering on the side with mousetraps; good enough that I've even caught a mouse or two. Now, show me how to make a gun like yours."

Madlin pulled her pistol from its holster and held it up between her and Dan. "There's no way you could make this. This is worlds harder than rune-carving."

"Piss off! You're not talking about rune carving; you want to cast spells," Dan said. "That's harder than your steel-whittling."

"How hard can it be, if a kid your age can do it?" Madlin clamped her mouth shut. She hadn't meant for it to come out like that.

Dan glared at her, unblinking, unflinching. The only movement in his face was the slight flaring of his nostrils as he breathed. "Plenty," he answered at length.

"Aether is dangerous," said Dan. He turned and looked off toward the Dragon Fangs. "Those words and gestures form a pattern in your mind as you focus on them." Dan held out a hand, palm upraised, and a shimmering sphere appeared above it. "With practice you can form the same patterns entirely in your head. Form them incorrectly and something unintended will happen." The sphere exploded, and Madlin yelped, diving for cover behind a sack of pumpernickel loaves. When she felt no pain, heard no aftermath, Madlin looked up to find Dan smirking at her.

"That wasn't funny," Madlin said. She sat up and brushed her jacket clean of burlap strands.

"Magic's not a funny business, but that doesn't mean you can't laugh about it. My uncle Rashan killed a lot of people with his magic, but he still jested with spells."

"I just want to find a way to get my collar off."

"Yeah, I guess that's got to be pretty annoying," Dan said flippantly. "Can't you just tinker it off? Seems easier than asking me how to magic it off."

"If I break the runes, the spikes on the inside will reappear and cut my head off. With the runes intact, I can't so much as scratch it. I don't know any way to 'tinker' around that. I need some sort of magic. Make it bigger so it can fit over my head. Make my skin hard as diamond. Isn't there anything that can do that?"

Dan nodded. "Sure, you'd just kill yourself trying it."

Madlin let out a beleaguered sigh and collapsed back into the wagon. She looked up into the canvas ceiling above and wondered what she could say to convince Dan to teach her.

"I've heard that heat makes metal expand," Dan offered. "Can't you get to a forge and just heat it up enough to pull it off?"

And melt the thing in the process? I'd burn to death before it got halfway hot enough. She didn't bother voicing her objection. She gave up and listened to the clop of horse hooves and turning wagon wheels as they meandered toward civilization.

"That kid's as much a genius as he is an idiot," Tanner said. He kept his voice low, mindful that eavesdropping from wagon to wagon worked both ways.

"What do you mean?" Jamile asked. She twisted in her seat, up front with Tanner as he drove.

"You'd think a boy that age would be all twistin' himself up in knots to get on a girl's good side, 'stead of riling her every chance he gets."

Jamile laughed. "You haven't been around a lot of boys then, I imagine."

"Naw, I guess not. Not since I was that age myself."

"I used to live in a sanctuary overrun with children of all ages. Dan's unusual in a lot of ways, but he makes a mule of himself the second he talks to a girl, same as any other. At least he tries to be the know-it-all, rather than beating up some poor defenseless lad to prove he's a man."

Tanner's eyes widened and he gave an exaggerated shudder. "Wouldn't want to be around for that. I could end up the poor defenseless lad, if he was lookin' to knock someone around."

Jamile smiled and bumped a playful shoulder into Tanner's. "Oh, it's all bluster."

"Don't get me wrong, kid's got nerves of stone, but he's got a temper, too."

"He seems to respect you, at least," Jamile said.

Tanner chuckled and shook his head. "He needs me 'til he's old enough that fellas will take him seriously by himself. He knows he can't go around buying ships and hiring coinblades looking like ... well, looking his age. Ain't like he's some old nutter of a sorcerer going round lookin' like a kid, he's just a smart kid is all."

"So what, he turns sixteen or eighteen and burns you up like a cinder?" Jamile asked lightly, still smiling from her earlier amusement. Tanner glanced over at her. Jamile always seemed to be smiling or joking. She had warmed as quickly as the weather as they'd ventured north, but Tanner couldn't get a read on her. Madlin was plain enough to judge: hotheaded, stubborn, demanding—a spoiled rich girl who was willing to dirty her hands a bit, but still a child at heart. Jamile seemed a decade older: composed, mature, patient. She carried herself like a woman too, unlike her friend.

"What is it?" Jamile asked, catching his eyes lingering on her.

Tanner blinked and looked away. He returned his attention to the road. "Nothin'. Sorry. Just don't need remindin' that I'm a dead man if he ever gets drunk and mad and I say somethin' that crosses his mind wrong."

"He wouldn't ..." Jamile said. Tanner raised an eyebrow. "Would he?"

"I know he don't look like much, but that kid's got nerves like a headsman. They got to him young; killin' don't even rile him. I killed plenty in my time, and I never sleep right the night after. Usually it's me or the other guy, and I can't help wonderin' when it'll be me on the wrong end."

"A lot of children put on a brave face, but they still get nightmares about things like that."

"Oh yeah?" Tanner asked. "How often do our kind get nightmares?"

Jamile straightened, and Tanner knew he'd made his point. Twinborn saw another world instead of dreaming; Jamile and Madlin saw the world of Korr, while Dan and Tanner split their time with Veydrus. There was no place for nightmares.

"Well, surely it must still bother him," Jamile protested.

"He's a warlock, sweet-thing," Tanner said, shaking his head. "Being from that other world of yours, you don't know the half of what that means."

Madlin woke with a start when an elbow bumped her cheek. It was a nap she hadn't intended to take. The darkness had passed in an instant, since Chipmunk was asleep in Korr; she had no awareness of either world. Her first look was to the sky outside, to judge how long she'd slumbered. In the process she noticed Dan snoring next to her. His had been the elbow that jostled her awake.

"Get off me, you oaf," Madlin said as she shoved him onto his side and freed herself from bodily contact with the boy. Dan's snoring continued.

It was late afternoon, with a reddened sky and long shadows bidding welcome to sunset. The monotonous clop of hooves and the gentle roll of the wagon threatened to lull her back to sleep, but she resisted the temptation.

Rummaging in the wagon's supplies, she found a meal of salted pork strips and some ale to wash it down. Madlin watched the young warlock's face while she ate, wondering at the mischief he was undoubtedly up to in Veydrus, awake in the middle of the night. There was no other explanation for him sleeping through her rough handling.

Shortly before sundown, the lead wagon stopped. The driver of hers followed their lead, as did the two wagons behind them.

"What's going on?" Madlin asked. It was her place to call the halt of a day's travel. All of them but Tanner and Dan were in her employ.

"Couldn't say, Miss Errol," the driver replied. "Want me to head up and ask?"

"No, you stay here. Keep your rifle handy."

Madlin hopped down and checked that her pistol was loose in its holster. A yawn snuck up on her unbidden, and she muffled it with the back of her non-shooting hand. As she walked to the lead wagon, she idly touched her neck where a collar would have been if she were Chipmunk. *Stop that*, she chided herself.

The caravan had arrived at a low stone bridge spanning a stream. There were guard houses on either side, and a chain struck across the span, barring their way. An official in a red coat with gold buttons was arguing with Tanner as Jamile looked on.

"That's not going to happen," Tanner said, waving his hands in front of him. Madlin was comforted to see that he didn't have a weapon in hand. The official appeared to be unarmed.

"I'm afraid I must insist, sir," the official replied. The man moved to step around Tanner, but Tanner sidestepped and interposed himself between the official and the wagons.

"Can't let you."

"Tanner," Madlin called out as she approached. "Your Kheshi's gotten a lot better of late, but you should let me handle this."

"Are these your wagons, lady?" the official asked.

Madlin looked the man over. He was paunchy and his straggly moustache had streaks of grey in it: a bureaucrat, not a guardsman.

"They are. What's the trouble?"

"Lady Emskarl insists that all goods brought into her lands be inspected," the official replied.

"And I told him it was none of his rotten business," Tanner said.

"Is there any kind of toll?" Madlin asked, ignoring Tanner.

"It depends on the cargo you carry. Consider it the cost of protecting your valuables, while you enjoy Lady Emskarl's protection."

Madlin surveyed the guard posts and the far bank of the stream. "I don't see her around here," Madlin said without returning her attention to the official. "When will she be joining us? We've got room in the wagons, of course. Hope she likes salted pork, because we've got it by the—"

"Lady Emskarl is *not* going to be joining your sorry little caravan," the official replied. Madlin knew even before she looked back that his face was reddening. "These lands are her protectorate, and while traveling them, you are subject to her laws and beneficiary of her protections."

"We don't need any protection. In fact, seems like we'll be protecting a little patch of land within a rifle's range everywhere we go. Maybe *she* oughtta be paying *us* for protection," Madlin watched the official's face as it turned a shade darker. Pureblood Kheshis were so obvious in anger, their pale skin striking a stark contrast when flush. Madlin scrunched her nose and shook her head. "Naw, we can just call it even I think. We'll take care of our own, and not trouble Lady Enkarl—"

"Lady Emskarl!"

"—her ladyship's troops while we cross."

Madlin heard the whisper behind her before she heard the approach of steps. "Hey, let her take care of this." It was Tanner's voice, but the footsteps weren't.

"Could you two kindly piss off and let ... me sleep in peace?" Dan drawled around a yawn. He shuffled past Madlin and stopped before the Kheshi official, rubbing the sleep from his eyes. "And who's this ape?"

"Guards!" the official yelled over his shoulder. Madlin watched the last shred of his patience as it crumbled between her jibes and Dan's thoughtless insult. She had been intent to bully the man, intimidate him enough that he would accept their bribe rather than risk his life to do his job. Dan's push had been too much.

Ten men in red uniforms poured from the guard houses with muskets in hand and short swords sheathed at their hips. Behind her, Madlin heard the sound of rifle bolts being thrown. They'd ejected an unspent cartridge apiece, Madlin knew, but it told her they were there behind her, ready to confront the Kheshis.

"Lay down your arms and surrender yourselves to the authority of Lady Emskarl," the official said as his men spread out. Madlin felt a cool wind cut through her, refreshing but out of place amid the languid warmth that had settled over the countryside. "You will step aside and allow—"

Madlin felt a shockwave, though it passed through her without harm. The Kheshi soldiers' muskets were jerked upward; most panicked and fired wildly into the sunset sky. Madlin's own men reacted and fired, though the effect was difficult to notice. From Dan's outstretched hand, black lightning crackled and leapt, lashing out to strike each of the Kheshis in turn. In less than the time it took for Madlin to release the breath that had caught in her throat, they all lay dead. All but the unarmed official.

Dan walked over to the man as the bodies lifted into the air and drifted toward the stream. The official backed away, but stopped with a jolt, as if he had struck a solid wall, though nothing was visible behind him. Madlin watched wide eyed, unwilling to blink.

"What part of 'piss off' was so hard to understand?" Dan asked, his face inches from the Kheshi's. Madlin could see the sweat bead on the man's face. The reddish hue had drained completely. The man stammered silently, his lips trying and failing to form words. He flinched and began shuddering when a chorus of splashes accompanied the bodies of his men plunging into the shallow waters of the stream.

"Quit scaring the poor bastard," Tanner said from behind her. Madlin couldn't tear her attention away from Dan and the Kheshi official to bother to look back.

Dan's head titled back. Madlin couldn't see his eyes, but she'd seen the expression on Dan's face often enough to envision them rolling. His shoulders rose and fell in a sigh. "Fine."

The Kheshi flew aside as if fired from a cannon, hitting the stream with a splash that sent water cascading over the far bank. He hadn't yelped or cried out, likely dead from a snapped neck the instant he was launched.

The chain across the bridge snapped and fell aside. "Road's clear," Dan announced as he walked back to the wagon. He yawned and stretched, his arms reaching out, fists clenching and unclenching. "And gut me, I'm wide awake now."

Madlin didn't sleep well that night, or at least, she lay awake a long while before sleep caught up with her. Jamile breathed nasally beside her, something in the northern air disagreeing with her constitution. It was a distraction—some small, constant worry for her friend's health that was far from serious enough to dwell on. Madlin listened to each catch in her breath, the different sounds she made as she wheezed. But Jamile slept.

How can she just sleep after watching that? Madlin wished she knew the trick, because she couldn't get the image from her eyes, even by closing them—especially by closing them.

Tanner had shrugged aside the incident, obviously inured to Dan's outbursts of violence. Jamile hadn't wanted to talk about it. The Errol Company guards had gossiped about it with her, none of them offering any reassurance at all. Madlin would have been neither surprised nor reproachful if any of them quit their jobs rather than stay with the caravan. To his credit, Dan had offered to share what he had pilfered of the Kheshis' dinner, but no one else was of a mind to share the spoils of his murders.

Madlin tried to picture the Kheshis with kuduk beards, and when finally she had the image fixed firmly in her mind, she asked herself: *Could I have done it?*

She meant Chipmunk, and she had to admit: *Yes.*

Chapter 4

"Lift is achieved by offsetting mass with a displaced volume that is lighter than air." –Introductory Flight, by Z.K. Orelan

The *Jennai* led the way over the plains of northern Ruttania with the *Cloudsmith* following in her wake. Vacuum pumps aboard both vessels were working constantly, straining to keep air out of the lift chambers that kept them buoyant. Dry, barren farmland sped by beneath them, less than one hundred feet below.

Chipmunk stood at the forward-facing windows of the bridge, watching with growing alarm as they drew closer to the ground by the hour. "We can't keep this up," she muttered. As much as they'd tried to balance the load from newfound supplies, their thunderail heist had put both airships overweight.

"You said yourself we have to get well away before we set down," Captain Bosley replied, though Chipmunk hadn't meant her comment for his ears. "I can turn us for the mountains anytime you like."

"I'm not even sure we have the lift to navigate the foothills anymore." Chipmunk held onto the railing and hobbled over to the starboard side of the bridge. The Homespires loomed to the east, a taunting warren of hiding places and kuduk settlements. A wrong turn around a peak could put them in artillery range of an aerodrome's defenses. All that was moot though, as far as Chipmunk was concerned, until they had the lift to keep safe amid the mountain range.

"There are cities all along the coast," Bosley reminded her. "If we don't get above cloud level, we're sure to get spotted on this course.

Her options were unpalatable. All the lift the ships needed was readily available; they just needed to abandon their hard-won supplies and strand their refugees. Chipmunk couldn't bring herself to give it serious consideration. If they set down, the craftsmen aboard both vessels could work on placing levitation runes on the airships, and Sosha and Chipmunk could empower them, supplementing the vacuum with all the lift they needed. It was the plan she preferred, but setting down in the open was an invitation to ambush should anyone spot them. They could also plot the course least likely to get them discovered as they crossed the shoreline, then put themselves out over the Sea of Kerum and find some refuge amid the islands of the Broken Chain. It seemed like the riskiest option, but only if they plotted wrong or were unlucky.

Chipmunk lost track of time as she mused, turning the options over one by one. She changed her mind each time some downside of her current favorite came to the fore of her thoughts. Problems only exist until a solution presents itself, her father had taught her. She contemplated taking a nap so that she could have

Madlin send word to her father via Jamile and Sosha. All the twinborn her father had gathered were spread between the crews of the two airships. Surely someone among them could formulate a better plan.

All the twinborn in one place.

For the first time, Chipmunk wondered whether they were taking too great a gamble. All the rebellion's twinborn in one place meant an unlucky encounter with a Ruttanian airship patrol could be the end of them. And they weren't even doing anything beyond acting as officers and taking their part in the fighting. Helpful, perhaps, but nothing that one-worlders couldn't handle.

"Signal the *Cloudsmith* to land. I have a plan."

The cargo hold of the *Jennai* was packed with Korrish twinborn from both vessels. Even with the cargo bay ramp down and compartment open to the air, the press of bodies made it oppressively hot. A table had been set up, and Chipmunk brought twinborn by the pair to hand out assignments.

"Leda and Raimy, you make your way to Juudun Sky. Should be about two days on foot. Take whatever supplies you need." The pair nodded their understanding and Chipmunk gave them a salute, which they returned. She'd adopted the fist-to-temple gesture used by the Takalish army in Tellurak as the official salute among the rebels. They'd never had one before, and she thought it was high time that they started acting like an army if they were going to be functioning as one.

"And remember," she called after them, "your twins aren't to leave Tinker's Island until further notice. Understood?" Leda and Raimy both turned and saluted again. That was the key: pairs. Just as she could relay information ship-to-ship via Madlin and Jamile, so could the whole of the rebellion keep in constant contact via other pairs of twinborn.

"How many more spies and infiltrators do you plan on sending out?" Erefan asked from the far side of the table. The Mad Tinker of Korr had his arms crossed and a neutral expression plastered over whatever thoughts he was keeping to himself.

"Another few pairs. Why?"

"They're not trained for this sort of thing," Erefan replied.

Chipmunk winced. It was a subject she'd hoped to keep quiet. There was no delusion among her troops, but it helped morale to treat them as if they were ready for anything. "Who's trained for any of this? We're all putting up our best effort."

Chipmunk leaned on her crutch and hopped around the side of the table. "Kinmi and Suben, you two will be—"

"Excuse me, ma'am," Kinmi said, "but could I get paired up with Syr?" Chipmunk cast a suspicious eye toward Kinmi, a cobbler's assistant who'd proven to be handy with mechanic's tools. Apparently, he'd also proven to be handy with the ladies.

"You talk to her about this?" Chipmunk asked. Kinmi nodded. "You gonna be able to keep your hands off each other long enough to do your job?" Kinmi grinned and couldn't meet Chipmunk's eyes, but nodded. "Fine. You'll pose as married freemen. Just keep a high neckline on any dress she wears until the calluses from her collar fade."

"Yes ma'am," Kinmi replied.

Chipmunk leaned over the map to point out the location of Kinmi and Syr's assignment. In doing so, she put her weight on her bad foot and grimaced in pain. Grunted words escaped through her clenched teeth; she hoped they hadn't been clear enough for anyone to hear—especially her father. Though she was a general, it seemed uncouth to use that sort of language in her father's presence. He had taught her better words than those.

"What was that?" Erefan asked.

"Nothing. I just said we were lucky to have—"

"Not that! It's that foot still, isn't' it? Sosha mentioned you were favoring it badly back at the thunderail."

"It's getting better. I was just careless and put my whole weight on it."

Erefan's eyes scanned her. Chipmunk felt like a misbehaving bit of clockwork that he was trying to troubleshoot. "I'll send Sosha over to have a look at it."

"No, it's fine."

Erefan walked from the cargo hold, holding his hands up in mock surrender.

In the privacy of her own cabin, Chipmunk fumed. She lay on her bed, bootless and with her foot propped on a pile of pillows. The overhead light was enough to read by, but hardly kept the whole of the room well lit; Chipmunk preferred the curtains drawn. Even with her cabin a story up from ground level while they were landbound, she feared that surreptitious looks might come through the cabin window out of curiosity mixed with ingenuity.

"I told him it was fine," Chipmunk protested as Sosha unwound the bandage from her left foot.

"And you've told me that three times before when I've found stitches ripped out. This foot is never going to heal if you don't keep off it. I can only imagine the scar that—"

Chipmunk had been intent not to look while Sosha worked, but she propped herself up on her elbows to find out what had caused Sosha to break off midsentence. "Scar that will what?"

Sosha didn't answer, but instead stood and drew open the little curtain covering the cabin window. "I need better light." Chipmunk shielded her eyes against the afternoon glare that came in through the west-facing glass.

"What's wrong? Did I tear another stitch?"

Sosha shook her head. "Not this time," she replied somberly.

"Good, wrap it back up and I'll get back to the bridge. And you don't have to sound so glum about being wrong."

Chipmunk tried to push herself up to a seated position, but Sosha's hand forced her back down. "The wound's gone septic."

"What? No." Chipmunk brushed aside Sosha's hand and sat up. She grabbed her ankle and twisted the injured foot around until she could see the bottom. The stitches were barely visible amid the swollen, discolored flesh. "But you washed it every time. That's supposed to stop infections."

"Every time you split it open, grime can get in there. I kept it clean as best I could, but you kept reinjuring it." Sosha's voice was small, apologetic. She couldn't look Chipmunk in the eye.

"Well, cut it open, lance it, whatever you need to get it cleaned out properly this time," Chipmunk said. "Just get it over with."

"It's not that simple, Rynn. Look at your ankle."

Chipmunk shifted her grip where she had taken her ankle in hand. Darkened lines stood out against her pale skin, like rivers on a map. She pulled her hands away and wiped them on her pants.

"It's on the inside," Sosha said. "The blackened blood is showing through the skin."

"What do you have to do?"

"I think you know."

Chipmunk shook her head. "No. No, you can't cut my foot off." She pushed herself back against the wall of her cabin, as far from Sosha as she could get, swinging her leg over the far side of the bed. She was only a half pace away.

"You think I *want* to?" Sosha asked. "Rynn, you're only going to get worse. This isn't a joke; if it lingers, it'll kill you."

"There's got to be another way," Chipmunk muttered, looking out the window. She turned to Sosha. "You're not doing anything until I talk to Dan."

"I don't think you're being rational, Rynn. He's already said he won't teach us spells."

"Maybe I can burn the taint out with aether. Maybe his world knows a medicine for it. I'm not giving up without at least asking him."

The room lurched just then. A shuddering of the walls and floor that had been absent during their time on the ground had resumed: the sound of the pumps and propellers. The *Jennai* was taking off.

"Poo!" Sosha swore daintily. "They're supposed to have waited for me. The *Cloudsmith* doesn't have anyone—"

"They're not worrying about the runes right now. We wouldn't be lifting if we hadn't been spotted. I left orders."

Chipmunk swung her perilously wounded foot over to Sosha. "Wrap it, quickly."

"You're not in any condition to go up there."

"None of us are going to be in any condition if we get killed."

Chipmunk arrived on the bridge with Sosha acting as her crutch. Outside the ship, rifles fired at assailants she could only guess about.

"Captain Bosley, report!" Chipmunk pushed past the captain and attending officers, and collapsed against the forward railing just in time to see a trio of liftwing airships buzz past. They were of similar design to the ones the rebellion had captured for their use, but they had the original repeater rifles still attached.

"We've got eight of them on us," Bosley replied smartly, like the sea captain his twin was in Tellurak. "We shot down a ninth."

"Have we launched our own yet?" Chipmunk looked out the window to get a sense of the battlefield. This was the first time they'd been caught out in open skies; none of them had battled in the air before. The enemy crafts looked like a scattered flock of birds, and indeed some of the distant figures she spotted might have *been* birds for all she knew. She drew her pistol and used the optics to get a better view.

"No ma'am," Bosley replied. "Seemed like we'd be sending Rennon to his death, setting the dogs on him nine-to-one."

Chipmunk nodded. "Good. You were right to keep him in. Those are better suited to hitting slow-moving targets."

"Like us."

"Like us," Chipmunk agreed. "Any damage to the vacuum tanks?"

"Hard to say. Pump gauges say we're evacuating just fine, but we won't be able to tell for certain until we're closer to full vacuum. For now, we're climbing at least."

"Well, we're already shooting at them. Nothing more to do for now but hope we get them all before we take too much damage to keep vacuum."

"Aye aye," Bosley acknowledged.

Chipmunk stood and watched along with Sosha and the bridge crew of the *Jennai* as the Ruttanian airships danced around them in the sky. They looped and climbed, dove and spun, raking the two rebel airships with their repeater rifles with each pass. The bullets plinked against the reinforced walls of the vacuum tanks, trying to turn the stadium-sized chambers into sieves. There was no way to judge the damage except by the vacuum gauges and their altitude. It was possible that the bullets were deflecting off the thick steel plating required to keep the vacuum pressure from caving in the tanks. It was just as likely that each pass jabbed a row of holes into the *Jennai* and the *Cloudsmith* like a sewing machine.

It was a surreal sight, beautiful in a way that only a layer of intervening glass could make it. They were spectators watching a theater performance of acrobats and knife-jugglers. Then on one pass, a Ruttanian airship lined itself up to make a run straight for the bridge of the *Jennai*. Chipmunk saw it through the sight of her pistol and drew back, startled. She looked through the window without the sight and confirmed that one was headed right for her position.

"Stand back," Chipmunk said to everyone. She looked through the sight and located the airship at greater magnification. She needed one hand to hold her balance, so keeping the gun steady gave her trouble. The airship grew larger by the second in her view.

Sosha put a hand on her shoulder. "Rynn, what are you—"

"Stand back!" Chipmunk shouted, shouldering Sosha aside and quickly reacquiring her aim.

Click.

The forward window of the *Jennai* shattered, allowing the wind and noise of the outside onto the bridge. Chipmunk watched through the sight, momentarily losing her target as she jumped at the sound of breaking glass. The Ruttanian airship was gone.

Leaning out the now-open window, Chipmunk watched the pieces of airship scatter as they fell. Her shot must have connected with the engine block for it to have torn the craft apart like that. She had worried briefly that her coil gun might have been too powerful to do major damage, that it might have just made a small, neat hole.

"Rynn, what were you thinking?" Sosha asked. Broken glass crunched underfoot as those on the bridge rushed to have a look at the falling airship.

"Nice shot, General," Captain Bosley commented.

"Thanks. Get someone to sweep up this mess." Chipmunk stood in place, not daring to set foot on broken glass again, even with proper boots to protect her feet. By the amount scattered on the floor, most of the glass shards had been blasted overboard to become a hazard to some scrub-farmer's harvest. Had the *Jennai* been hovering instead of motoring full ahead, hardly any would have blown back inside.

Chipmunk took a few more shots out the window to be thorough. A volunteer was already at work sweeping up broken glass with a silver-plated dustpan and a wood-handled brush from the janitorial supplies in first-class. Only the top and back of the sweeper's head were visible to Chipmunk as the man bent over his work. She didn't know his name. It was not so long ago that she had been the nameless peon who toiled at floor level, now she ordered others to do such work for her. She made a mental note to learn his name once the bullets were done flying; it was exactly what Mrs. Bas-Klickten would never have done, and that made it worth doing.

Footsteps hammered the stairway up to the bridge. "General! General Chipmunk!" The voice grew louder as the footsteps approached. The door of the bridge flew open and a panting Innin stumbled in. "Two of the Ruttanian airships are breaking off the attack."

Chipmunk slammed the butt of her pistol on the railing. "Damn those cowards! What heading?"

"South-southeast, about oh-nine-five," Innin replied.

"Rennon's going to have to go after them," Captain Bosley said.

Chipmunk shook her head. "They have a head start. There's no reason to think our airship's any faster than theirs. It's the same model." Her mind whirred. Captain Bosley got half a word of comment out of his mouth before Chipmunk's raised hand cut him off. The crew remained silent as the wind blew around them and the propellers hummed.

"I'll go," Chipmunk said. "I can try overloading the runes and see if I can make it go faster than they were designed." She hobbled along the railings and headed for the door.

Sosha cut her off, blocking the railing and offering no assistance as a shoulder to lean on. "No, Rynn. You're in no condition to be walking, let alone flying."

"It's either you or me," Chipmunk replied. "And I know you won't pull the trigger even if you can catch them."

"General Chipmunk," Sosha said, relenting on the use of her official title, "it is inappropriate for you to risk yourself on a dangerous mission with low prospects for success."

"I'm afraid she's right, ma'am," Captain Bosley agreed, sounding relieved not to have been the one to broach the subject.

Chipmunk searched the eyes of the crew for signs that she had support on the matter. Each man and woman met her gaze, but what she saw was support of a different sort: hard, stoic eyes, firm set jaws, unwavering attention. She wasn't one of them—she was their leader. Perhaps they admired her willingness, but she saw no sign that any of them were eager to let her run off to pilot a liftwing after the fleeing kuduks.

She hobbled back to the broken window and looked out to the northeast. The low-lying foothills of the Homespires beckoned, promising safety if only they could couch themselves among the rolling landscape without embedding themselves in it first.

"Slow to quarter speed. Set a heading two-nine-zero. Signal the *Cloudsmith* to do likewise."

"Yes ma'am. Into the mountains," Captain Bosley replied. He took the wheel as one of the officers cranked back the engine power to the propellers.

"Not that far. We just need to find a place to put ourselves back together a bit. We need lift, and we can't get it without some upgrades. Set us down in the first valley deep enough that we can't be seen from the plains."

"Aye aye, General," Captain Bosley acknowledged.

"Do you ever get the impression that we've mixed up our jargon a bit there, Captain."

"A bit, maybe," Captain Bosley agreed. "But I won't worry myself over it unless I start calling you Miss Errol, or General Madlin." He winked.

The western half of the valley was already blanketed in shadows as the eastern rises clung to the sunset light. The *Jennai* and the *Cloudsmith* had set down so close together that their vacuum tanks were dangerously close to touching. Chipmunk had ordered them rearranged five times before they were parked to her satisfaction. Crews were already on the access ladders, checking for damage, and would continue until the evening light failed them.

Chipmunk stood off to the side of the airships, watching the work by her father's side.

"Your plan had merits, Rynn," Erefan admitted. "But we didn't put off enough weight for it to matter."

"Enough to maneuver the foothills, at least."

Erefan shrugged. "In, yes. Out, we'll have to see about."

"We're going to have to use runes."

Erefan glowered at her in reply.

"You've seen what my coil guns can do. Why do levitation runes bother you?"

Erefan plucked Chipmunk's gun from her holster before she could object. "If this little trinket fails, what happens? No shot. Buoyancy rune fails, we fall from the sky."

"And if this one fails," Chipmunk pulled down her scarf, baring her slave collar, "my head comes off. When did you become such an old woman?"

"I started worrying more when I realized you'd stopped altogether. You're letting this General Chipmunk business get to your head. When I've gotten the world-ripper on Tinker's Island built, we'll be able to get around easily. Until then, we just need to keep ourselves safe."

"You don't trust magic, but you'll trust that machine of yours?" Chipmunk asked. "You can't tell me that thing isn't magic."

"It's just a science we don't understand. Kezudkan used a rune-powered dynamo for the spark, but the device is scientific in nature, I'm sure of it."

"If I hook a bunch of dials and switches to the runes, would you feel better about levitation? That's all I saw on your machine."

"Before you blasted it."

Chipmunk's brow knit. "It was a magical device, controlled by comforting little dials from a lab-grade spark supply box."

"Sosha told me about your foot," Erefan said, lowering his head. Chipmunk took the change of subject as a victory, since her father rarely admitted a lost argument directly.

"It's her fault. If she'd sewn it up better—"

"She warned you to stay off it, and look what it got you," Erefan snapped.

"Well, I'm going to take a crack at it myself, once I've slept," Chipmunk shot back. "Sometimes it feels like I'm the only one around here actually trying."

"What, you think you're a better nurse than Sosha now? You let your foot go septic without even noticing."

"Well, I'm going to see if my Veydran friends can help. Korr and Tellurak don't seem to be offering me any options."

Erefan crossed his arms. "Magic isn't a cure-all."

"You know, from what I've heard, it is."

Chapter 5

"An understanding of metallurgy is fundamental to the tinker's trade. Without suitable materials, dreams remain trapped in the mind." –The Tinker's Handbook, Vol 1., Foreword

The new workshop had been just another old warehouse two months ago. It had been repurposed; the barrels and crates that had cluttered the corners had been replaced by the trappings of a new sort of industry. A smelter took up one corner, smaller than the one in the foundry and made for processing a single material: copper. The workshop was devoted to the single purpose of working copper, drawing it out into long, thin strands, or casting it into shapes of cunning design.

The transformation had taken place with all the focus and relentless drive that Cadmus Errol was known for. He had laid the groundwork for the facility over years of sketching and figuring in his head. Because his timeline in Korr had been greatly accelerated by Kezudkan's eagerness, he had been forced to focus on preparing his people for the great escape, which ended up not happening quite how he'd planned it. In an ideal world, Cadmus would have been ready with a second machine before he ever made use of the one in the daruu's workshop. But neither Tellurak nor Korr were ideal worlds.

The Mad Tinker stalked his newest factory, peering over the shoulders of workers and stopping to confiscate production orders long enough to peruse them before handing them back. Nothing exceeded his expectations, but nothing fell short of them, either. He knew his people. There were mechanics among the twinborn who had worked with copper in Korr, who knew the workings of a wire-pulling machine, even some who had worked with spark before—not that there was any spark on Tinker's Island yet.

One of the twinborn foremen approached from across the factory. "Morning, Cadmus. How's Rynn?"

It sounded odd hearing his daughter's Korrish name on his men's lips. They'd always called her Madlin, even when talking about Rynn. It was often easier for everyone to use names from a single world, but those days were fading to distant memory as the distinctions became important.

"Morning yourself, Mr. Grandle. Rotten," Cadmus replied. "She's off on some miscalibrated trial to find magic that'll fix that foot of hers."

"Hey, I didn't even believe in Veydrans until a few weeks ago," Grandle said. "Maybe they've got some tricks we don't know."

"Tricks?" Cadmus scoffed. "Need more than tricks; Rynn's gone and got septic rot. I was up predawn, caught myself sketching up mechanical legs."

"Least we've got Sosha. Hate to have drawn lots to see who does the job."

Cadmus glowered at Grandle. "You always so cheerful about medical butchery? How's my dynamo?"

Grandle straightened up, reverting to a more subordinate posture. "All to plan, tinker. We're just waiting for the wire production to catch up to what we need. They're getting a better yield every day, but it's still slow compared to the factories in Cuminol."

"Well, I don't expect to let a bunch of kuduks show us up. I expect us to be up to full production by the end of the week." Cadmus gave a nod of dismissal and headed for the door. He had other appointments to keep.

Grandle fell into step behind him. "One other thing, Cadmus. We're all set to tie into the main shaft for the dynamo, but Rynn had an idea."

Cadmus stopped short, causing Grandle to stumble to avoid crashing into him from behind. He twisted around and met Grandle eye to eye.

"She pointed out that we'd lose use of the workshops while the dynamo was on if they were all sharing the central shaft," Grandle said. "She thought it would be worth trying to rune the dynamo to run on aether."

"I'm not trusting in aether to—"

"She said it could run in either mode."

"I see you two have discussed this at some length. Anything else you and my daughter have plotted behind my back?"

Grandle reached inside his jacket and withdrew a folded sheet of paper. He handed it to Cadmus as if it might spring alive and attack as soon as the tinker touched it.

"You drew this, runes and all?" Cadmus asked. He looked up, and Grandle nodded. Cadmus crumpled the sheet and stuffed it into Grandle's hands. "Your penmanship's like rat droppings and you draw worse than a drunkard with busted spectacles." Cadmus resumed his path to the exit.

"But sir—"

"Don't you go sir-ing me. I don't own you."

"But Cadmus, Rynn already arranged interviews for the rune carvers." Grandle blanched as Cadmus whirled on him. "It wasn't me. She just told me that they were ready to meet you today. She got someone else to gather them up; I don't know who."

"Just who's in charge around here, anyway?"

Grandle sweated a moment as if unsure how—or perhaps whether—to answer. "It seems more of a bi-world arrangement these days. You run Tinker's Island, Rynn commands our forces in Korr."

Cadmus let his breath vent through clenched teeth. He hated liars, bootlicks, and lackeys. As much as he might wish it otherwise, Grandle was technically correct. It was a sort of correct he had to respect, even if he didn't like it.

"Fine. We'll rune the dynamo—just as a contingency!" Cadmus shook a finger for emphasis. "I'll meet with the carvers once I've seen about getting us more copper."

Cadmus took as few meetings in his office as possible. It was a cluttered place, filled with paperwork that would be collected by his assistants at day's end whether he looked at it or not. A small stack of important documents set to one side required his attention—contracts, treaties, and the like—but the rest was merely for his perusal. Like a castle's torture chamber, it was a place for the unpleasant necessities of leadership that a civilized society would have been better off without.

The Mad Tinker perched on the edge of his seat with his elbows on his desk, chin resting on his interwoven fingers. Across the table sat a younger man, hale and full of vigor, trying to slink below the tinker's view. His visitor was the son and trade representative of Mr. Amin Sutz, a shipper whose vessel had just delivered copper ore that Cadmus had been long anticipating.

"Say that again, more slowly, Mr. Sutz. I'm hoping that I may have just misheard you."

Jaffry Sutz reached a finger inside his collar and tugged it away from his neck. "I'm ... I'm afraid not, Mr. Errol. You see, there's a new wing being built for the Kheshi royal palace, and they want it out of copper, to match the rest."

Cadmus pounded a fist on the table, causing Jaffry to flinch. "Rot them! I'm paying five times what it's worth as it is. You can't tell me they outbid me."

"My father made the commitment before your order. He had his trade license in Khesh to think of."

"You get that ship sent here instead of Khesh and I'll make sure you won't need to deal with them anymore. I can keep you in coin 'til the end of days."

"I'm sure my father wouldn't like to see his trade with Khesh cut off entirely. He wouldn't—"

"I'm not talking about your father. I'm talking about you. Mr. Sutz, you strike me as a man being forced to play against weighted dice. If it were up to you, would you sell me the ore, or deliver it to Khesh at a fraction of the price?"

Jaffry stood, straightening himself and smoothing the front of his shirt. "This is my father's legacy to me. I can't soil the family name on a single deal, especially one with this importance to the Kheshi royal family."

Cadmus swiveled in his chair and faced the window. He could see the harbor below, where his copper ore was being unloaded from the *Kimba's Pride*. It would be the last ore to arrive at Tinker's Island for over a month, and unless he acquired a substantial supply soon, production would have to be suspended. Copper was the cheapest and most widespread conductor on Korr, and Kezudkan had procured it in vast amounts for the first world-ripper machine's construction.

But Kezudkan had fallen on hard times. Copper was the cheapest reasonable conductor, not the only, nor even the best.

He spun his chair back to face Jaffry. The young man had his hands clasped in front of him, fidgeting. "What about silver?"

Jaffry cocked his head and blinked. "Silver, Mr. Errol?"

"Yes, shiny stuff, prone to tarnishing, used in tea sets, tableware, and hundred-fonn coins. Your father deals in all manner of ore. Does he have any silver?"

"Well, yes, I suppose. How much are you talking about?"

"Same as the copper. Silver's heavier by about fifty percent, but the same volume would do."

Jaffry's mouth opened, but no sound issued forth. He stayed like that way for a moment. Cadmus could envision the gnashing gears in the man's head as his brain came to a halt.

"Mr. Sutz," he prompted.

Jaffry licked his lips and came around. "I don't know our silver holdings, but we haven't got *that* much, I'm sure."

"I'll take all you've got. Ore, coin, trinkets, all at standard market value."

"I ... I can't even calculate what that would cost. I don't know how much credit my father would be willing to extend, even to you, Mr. Errol."

Cadmus stood and strode around the table. Hooking Jaffry Sutz by the arm, he took the young trader in tow as he left his office. "Allow me to show you something."

Jaffry said nothing as Cadmus led him through the halls of the Errol Company headquarters. They passed offices, clerks, accountants, and supervisors; anyone who caught Cadmus's eye gave a nod of greeting as he passed. Jaffry elicited a few second glances, but no one questioned what the Mad Tinker was doing with the Acardian gentleman in his grasp. Farther into the facility, they passed guard posts with locked metal doors and men with rifles. The exchanges with the Errol Company security personnel were brief, direct, and impersonal.

Within the bowels of the building, three stories down and reachable only by steam lift, they came to a set of steel doors and another, less formal guard post. Anyone who had made it thus far was past the point of dealing with armed resistance.

"Orris, open the vault," Cadmus called out as the lift gates opened.

Orris looked up from his book and took his feet down from the desk. "Really, Cadmus, I take shifts down here for the quiet. Can't you awe the merchant brats with your dragon's hoard on Averi's watch?" Despite his complaint, Orris stood and took a ring of keys from his pocket.

"Averi's not half the showman you are," Cadmus shot back as Orris fiddled with the first of a half dozen locks.

"So this is a gawk-show, then?"

"Mr. Sutz here was balking at extending us credit for a shipment of silver."

Orris looked over his shoulder as he turned one of the keys in a lock. His brow knit in a perturbed frown. "When did we start buying on credit?"

Cadmus didn't answer, but watched Jaffry's face as Orris unlocked the vault. He rarely took anyone down to the vaults, especially not suppliers. It was a fit of pique as much as any practical reason, Cadmus admitted to himself, after having his financial means questioned. Seeing the expectant wonder in Jaffry's eyes made him wonder why he didn't do it more often.

"Behold!" Orris said with a melodramatic sweep of his arm as he pulled open the door. "Cadmus Errol's treasure trove." Cadmus gave Orris credit for keeping a straight face, despite a smile that looked ready to burst from his lips at any moment.

Cadmus pulled Jaffry along, but the younger Mr. Sutz balked. Inside the vault was not a haphazard hillside of gold as dragons were known to sleep upon in fairy stories, but a warehouse of coin. Shelves lined the walls, stacked with strongboxes. Crates covered the floor, and the one nearest the door was open to reveal that it was filled halfway to the top with trade bars, the finger-sized gold currency that rich men used to buy horses and ships. Most impressive of all were the kings' bars, gold bricks large enough to pass as masonry in a chimney. Too heavy to lug around, they were deemed too heavy for common theft as well. Kings' bars were meant to be stored, not spent, and the only time anyone used them in barter were for payment to mercenary armies, the purchase of land, or as tribute to foreign rulers.

Cadmus let Jaffry gape for a long while.

"There's not much in there besides gold," Cadmus said. "It's denser, so it takes up less room than silver or minted coin. If you can sell me enough silver that I can't pay you in coin, *then* we can talk about my credit."

With Jaffry Sutz's ship relieved of its ore and Jaffry himself loaded with dreams of gold, Cadmus found himself light afoot heading into his afternoon meetings. What good was a miser's fortune? There was a war to win in Korr, and the rebellion was poised on the fulcrum of disaster. The sooner he had a functioning world-ripper, the sooner Erefan's forces would be safe. The realization that he could supplement his copper supply with silver, perhaps even lightsteel or other uncommon conductors, was a key worry hammered into a solution. Even the prospect of being cooped up in his office for much of the day couldn't dampen his spirits—until the first appointment arrived.

The appointment book was filled with a motley cast of unlikely runesmiths. Beside the list of names and times were annotations as to the qualifications of each: a metal sculptor, a silversmith, three printing engravers, a scribe, two mechanics, and three twinborn who'd seen runes on a daily basis, one of whom worked on dynamos as an assistant cableman.

Cadmus's interviews were scheduled in alphabetical order. The first man was Ronley Briarford, the silversmith. He had a craftsman's handshake, firm and rough, an honest worker's grip. When questioned about his qualifications, Briarford produced a sheet of silver and filigree tooling. Before Cadmus's eyes, the silversmith carved his best approximation of the runes on Grandle's instruction page. Cadmus had seen the runes on Kezudkan's dynamo and knew that Grandle's engravings wouldn't be functional, but they were a fair copy of what the man had seen. By the time Cadmus called an end to the interview, he knew he had at least one candidate who might carve working runes once he was shown a proper drawing of them.

The second interviewee was a mechanic from his rifleworks by the name of Abe Dakinshi. He was a Takalishman older than Cadmus by a dozen years, who had been working on firearms since before Errol Company was founded. He was a trigger specialist, capable of fashioning any part of a gun but selected to work on the painstaking details of the smallest, most finicky pieces. He used an awl and an old piece of steel to scratch his sample runes. Cadmus had known the man for years, and kept up an amiable chat to stave off the cringe-worthy sight of the man's carving. By the end of half an hour, the man had butchered a handful of runes and caught Cadmus up on the health and tidings of his family.

A twinborn named Frent and a printing engraver by the name of Vander Heckleston failed to impress Cadmus in the least. He complimented them on their willingness to take on a new assignment, but cut their interviews well short.

Still behind schedule from Abe Dakinshi's interview, Cadmus was tempted to cut the scribe from his roster of potential recruits. A steady hand was admirable, but pen and ink were a long shout from working with metal. A moment's internal debate resolved that he should meet the man, just to be thorough.

When Erund Hinterdale sat down across the desk from him, Cadmus found himself intrigued. The scribe was tall and slender, the sort of build that few can maintain while working a manual trade. When Cadmus offered his hand across the desk, the scribe's grip was iron-strong, though his skin was smooth as a prince's. What struck Cadmus was the man's ease. Even Abe Dakinshi, who had worked for Cadmus since Tinker's Island was founded, seemed on edge in his interview. Erund Hinterdale lounged in his seat, respectful, attentive, but clearly nonplussed.

"You've heard what that job entails, I imagine, Mr. Hinterdale," Cadmus said. It was a statement that left room for interpreting it as a question.

"Erund, if you don't mind, Mr. Errol," Erund replied. "And yes, I've heard a stray rumor or two."

"I'm going to show you a series of patterns, and then you will copy them as best you can. What medium will you use?" Though Cadmus knew the answer, he had asked the other candidates, so it seemed only fair.

"Acid and steel," Erund replied. He drew a piece of sheet metal from inside his jacket along with a thin glass rod and a stoppered vial.

Cadmus raised an eyebrow. "Interesting choice."

Erund shrugged. "I can write them in pen and ink if you like, but I didn't think that would prove much unless you were making this machine of yours out of paper."

"Indeed," Cadmus said. He handed Erund the paper. "Begin."

Erund unstoppered the vial, letting an acrid scent waft into the office. He dipped the glass rod in the acid and shook a droplet back into the vial before it fell on Cadmus's desk. With broad strokes, the scribe made copies of each of the runes on Grandle's sheet, though far larger than those penned runes had been. A trail of vapors sizzled in the rod's wake as the acid etched the steel. After a few moments, Erund produced a rag from his pocket and wiped the glass rod clean, then handed the metal sheet to Cadmus.

Cadmus held the steel up to the light, angling it to check the etch. It wasn't perfect, but the lines were of more uniform depth than he had suspected. Held flat before him, the runes looked like they came from a Korrish school primer, formed large and perfect. A scratching sound broke Cadmus's concentration and he found Erund had appropriated a fountain pen from his desk and was writing on the back of Grandle's sheet of example runes.

"What do you think you're—"

"Here," Erund said. He handed the paper to Cadmus. The ink was still wet, but there they were: Korrish runes. "Let your other candidates work from these instead. It ought to make it easier on them."

Cadmus had overlooked something with the distraction of the acid-work. The runes weren't copies of Grandle's; they were how the runes ought to have looked. He glared at Erund Hinterdale from below a furrowed brow. "How did you know to make these? Who else are you?" He was unaccustomed to twinborn showing up unannounced in his office.

Erund reached to a chain around his neck and pulled medallion from below his tunic. It was pewter, fashioned in the form of a letter "S" wrapped around a quill. "I'm also an expert scribe, or would be if I was still in Acardia."

"That's not an answer to my question."

"Surely it is. I've come across alphabets in more languages that you can imagine exist. The Society of Learned Men has used my services to transcribe ancient works so that they can pore over them at leisure without exposing the originals to undue wear. These characters you showed me are ones I've seen before, though I couldn't say what they mean."

Cadmus leaned back in his chair and looked the Acardian scribe over. He was lighter skinned than most twinborn, pale as only Acardians and southern Kheshi are known to get, and with hair the muted brown of transmission fluid, he certainly wasn't Kheshi by birth. Few Korrish were so pureblooded. Thanks to centuries of commercial transport of humans by the kuduks, geographic distinctions were shades of brown and tan. He had seen Acardian-looking Korrish only a handful of times, but they existed.

"Try another one," Cadmus said. "I've looked for books with runes like these in them. They're just not to be found, even among the Society of Learned Men. I believe you that you've seen the runes before; I couldn't have made them prettier myself."

Erund smirked and put up his hands. "You've got me. I was like you until about six years ago. Now, this is the only world I've got."

"One-worlded, huh?" Cadmus asked. Erund cast his eyes down and nodded. "Where were you from? Who else were you?"

"I lived in a humans-only village outside Cuminol. I worked as a scribe, since I was one of the few who could read." Erund glanced up as he spoke, but averted his gaze again quickly.

Cadmus switched to Korrish. "Who is the enemy of all humans?" Among freemen humans, it was a phrase taught to every child.

"Pardon?" Erund asked.

Cadmus repeated the question.

Erund squinted and put a hand to his ear. "I'm sorry, my ear for Korrish had gone soft. Who is what now?"

There was some glimmer of comprehension—or was there? Perhaps something in his tone had conveyed the heart of Cadmus's question. Confidence schemes were an art that Cadmus had never patronized, but he knew the principles: skilled observation, inference, vague answers, leading questions. Was Erund playing three-cups and a marble with him? From Madlin's reports, the Veydrans she was traveling with could puzzle out bits of Korrish by the sound. There were plenty of ways to glean bits of Korrish geography from the Tinker's Islanders, and it wasn't likely that any of them would refer to a humans-only sky as a village.

"Well, despite the rusty ear, I think I've found my man," Cadmus said. He stood and extended a hand to Erund once again. The scribe—and likely infiltrator—relaxed visibly and gave an amiable shake, less focused on impressing with grip than in the vigor of the shaking. Cadmus clapped Erund on the back and guided him out the door of his office. "We'll get you clearance to the dynamo workshop. You can start tomorrow on some practice metals."

While they walked among the offices of Errol Company, Cadmus searched for someone. It wasn't a particular twinborn he sought, but rather one with a particularly quick mind and the proper tool at hand. He made a few cursory introductions, pointed out bits of trivia about the construction of the building, all biding time until he found what he was looking for.

Mazzin Daug was the man who caught the Mad Tinker's eye. He was a Takalishman who was quarter Feru by his mother's side. He had grown up the son of a soldier in Tellurak and his twin was a freeman pub bouncer in Korr. He was bull-necked and barrel-chested, looking like a statue whittled from mahogany and left to the elements for a year. "Mazzin, come here a minute. There's someone I'd like you to meet."

"What's that, boss?" Mazzin asked as he approached. "New fella comin' on?" He extended a meaty hand, slashed across with light-colored scars.

"Mazzin, this is Erund Hinterdale," Cadmus said. As Erund extended his hand, the Mad Tinker switched to Korrish. "*Ventilate this imposter immediately.*" He chose long words in the hope that the Veydran spy wouldn't puzzle it out in time.

Mazzin was a soldier's soldier. He knew his commander's ruse immediately. He drew his pistol—the thing Cadmus had primarily looked for in a rescuer—and fired, putting a bloody hole in the center of Erund's chest. The false twinborn's eyes went wide in surprise, or shock, or fear. When he fell dead to the ground, it no longer mattered the cause of the gaping eyes that stared off at an accountant's door nearby.

"Get someone to help you get him down to the furnaces. Incinerate the body. Make inquiries and find out if anyone else was here with him, and take them into custody. I want this mopped up quickly."

Cadmus watched as the body was removed from the halls of Errol Company headquarters. No sooner had four workers trussed the corpse up in a tarp, than a pair of janitors appeared on the scene to scrub away the blood. It did Cadmus's heart good, seeing the efficiency of his people. They had suffered a close miss that could have put all these fine men and women in peril.

"Dammit Madlin, this is the trouble in trucking with Veydrans."

Some days, you are just in the wrong place at the wrong time. Mazzin had been seeing about a discrepancy in his weekly wage when Cadmus had recruited him for an impromptu murder. Guilty or not, the man hadn't been tried, but Mazzin hadn't been given time to think. The order was clear; Cadmus's tone was urgent. It had been more a reflexive response than a decision.

To keep matters quiet, he was also assigned the task of finding Erund Hinterdale's associates on Tinker's Island and arresting them. The man had only arrived days ago, and the only lead Mazzin had to go on was a wife. The thought that he'd killed a family man sat in Mazzin's stomach like a ball of lead: heavy, poisonous, and with no quick way to be rid of it.

The Gilded Coin was Cadmus's attempt to extort money from wealthy visitors to the city. Whatever else might be inferred from the man's actions, Erund Hinterdale had money. Flanked by two one-worlder guards he'd brought along as much for company as for their aid, Mazzin knocked on the door of room 412.

"Open up," Mazzin called through the door. "Official business."

He didn't have to wait long. The door opened and revealed a woman as tall as he was. She was thin past the point fashionable ladies strove for, with a fair face and reddish gold hair, and was wearing coveralls belted so tightly that it looked as if she must be about to snap in two.

"Official, huh? What sort of official comes with a drawn gun and two fellas along for muscle?" she asked.

Mazzin ignored her question. "Juliana Hinterdale?" She gave a lopsided smirk and nodded. "I am Mazzin Daug, Errol Company security. I'm going to have to ask you to come with us."

"What's this all about?" She crossed her arms and made no move to exit the room.

"Your husband threatened Mr. Errol and was shot dead."

"Wait, you said your name was Mazzin?"

"Yes ma'am, now if you'll please come with us, we have some questions we'd like answered."

Juliana raised an eyebrow and called over her shoulder. "Sweetheart, wasn't Mazzin the name you mentioned to me?" The reply from within the room was muffled by one of the interior doors.

Mazzin heard a door open and the slapping of bare feet on the marble floor.

"Oh, not you again," Erund Hinterdale replied as he stepped beside his wife, soaking wet and wrapped in a towel. "Listen, I've played along enough for one day, all right?"

Mazzin stood frozen. One of his men bolted, but only managed to run two paces before he hung suspended in the air.

"What do we do with this lot?" Juliana asked.

"Did you tell anyone else about my wife yet?" Erund asked. He wagged a finger at Mazzin. "No lying."

"N-no," he managed to say.

"Seems simple enough, then," Juliana said.

There was a blinding flash, then nothingness.

Mazzin stood in Cadmus's private workshop, where the Mad Tinker was relaxing over a pile of sketches for his great machine. It was dusk, and the red of the sunset cast the room in a hellish light. "Nothing at all?" Cadmus asked.

"He seems to have come alone," Mazzin replied. "He had a room at the Gilded Coin, but he had few possessions, and nothing so useful as a journal or letters. It seems he was a bit of a loner, only a handful had even recognized the name."

Cadmus set his pencil down and paced in front of the window. "What could he have wanted?"

"I can keep making inquiries, tinker."

Cadmus stroked his chin. The puzzle made no sense without more pieces, but Tinker's Island seemed an unlikely spot to turn up more. "No, I'll make inquiries in Korr. Thank you, Mazzin."

"Goodnight, tinker. See you on the other side."

Chapter 6

"If you want to get rich at a festival, rob a thief. He's already picked everyone's pockets clean."
–Tolian the Quickfinger, from the play Prince of Alleys

The streets of Bouo were never quiet, but during festivals it was a merry riot in the streets. Madlin had lost the count of days as they crossed Khesh, but she didn't need a calendar to know the Serpent's Tribute had arrived. Even with a light rain falling, the people of Bouo were out in celebration, many decked out in costumes adorned with green feathers meant to look like serpent scales.

As the wagons crept through the streets at less than a walking pace, Madlin hunched inside with a hand on her pistol grip. The crowds were too thick for her liking, the costumes garish and bewildering to the eye. News of her trek across northern Khesh could not have gone without rumors arriving well before the wagons. If anyone had intentions of ambushing them for their cargo, the crowd could conceal any number of assailants among the revelers.

Dan plunked himself down beside Madlin. "None of the serpents are real, you know. I don't think you're going to need the gun."

"If this were Korr, and this was someone else's money, I'd be looking for a way to boost it," she replied.

"Maybe, but it's crated up. It's not like someone is going to cut your purse strings and sneak off with it. Besides, half this lot's already drunk and the rest are trying to catch up." Dan extended a handful of sweets in a tiny wicker basket. "Here, try one. They're pretty good."

Madlin leaned away from the basket. "Do you know what those are?"

"Fella hawking 'em said they were sweethearts."

Madlin gave him a sickly smile. "Yeah, fried chicken hearts glazed in sugar." She watched for Dan's reaction, but he kept chewing as if he hadn't heard her.

"Funny, you'd think they'd have given them a cleverer name." Dan popped another into his mouth. "Really, you can hardly even taste the meat inside. They could have sugared black beans or peas or something and you'd never tell the difference. There some special Serpent Day thing about chickens I don't know about?"

"Can you maybe *not* eat those right in front of me?" Madlin asked. Her stomach was turning sour with the squishy noises of Dan chewing as he talked.

"What, are you squeamish?" Dan asked. He opened his mouth wide, showing half-eaten sweethearts within. Madlin cringed away from both the sight and smell. Dan laughed. "That's what you get trying to make *me* sick telling me what they are when I've got them in my mouth. You don't get to be warlock by tossing your lunch over every little thing, but I know that trick. I invented that trick."

Madlin watched a troupe of actors putting on a makeshift performance for an audience within elbow's reach. Three of them were dressed as fishermen, and a fourth wore an elaborate serpent costume with scales of oxidized copper. "You don't strike me as the inventing type. I bet you'd find tinkering pretty boring."

"You said it, not me. I've got nothing against you tinkers, but I just don't need machines to do my work for me. It's fine for people who can't do magic worth horse snot, like Tanner."

"Tell me, Dan, what do they do when people get sick in Veydrus?"

There was an elaborate sigh from above Madlin, and a basket of sweethearts showered her. "Piss off, Madlin. How many times are you going to try to thief-talk me into giving you magic lessons? Lather up any more jelly on my bread and I'll rot my teeth."

"It's a fair question!" Madlin protested, flicking the foul treats off the wagon and into the crowd.

Dan grabbed hold of one of the supports for the wagon's canvass covering and swung around into Madlin's field of vision. "Fine then. For a sniffle, we drink dragon piss. For fever, we lie naked under a full moon. If someone breaks a bone, we take them to the smithy and alloy the bone with iron, then weld it back together. Festering wounds must be bathed in virgin blood. Should anyone show signs of hysterical madness, we treat them with land and title."

Madlin listened to the tirade with her lips pursed. "How's the virgin blood thing work?"

Dan's face grew solemn. "You're serious about this one, aren't you?"

"If I can't find a way to cure septic rot, they're going to cut my foot off."

"Make sure they've got hot tar on hand to seal it," Dan said. "I've watched it done after a battle. Nasty business. If it were me, I'd almost rather let the rot take me. Then again, it's not me."

"What would you do if it was?"

Dan studied her. Madlin had not grown accustomed to the vast age that crept into his eyes when he took something seriously. She couldn't tell if he was using the aether vision he had told her of, or if there was some evaluation being made of her. "I'd keep it to myself, fix it quiet, in the middle of the night, when no one was around." He bobbed his head, prompting Madlin for a sign that she understood his double-meaning.

"Good enough," Madlin replied. She checked over her shoulder, and Jamile was still on the next wagon ahead, sitting with Tanner. "I'll find you once everyone else is asleep."

"I've got a price though."

"What's that? Ten percent of a gold mine not enough?"

"My share's only five once Tanner and I split it, but I'm not asking for more gold. I've got two conditions."

Madlin's hand strayed to her pistol. No-Boots had tried a similar tactic on her once. What was it about adolescent boys? "What kind of conditions?"

"First is for your own protection. I'm going to use a spell to watch through your eyes. If anything goes wrong, I'm waking Jamile."

Madlin shrunk back. "You can *do* that?" Dan shrugged and nodded. "I don't like the idea of someone else watching what I see."

"Just don't go bathing or taking your clothes off in front of a mirror. I'm guessing Jamile and your father aren't keen on you using magic, or you wouldn't keep looking over to see if she's listening. I'll help you, but I don't want you killing yourself, either."

Madlin mulled over Dan's condition. The thought of another mind lurking behind her eyes sent a cold shiver through her despite the warm Kheshi rain. It sounded similar to her own slumbering consciousness watching Chipmunk's antics, but without the lifelong familiarity, sisterhood, and trust. Some part of her had always wondered whether she and Chipmunk were even really separate people, and not king and crest of the same coin. Dan's presence would be alien. "Will I be able to tell you're there?"

Dan held up his palms. "How would I know? I don't let anyone use magic on me."

"That's not exactly reassuring," Madlin replied dryly.

"It's like a wolf pack," Dan replied. "Biggest wolf doesn't get rolled on his back for anyone. Doesn't mean the others have it so bad though. I'm the lead wolf wherever I go when it comes to magic. You want my help, you're gonna have to learn how to behave in the pack with the rest of them."

"What says I won't take your advice, then renege?"

"For your own good, I'd check on you anyway. You haven't got a sorceress's mind. You want to learn about magic, but you put your trust in things like locks and guards with rifles. I could slip past any guard you post and get through any door. So, are you just pissing in my ale here, or are you going to agree to my first condition?"

Madlin couldn't see another way. If Dan had a mind to, she suspected he could make good on all his boasts. He had already proven that he wasn't deterred by guns. Why would a lock on the door of a rented room pose any greater challenge? "Fine. But let me hear your other condition before I agree."

"When we get settled into an inn, we ditch this bumpkin festival and find a game of Crackle somewhere with good liquor," Dan said. He hopped down from the wagon and fell into stride a pace away. He was tall enough that he only looked up slightly to see eye to eye with Madlin.

"Serpent Festival not to your liking?" Madlin asked.

Madlin had heard many descriptions of Bouo. To most foreigners, it was the bazaar of Mongrel Khesh. To frequent visitors, it was a pit of vice and corruption. To the locals, it was the soul of the Kheshi Empire. To the southerners, it was the leak where filth from across the seas seeped into the continent. It was crowded, raucous, colorful, and diverse. She had never heard anyone refer to it as backward or countrified.

Dan gave her a withering look. "Amateur pipers on every corner, warbling out the same tired ditty without end. Kids dressed in feathered hats, pretending to be dragons—"

"Serpents," Madlin corrected.

"It's all the same to them. None of them has seen a real dragon; no one gets to be eight years old still believing they're real. Food's not half bad for Khesh, but it's all sugary and it'll sour my stomach if I eat much more of it. I'd just rather have a bit of a good time fleecing the locals at cards."

"What do you need me along for, then?"

"Tanner's too good, and I'm sick of following him everywhere anyway. I need someone of age to get me in and swap drinks with me. I'll order whatever you like, so long as you get me whiskey or ale—I'll let you know which before the serving girl comes 'round."

"You sure this isn't just an excuse to hang around me?" Madlin asked. Perhaps the direct approach would get Dan to falter and reveal his intentions.

Dan rubbed at the side of his face. "Not sure how to break this to you, but I see plenty of you these days. I'm not dog tired of you like I am with Tanner, but unless you get up and dance on the tables, I don't expect to see anything I haven't already outta you."

Madlin frowned. "I don't dance."

"Doesn't surprise me," Dan replied.

Rooms were impossible to find in Bouo during festivals, but certain sums of money shifted the impossible through unlikely and plausible, and into the realm of the done deal. Five rooms on an upper floor and space in the adjoining carriage house for their wagons, and Madlin's caravan was settled at the Silverhorse Inn. They'd paid triple the usual rate and had to bribe the occupants to vacate, but with Madlin's money and Tanner doing the talking, it had been arranged.

Madlin threw the satchel with her personal belongings onto the bed and slammed the door shut behind her. The room was cozy for the price it had commanded, but it was all hers. It had been far too long since the last time she had accommodations all to herself in Tellurak. It had doubled their expenses to take on an additional two rooms so that no one but the guards were sharing, but it was worth every fonn.

Cares left aside for the moment, Madlin collapsed onto the bed crossways and luxuriated in the feel of a proper mattress beneath her. The music from the Serpent's Tribute festival wafted in through the slats in the windows, though she had chosen a room that backed onto a little-used side street that was barely more than an alley. It was just as well; pure silence wouldn't have been any greater comfort.

Madlin's unwinding was cut short by a quick series of raps on her door. For a moment, the thought of ignoring the summons and pretending she wasn't there crossed her mind, but the moment passed. She stretched as she rose, and checked to see which tagalong had come first to claim her, Jamile or Dan.

When she opened the door, she found the young warlock waiting patiently, his hands clasped behind his back.

"What've you got back there?" Madlin asked.

Dan looked puzzled for a moment, then held his hands out in front of him, palms up. "Nothing. By the winds, you're paranoid."

"My father always said that was a lazy man's word for cautious."

"There's caution, then there's worrying about what your bodyguard has behind his back," Dan said.

"Oh, so you're my bodyguard now?" Madlin asked. "When did I hire you?"

"About the time we wandered into Kheshi territory armed, and you had promised me a sizable fortune in gold that you hadn't delivered yet."

"Does that mean I can leave my pistol behind? You'll be there to defend my life and honor?"

"Do what you want with your honor, but I'm seeing you alive to Tinker's Island if I have to burn Bouo to the ground to do it."

Madlin checked that the pistol was loose in its holster. "Guess I'll keep it on me then. Where are we headed?"

"Someplace that will play Crackle with trade bars," Dan replied. "We'll look around until we find one."

"Might take a while. You willing to go dry that long?"

"This is the sort of festival where you can carry a tankard in the streets with no one blinking, but any respectable place won't serve me one in the first place. I get thirsty, I'll just send you in someplace to grab me a pint."

Madlin looked down the hall in both directions. "You seen Jamile? I was guessing at which of you would come for me first."

"She left with Tanner as soon as they dumped their bags."

"Oh," Madlin said. She hadn't even been considered as a sightseeing companion, it seemed. *Well, we already saw Bouo together once*, she rationalized. It still stung to be brushed aside so easily after they had spent so much time together these past months. Perhaps too much time. Maybe she needed space.

Dan waved a hand in front of her face. "You in there? Come on, I said let's go."

"Of course. Lead on."

Jamile laughed and twirled around as a troupe of dancers passed through the crowd, leaping and careening around the pedestrians. A green feathered bonnet graced her head, purchased as soon as she and Tanner had joined the throng in the streets. Her gait bounced in time with the beat of the music.

Tanner looked over and gave her a world-weary smile. "You getting your money's worth out of that bonnet?"

Jamile hadn't stopped smiling since they joined the revelers, and she turned it in Tanner's direction. "I've never seen so many happy people in one place before."

"Mad Tinker's place must be a ship's hold full of laughs," Tanner said. He dodged out of the way of a drunken old man in a green shirt with feathers on the shoulders.

"It's not a bad place, but no one would ever call it merry," Jamile replied. "I think it's that there's no children, or at least no more than a handful." To emphasize her point, Jamile found a girl of eight or nine years in the crowd, took her by the hands, and whirled about with her for two measures before releasing her back to her mother's company.

"I guess." Tanner passed a coin to a street vendor's hand, and took a spit of chicken and red peppers in return. "I used to go in for this sort of thing when I was your age. I used to think it was easier talking to girls when I was drunk. Realized since then it is just as easy when they are."

"Listen to you, the bitter old bachelor. You'd think you were fifty," Jamile teased him. She slipped her arm around his and tried to pull him into a dance. Tanner held his spit of chicken aloft and away from her as he pulled free of Jamile's grasp.

"Knock off—"

"Not 'piss off?'" Jamile asked. "I hear that enough from you and Dan both."

"Give a fella a bit of credit for trying, would ya? You're still a girl. I'm not a complete clod. And yeah, that bit of color works well enough in both worlds, allowing for translation."

"I'm a grown woman you know, and I've heard coarser language than you might imagine."

Tanner gave her a skeptical eye up and down. "You're shaped like a proper woman, but I can't take you seriously as one in that hat. That thing's ridiculous."

"You always so serious?"

"It ain't serious, it's paranoid. Fun's fun; I get it. But this place has cutpurses and worse, and I've had an enemy or three in my day."

"Bouo is civilized. How much worse can we expect?"

"Imagine me or Dan, if we weren't all friendly like."

The smile faded from Jamile's face. "Tanner, I never meant to pry, but are you in trouble here?"

The smile migrated onto Tanner's face. "Naw, nothing like that. Just that me and some former associates used to operate a lucrative business in these parts, and it was the sort of operation that stepped on a few toes—I was gonna say once in a while, but it was pretty well close to daily, when we were thick in it."

"You and Dan used to live here?"

"Not him. It was before his time. We had a Tezuan-trained sorceress, a former Acardian sergeant at arms, and a Takalish warrior scholar—all twinborn."

Jamile raised an eyebrow. "Quite the coterie you had there."

"Yeah, it was—if that means what I think it means."

"A little group."

"Yup, that it was," Tanner said.

"So what happened? You met Dan and moved on to serve the great warlock?" Jamile teased.

"We had a crazy job planned, split up all over two worlds, keeping in touch through some half-cracked plan of switching messages back and forth between worlds."

"Madlin does that," Jamile noted.

"Well, that girl's barely more than half-cracked herself. Anyway, we got all split up, a couple links in the chain got killed, and I never heard from any of them again."

Jamile hooked her arm around Tanners and leaned against his shoulder as they walked. "That's so sad. Have you tried looking for them?"

Tanner shook his head. "No. Not hard, at least. One I saw die right in front of me, terrible mistake made by a good friend of mine, but when you're out in the dead of night with blades out, things like that can happen. Another I always suspected would go his own way. We weren't exactly friends, but we understood each other enough that I didn't expect a goodbye out of him. As for the sorceress ..."

Jamile waited as Tanner took a bite from his skewer. "What about her?"

"She either got what she wanted and never looked back, or died trying," Tanner said with his mouth full.

"Were you two lovers?" Jamile asked. She could see the pain clearly etched on Tanner's face: the tightness around the mouth, the slight furrowing of his brow.

"Naw. Don't mistake me, I'd have taken her in a snap." Tanner snapped his fingers. "She wasn't too much older than Dan when I first met her, but by the time she grew up, she knew me for who I am. Even if she weren't too young by a bucket of years, once a girl knows you, it's too late."

"That's not very romantic. So you're saying all romance dies when you get to know someone?"

"It's fine after she already loves you. You got her then; she's inclined to forgive a few things. Work as a coinblade beside someone for a few years, you're a killer, first and last in their head."

"If the killing is in a good cause, I could see her thinking the better of you for it, even if not every girl would."

Tanner halted dead in his tracks, and Jamile jerked to a stop right along with him, since she was latched onto his arm. He looked down at her and waited until he had her eyes fixed on his before he spoke. "If it had been, yeah, she probably would have." Tanner resumed walking and Jamile stumbled a step before she fell into stride with him. "Worked for the fella she ran off after."

They walked in silence for a long while after that. Jamile turned her attention to the revelry around them, rather than the man on her arm.

Madlin sipped a syrupy fruit drink so sweet it made her teeth ache. Across the table from her, hazy in the gloom of pipe smoke in the windowless gambling house, Dan took a long pull from an ale tankard. It had taken less effort than Madlin had expected to find a haven free of the boisterous festival cheer. Half a dozen tables were packed together with just enough room for the servers to navigate the jumble of chairs and bodies. Madlin had put her back to a wall, but Dan had foregone any such precaution.

The proprietor had balked twice before letting them in, firstly because they were both so young—Dan's plan for tagging along with Madlin hadn't accounted for *her* age being questioned—and secondly because children aren't known for carrying much money. Once Madlin smoothed out the latter objection, the former dissolved readily.

"I fold," Madlin muttered. It didn't matter whether any of the other players heard her, once she threw her cards away. The table held ten players, and pure chance would hold that she'd only hold the best cards one hand in ten. She hadn't counted, but it seemed like far longer than that. As play passed to her left, two more players folded, another called the bet, a fold, a fold, then it came to Dan.

"I raise," Dan said. He had a sloppy, drunken grin plastered over his face, and he kept his tankard in hand instead of his cards. With his free hand, he shoved five trade bars into the middle of the table.

There was a grumbling around the table. Madlin could only guess at the sort of scum they were gambling with, who kept to darkened card halls but had coin enough to pile it high like fortress walls in front of them.

At least one, she had gathered, was a local syndicate lieutenant, and another was one of his underlings. The gentleman in the Acardian suit coat was a diplomat who probably shouldn't have been seen in such company. The Takalishman to Dan's left hadn't said a word not directly related to the game, and the steel in his eyes kept her gaze from lingering on him. Another pair stank of brine and salt, and had taken seats flanking her. By their weathered skin she guessed they were sailors. By their belt knives and flintlock pistols, she suspected they weren't the friendly sort. A hulking, fair-skinned southern Kheshi had managed to say even less than the Takalishman, despite chattering non-stop. He spoke of weather and women, and bold deeds he was clearly exaggerating beyond credulity. Despite a good run of cards, his pile grew slowly as he drank his winnings as fast as they arrived. The last member at the table, the only one still in the hand with Dan, was a local with hair so thick with grease it seeped into his words. A mongrel if ever northern Khesh could claim one, he appeared to be a mix of Feru and Takalish, but had pale blue eyes. His name was Zinn.

"Who let this little rotter in with us?" Zinn complained, studying his cards. "Kids ain't got no business playin' cards."

"You're just sore you're gonna lose your shirt money," Dan replied, grinning like an idiot.

Zinn's brow knit and he glanced up from his hand.

"That not it?" Dan asked. "I was assuming you were playing to be able to afford something better than that used handkerchief with sleeves you're wearing."

"Swallow a knife, you little runt."

"Didn't bring one," Dan replied, nonplussed by the threat. "I'm *completely* unarmed." Still holding his tankard, Dan threw his other arm over the back of his chair.

Madlin felt a chill in the pit of her stomach as she heard the goad dig in, plain as if Dan had poked Zinn in the chest.

"What, you think your sister with her fancy pistol's gonna hide you under her skirts?" Zinn said, his voice rising a hair.

"I'm not—" Madlin stopped herself as she drew attention from all around the table. She wasn't eager to test out Dan's protection while he was inebriated. She let the multiple inaccuracies in Zinn's retort pass uncorrected.

"Why don't you quit yapping like a fishmonger and call my bet," Dan said.

"You're trying to run me off this one, ain't ya? You ain't got half the hand you'd like me to think, huh?" Zinn asked.

Madlin put a hand to the grip of her revolver and made sure it was loose and that it wouldn't hit the underside of the table if she tried to draw it in haste.

"Price to find out's right there on the table." Dan craned his neck to better see across the table. "Oh, looks like that would clean you right out. You could probably sell that paring knife at your belt for enough to eat tonight. I'd feel bad starving you on a festival day."

"No one can be this much of a prat with a winning hand. I call." Zinn slapped his hand on the table, showing a flush to the queen.

"Oh, now I see how you had such a tough decision. You had your head up your arse," Dan replied. He tossed his own cards down to reveal two aces, matching the two from among the common cards.

"You little—" Zinn began.

"Hey now!" The huge southern Kheshi stood and reached for the discarded cards. He flipped them by the handful, over the vocal protests from the other players. The dismay over the breach of Crackle protocol faded into a different sort of fury when the cards were shown. "I threw down the ace of swords. Where did you get a second one?"

All eyes turned to Dan, who just sighed. "Your eyes are going, friend. Might not fit your proud warrior image, but you should look into a pair of spectacles. That's no ace."

Madlin had looked away along with everyone else, and when she looked back, the card trapped under the Kheshi's meaty finger was the two of swords, not the ace.

"How did you—"

"I didn't do anything," Dan replied. "*You* just spat in my eye by calling me a cheater to cover your bad memory and fading eyes, old man." He reached out and pulled the pot into his stack of coins and trade bars.

The Kheshi looked around the table. "You *saw* it, all of you! This little imp is a sorcerer."

"Am not," Dan replied indignantly. He tried to maintain a look of offended pique, but a grin fought its way back to the fore.

The Kheshi shouted something in a language Madlin didn't recognize and leaped across the table. Coin, cards, and scoundrels all scattered in the Kheshi's wake. A simmering hatred brewed among gamblers of a certain ilk. The suspicion that everyone was out to cheat them bubbled just below the surface, and came to a boil the instant proof was offered. The whole room erupted in chaos as offended gamblers took out their frustrations on the accused cheat—whoever they guessed it was, once the room had devolved into a general melee. Other, more opportunistic sorts scrambled for the scattered coins and sought the nearest exit.

Madlin drew her revolver and pressed herself as flat against the wall as she could, abandoning her chair as an untenable position. A young woman might have made a tempting target of opportunity, but most Kheshis were peculiar about honor when it came to women. She might be carried off as a prize at the end, but unless she waded in among the brawl, she didn't expect anyone to come after her. The gun helped on that account.

When Dan was buried under a muscled brute three times his heft, Madlin worried for his safety. Her glances around the room strayed often to the door, looking for an opening to bolt. When no one seemed likely to clear a path for her, she waited and watched the combat. Men fell upon one another with tankards, fists, and the occasional knife. She didn't see anyone with a firearm drawn besides herself. Two of the serving girls were pressed against the far wall of the card room, using their drink platters as shields.

As she watched the action, she saw the serving girls edging around the periphery of the room. Someone had taken them in tow and was sneaking them clear. Dan! Madlin hadn't been able to keep track of him, and had assumed he was still on the ground somewhere in the worst of the rumble. He had the hood of his cloak up, but by his build and manner, she knew it had to be him.

As Dan reached the door and ushered the two relieved serving girls through—Madlin's ire rose as he swatted one on the backside to urge her into the front room—he looked over to her. "Time to go!"

Madlin gestured to the clutter of tables, chairs, and angry, drunken gamblers littering her path. She was startled as they slid out of her way, and in her fright almost believed that she had somehow done it. But Dan beckoned to her with the path cleared, and she rushed though the parted furniture and out the door.

"Thanks," Madlin said, short on breath after finding she'd been holding it as she cowered against the wall. "What possessed your pox-rotted mind to start a fight?"

Dan opened his mouth, then closed it and raised a finger. "Just a moment. Almost forgot something: Don't start something and leave it unfinished." Dan pulled the door to the card room closed, but just before it latched, a tiny spark flew from his finger.

Click. The door shut. From within the room Madlin heard a sound that few from Tellurak would know: the ignition of a gas burner, or at least something that sounded like one. There were screams from within.

Madlin was aghast. "What did you just do?"

"Two reasons for everything," Dan said, mimicking the cadence of a professor's lecture. "First, I won." Dan hefted a sack slung over his shoulder beneath his cloak. "Second, I showed you how dangerous magic can be. You sure you want to learn magic that will make you scream like that if you misstep?"

Madlin gave a tight nod. She wasn't sure, but neither was she about to spoil her hopes of saving her foot.

"Let's get out of here. Takes a lot to rile the constables in this lawless town, but this should do it."

Dan took Madlin by the hand and led her out into the streets.

Chipmunk awoke in a darkened cabin, alone. She was aboard the *Jennai*, still parked on the valley floor, undergoing repairs. The quiet wrapped around her like a blanket, isolating her from the world outside. She could hear her breath quickening as she prepared to put Dan's advice into practice.

It was so simple, or at least it sounded simple the way he explained it. The act of using aether cleansed the body. "*It's like fire in your veins,*" was how he had put it. Chipmunk had never felt the fire. Apparently, empowering simple rune structures wasn't enough to have a noticeable effect. She needed something that channeled more power through her.

For a moment, Chipmunk had forgotten about Madlin, but she found her thoughts drifting to her twin's circumstances. Madlin was asleep fully clothed with the exception of her boots and gun belt, locked in a room with a thirteen year old madman. It was hard to think of Dan as anything less after his display at the gambling hall. There had to have been fifty people killed in the fire, and for what, to test her resolve? It had almost worked in deterring her, but she wasn't willing to give up on curing herself so easily. Chipmunk touched her forehead and rubbed away at the memory of Dan's fingers on Madlin's skin.

"I can wake up at any time, just you remember that," Chipmunk whispered to the darkness. By his description of the spell, Dan would be able to see and hear through her, but that would be all. She kept her hands away from her sensitive areas, in case he had lied. Madlin was at the whim of Dan's self-restraint, which was scant comfort.

She found the curtain to the cabin's window and let in enough moonlight to see by. In the washed out light, she found her right boot and her crutch; she planned to keep off her infected foot entirely. It was more awkward than using the foot for balance, but less painful.

The corridors of the *Jennai* were guarded, but only by sleepy soldiers with little concern that they might find trouble. Chipmunk had little to worry about from them, since she was in command. If anyone could wander the ship at night, it was her.

"General Chipmunk?" one guard whispered at her approach. He spoke Acardian. "Is that you?"

"Anyone else stumbling about on a crutch around here?" Chipmunk replied.

"Anything I can help you with, ma'am?"

"Bucket of water," she replied. It was hard to make out the soldier's reaction in the scant light from the corridor windows. "For my foot," she added.

"Of course, ma'am," the soldier said, sounding relieved. Chipmunk couldn't imagine what else he might have thought she needed a bucket for, unless perhaps she was planning on scrubbing floors in the middle of the night. She stood and waited as the soldier went off to find her one. There were a great many demands placed on her in her position as General, but at least there were certain perks as well.

The soldier came back minutes later with a steel bucket in one hand and a jar in the other. The bucket looked like it was from the coal room, rinsed off. The jar she had no ready guess for.

"What's that?" she asked.

"Biggest bucket I could find. Hope it fits your foot. Oh, and I found some epsom salts. Thought it couldn't hurt."

"Thanks," Chipmunk replied. "Bring it to my cabin, will you?" She gritted her teeth at the slip, and hoped the soldier didn't notice that, either. She was still in the habit of asking for things, rather than giving orders. She caught herself doing it too often, habits long ingrained in her because she had always been a follower, and in Madlin because she had grown up in equality-conscious Tinker's Island.

The soldier didn't make use of the offered option to decline her request, and followed after her halting gait. To the man's credit, he didn't patronize her by offering his shoulder or arm for support. Chipmunk used a corridor wall to help balance.

"What's your name, soldier?" she asked just as they arrived at her cabin.

"Calair, ma'am. Renfry Calair." It was a Hurlan name, which made the Acardian understandable. Hurlan had its own language, but few spoke it outside their borders. Acardian was a sister tongue and taken up by most Hurlans who traveled.

"Well, Freeman Calair, thanks for your help."

"If you need anything, I won't be far," Calair replied.

Chipmunk shut the door and set the epsom salts aside. It was a thoughtful gesture, but she had no intention of putting her foot in the water. She sat down on the bed and took a few deep breaths to steel herself. She went over Dan's lesson:

"You don't know any real spells, so you're going to need to try the other way. Remember how I said I keep warm with aether? Well, it's like that, but you're going to go a bit hotter. You need to burn the rot out like a fever. Draw in aether and hold it. Let that burning sensation thrash around inside you. It's going to hurt, but that's how you know it's working."

The bucket was for the aether when she was done with it. She hoped it would be enough, but she was willing to risk melting metallic walls and floor panels if it came to it.

Another steady breath: air in—hold for two beats—air out. Chipmunk let her muscles relax. Lying back in bed with her back to the wall, she picked up her left foot and crossed it over her knee, where she could see it in the pale light. She hadn't noticed before, but there was an odor to it that shouldn't emanate from living flesh. The safety pin came away easily and Chipmunk slowly unwound the bandage, dreading the sight beneath.

The foot was dark, far darker than Sosha's skin, a deathly hue that benefitted from insufficient light. The surface was wrinkled and puckered, like something beneath the skin was eating away at it—which she supposed it was. Chipmunk closed her eyes, reminding herself that in a few minutes, the rot would be gone. Dan might have been many things, but he had never set her amiss on magical matters. It had to work.

Chipmunk calmed herself until she felt adrift, risking falling back to sleep, but needing the freedom from distraction so she could concentrate. She drew in aether, just a trickle. There was no cause for rushing things. A little warm glow welled inside her, like the feeling of gulping hot cider on a cold day. The cool inrush of the aether chilled her around that growing ball of heat in her core. It wasn't long before the heat began to spread throughout her body. She was no expert on anatomy, but it didn't feel like it flowed through blood vessels, but poured down her limbs like they were made of dry sponge, soaking in water.

There was no concept of time. She wished that she hadn't left her pocketclock with the ship's navigator, so that she would have something to ground herself. Brushing aside that unhelpful thought, she kept up the flow of aether as she warmed. The chill of her draw was no longer enough to overcome the aether already within her. The pleasant warmth had grown to the heat of a steam room, of standing too close to the boiler. She cut the flow and waited to see what happened as the stored aether worked its way around inside her.

The tinker's brain in Chipmunk's head told her that with the inlet valve closed, the system should maintain a steady temperature, less heat lost to the air over time. The principle held for any liquid or gas—aether was neither of those. Despite containing the same amount of aether, the burning sensation kept growing. A furnace door opened, and Chipmunk stood right in front of it, unable to back away from the waves of heat pouring forth. Instinctively she put a hand over her mouth to protect her lungs from the blistering air she imagined around her, though the cabin was cool everywhere but inside her body.

The furnace cracked and split; lava spewed forth, washing over Chipmunk. Her whole body felt like it burst into flame.

She had waited too long, she knew at once. The fascination with the process and a struggle to understand how it could defy all the physics she knew had cost her time she should have spent mitigating the effect. Chipmunk's eyes snapped open and sought the water bucket. A scream tore itself loose from her throat as she forced the aether into the bucket. The surface steamed instantly, and within seconds it was boiling so violently that the bucket shook and danced along the floor.

As she struggled to force the aether from her, black spots swam in her vision, rimmed in purples and greens. There wasn't enough light for her to have seen such colors. Everything in the room was shades of grey. Until it all went black.

Chapter 7

"Great power and knowledge makes them wanton as children. Would that the mighty sorcerers held the wisdom of a common shepherd; to each look after his own and leave the greater world in peace." -Tallax

The audience hall of the Imperial Palace of the Kadrin Empire murmured with conversation and lilted with the harmony of flute and lyre. There was no pressing business on the schedule, just a series of minor matters to bring to the empress' attention. The audiences were spaced out to stave off the boredom of the court hangers on. During the ample breaks, servants with trays of delicacies drifted among the self-important and important alike—and were wise enough to tell them apart. Knowing whether the last goblet of wine should be given to Lord Allard's daughter or one of the empress' knights was a key to long, fruitful employment. No one got rich serving in the palace staff, but few servants were better off.

A slim black hurricane threw open the doors of the audience hall, sending the door guards scrambling. He strode through the polite gathering with the grace of a pig farmer in his own sty. The servants who knew their business would sooner offend the empress than earn the ire of Danilaesis Solaran, the future warlock of the Kadrin Empire.

On the dais, Empress Celia conversed with the high sorcerer, Danilaesis's grandfather, Axterion. The two carried their conversation in low tones, with Axterion craning his aging body over the throne to maintain a semblance of privacy.

Axterion looked up, his bushy white eyebrows knitting themselves into one jumble of scruff in disapproval. "What do you want, boy? You should be in ..." Axterion paused and scratched a finger at his bearded chin. "Astronomy, if I'm not mistaken."

"Clear the hall, I've got more important things on my mind than stars. Nothing this rabble needs to concern themselves with," Danilaesis replied. He continued to the base of the dais, but didn't set foot on the steps.

"Since when did I say you could go about dressed up as a warlock?" Axterion asked. "I thought I had them put your last outfit in the hearthfire."

"Letter of the law, Marem did. I cast a ward over the fabric to keep it from burning. I just picked it out once she was gone and sent it to the wash woman to get the smoky smell out. Now just order the hall clear so we can talk about things that matter."

Axterion looked sidelong at the empress, who had watched the exchange impassively. "Very well," Empress Celia said, her voice carrying throughout the hall. "Clear the room."

Guards slipped in from the corridors and helped usher courtiers through the doors. There was muttering and grumbling, but no open protest. Danilaesis knew he was despised at court; it was a goal of his. He could no more stand the fawning, vapid noble proxies than they could tolerate him.

"Send the listener away as well," Danilaesis said, once the hall was empty of all but himself, Axterion, and Empress Celia. "I'll fetch him when we're done."

"Kaelmar, you may go," Axterion said. Though there was no sound, Danilaesis could see the aether shadow of the man, even through the warded palace walls. Normally he would remain on hand to summon the courtiers to return once a private audience was ended. Danilaesis wanted no Fifth Circle sorcerer involved in hearing his news.

"Warlock Danilaesis, what would you speak of?" Celia asked, drawing a frumpled glare from Axterion at the use of Danilaesis's title. Danilaesis had always liked her. She was brutal and shrewd, taking over true rulership of the empire from Emperor Sommick, who did nothing but drink and eat and sire heirs. Celia was young enough and comely enough that despite being more than twice his age, Danilaesis could still harbor boyish fantasies about killing the emperor and taking her for himself. Her sorcerous ability to keep her youth certainly helped.

"I saw it."

"That other world you mentioned?" Axterion asked. "Korr?"

"It was only a glimpse, but it was enough. It's real," Danilaesis replied. The gleam in his eye would have spoiled his deception had he tried any.

"Why is this so urgent?" Celia asked. Her hands clung to the arms of her throne, like claws. Danilaesis could never decide if it was anger, impatience, or just the desire to get up from the throne and pace about in un-empresslike fashion that made her do it.

"This is a world where you'd be a formidable sorceress, Empress," Danilaesis replied. Before taking the throne, Celia had been nothing more than a Sixth Circle sorceress with a prominent patron. Danilaesis could twist her like a cloth-knot doll. "They have airships that fly on the barest hint of aether, based on designs far cleverer than the *Daggerstrike*, or the sea ships we've converted."

Axterion took two shuffling steps with the aid of his staff, and lowered himself into his cushioned chair near the royal thrones. "Yes, I can see how that could come in useful. Ghelk still fears to move against us, but the rest of the Megrenn Alliance is pulling themselves together faster than we are."

"Even if they make their own airships, they won't be able to make them like these," Danilaesis said. "We'd rule the skies, maybe even pin the dragons in their lairs and keep the goblins in check."

Axterion shook his head. "No, much as I like the idea, your grandmother always cautioned against the pollution of the worlds. Unintended consequences.

Maybe the goblins get a hold of one and make five for every one we build. They could, I reckon."

"Quit being death's herald," Danilaesis said. "Think of it: we sweep the Megrenn Alliance clear, then drive the goblins to extinction."

"Dragons would never allow it," Axterion said. "I know Rashan killed one, but you're no Rashan—"

"Yet," Celia said.

"Thank the winds!" Axterion added. "There's ways to deal with folks besides killing, or are you skipping those classes, too?"

"'Never suffer an enemy to live, once they offer violence,' my uncle always said," Danilaesis replied.

"Look where that got him," Celia replied. "I saw that desperate paranoia firsthand. Anything you saw from him but madness was a painted facade. In the end, he was only happy when killing."

"Yeah, two hundred forty two years, and we can't even be sure he's dead," Danilaesis said in mocking tone. "Saved the empire in four wars. What a waste of a life."

Axterion's eyes narrowed. "Just how did you see Korr?"

Danilaesis smirked. "You got me. Yeah, it was one of the tricks Rashan showed me. He never could say no to teaching me spells. Said I was one of the few bright hopes in the empire. I can only assume he included the two of you in that sentiment as well." He slathered on the sarcasm at the end, lest the dullards misconstrue him.

"Whose eyes did you use?" Axterion demanded.

"Twinborn girl named Madlin. All fully consensual," Danilaesis swore, holding a hand to his heart.

"What price are they demanding for knowledge of these airships?" Celia asked.

"I don't plan on paying them anything," Danilaesis replied. "I'm going to convince them to build them in Tellurak and in return for empowering them, I'll get to see the plans."

"So you would arm one world with devices and teach magic to another?" Axterion asked, pointing an accusing staff at Danilaesis.

Danilaesis spread his hands. "I keep telling you, I only taught them enough to draw aether and vent it off. I'm no fool."

"Good." Axterion grunted. "You've got as much business teaching spells as you do leading troops into battle."

"You didn't need the hall clear for this," Celia said. "You could have come to me later, in private."

"Neither of you has ever flown on an airship, have you?" Danilaesis asked.

"Blasted things aren't safe," Axterion grumbled.

Danilaesis grinned. "These are. The stories I've heard, they have hundreds of troops aboard, like little cities. How can I keep that to myself until classes end?"

"In the future, you will find a way," Celia said. "Go bring back the listener and have the court sent in."

"You'll see one day," Danilaesis said, holding up a finger. "These airships will sort out our Megrenn problems, and you'll be kissing my toes." He spun on his heel and stalked off.

It seemed for a moment that he was going to have the last word. The door was within his reach, when Axterion's gruff voice echoed across the black marble chamber. "And take off that costume. You're no warlock yet."

There were few pleasures sweeter than subverting his grandfather's edicts. After Danilaesis found the listener and gave him leave to refill the audience chamber with its usual complement of toadies, he searched among the courtiers. He had caught the eye of Lord Allard's daughter on his way in, and sought to find her again. Sybissa was close to him in age and fair as a spring flower. He parted her from her chaperone as the herd flowed by, and extracted her from the mass of rich, pompous slackwits. She was no better than the rest in that regard, a blushing mess of giggles and shy glances that he led to less populous palace halls. Keeping Dan's promise to Madlin not to take ungentlemanly advantage as she slept had taken an act of willpower that required repayment. He needed a willing vessel for his yearnings just as urgently as Madlin's twin had needed a bucket of cold water for her trapped aether. The difference was that Danilaesis knew how to handle his own dilemma.

Chapter 8

"I have felt fate's kiss, that I had friends who would act from their hearts, rather than do what I asked of them."
–King Jouron, in The King's Lament

Chipmunk sat in bed with a makeshift drafting board across her lap. She wore her kuduk-made spectacles and a woolen nightshirt that reeked of stale sweat. The curtain was closed, but an extra light installed by the head of the bed provided plenty of light to draw by. A side table was littered with sheets of paper. Some were reports or manifests, but most were her own sketches. The blankets were littered with pencil shavings from the small knife she used to sharpen it; the knife itself lay amid the shavings.

Time was forgotten. The heel of Chipmunk's hand was grey with graphite dust, and her eyes were heavy with uncounted hours of staring.

There was a knock at the door. She looked up, but said nothing. Her pencil stopped mid-line.

"It's me," Sosha's voice called through the door.

Chipmunk reached to the bedside and drew her coil pistol. "Don't even try coming in here."

"I'm just trying to—"

"GO AWAY!"

She listened as Sosha's footsteps faded down the corridor.

It took a moment for Chipmunk to slow her thoughts enough that she could lose herself in her work once more. Drawing wasn't the same as working in steel, but she could envision the result from the lines on paper. She had progressed past the stage of wild imaginings and had moved on to practical schematics to hand over to the welders and mechanics.

There was another knock at the door. "Who's there?" she snapped.

The door opened before she thought to draw her coil gun. It was her father. "Why'd you chase Sosha off?" Erefan stepped inside and shut the door behind him.

"Because my Eziel-damned foot is killing me," Chipmunk replied. She slammed her pencil down on the bed. It lacked the satisfying snapping sound she would have preferred to punctuate her statement.

"That doesn't make any sense. You haven't got a—"

"Because that butcher cut it off!" Chipmunk shouted. "And yes, it still hurts; gut me if I understand how."

"Maybe you should try asking that one to your Veydran friends. They're the ones who nearly got you killed."

"No thanks to you," Chipmunk replied. "At least Dan was willing to try."

"At full risk to you," Erefan replied, crossing his arms. "He wasn't in any danger, but he nearly baked you alive."

"I knew the risks."

"Yes, but you didn't understand them," Erefan said. He sat down on the end of the bed. "You're pestering the forces of the universe, and they're going to swat you like a fly. You don't work around live spark without rubber gloves. You don't weld without goggles. What make you think a rusted bucket of water was going to protect you from aether. You might as well have kept an onion in your pocket for all the good it would do. Stupid, superstitious nonsense, all of it."

"All I know is Dan tried to help me and Sosha cut my damned foot off."

"I heard you gave Captain Toller a time of it about letting Jamile aboard the *Darksmith*."

"You can thank my Veydran friends for that one, too. They convinced me to let you deal with her when we got home. Dan kept me from shooting her when I woke up."

Erefan scanned the bedside. Before Chipmunk could guess ahead of him, he picked up the coil gun and held it out of reach as she made a grab for it.

"Gimme that back."

"Why, so you can shoot Sosha when she comes to change your bandage? Rynn, you've got to get this temper of yours under control. People are looking to you for guidance—Eziel help them—so you can't go sulking off by yourself when unpleasant realities crop up."

"Unpleasant realities?" Chipmunk grabbed her collar and lifted her chin. "*This* is an unpleasant reality. You want to help, find a way to get this thing off without killing me. *This*," she whipped back the blankets to show a bandaged stump just below her knee, "is Sosha's incompetence and a missing foot. She's no physician, and I don't want her for a nurse, either."

Erefan studied the coil gun idly as he sat. "You know, I found myself in Tinker's Island, sketching up plans for mechanical legs the other night." He set the gun down in his lap and sighed. "My only daughter is maimed, and all I can think of is to make replacement parts. I don't know what to do for you, Rynn. Sosha does. Jamile does. If it hadn't been for her, you'd be dead by now twice over. Once from the black rot, and once from the burning blood."

Chipmunk glanced down to her arm, where a scabbed puncture wound by the crook of her elbow reminded her of the transfusion of blood she'd received. Missing limbs, someone else's blood coursing through her ... there was nothing natural about medicine.

"Any of the leg designs seem promising?" Chipmunk asked.

"Not yet," Erefan admitted. "I won't go a half-measure on this. We don't have the facilities here, but once we get the world-ripper running, I'll have one through from Tinker's Island."

"We're not running."

"I know."

"Want to see what I've been working on?" Chipmunk asked. She turned the drafting board away from Erefan, pending his answer.

Erefan made a pretense of trying to peer over the top, but he had no angle to see from where he sat. "Two days of secrecy, and suddenly you're eager to share?"

Chipmunk hooked a thumb at the side table. "Reports are saying most of the holes are patched. We'll lift soon if I don't show you."

"What is it?"

Chipmunk said nothing, but handed the sheet of paper to Erefan. His raised brows told her she had piqued his curiosity. "No vacuum at all?" Erefan asked. He laid the sheet on the bed between them. It showed the two airships joined together by a series of welded scaffolds, with the giant vacuum tanks sectioned into multiple stories of compartments for crew and equipment storage, with stairways down into the gondola.

"We're already having trouble keeping enough vacuum to stay aloft. There's a limit to vacuum we just can't get past. Levitation runes are the only way we'll be able to keep these things above cloud level without dumping crew and supplies, and I don't think that's how this war's getting won."

"This could take months," Erefan said. "I don't think we can remain undetected that long."

"We don't need to do it all at once. I had the ships park this close because I had some inkling of how I wanted to do this. For now, we just need to join the two ships, make sure the walkway between is safe, and get enough levitation runes carved that the vacuum can get us cloudborne. From there, we'll find someplace remote to set down and finish the work. We'll get supplies from Tinker's Island once the machine is ready." Erefan was bobbing his head along as she spoke.

"I like it."

Chipmunk smiled.

"I think that's the first smile I've seen from you in days," Erefan noted.

"First time I forgot about my foot for long enough," Chipmunk said. Her smile vanished.

"Oh, enough of the self-pitying twaddle. You'll heal up, we'll build you a proper tinker's leg, and you'll get on with running a rebellion. Oh, and just an observation, but 'General Chipmunk' sounds like something you call a little girl who wins all her games of Tunnel Hunt. I haven't laughed out loud in front of any of your troops yet, but I can't promise I won't. I've heard it from a few others as well." He stood and headed for the door.

"I'll take it under advisement," Chipmunk replied dryly.

Erefan held up the coil gun. "And I'll be sending Sosha along shortly. You need tending to, and she's the only one qualified. I don't care if you're not crying and hugging, but you're going to remind yourself that she saved your life." The door closed behind him.

The book in Chipmunk's hands was a soggy romance of questionable literary value. It told the tale of a pair of young kuduk lovers kept apart by family politics and bureaucratic tangles that were fifty years out of date. There hadn't been many books aboard either ship when the rebellion stole them, and it sounded like the best of a bad lot. It had the advantage of possessing a large cover, which Chipmunk held close to her face so she couldn't see around it. She glossed over the fact that the characters were kuduk, and replaced them with humans in her imagination in an attempt to lose herself in the pages.

At the far end of the bed, Sosha was tugging, prodding, and washing. It wasn't happening to Chipmunk, it was happening in another world, a land outside of fictional Sweetrock Deep, where Chipmunk stood beside Melody Steamheart as a magistrate attempted to explain why her marriage application had been referred to the Moral Hygiene Committee. Chipmunk found herself skipping long passages that detailed the appeals process and why Melody and her betrothed couldn't get an exemption. She winced as Sosha applied an ointment that tingled, catching her off guard and sucking her back to Korr.

She knew Sosha was nearly done, so she skipped to the end of the book and skimmed the last few pages. License approval. Wedding plans. Marries Thunder Hardstone. She frowned and flipped back to earlier in the book. Her beloved had been Hammer Deepspike. Chipmunk shook her head. Either the author lost track, or there was some twist in the pages she had skipped. She didn't care enough to investigate which.

By the time Chipmunk had wrung the book dry of the faintest droplet of interest, Sosha had finished and Chipmunk's leg was snug in a fresh bandage—what little of it remained.

"You sick of this room yet?" Sosha asked.

"Sick of the company," Chipmunk replied, still holding the book between them, stuck at the final page.

Sosha hooked a finger over the top of the book and pulled it down. "You need to get up and move around."

"I don't want anyone to see me like this." Chipmunk yanked the book free and snapped it shut.

"What's there to be ashamed of? You escaped kuduk slavery and were wounded in the effort. You've paid in blood. The Tellurak soldiers see that and they know they're following someone dedicated to a cause."

Chipmunk raised her chin and showed off her collar. "This isn't enough of a reminder for them?"

Sosha tilted her head. "Our people know what it means; a lot of them wore collars until your father freed them. The Tinker's troops? They see it, but it doesn't hit them in the gut. I don't think anyone knows the frustration of not being able to get a collar off unless they've worn one." Sosha held out a hand. "Come on, show them their general isn't bedridden."

"What, are you going to carry me? I can't get around on a single crutch with one leg."

Sosha winked. "I've got a surprise for you." She stood and slipped out into the corridor. Seconds later, she reentered with a new pair of crutches. They were cobbled, but cobbled by someone who knew their business. They were of slimmer construction than her own crutches had been, though still based in steel pipe. The shaft was jogged so that the welded grip two thirds of the way up was in line with the lower end. Cushions at the top were repurposed from the chair arms from the lounge in first class. She didn't recognize the rubber ends they'd attached to the bottoms to keep traction on the floor.

"Who made those?"

"Do you have to ask? Your father finished them yesterday, but I didn't want to force you up so soon if you weren't willing."

Chipmunk took one of the crutches and hefted it. It was lighter than hers, partly due to thinner piping, partly due to a single-post design, compared to hers with its two pipes coming together like streams into a river, with the grip across. The grip of the new crutch jutted from the side and was wrapped in cloth tape. She took the second crutch from Sosha and scooted to the edge of the bed.

Her balance was awkward as she swung herself around; her left side felt too light. She kept the bandaged stump clear of the blankets as she moved, lest she catch it on anything, wary of the pain she expected. It hurt enough already without more help. Chipmunk arranged the crutches under her arms and used her good leg to hop to her feet—or rather, her foot.

"How do they feel?" Sosha asked, craning her neck around to meet Chipmunk's gaze as she watched the floor.

"Right one's fine. Left one still feels like someone stuck my leg in a furnace."

"No, I mean the crutches. Length? Grip? Weight?"

Chipmunk took a few experimental hops around the cabin, mostly turning since that was all the room there was. "Fine for now. I'll let you know after an hour or two on them if I feel the same way."

"Good, so you will be getting up." Sosha beamed.

Chipmunk looked down to her nightshirt. "Well, I'll need to put something on. Even though it's warm about, I probably shouldn't go out like this."

"I borrowed a skirt for you," Sosha said. "I put it in your footlock—I put it in the trunk at the end of the bed."

"Foot," Chipmunk said. "You can say the word. It's not like I'm going to forget I'm missing one if you don't say it for long enough. Foot, foot, foot."

"Fine," Sosha replied. She opened the footlocker and threw a clean shirt and the aforementioned skirt on the bed. "Let me give you a hand."

"I can dress myself, it's not like I'm—" Chipmunk stopped herself. She was. Maimed, crippled, an invalid, whatever the term, it fit her now. "All right, just be quick about it."

The ends of Chipmunk's crutches sank into the soft soil each time she planted them. It was easier than navigating the *Jennai* with its slick metal floors and stairways. The outsides of both ships swarmed with workers, some skilled tradesmen, some just pitching in to help out. She could tell the two groups apart by a moment's observation.

It was the largest she'd ever seen one of her drawings become in real life. A lattice of short bars ran between the vacuum tanks of the two ships, angled against one another to prevent twisting and racking. At ground level, a more elaborate scaffold was being constructed between the forward starboard gangplank of the *Jennai* and the forward port gangplank of the *Cloudsmith*. When they had more materials, they'd build additional crossings and lay a proper floor, but for the time being they just needed a way between ships other than signaling.

"Ahh, General Rynn, there you are. We're having some trouble with the ..."

"General Rynn, good to see you up and about again."

"Excuse me a moment, General Rynn. Can you show me where we're supposed to put ..."

There was a trend developing, and she didn't care for it. There was a hint of artifice in the use of her name among the rebels, the use of her full title when there was no need for such formality. As with most artifice, she suspected her father foremost. He had made it clear upon first hearing her human name that he didn't care for it. It seemed that he had taken advantage of her convalescence to rewrite the personnel records, starting at the top. Worse, she couldn't think of a way to reverse the trend without coming across as petty and rude.

For all the questions and consultations, her plan was roaring into action. It had only been a few hours, and the shape of the combined airship was already taking form.

"Who's carving the runes?" Chipmunk asked. She didn't need to look to know that Sosha was still clinging to her like a shadow.

"They're inside the ship," Sosha replied. "We've got a jeweler's assistant and a cobbler who proved handy with an awl. Your father marked the spots with chalk. I think he put them where you said, but it wouldn't surprise me if he had his own notions."

"Getting to know him a bit, are you?" Chipmunk started moving again, idly touring the ships while getting accustomed to the crutches.

"The man would tell the sun how to shine if he could find a way to talk to it."

"Probably have a way worked out to get it to shine through a cloudy sky, too."

"What's that sound?" Sosha asked.

Chipmunk paused and listened, straining her ear to catch anything that sounded out of place. She shook her head. "I don't hear anything."

"Just wait."

A low droning grew slowly, echoing oddly among the steep hills. There were shouts from the workers on the vacuum tanks, who had the higher vantage, but Chipmunk had already deduced the source of the noise.

"Is that a—?"

"Airship!" Chipmunk shouted. "Everyone on board, NOW! Pumps to full. Lift off and prepare to fire once you see them." She hopped along as quick as she could, using the crutches when she felt overbalanced. It was still slow going. She heard the vacuum pumps aboard both ships kicking on, it wouldn't be long before they began to lift.

All over both vessels, workers scrambled to get inside. The ones working on the vacuum tank lowered their welding gear and slid down the external maintenance ladders. On the ground, rebels swarmed over their hard-won building materials, reloading the cargo holds with steel bars and sheets than had been laid out for the workers.

A shadow fell over the valley floor. Chipmunk turned her gaze upward to see the Ruttanian army vacu-dirge that blotted out the sun. One of her crutches caught the ground at an unexpected angle while she wasn't watching her footing, and the ground came up to meet her, face on.

"Torvar, Beele, get over here," Sosha shouted from close by. Repeater-rifle fire rattled down from above, sending up clouds of dirt in a neat row not far away.

Chipmunk tried to keep her grip on her crutches, but someone yanked them out of her hands. Suddenly she was hauled up and two solid-built men lifted her onto their shoulders with her arms around each of their necks. She flew along, borrowed skirt trailing in the wind. They had her aboard the *Jennai* before half the workers had made it aboard. Sosha tried to follow, but Chipmunk retrieved her crutches and waved her away.

"Get to the *Cloudsmith*. Find the runes and get them working quick as you can."

"Aye aye, general," Sosha said with a quick salute before she ran off.

"Get the coil guns ready and fire on that enemy ship as soon as you have a shot!" Chipmunk shouted to no one and everyone at once as she made her way to the support pylons that attached the vacuum tank to the gondola portion of the ship. She could only hope that her father hadn't made too many alterations to her plans.

The rearmost support she had designated was bare of runes and no one was working on carving any. The next was in the same state. She cursed her luck for having started at the wrong end of the ship. At the midpoint of the ship she found the cobbler working with his awl. The rune structure was half-finished and crude.

"Tell me this isn't the first one you're still working on," Chipmunk said, puffing for breath.

"No ma'am. I'll have this one good in five or ten, give or take a few, but the ones up front 'o here is done drawed up."

Chipmunk looked over the runes. They were a series of straight-ish scratches where they needed to curve, and weren't very deep or uniform.

"The others look like this?" she demanded.

"Yah-huh," the cobbler replied with a nod.

Chipmunk snatched the awl from his hand and held it between her teeth. "Go fine 'nother," she mumbled as she hopped off to the next pylon. The awl tasted of steel and leatherworking oils and sweat. She wanted to keep her lips off it but she couldn't risk the time lost if it fell from a toothy grip as she tried to run on crutches.

The pylon at the mid fore sported a complete set of shoddily-scratched runes. Chipmunk leaned in close, even pulling her spectacles up to get a detailed view. Definitely not touching. Runes were more than a shape to fool the eye, they were conduits of aether. There were places where lines didn't touch in some runes, but only where they were damned well meant not to touch. A cluster of scratches was no more a functioning rune than a jumble of wire scraps was a spark circuit.

Chipmunk put her spectacles back down and leaned against the wall for support. Her crutches fell to the floor with a pair of clangs. She needed both hands to work the awl as she scratched in among the cobbler's runes, connecting the mass of lines into working runes. She heard shots fired all the while she worked, both the Ruttanian repeater-rifles and her own troops' Tinker-made weapons. She hoped there was coil gun fire as well, but there was no way for her to hear the quieter weapons through the walls of the *Jennai*, let alone over the firing of the black-powder weapons.

How long she worked, perhaps half an hour, perhaps a handful of minutes. It was the close, hands-on work in which she loved to lose herself. The tool was ill-suited to the job, and the circumstances manic, but there was a meticulousness that drew her into the minutiae and let her block out the distractions around her.

There. Finished.

It took several blinks to get her eyes to stop trying to focus in tight on the tiniest of scratches and take in the runes as a whole. A change in the feel of the floor plates told her that they were airborne—they likely had been for some time. Somehow she had failed to take note as the ship listed heavily to port. The shift had leaned her into the wall she was working on, else she might have been thrown to the floor by the change in altitude. Sosha's runes must have been in better shape.

Time to right this ship.

Chipmunk pressed her hand to the runes and drew in aether. The clean, crisp feel that washed into her brought with it a foreboding memory of the last time she had delved into sorcery. This time, however, she kept no aether stored inside her. As it came in, she poured the aether into the rune. The metal of the ship groaned in protest as the load upon it grew, as the pylon tried to float up, pushing against the vacuum tank and pulling on the gondola.

It wasn't until much later in the day, when her troops and officer had all reported in, that she learned her first great lesson about airship combat: altitude is victory. Get enough air beneath you, and your adversary can't get a line of fire on you because of the bulk of their own vacuum tank getting in the way.

By nightfall, they were on the ground again, salvaging the enemy airship, repairing their own, and continuing Chipmunk's modifications. The pocketclock was wound and ticking; the Ruttanians knew where they were.

Chapter 9

"If I had invented politicians, I'd have scrapped them after the first prototype as a flawed idea." –Kezudkan Graniteson

The Eversall Civic Auditorium was a structure meant to echo. Its vaulted ceiling and bare stone surfaces were expertly crafted to spread sounds from the front of the chamber to all those in attendance. Despite its name, it was intended for public government proceedings, not theater performances—though Kezudkan sourly conflated the two when it came to politics.

The barrister at Kezudkan's side was a model of the profession, with a beard combed, curled, and dyed boot-polish black. His daruu solicitor sat on the far side of the witness table, flanking the barrister. Dunmurok had advised Kezudkan since they were both young men, and his advice had included hiring a strop-sharp kuduk to speak in front of the city council.

The auditorium held quite a crowd. The galleries were only ever filled when scandalous trials were conducted. Murderers, traitors, and corrupted officials had the masses slavering for justice. An investigative hearing into a matter that faded from the newspaper headlines over a month ago was only enough to pique the idle minds of a few citizens, and then only because of the bizarre circumstances involved.

Of the nine council members seated at the head of the room, the centermost spoke. "Kezudkan Graniteson, this hearing has been convened to unpuzzle the origins of what has come to be known as the Great Eversall Revolt. I would first like to convey this council's disappointment at the tardy and lackadaisical manner in which you have chosen to treat our summons. While I have every intention of delving to the bottommost shaft of this affair, you have complicated matters needlessly by your delays."

The barrister stood. "Lady Chief Councilor, please accept my client's contrition for the delay in appearing before this council. Mr. Graniteson was away from Eversall at the time of the incident, attending to the health of his sister. As he was not a witness to the preceding events, it is very likely that Eversall's investigators have more knowledge of the events in question than my client. However, he is here of his own free will and eager to provide answers to any questions, however insignificant a help they may be."

Kezudkan glanced behind the back of his barrister, and caught Dunmurok's eye. The daruu solicitor gave a nearly imperceptible nod that said: *I told you he was good.*

The chief councilor peered down at Kezudkan through gold-rimmed spectacles. "Does the witness wish to make a preliminary statement?"

"My client has no preliminary statement," the barrister replied.

Chief Councilor Elaura Korsger nodded an acknowledgement and leafed through the documents in front of her. She perused one of them briskly, then leaned forward and turned to one of her colleagues. "Councilor Derrath, proceed with the inquiry."

At the far end of the raised desk behind which all the councilors sat, a grey-bearded kuduk took up a sheaf of papers and cleared his throat. "To begin, Mr. Graniteson, let us clear up a few details ..."

The inquiry began with the chief councilor outlining trivial details about Kezudkan personally: his birth date, parentage, academic and professional credentials, and the nature of his varied business concerns. Then another of the councilors took over and spent the rest of the morning reading into evidence the official accounts of the slave escape, the investigation of the Graniteson Estate, and the subsequent actions of the human rebels who had presumably risen in the wake of the escape. The barrister objected to the latter, saying that there was no conclusive evidence that the upswing in rebel activity was tied to the Eversall Revolt—he tactfully left the "Great" off the beginning, which Kezudkan appreciated—and the objection was sustained.

At least I'm not getting the whole muddy rebellion lumped down on my shoulders.

The inquiry proceeded to matters of property and structural damage throughout Eversall. The numbers were staggering, likely inflated of course by citizens looking to profit from the tide of insurance claims, but staggering nonetheless. The barrister stood time and again to raise objections of relevance, given that Kezudkan was not responsible for the behavior of escaped slaves, citing Article IV, section 8a of the Slave Code. Whatever he was paying the barrister was a pittance compared to the expense that would come of having every insurer in Eversall fall on him like a swarm of rats to cover their losses. The kuduk barrister was like a champion from the ancient days of trial by combat, taking up his lord's banner to defend Kezudkan against all slander.

That lofty comparison screeched off the rails as the subject shifted to Kezudkan's personal dealings.

A councilwoman named Gurta Glondreigh had taken over, the fourth councilor to have a turn at the questioning. "Our investigations have revealed, Mr. Graniteson, that you have incurred a substantial debt. Additionally, we have obtained records from Slave Welfare indicating that you had an unusual number of slaves present in your home."

The barrister rose, popping up like a spring-box puppet to attack all statements the council made. "Lady Councilor, if you please, my client's temporary financial encumbrance was not a burden upon the household. My client is accustomed to a certain quality of living that requires a robust staff of slaves. The sheer quantity of humans my client owned may have made it statistically more likely that one would carry the seeds of rebellion within its head, but you cannot fault a man for living in a style to which had become his habit."

"I can if the debt was secured against the value of those slaves," Councilor Glondreigh replied. The barrister's head snapped around to glare at Kezudkan. There was a murmuring in the gallery of the auditorium. The sort of kuduk who came to watch dry legal proceedings was the same sort who found financial malfeasance titillating.

"I would ask for a short recess, so I might consult with my client," the barrister said.

"Denied. We've tapped all around the vein with our hammers, I will not adjourn the proceedings the instant we strike ore. Mr. Graniteson, if you have not fully informed your legal counsel in regards to your finances, I would ask that you answer these next few questions personally." Councilor Glondreigh ignored the barrister and focused her full attention on Kezudkan.

"Lady Councilor—" Kezudkan began.

"Stand when you address the council, Mr. Graniteson."

Kezudkan leaned on his cane and levered himself to his feet. He had been sitting far too long and far too still. His knees and hips ground like millstones as he straightened to his full height. "Lady Councilor, if you wished to plumb the deepest corners of my financial dealings, you should have summoned my accountant to the inquiry."

"Nonsense, Mr. Graniteson," Councilor Glondreigh said in a patronizing lilt. "We've spoken to the accountant listed on a number of your official filings. The poor gentleman was unaware that you were daruu. He had only corresponded infrequently with you, and his major dealings with you involved checking sums in ledgers delivered by your innumerable slaves. I rather suspect that you know every bog and cubby of your finances. How deep is your personal debt?"

Kezudkan held up an empty palm. "Without ledgers in front of me?" he scoffed. Finding nothing but stern faces among the councilors, he knew he had to venture a guess. "Seven, perhaps eight hundred thousand tenar." He took a few pacing steps to limber his joints as the gallery gasped.

"And the total value of the slaves in your estate, prior to the revolt?" Councilor Glondreigh asked.

"Triple that, at the least!" Kezudkan exclaimed, turning to shake his cane at the councilor.

Councilor Glondreigh laced her fingers in front of her. "Mr. Graniteson, do not test the council's patience. We have the records for each of your slaves from the files at Slave Welfare."

"Then what the quakes are you asking me for?" Kezudkan snapped. "Market prices, finding the right buyer, slave prices aren't so simple as Slave Welfare would make it appear. They need a number for the bookkeeping, but those aren't numbers a banker would care about."

"Are you an expert in the buying and selling of humans, then, Mr. Graniteson? You think yours were worth well more than the amount obtained by summing the individual values from Slave Welfare."

Kezudkan fought back the urge to shout that Erefan had been worth more than all his debts combined, with change to build a new wing on the estate. Instead he replied, "I've been to enough auctions to know my way around a sale."

"Very well, Mr. Graniteson. Let the record show that the witness disputes claims that his assets were insufficient to cover his debts, but does not deny that the collateral for his debt was his household staff of humans, which has now conveniently disappeared via revolt."

The Chief Councilor spoke up. "Are there any further questions you'd like to ask, Councilor Glondreigh?"

"No, there are not."

Kezudkan pivoted and aimed himself for the comfort of a low, stone seat beside his barrister, but a voice from the council stopped him. "One moment, Mr. Graniteson. I have another topic which I rather suspect your counsel will have no knowledge of."

The barrister popped up. "Objection, Chief Councilor. Councilor Oerteron is presupposing."

"Very well, then," Councilor Oerteron replied, acceding to the objection before the chief councilor could rule. "Would you care to explain what Mr. Graniteson was doing with the following items ..." The councilor went on to list the entire contents of a thunderail car that Kezudkan had hired, the switches, the relays, the miles upon miles of copper wire, the enormous quantity of lodestone. Kezudkan found it at once both fascinating and appalling that they had such a detailed inventory when he had gone to considerable expense not to have those items appear on any official list.

The barrister listened with glazed eyes and a posture that showed more patience than attentiveness. "My client is a hobbyist after a grand fashion. The materials you mentioned were for the construction of scientific equipment whose purpose and fabrication are beyond my layman's understanding."

"Why then," Councilor Oerteron asked, "are the records of these purchases falsified at every point along their travels? I prosecuted the Ten Banks debacle some years back, and I don't recall their machinations being so elaborate as Mr. Graniteson's."

"I believe my client was merely taking excessive precaution against—"

"Sit down, young man," Kezudkan said with a sigh. He took his cane and gently prodded the barrister back down into his seat before using it to rise once again. "Well played, Councilor, well played. I give up my charade. I had hoped to keep my invention bottled up a while longer, but you'll have it out of me in the dungeons, I'm sure, if I don't lay bare the recesses of my affairs before you."

The chief councilor spoke up. "We no longer have dungeons in the manner you—"

Kezudkan's cane slammed against the edge of the councilors' desk, stunning the chief councilor into silence.

"If you wish me to spill forth the dregs of my soul, kindly chew on your beard while I do so," Kezudkan said, despite the fact that Chief Councilor Elaura Korsger could no more grow a beard than he could. He cleared his throat and continued, sauntering up and down the length of the bench. "While my well-meaning barrister chipped at the surface, he underestimates me more egregiously than this council does. Science is a field where you may prove your theory if ten men can all solve a math problem the same way. I am a bit of a tinker myself. I like to see things work. When I was a boy, there was no spark, except what came from sky-storms or scuffing feet upon a deep pile rug. I watched its rise, saw its potential, and wanted to try my hand at it."

Kezudkan spared a glance at the spectators as he turned at the end of one lap. They were hanging on his every word. Considering all that he was about to lose, they ought to be. "As I advance in years, I find myself less tolerant of the laborious aspects of invention. I found a human, some years back—a freeman—and conspired to force him into selling himself to me. Not to bore you with the details of how, but this human was one I had to have. He had a tinker's mind and endless energy. His name is Erefan—you'll find it in your records there—the finest human I've ever known. He built me anything I asked him for, and half the time I didn't even have to tell him how. I paid a barroom ditty for him and he's worth a symphony. As years went by and my family moved away or died off, he became the only voice in my estate worth hearing. Vile as it may seem to you, I grew friendly with this Erefan, and we spoke often. Together, we designed and built the most marvelous machine that Korr has ever seen."

"Where is this going, Mr. Graniteson?" Councilor Oerteron asked.

"Councilor, you wished to know what I was doing with those materials? Why I kept the shipments secretive?" Kezudkan asked. The councilor nodded. "The obvious answer is that the materials were for the machine I mentioned. The subtle answer is that this machine required more spark than any one man has likely ever had need of. It was simply too much for the civic spark to provide. I knew General Spark Services would have been pulling their beards out if I had set up a personal dynamo the size I needed, so I took great pains to disguise the shipment, especially the lodestone."

"Are you telling us that the destruction of the lower three floors of your estate were the result of this machine you built?" Chief Councilor Korsger asked.

"No, not that," Kezudkan replied. He took a few paces for a dramatic pause, the clopping of his cane on the stone floor the only sound in the chamber. "No, I am fairly certain my slave Erefan used my machine to gather an army, and used explosives to destroy it so that I couldn't use it to track him down. You see, my machine permits instant travel to or from anywhere." There were gasps and muttering, not just among the spectators, but between the council members as well.

"Order! Order!" Chief Councilor Korsger shouted, banging a gavel to draw attention back to the front of the chamber. "Mr. Graniteson, if I understand correctly, you are claiming that your slave commandeered an experimental device of vast potential utility and used it to rally an army from across Korr? How is it that this slave was allowed unsupervised access to such a dangerous piece of equipment?"

Kezudkan turned his back to the council as he retrieved a mug of water from the witness table. Oration was dry work. "The crazed rat-eater worked twenty hours a day on the thing. Had to boot him out on holiday to get him to stop, and lock the estate doors behind him. Humans are obsessive creatures; terribly useful trait if you find a good task for it."

The barrister stood. "I must insist that my client refrain from answering any further questions, on the grounds—*Mmph.*"

Kezudkan put the tip of his cane to the barrister's gut and set him back down in his seat, driving the wind from the man at the same time.

"You may wish to heed your counsel's advice," Chief Councilor Korsger said. "In light of these facts, we may have to adjourn and reconvene at a criminal hearing."

Kezudkan waggled a finger in the air. "Article IV, section 8a, I believe exempts me from liability for the actions of a runaway slave."

"He was in your workshop, by your own admission," Chief Councilor Korsger replied.

"He was a runaway the moment he used my machine for his own purposes," Kezudkan countered. He spared a glance over his shoulder and tapped at the floor with his cane.

"Mr. Graniteson," Chief Councilor Korsger said, "I'm afraid we cannot accept your—frankly dubious—claims without proof. I am afraid we are going to have to adjourn this hearing until such time as we can arrange a criminal inquiry into the events that took place within the Graniteson Estate on the night of the revolt."

A side door to the auditorium opened, and two bailiffs entered, pulling a steel cage on wheels. "Oh, so this is the part where you declare me to be a risk of flight, and cage me until your inquiry? No, no I think I'd rather prove you right than win the moral victory." He shook his cane at the chief councilor.

On cue, a crackling spark leapt from the nothingness a pace away from Kezudkan. It hung in the air, writhing and twisting as it grew to outline the edges of a circular opening in space. Through the hole was a scene of metalworks and spark. Humming dynamos crackled in rows, pumping spark into a sea serpent of copper wires, its tentacles spread across the floor. A cloaked and hooded figure sat at a formidable looking set of dials and switches.

"My proof," Kezudkan declared to a stunned audience, then stepped through the hole. It closed behind him.

"You're quite a showman, Kezudkan," Draksgollow said, pulling back the hood of his cloak with his mechanical hand. "Wish I could have heard the speech."

"A man can't just disappear when an inquiry is ongoing. He's got to disappear so that folk don't want to find him," Kezudkan replied. "I think they'll be happy to just have my creditors write off my debts as a loss and stop trying to find me."

"Bit of an optimist, aren't you?"

Kezudkan put a hand on the controls of the wondrous machine. "I don't think anyone's going to be finding us."

"Plenty of people know I'm here," Draksgollow said. "It's a business interest of mine."

"Ahh, but machine three we will move to a secure location: somewhere remote, somewhere comfortable. I suggest you move your office there, and anything utterly essential. We can keep this facility running for as long as it remains undiscovered."

"I take it back, you're paranoid," Draksgollow said.

"Not paranoid, prepared. I won't forgive Erefan for what he tried to do to my sister. So long as that man still walks one world or another, I won't allow my guard down."

Chapter 10

"I won't get on a wooden boat ever again. Our steam ships have double hulls and sealing hatches and compartments. I refuse to trust my life to glorified bucket and the whim of the winds." -Cadmus Errol

The Katamic Sea fought the passage of the *Darksmith* with the weary sense of duty of a swordmaster sparring with a recruit. There was no question the sea could win the match any time it liked, but it badgered and tested the *Darksmith*, poking and prodding to see if the captain knew his lessons. When a trail of pink sky appeared over the port railing, the crew knew that the Katamic had played out its wrath. The storm clouds limped away to the east, their rains exhausted, leaving heaving swells in their wake.

Tanner had little love for ships, despite owning one of his own—off somewhere shipping who knew what for a pittance of honest coin on the side. He had developed a grudging respect for the service they provided, getting him off one forsaken continent and depositing him on one where he hadn't worn through his welcome. Khesh was a large enough landmass that it took a long time to use up, but he wasn't sad to be rid of it.

"Some storm, huh?" Dan said from behind him. Tanner could hear the idiot grin in his voice. Tanner attributed the boy's lack of fear to the venom that ran in his veins.

"Yeah," Tanner agreed. He watched the sun slowly edging over the horizon. Somewhere he had heard that red-tinged skies were a favorable sign—probably from someone who had never seen a city burn. "We're lucky this iron beastie doesn't go in for sails, or we'd be half a day waitin' for repairs to the rigging."

"What do you say I carve a few runes on her and we—"

"And we lose ten percent of a gold mine for robbing the Mad Tinker?" Tanner asked.

"Eat a blade, old man. You know I was just joking," Dan said.

Wish I was sure, kid. Tanner sized Dan up as an opponent, something he did by reflex to most men he met, and was doing with Dan more often by the day. The boy was within his sword reach, a bit *too* close, in fact. He'd have to take a step back as he drew to have room to thrust. He could have Dan spitted on the end of his runed sword in two blinks—which was probably one blink longer than he would have.

"Just watch who you're sayin' stuff like that around. The bossy one's got a short temper and a quick trigger finger."

"Yeah, and none of them speak Kadrin," Dan pointed out. "Besides, I'm not afraid of her."

"And there goes our ten percent, again."

Dan let out a theatrical sigh. "What am I supposed to do for fun around here? You're glooming off out to sea, the captain and crew seem to think I'm a mythological creature, and the two girls are dense as lead."

"So, you tried after all, huh?" Tanner asked. He turned and rested his elbows on the ship's railing. "I was wondering if you'd noticed them."

"Well, Madlin a bit. It seemed like you were interested in Jamile, so I left her for you, seeing as you never get the skirt of a woman outside a whorehouse. Seemed sporting to let you have a go first."

"Yeah, you little jackal? I don't see Madlin stumbling around all doe-eyed and swooning over you. What happened, your voice break in front of her and remind her you're too young for shaving?"

"Nah, it's like a dog humping a chair leg. That girl's got no interest in men, if you ask me."

Tanner chuckled. "Maybe she's just got no interest in boys. You think of that?"

"Nah, if she wants a man, she'll build one out of springs and pipes. Then she'll probably come begging after me to teach her magic to make it real."

"Why don't you just show her a little something simple? She'll be months trying to get it right."

"Yeah, and maybe I can give her just one utoru berry, too," Dan said. "She'll be after me the next day, looking for more, and then more. I don't need an apprentice."

"Well, you're welcome to try your luck with Jamile. Ain't nothin' between us. Funny how old a young girl can make you feel sometimes. Feel like one of them crusty old bastards who hangs out in taverns grabbin' the serving girls' rumps and droppin' tips on the floor."

"I won't be old like you for fifty years," Dan said with a grin.

"You can take your life extension and cram it up your arse, you sorcerous little turd," Tanner said with a dark look.

"Bit of a recursive metaphor, don't you think?" Dan asked. "I mean—wait, what's that?"

"What's what?"

"Can't you feel it?" Dan asked. He shook his head. "No, of course you wouldn't. Something out there is drawing aether. A real draw too, not the piddling summer breeze you've got, but a storm in the aether." Dan's eyes took on an ominous gleam. Back in Veydrus, he had never known Rashan Solaran well, but those who did had told stories of the look in his eye when the prospect of battle arose, straddling the line between madness and a child getting his age-day presents.

Tanner pushed away from the railing. "We've gotta tell the captain—"

Dan caught him by the arm. "And tell him what? That the witch-boy's seeing things and he better get ready for numpshins and gollywocks that are coming to get us?" Tanner stopped pulling and Dan let him go. "I'll handle it when it gets here, whatever it is."

"We should at least let the girls know," Tanner said. "We can't just keep it to ourselves."

Dan waved a dismissive hand. "Do whatever you want." He headed for the bow, sauntering as best he could with the shifting deck beneath his feet. "I just made it up. There's nothing coming. Go have a game of Crackle and drink yourself stupid for all I care."

Kthooom.

The sound thudded through the walls and floor of the darkened cabin. From across the room, Jamile whispered, "What was that?"

"PIRATES!" the shout from out on deck removed all doubt.

Madlin threw back the sheets and fumbled for her clothes as she wriggled out of her nightshirt. When the two activities got in the way of one another, she gave up removing her nightwear.

"What are you doing? Madlin, you can't go out there!"

"You stay put," Madlin ordered. "I'm going out to find out why Toller is chasing pirates again, despite my orders." She hopped into a pair of trousers and pulled a jacket on over her nightshirt. On her way out the door barefoot, she snatched up her gun belt, buckling it on as she searched the deck for the captain.

"Turn us to starboard, heading oh, five, five!" Captain Toller's voice carried over the sounds of the crew taking battle stations. He was dressed much like Madlin, with his captain's jacket over bed-trousers and a bare chest. Toller had taken the time for boots, however.

"What's going on?" Madlin demanded. "I thought we've been over this? No pirate-hunting."

"It's not us," Toller insisted. "They were firing on us before we even caught sight of them. First ranging shot was well short."

"Well, turn us about and evade them."

"Not that simple," Toller replied. He marched over to the ship's guns with Madlin in his wake. "Momentum is against us. We're being carried right toward them. If we turn and run, we'll give them a chance to fire on us with no danger to themselves."

"I thought this ship could bounce cannonballs off its hull like they were peas."

"Your father's claim, not mine. Plus it doesn't do us any good out on deck if one comes in high."

Kthooom.

"Shit!" Madlin swore, ducking her head. The splash came on the far side of the ship. Whoever was out there in the darkness had the *Darksmith* inside their range.

"Where's Dan?" she asked suddenly. "Maybe he can do something to—"

"Fine," Toller snapped. "Just get out of the way."

Madlin wove her way around the flurry of activity from the crew, cursing herself for leaving her feet bare as the deck plates sucked the heat from her skin. She spotted Dan at the bow of the ship, a pace away from the ship's telescope, watching the water by starlight. He was lounging against the forward railing, propped up on an elbow with his ankles crossed. Madlin broke into a run.

"Dan!" she shouted. He didn't turn, but she caught a flinch of his head that told Madlin that he'd heard her. "Dan, do something."

She came up beside him, huffing for breath. He turned with the languor of a waiting lover and graced her with an easy smile.

"Not yet. Let your friends play with their tinker toys a while longer. Once we get close enough, I'll handle things."

"What about a fog?" Madlin asked. She pointed out to the suspicious bank of fog on the water where the cannon fire originated. "Hide us like they're doing?"

"Oh, they're not hiding. Not from me at least."

"Dan!" Madlin grabbed him by the shoulder and turned him to face her. In the starlight he looked so young, his beardless face smooth and shining. "This isn't a game. If you can help us, then do something."

"So you're looking for my magic to solve all your problems again? I remember that not working out so well for you last time."

"This isn't the same at all. This is *you* using your magic, not me trying to follow your instructions from another world."

A gleam of mischief crept into Dan's eye. He gave a quick glance down and back up, taking in all of Madlin in a blink's time. "What's it worth to you?"

Madlin's face flushed and twisted into a scowl. "How dare you!" Dan was tall and willowy, with a lot of filling out to do in both limb and torso before he'd have a manly frame. He was also still leaning on the railing. Madlin put both hands to his chest and shoved.

Dan let out a startled yelp as he pitched over the bow of the ship.

Madlin let out a gasp of her own, only slightly less surprised by her action than Dan had been. She bent over the railing and saw a flash of spark where Dan bounced off the hull before splashing into the water.

Kthooom.

Kthooom.

The first shot hit the water not far from where Dan had gone in, sending up a spray that soaked Madlin's hair and trousers, though her jacket at least proved resistant to water. The second hit with a great crash and a clatter of protesting metal. It sounded nothing like she would imagine if the shot had ricocheted off the steel hull.

"Hit on the starboard, above the waterline," one of the crewmen shouted. There were unintelligible shouts from below decks that hinted at injuries or repair efforts, possibly both.

Madlin felt her breath quickening. She leaned out over the forward rail again and looked for any sign of Dan. She didn't know why she should expect him to still be there when the *Darksmith* had continued on course after he fell. Still, Madlin watched the choppy froth at the bow and waited for evidence that he might have clung on or used his magic to bob to the surface. There was nothing.

The *Darksmith's* guns opened fire, targeting the unnatural fog that clung to the Katamic like a burr, blotting the reflected starlight from the water's surface. The return fire drowned out any hints of whether their shots had been effective.

Kthooom. Kthooom.

Kthooom. Kthooom.

The hidden ship opened up with their full broadside. Madlin felt the *Darksmith* shudder with multiple impacts, but she couldn't get a count. She clung to the forward railing to avoid getting pitched headlong into the Katamic after Dan.

When the initial jolt passed, Madlin leaned over the rail again. "Dan!" she screamed. "Dan, please! Get up here and do something!" There was no answer, no response from the Katamic that indicated a boy was listening from down below the surface.

"Hit below the water line," a crewman shouted. "Man the pumps!"

The *Darksmith's* deck guns fired, cracking the air, but providing no sound of a hit within the fog. That fog was growing closer, or the bank was growing, it was difficult for Madlin to tell which.

"Get us out of here!" Madlin shouted in the direction she had last seen Captain Toller. "Full about, bring the engines to full!"

"You don't command here, Miss Errol," Toller shouted back. "Get below and see to those pumps, tinker."

Kthooom. Kthooom.

Kthooom. Kthooom.

The *Darksmith* shook. The deck was blasted with metal fragments as one of their own deck guns was hit, sending shrapnel among the crew. The screams of the wounded and shouts for help joined the chorus of orders and the occasional prayer.

Madlin dashed across the deck, her bare feet sliding and skidding on the cold, wet steel. She caught herself against the mount for the bait sail, then hooked her arm around the magazine holding shells for the starboard deck gun. At the far end of the ship, she caught hold of the door handle leading below as the *Darksmith* shook under the force of her own guns.

There were handrails to both sides of the stairwell that lead down into the hold. Madlin clutched both of them as another pair of strikes had the *Darksmith* convulsing in what she hoped were not its death throes. The emergency magnesium lights threw the corridors into a surreal chaos of brilliant white and harsh shadow. Crewman jostled past each other, some carrying tools, others looking to get out of the way or escape onto the deck. Madlin pushed past them and found herself ankle-deep in seawater. It was an ominous sign, with another deck below and a smaller cargo hold below that one, that water was already flooding the corridor.

"Status?" Madlin shouted. "How bad is the damage?" Everyone else was shouting too. She could only hope that someone recognized her voice and realized that she was better qualified than the ship's mechanic.

"Three hits below level," a voice shouted over the din. "Engine's out." Madlin tried to pinpoint the speaker, but elbows and shoulders knocked her around like a billiard ball as she wove through; it was hard enough keeping her bearings. Someone stepped on her foot, and she cursed in Korrish and shoved a deckhand away from her.

She ducked down a side corridor and saw a bulkhead, shut but leaking a fine spray of saltwater along the lower edge. They'd need caulking or a welder to seal it, and welding a pressurized leak was daredeath work. If it was the worst of the damage though, Madlin would have been shocked. The ship was already listing to starboard, so there had to be other compartments open to the sea. She threaded her way through the main corridor before giving up and shouting, "Clear a path!" Enough of the crewmen obeyed that she was able to squeeze through to the engine room.

"Holy Eziel, save us," Madlin whispered when she saw the engine. It had taken a direct hit. The engine room was taking on water through two head-sized holes in the hull, and a pair of men were manually working the bilge pump to stem the influx of Katamic ale. The engine itself was a wreck of shattered steel and cast iron, hopelessly irreparable. The scent of brine should never overpower the odors of grease and charcoal in an engine room, but the furnace was cold and soaked, the engine shredded and washed with seawater. Something incongruous caught Madlin's eye, something no one who hadn't taken a steam engine to pieces and reassembled it a hundred times would have noticed: a piece that didn't belong. It was an apple-sized sphere, embedded in the side of a ruptured boiler. Madlin pulled a pocket knife from her jacket pocket and pried it loose. It was a cannonball, a perfect sphere that had been flatted on one side by its impact on the *Darksmith*. What stood out were the runes carved all over the iron surface.

The hulls of the Errol Company steamships were designed to withstand cannonfire from even Acardian-made long guns. They had no protections that would stop runed projectiles. Madlin couldn't tell what the runes did precisely, but it was simpleton's guesswork to figure it was for punching through steel hulls.

Madlin noticed something as she finished examining the cannonball. It was a peculiar quiet, one of the loudest she'd ever heard, in fact. The ship's crew was still scrambling to enact makeshift repairs, and the bilgeworks still pumped away as two men powered the see-saw handle. There was still the waterfall crash of water spilling into the ship. What had gone quiet were the guns. Neither side was firing.

There was nothing Madlin could do to weld the gaping holes in the hull. There was no point in taking a shift on the bilge pump; her arms would never keep pace with the hearty lads her father employed for such tasks. There was nothing salvageable about the engines, and she doubted her revolver would be of much aid unless the fighting came deck-to-deck, as it did in cheap swashbuckling stories that glorified piracy. Madlin could only think of one way she could lend aid. She dropped the cannonball in the wreckage of the ship's engine.

The nearest wall was as good a place as any. Madlin scratched at it with her knife, the hardened steel of the blade able to gouge lines in the low carbon steel of the engine room wall. Steam ships weren't made of wood, like sailing ships. No piece aboard could float on its own; it relied wholly on water volume displacement to maintain buoyancy. It was time to add a little levitation to that equation.

Jamile cowered in the corner of her cabin farthest from the window, bunched up in a blanket and wedged behind the bunk bed. There was nothing she could do until the fighting was over. She'd only be in the way, and she doubted she could keep her footing, let alone stitch a wound. The world shook and rocked and shifted, attempting to dislodge her from her haven. At any moment a cannonball could rip through the wall of the cabin and end her life in an instant.

The shouts of the crew were all muffled and incoherent. She felt their sense of urgency, of fear, of panic. She knew Madlin was probably one of those voices, trying to do something to help. Jamile wished that Madlin hadn't run off, hadn't left her alone. She was too scared even to cry.

The guns had been silent for a time Jamile hadn't thought to measure. It wasn't like lightning, where you could play the game of counting seconds until the thunder came to guess how close the storm was. The guns were thunder without lightning, and the storm was all around her. In that lingering absence of guns, she heard ... cheering?

Had the *Darksmith* prevailed? Jamile hugged the blanket around her body and tiptoed over to the window, the icy steel of the floor hurrying her along. She could see nothing. Whatever battle was taking place was on the far side of the ship.

Jamile dressed hurriedly. She pulled on a dress over her nightshirt, ridiculous as she felt doing so, and a jacket over that. She slipped her shoes on, and noticed that Madlin's boots were still in the cabin, though they'd been thrown around like everything else. Jamile picked them up on her way out the door.

On deck, the crew was gathered along the starboard railing—which was decidedly lower than the port, though no one seemed bothered by it right then. The night was lit by the stars above and the fires burning aboard the sailing ship a few hundred paces distant. The pirate ship that had been battling them was a magnificent specimen, with three masts and elaborate rigging supporting more sails than Jamile could count. Her difficulty in counting was compounded by the fact that nearly all of them were ablaze.

Her first thought was that the *Darksmith's* gunners had hit their target. Then she saw it. Half the fires on the pirate vessel went out at once. There was a flash of light and a bolt like lightning arced across the ship, striking a shimmering globe that appeared around one of the man-shaped silhouettes on deck. That figure dodged among a knot of larger silhouettes who fell away in short order, wounded or dead. The crew of the *Darksmith* hooted and cheered as if they were spectators at a crashball game or a pit fight. They shouted encouragements, suggestions, and some general purpose invectives against the pirates. All but one.

"Dan!" Tanner shouted, his voice as discordant as a fan of a rival side attending a visiting match. "Don't start a war! Dan, get back here!"

Jamile edged her way down the angled deck until she was behind Tanner. "Is that Dan over there?" she asked, feeling stupid for having asked the obvious first off. "What's he doing?" There was some part of Jamile's mind that would not allow a thoughtful, insightful question to form until she had been assured of the reality of what she was witnessing.

"Bloody-handed fool's going to get us all killed," Tanner muttered over his shoulder.

"It looks like he's handling himself well," Jamile replied.

Tanner grabbed her by the jacket collar and pulled her close. "It's not here I'm worried about. This isn't piracy anymore, it's politics." Tanner checked over both shoulders, but nobody was paying them any mind. The flashes of aether on the pirates' ship had them all mesmerized. "They're my kind, Zayne and his boy. Dan kills them and it's war in Veydrus."

"Then why is Dan—"

"Because the kid hates the idea of war as much as he hates honey candy and tupping chambermaids," Tanner said.

"What can we do?" Jamile asked.

Tanner turned away and looked to the pirate ship. There was a blue flash, like a ray of colored sunlight, followed by a crack and a lumberjack's groan as one of the masts split and toppled. "Nothing."

Madlin slumped against the open hatch of the engine room. Three rune patterns glowed a faint blue in the dark; the magnesium lights had burned out. The bilge pumps had seen three shifts of workers and with the aid of the levitation runes, the pumps were starting to make headway. The knee-deep water had receded back to Madlin's shins. Much as she's pressed her father to upgrade Tinker's Island with spark amenities, she was just as glad now that the *Darksmith* was run on coal and lamp oil.

There was a dull ache within her, like sunburn on the insides of her veins. Three sets of runes hadn't seemed so daunting a task, but she knew better than to draw assumptions about how aether worked. If there was rhyme or reason to the arcane, it escaped her. Its workings seemed faulty based on all she knew of physics.

The cheering persisted up on deck, and the curiosity was too much to bear now that she had exhausted what she could do with runes for the time being. Madlin sloshed through the indoor portion of the Katamic until she reached the stairs.

Out on deck, the scene was something from a storybook. As the crew of the *Darksmith* shouted encouragements, a wizards' duel played out on the decks of an Acardian heavy frigate. Its sails and rigging blazed with fire and one of her masts lay in the water like a gangplank to the bottomless depths of the sea.

Madlin shambled across the deck like a sleepwalker, transfixed. Flashes of blue and silver, red and fiery orange stabbed and crackled back and forth across the deck of the Acardian ship. Shimmering auras flashed into view around the combatants as some form of protective magic thwarted each attack. The action was too far away for her to make out details, but one of them had to be Dan.

"Madlin," Jamile called out. She was standing at the railing beside Tanner, though in the starlight she could only tell by his foreign clothes and the sword at his hip. "Dan's fighting off Zayne's pirates by himself."

At least that explains where he went. In the confusion of the attack and her hurried repairs, she had forgotten about him.

Madlin kept an eye to the battle as she joined Jamile and Tanner. Captain Toller fell in beside her before she arrived.

"I heard what you did down below," Toller said. "You've probably saved us from a float home in the Katamic."

"We're little better than a raft right now," Madlin replied. "We've got no engine, no rudder control, and most of the lower decks are filled with water. Even if we rigged an engine, the coal's soaked."

"How long will the runes keep us afloat?" Toller asked.

Tanner perked up. He hooked a thumb at Madlin. "This one's runecarving is all that's keeping us up?"

"Dunno," Madlin replied, ignoring Tanner. She pointed to the battle. "Longer than that one's going to last."

"They look evenly matched," Jamile said. "This might go on for hours."

Madlin shook her head. "Half the ship's aflame. It's only a matter of time before—"

KTHOOOOM.

The Acardian frigate was split in half as a great billowing gout of flame and smoke exploded out the side.

"... it reaches the powder."

The midmorning sun made the Katamic sparkle and shimmer, bright enough to hurt any eyes that lingered too long. Madlin sat on the aft deck, starboard side, letting her feet dangle over the edge of the ship. She stared off ahead as the current carried them along, watching for signs of life among the wooden wreckage of the ship, which she had learned was the *Fair Trader.* Four of the pirates had managed to swim to the *Darksmith* and were locked up in a soggy crew compartment below decks. At times she thought she could see movement among the debris, but the two spyglasses aboard the ship were in great demand and she hadn't the energy to argue for a longer turn.

Tanner and Jamile had gone to bed—separately, as far as she knew. The two seemed to be growing closer as Jamile and Madlin argued more and more often, so the other possibility wouldn't have surprised her. Captain Toller was working with his navigator and the nautical charts to determine where the current would take them. She had spent a few moments watching them before growing bored and frustrated. They had no idea where they were thanks to the ship's compass being damaged in the battle and the fact that neither of them could find a sextant. The current maps were bunk as far as Madlin could tell, anyway—more of a guideline to the lay of the shipping lanes than a means to calculate a course.

Of Dan there had been no sign. If he was the storybook warlock he claimed to be, he should have survived. If he was the spiteful little shit she had grown to consider him, he was probably already aboard and was just making her worry.

On the subject of the Mad Tinker, there was agreement among the three Korrish twinborn aboard: he needed to know nothing until they knew where they were. For a man with a thousand worries, adding one he could do nothing about would benefit no one. For now, they would bide their time and see where the current took them.

Chapter 11

"When Jennai died, I swore I'd raise Madlin right, have her follow in my footsteps. Maybe I should have worn daintier shoes." -Cadmus Errol

A steady rain fell in what they'd come to call the Valley of Twisted Steel. The *Jennai*—which had absorbed the *Cloudsmith*, name and all—sat with engines at idle as welders worked under tarpaulin tents to connect the two ships more securely. After the attack three days prior, they had set down near the wreck of the Ruttanian vacu-dirge and set about salvaging materials at once. Crews in breather-cloth masks cleared kuduk bodies from the site and stacked them for the crows at the far end of the valley; they weren't worth the risk of a smoke plume to burn, or the effort of digging a grave to bury.

Mechanics and welders stripped the outer structure for beams and hull plates, but Chipmunk waited until the interior of the ship was cleared before leading salvage crews aboard to go through the lighter supplies. It was awkward as a snake in shoes getting around on her crutches, both for the frequent jutting of parts from one cabin into another and for the fact that the majority of the walking was done on walls, as the hulk had settled on its side.

"Grab those charts," Chipmunk ordered, pointing to a pile of papers that had survived the fires and shards of blasted glass that sweepers had already cleared away. "The spy glass, too."

"Lens is shattered," one of the workers reported, holding the offending spyglass for her to see.

"Take it anyway. I might be able to grind a new one," she replied. She pointed with a crutch to a hatch in the adjoining wall, oriented sideways from waist to head high. "Let's check the briefing room." The Ruttanian ship was the same make of Horlaide Company airframe, with only minor differences in accommodations and armaments differentiating them. She knew the layout, even sideways, nearly as well as she knew the *Jennai.*

"Aye, General Rynn." Another of the salvage crew took three hearty tugs on the handle before the catch released, letting the door swing open into the next room with a clang that had Chipmunk and the rest of her team clutching at their ears. Chipmunk managed to keep one of her crutches tucked under her elbow, but the other fell to the floor.

"Let me get that for you, General." If it weren't for the fact that she went to bed each night with hands sore as a brawler's and arms that ached from holding up her weight all day, she'd have felt as if she were the laziest human in the rebellion.

Her troops and workers went out of their way to not only follow orders, but anticipate them. They coddled her every opportunity they got.

"Thanks," she muttered as she rebalanced herself on three points instead of two. "First two of you in there, give me a boost up."

With her crew's aid, she went from one compartment to the next, picking through the debris of over a hundred kuduk lives that had been lost in the crash. The bodies at the valley's end had all of their pockets emptied, their rings pocketed, their wallets' contents bundled into the rebels' little treasury. The crew quarters contained far more useful—and occasionally heartrending—loot. They found books and magazines, extra clothes and uniforms, sweets, bottles of liquor, and a few pocketclocks. From all the ship, they also found seventeen decks of playing cards, eight pairs of dice, and a chessboard with most of the marble-carved pieces broken. Walls in the crew quarters were often adorned with flashpops stuck to the walls with painter's tape. They came in two basic styles: flirty images of kuduk women, and various family flashpops with wives and children.

"Peel those off the walls," Chipmunk ordered after the fifth room with the portraits. "I'm sick of kuduks staring at us while we work."

"Yes ma'am. But what do you want done with them?"

Chipmunk thought a moment. Shredding them didn't seem fitting. There would just be bits and pieces of kuduks staring up from the floor with their sepia eyes. Burning seemed like more trouble than the portraits warranted. "Pile them up in a sack and leave them with the bodies of the ship's crew."

There was so much to salvage in the rooms. Chipmunk had to order personnel rotations to send sacks of plunder to the *Jennai* and fresh legs and backs to continue gathering. While she lifted nothing but her own weight and carried nothing but her crutches, Chipmunk was growing weary from the exertion.

"Can't we just take this whole ship in a sack and sort it out later?" Chipmunk mumbled. She intended the comment solely for herself, but a woman from her salvage crew overheard.

"If the *Jennai* can lift while it's full o' holes, why not this heap?" she asked.

The gearworks in Chipmunk's head made a grinding, grating sound as a lever wedged a new pinion into her thinking engine. "One hour break," she called out. "Someone give me a lift out."

The planning room of the *Jennai* had a central table strewn with maps and charts that gave detailed accountings of the surrounding terrain. Atop the pile was the log book from the Ruttanian ship *Sulfurous*, lying open to its most recent entries. Pages scattered around the table bore hastily scratched calculations, and more were being added by the minute.

"Best case, I think we've got at least a day and a half before the Ruttanian Air Corps finds us, assuming they sent a ship as soon as the *Sulfurous* didn't return on schedule," Chipmunk said.

Erefan shook his head. "Not conservative enough. You're making assumptions that might not be true. What if they weren't scheduled to turn back?" He pointed to the map. "What if they weren't a patrol, but traveling point to point. If they were heading—"

"Wouldn't they be here already?" Chipmunk asked. "If Twincrag Sky Aerodrome sent out a search vessel as soon as the *Sulfurous* failed to arrive, it would have been here ...." She scribbled as she talked, lines of numerals and mathematical symbols, "... eight hours ago, at least." She flipped the page around so that her father, Kandrel, Bosley, and Sosha could see her sums.

"Could be that the Tephis Aerodrome cables Twincrag, has them investigate when the ship goes missing," Kandrel suggested. Bosley and Chipmunk bent over their sums to calculate.

"They'd be here in anywhere between an hour to three, depending on the local winds," Erefan said, interrupting the hasty mathematics of his daughter and the ship captain. "I figured that scenario already. It's more likely than the worst case, but it still means we ought to get our arses off the grass and above cloud level."

"I think it's worth the risk staying," Chipmunk replied. "The most likely scenario in my mind, Ruttanian Air Command doesn't brown their trouserbacks the minute an airship is late. Plus, we're assuming that if they hadn't encountered us when they did, the *Sulfurous* was heading straight back to dock."

"It's the only assumption that lets us even begin calculating scenarios," Erefan said. "We don't get trial runs at this. We figure the least time we have safe on the ground, and make sure we're off it before anyone's the wiser. Rynn, I taught you all this, why are you being so obstinate?"

Chipmunk slapped her pencil down on the table. Silence hung in the air for a moment before she spoke. "That's *General* Rynn," she said. "And it's not my job to play safe and hide. This is a rebellion, not an emigration, and certainly not a gutted math problem. It's good information to have, but it's not the only consideration. That ship has enough steel to complete all our modifications, and room to house another few hundred troops once we fix it up a bit. It's also got more supplies than we can fit aboard the *Jennai*; we're busting out at the rivets of this teakettle as it is."

"How long will the runes take?" Bosley asked. The question was as good as taking her side, as far as Chipmunk was concerned.

"I'll round up some likely candidates and teach a class on carving them. Sosha will take a sample rune around on a piece of sheet steel and we'll see if we can find anyone else aether-capable among the troops. The levitation rune's simple enough, there are just going to be so many around it'll look like a typesetter went mad. I'm hoping in two to three days we can take the *Sulfurous* in tow."

"You called yourself Rynn, you know," Sosha said. She sat in a chair at one end the cabin. At the other end, Chipmunk sat on the floor working on a book-sized piece of steel with a screwdriver and a hammer, making tiny, elongated dents that would eventually form Sosha's test rune.

"Slip of the tongue," Chipmunk replied, not looking up from her work. With a sharp rap and a clatter, she dented the metal again. It jumped with each strike, and every time she had to re-orient it before she hit it again. "They knew what I meant."

"Have you ever seen a live chipmunk?" Sosha asked.

"Not for real, just a diagram in a wildlife book. It's too cold for them up in Tinker's Island," she replied. It went without saying that Eversall Deep had no woodland creatures dwelling in its depths. She looked up. "Don't you have patients to look after?" The firefight with the Ruttanian Air Corps had left five dead, thirteen injured.

"We used to have them around the sanctuary," Sosha said. "They're cute, inoffensive little creatures, adorable little puffs of reddish-brown fluff with black streaks in their fur. I used to try to catch them when I was little. If you held still enough, they might forget you were there and come close, but the second you flinched, they'd bolt. None of the children were quick enough to catch one, but it was great fun trying."

Chipmunk hit the steel again, and the rune grew incrementally. "Is there a point to this? Some joke about me being an easy chipmunk to catch, now that I'm hobbled."

"No, nothing like that," Sosha assured her. "It's just ... how old were you when you got that name?"

Chipmunk set the steel aside and pursed her lips. "Twelve, maybe?" she ventured after a moment's consideration. "Why?"

"It's just, well, it's just a *cute* nickname is all," Sosha said. "I'm sure it had something to do with your hair, but it's also just a scared, fuzzy little creature that lives in a hole in the ground."

"Well, maybe when I was twelve, that was a pretty good description of me—minus the 'fuzzy' that is. I'm not a scared little girl anymore though, and I live wherever I want."

"Maybe when you were twelve, it was a good name for you," Sosha said. "It doesn't suit you now."

Chipmunk snorted. "What, I need a new nickname? What do *you* think I should go by?"

"Just Rynn," Sosha replied. "Maybe with something tacked on as a surname."

"Rynn's a kuduk name. I don't—"

"Your mother gave you that name," Sosha said. "Your father said as much."

"Kuduk-approved then," Chipmunk replied. "There's probably a Rynn in every city in Korr."

"But only one in Eversall?"

Chipmunk shrugged. "Far as I know."

"Then you can be Rynn of Eversall. Maybe we can start a trend, giving humans surnames, like full citizens."

Rynn set her screwdriver down and leaned back against the bed. "You're serious about this one, aren't you?"

"This rebellion's going to grow, and if newcomers don't take you seriously, they're going to look to someone else to lead them."

"You're saying no one will take General Chipmunk seriously? I'd lose the army over my bloody name?"

"They're tiny, harmless little rodents that make squirrels look like shining knights by comparison."

Chipmunk tried to picture herself meeting someone named Squirrel, taking orders from a woman called Mouse, following Kitten into a battle. She'd been Rynn before, mostly when miserable, sweat-soaked, and working under a kuduk boss. It was a cloak she could wear when she needed an authentic disguise. She answered to it readily from long habit. Maybe instead of burying her birth name, she could reclaim it instead.

"Fine. You and my father win this one," Rynn said.

The cargo hold of the original *Jennai* was cleared out to make room for eleven students to work. The loading ramp was lowered to allow fresh air and light in from the valley, and the grassy lowlands just beyond the craft were piled with the former contents of the hold. Coils of rope rested on barrels of salted meats and fresh water. There were piles of scrap metal from the thunderail harvest mixed with bundles of cloth and casks of ale and wine. Anything not of immediate need had been dragged out and left until they were ready to depart.

"This isn't going to be too hard," Rynn said, raising her voice above the sounds of the construction going on just a few dozen paces away. "It's just like making your letters, except there's no using quick-script and no sloppy lines. Other than that, they're the same characters you read in the newspapers, just bigger and lined up touching in particular ways.

Each of her students had a crate for a workbench and one of the chairs from the dining halls. They were armed with various improvised chisels ranging from screwdrivers, to awls, to butter knives, and a few proper hammers mixed in with hard heavy objects that could at least be counted on not to break when striking a make-do chisel.

"This is what you're trying to make," Rynn continued. She held up a painting from the formal dining hall, depicting a dignified elderly kuduk in the uniform of an Air Corps general. Flipping the painting around backward, Rynn showed a painted copy of the levitation rune structure large enough to be seen from anywhere in the hold. "Your first ones we'll call practice, but any that work will get welded to the ship, so try your best."

Each student had a stack of thin steel plates beside their crate, rough and spattered around the edges where the welding torches had cut them from the vacuum tank of the *Sulfurous*. Each plate was roughly the side of a ledger page, and thin as shirt cloth. The students took a plate each and in moments they were playing the amateur blacksmith concerto. Rynn gritted her teeth to keep from wincing as her pupils tormented their steel work pieces.

She wandered among the rows of crates as unobtrusively as she could. The general din of the hammer-work drowned out the rhythmic thumps of her crutches against the floor. She glanced from sheet to steel sheet, watching the runes take shape in various states of deformity. The worst of them looked as if a woodpecker with the strength of a hydraulic piston had taken its anger out on the steel. Only two looked as if they might hold aether when they were completed.

A discordant clatter startled Rynn, and she spun to see what had happened. The hammering slowed as many of the student rune-carvers turned and did likewise.

"Flog this!" a stubble-headed young man said. He had no sheet left on his crate; he had been the one to throw his across the hold. "Sorry General, but this ain't gonna work." He held up a letter opener and the pipe wrench he'd been hammering with. "Yank someone else's dangles." He let the wrench and letter opener tumble from his hands to crash on the floor, then turned to walk away.

"Wrong way," Rynn said. The man stopped and turned to look at her over his shoulder. He was a few years older than Rynn was, a one-worlder whose name she couldn't recall. All she remembered about him was that he was swept up with a group of quarry slaves and knew his letters. "That's back into the ship."

"Yeah, and?"

Rynn tucked a crutch against her side and hooked a thumb toward the open ramp. "Deserter's exit that way."

"I ain't never said I was deserting!"

"You just stood up and walked out on your commanding officer without leave. You refused an assignment. You just quit on your comrades," Rynn said. All the hammering had stopped. All eyes in the hold were on General Rynn.

The would-be deserter's breath quickened. He looked to both sides for signs of anyone coming to his defense. Rynn had clearly shown that she was in charge, or so she thought. But a fundamental quality of mankind escaped her: some humans are irrational, especially when they feel cornered. The deserter snarled. "Who do you think you are, anyway? Just some cripple with a slave collar." He rushed her.

Rynn's eyes went wide at the unexpected turn of events. She had grown so accustomed to being obeyed and deferred to that certain laws of the natural world had gone overlooked. The most prominent of these was that of mass and velocity combining to create momentum. The deserter was a head taller than her and muscular from working all his life in a quarry. Rynn fumbled with her crutches to draw her coil gun, but there was too little time and too many objects to manipulate. He hit her midsection with his shoulder and Rynn was lifted off her foot, the breath driven from her lungs. A second later, the two of them crashed to the unforgiving steel of the hold floor. She tried to keep her head up, but the impact snapped it back and everything went black.

What could only have been a few seconds later, she pushed herself up to her elbows, watching dizzily as four of her students subdued the deserter. He hadn't been the only one in the class who had been a laborer, and stout bodies with thick arms were in plentiful supply. Other helpful hands kept Rynn from rising, murmuring assuring words and clucking over her like nurses. She had just banged her head, she wasn't bleeding out.

"Haul him down to the valley," Rynn ordered. Drawing breath to speak hurt her ribs, both front and back.

The deserter thrashed in the arms of his captors and spat vile threats. He had lost what semblance of civility he had earlier. One of her "nurses" shook his head. "Some just can't have a taste of freedom. They get themselves drunk on the stuff; can't tell 'em nothing."

"Help me up," Rynn muttered.

"General, you shouldn't be—"

"Just help me stand." Though she didn't raise her voice, there was an edge to her command, the weight of an order. Someone pushed crutches into her hands and someone else grabbed her beneath the arms and lifted her like a child, letting her dangle until she got both her foot and crutches settled under her. She bit her lip to keep from crying out at the pain that shot through her ribs. "Thanks."

At the bottom of the ramp, the four students holding the deserter hauled him into the grass. "That's far enough," Rynn shouted, trying to keep her rib muscles taut to ease the pain of raising her voice. "Hold him right there."

Rynn took a few steadying breaths with her self-appointed nursemaids to either side, ready to catch her if she stumbled or collapsed. She hobbled to the top edge of the ramp. "I'd have let a deserter go. This is a volunteer army; there are no slaves here. But humans don't fight among themselves. By attacking me, you sided with our enemies." Rynn drew her coil gun from the holster at her hip. The deserter's eyes widened and he renewed his struggles to break free, but to no avail. "I can't just let that go."

Click.

There was a hiss of displaced air, followed by wet thump a fraction of a second later. The deserter collapsed with a half-inch hole in the middle of his chest, and the four who held him let him crumple to the ground.

"Thank you all for your help. Let's get back to work. All the clocks in Korr won't stop for us."

Chapter 12

"The only thing better than enough, is more." - Neiron the Kingthief

Cadmus stood by the edge of the water as it rushed over Wheel Falls. His hat was wool-lined canvas and his long coat was oiled with linseed against the freezing spray. Thanks to hot springs and curious mineralogy, the Iceless River flowed year-round despite the frigid temperatures. Errol Company was the river's constant tormentor, chaining it against its will to power their machinery. Four waterwheels harassed its plummet over Wheel Falls, forcing it to supply torque to a series of shafts and gears that distributed that rotational energy to the factories—and now to the new dynamo.

"What if we dam the thing?" Cadmus shouted over the crash of water and the creaking of the great wheels. "We can build a sluice and let the water out in force when we power up."

"How long would that last us?" Enderburt asked in reply. "A minute's reserve would still take a blasted big dam. By the time we get done thinking it out on vellum, I bet ya we'll find it simpler just to make a proper dam of the whole falls and be done with it. Tear out the wheels and go full spark." Enderburt knew his spark as well as anyone on the island except Cadmus and perhaps Madlin. He worked as a maintenance assistant in the hydrospark factory in Kupak Deep. They produced spark wholesale, enough to ship it out of the city on heavy wires.

"Give me a solution I can have in a week," Cadmus replied. "We'll work on a solution that'll eat three months when I've got three spare months to feed into a spark dynamo. That isn't today, Mr. Enderburt."

Enderburt took off his own rain hat and scratched at a greasy crop of grey hair. "Not sure this end's gonna cough out any more spark than we're getting already, unless we take it to scraps and build new." He walked over to the edge of the falls and peered down. Cadmus gave him a moment to think. Enderburt was one of the few worth consulting on design matters, even if his thoughts took time to coalesce. "All your talk about dams and sluices ... what you're looking for is a spark condenser, really."

"Enderburt, I'm having all I can tolerate just getting copper wire made in this backwards world," Cadmus replied. "You expect me to fashion condensers in a week?"

Enderburt shrugged. "Ain't never been surprised by you yet, Cadmus. I just figure you want something built, it gets built."

Cadmus walked up and stood beside Enderburt at the falls' edge. Tinker's Island spread out below them to the south, little snow-crested buildings. Smoke rose from more structures than not, whether from hearth fires bellowing wood smoke from their chimneys or factory smokestacks belching black coal soot into the sky. The whole city ran on steam and clockwork. Converting them to spark on the quick was proving daunting; there was just too much basic infrastructure that needed to be built.

"Well, thanks for the confidence. I'm no miracle worker though, much as I'd like to be. I'm just taking the best of Korr and making it ours. They've got an eighty year head start on us on spark though, and it's still in its infancy. There's new spark inventions every day—or at least there were a dozen years ago, when I got to see them. Steam and gears, nothing's changed about those in a hundred years. Anything new's just paint over something older. Someone's always thinking up a new dynamo or a condenser. Last time anyone tried to store physical energy, they still just came back to springs and flywheels. It's not as if—" Cadmus looked up blankly in Enderburt's direction and blinked. "It can't be that simple. Can it?"

"Sorry, what's that?" Enderburt asked. "You got to rambling and I went back to thinking how I can dam this whole falls off for you in a week—steam cranes, and lots of 'em. Best I got so far."

"A flywheel. Falls spins up the flywheel, flywheel turns the dynamo shaft."

Enderburt nodded along, though his mouth twisted beneath a skeptical frown. "Crude. Might work, but a bodge of a job it'd be."

"Look, Madlin's going to be back in a week, and if I don't have that dynamo powering the world-ripper, I'm going to have to let her use those daruu arts to get it working. Do you want that?" Cadmus asked.

"Naw," Enderburt replied. "Sweet girl like that oughtta lay off that rubbish."

"Speaking of that 'sweet girl,' how's the welding going on that kuduk airship?"

"Back's twisted up like a candy swirl, to be honest. Feels good puttin' to work for a human boss though, so I don't complain," Enderburt said. He scrunched his face briefly. "This ain't complaining, so you know. I only mentioned the back cuz you asked. I mostly just feel for the poor saps making the rune plates. Feels like we oughtta just have a kick press and a die and just stamp 'em all out in an hour like they were griddlecakes."

"Well, if I can get the machine working, we might just arrange that," Cadmus replied.

World-Machine Theater, they called it. Twinborn and one-worlder alike came with meals from the mess hall with tankards of their preferred ales to sit and watch scenes from another world flash across the aperture of the giant frameworks of copper and steel. With the lights turned out, the only illumination in the room came from distant parts of Tellurak, aside from a few lights near the controls so Cadmus could see dials, gauges, and his notes.

Cadmus was weary to the bone, and feeling his age more than usual. He'd spent the afternoon getting efforts underway to build a giant flywheel for the dynamo, efforts that had ultimately involved him dirtying his hands in the foundry. Those hands ached and chafed from the shovel he'd used for hours as he helped dig a trench that would become the mold for the flywheel. Working with the hobbled machine in search mode was relaxing by comparison.

He had never intended for the world-ripping machine to become a form of entertainment, but once his employees began concocting excuses to be in the presence of the machine while it was on, he gave in to popular demand. And it *was* entertaining, he had to admit. Though his time with Kezudkan had dulled him to the sheer wonder of looking across vast distances in space, and even between worlds, it was still a marvel, and more so to those who were seeing it for the first time. While Cadmus browsed remote corners of Tellurak for news, the audience treated the images like a play, or a circus, gawking slack-eyed for hours, if he let them.

The last hour had been spent on a tour of harbors across Takalia, Acardia, Hurlan, and Khesh, as Cadmus looked for ships that wouldn't be due in Tinker's Island for days or weeks. He started east and chased the setting sun as he hopped from one city to another, cross-referencing with a map of Tellurak that was marked to correspond to the machine's controls. He recorded ship names in a log book and made guesses at their status based on what he could see of crates and sacks.

Satisfied with his shipping updates, Cadmus slumped in his chair. The world-ripper was left viewing the harbors of Darkport, watching the sunset over the low hills west of the city. "Requests cost a pint apiece," he called out to the audience. He needed something to dull the day's aches. Since none of the anti-inflammatories of Korr were available to him, he settled for treating the feeling of them, rather than actually reducing the pain.

The request came along with a pint of Acardian lager, fresh from the tap. It was from a foundry worker named Flenthan who had just arrived and gave up his own drink, untouched. "I want to see me some of them critters in the Savage Lands. Something big with fangs the size of dock pillars."

There was a chuckle from the audience at the whimsical request, but Cadmus just nodded as he sampled his payment. "Let's see what we can find."

With no listing of coordinates, Cadmus left the screen active as he spun the gross adjustment dials and sped the view in the direction of the setting sun. Most of the audience had to turn away as the illusion of motion overwhelmed the senses—especially with sensations of weak knees and nausea. Hurlan passed below in a blur of hills and trees, cities and villages blinking past too fast to even guess at names for them. The sun rose on the horizon as the view outraced Tellurak's rotation. The Katamic Sea appeared again on the far side of Hurlan, and the view continued to speed over the water, the glistening reflections of the sun's light dazzling the eyes of the stalwart few whose nerves could stand the sight.

Cadmus wondered if there was a proper name for the ocean between Hurlan and the Savage Lands. In ancient Garnevian, "Katamic" meant "universal" or "unending," but it was only a name. The official boundaries of the Katamic Sea were roughly Acardia, Takalia, Khesh, and Krang, but it was used for the sea around Tinker's Island, as well any other place that sailors from within its hazy borders traveled.

"Here we come," Cadmus said, slowing the view as land appeared on the horizon. The Savage Lands were half fable to any one-worlder from Tellurak but merely a mirror of the Lumberlands to the twinborn of Korr. After a blink of white sand on the beach, the view sped inland. Cadmus eased them up over the tops of the thick, shining green jungle that choked the landscape as far as the horizon. "The Savage Lands," he proclaimed grandly. "A place untamable by men—unless you bring along a hundred repeater rifles and fire at anything that moves." Chuckles identified twinborn in the audience, since they knew that was how kuduks had tamed their version of the Savage Lands and plundered it for lumber—a pricey commodity in tree-poor Korr. "Let's see if we can find Flenthan his monster."

The view plunged through the canopy and into the gloom of shadows below. They had traveled into the deep jungle, where trees were as wide as a man stood tall, and branches hung with vines and moss. Things moved before the eye noticed they were there—lizards, insects, snakes, birds. Everything seemed alive, wondrous, potentially deadly. An insect floated past as the view drifted along, only to be plucked from the air by the tongue of a tree frog the size of an ale keg.

"That doesn't count!" Flenthan said for all to hear, drawing laughs.

Up ahead, one of the trees shook. The world-ripper conveyed no sound when it was merely viewing, but the imagination supplied a crash of underbrush, a creaking and crackling of mistreated wood. "This seems promising," Cadmus said. He angled the viewer and lowered it as he brought it closer to the shaken tree.

If the viewer did one thing exceptionally, it conveyed scale. Everything was as lifelike as if it were on the other side of a pane of thickened glass. The beast stood twice the height of a man, cat-like in form, but with a savagery the oozed through the viewer and into the stomachs of the audience on Tinker's Island. The creature was striped in alternating light and dark, though the precise colors were impossible to tell in the low light. It dipped to one side and butted its back against the tree, rocking back and forth, sating an itch and sending shudders through the whole trunk. Bark sloughed off against the massive cat's fur, and it shook itself clean of debris after it finished. The cat then sat on its haunches, twisted around, and began grooming itself with a tongue like a bath towel. Cadmus edged the viewer ever closer, getting right up next to the stationary beast. Between licks, hints of its fangs glinted.

"How big's a dock pillar, anyway?" Cadmus asked.

"About that big, I'd say!" Flenthar agreed amiably. Cadmus knew the tooth was probably only two or three inches in diameter, and that a dock pillar was closer to eight, but he had no intention spending all night monster-hunting in the Savage Lands.

Cadmus let the audience marvel over the beast a few minutes longer, chattering among themselves and coming up with pithy remarks. "Wonder if them beasties like the taste of kuduk." "We're going to have the finest zoo anywhere, once this thing's ready to really go places." "I'd like a coat out of that fur."

Cadmus raised his voice to carry over the buzz of conversation. "Where to next?"

"How about seein' if you can find the *Darksmith*?" someone suggested.

"Tempting," Cadmus replied, "but it's dark over that part of the Katamic now. I'd never find a moving target in a space that size. It would be like ... like ... dash it to shambles, like finding a bloody analogy in the bottom of a tankard." Cadmus accepted the laughter at his own expense with cantankerous good humor. "Sure, how 'bout one of you comes up with the inventions *and* acts the rutting poet about it, spewing flowery nonsense for the crowd? Next suggestion."

"How about one of them little islands in the warm waters. I heard they don't wear hardly nothing," a voice called out.

"Do I need to get you limp-wits a map and a clock? It's well after dark there, it's almost due south of us, skipping over Takalia," Cadmus replied, using the technical barrier as a glove to avoid touching the moral question of spying on underdressed islanders.

"How about a look at the Princess of Khesh?" the same voice suggested. It was punctuated by a meaty slap and a yelp from the offender.

"Thank you," Cadmus said to whoever had doled out corporal morality on his behalf. "I will admit that we *could* do those sorts of things, but I assure you that we *will not*, even if I have to place a guard. We are neither savages nor juveniles, and we're not going to behave like either. Now, does anyone else have a suggestion before I shut this thing off for the night?"

"How about looking in on Powlo at the new mine?" Greuder suggested. It was a voice that Cadmus could easily pick out of a crowd of fifty-odd in a darkened room. It made sense too, since Powlo was one of Greuder's recruits, from back in the days when he still worked as a field agent.

"It's after dark there, too, but at least they'll have lights," Cadmus said. His hands set to work on the dials, and the view of the Savage Lands whooshed by, leaving streaks of color in the viewer. It was a shame that the targeting coordinates were relative to the machine, because from Kezudkan's workshop, Cadmus knew the settings for the Kheshi mining operation by memory. Instead, he had to blunder around the Kheshi countryside by starlight.

The audience chatted among themselves. A few who thought highly of their nocturnal geography shouted out instructions as Cadmus searched—some helpful, most not. Several availed themselves of the lull to supplement their refreshments, including a pint of a dark stout that Greuder offered in payment for his turn.

Fortunately Cadmus knew the Dragon Fangs by their peaks, same as those of the Homespires in Korr. The nighttime made the task of identifying peaks tedious, but eventually he caught sight of a tiny community nestled against the mountains. There were only a scattering of buildings, but the location was right, and he didn't expect to find much more there.

"Got it!" Cadmus said. Those who hadn't been watching the process turned their attention back to the wondrous machine once more, and everyone started settling back into their seats. It took the operation of multiple dials to guide the view down on something resembling a bird's flight toward the mine entrance. Though it would have been easier to adjust the axes of translation and rotation one at a time, Cadmus figured that it was more about showmanship than just finding a target with the least effort.

"Anyone want to wager whether Powlo's gotten to gold yet?" Greuder asked, standing up and addressing the crowd.

"Naw, you probably already worked out with him what he's dug up," someone replied. There were murmurs of agreement from the audience, and Greuder found himself with no takers for his bet.

"I'll bet you a week's wages that he hasn't yet," Cadmus said.

"You're a funny man, tinker," Greuder said with a low growl in his voice. "Since you don't pay me anymore."

"I admit, it would be a much richer bet if you weren't retired," Cadmus replied, still working the view on its swoop toward the mine. "Want to hire on as a cook, just to make the wager worthwhile?"

"I'd teach those stove-torturers of yours a thing or three, that's for sure," Greuder said. "Who'd you think—MERCIFUL EZIEL!"

The minor distraction of the Mad Tinker's banter with Greuder was forgotten in an instant as they saw the scene unfolding within the newest Errol Company mine. Helmeted figures in dark clothing were dragging bodies out of the mine. The darkness made more detailed observations impossible from a distance. Cadmus spun the dials frantically to get them a closer look.

Kuduks.

In Tellurak.

"Get guns!" Cadmus ordered. "Grab whatever you can, pistols, rifles, just get here and get ready in a hurry."

The audience scattered. There was no question of what Cadmus intended to try. The viewing party had turned into a rescue mission. Cadmus slung the view through the entrance and down the main tunnel of the mine. Blood smeared the floor in streaks as kuduk soldiers dragged body after human body from the tunnels. Rifles leaned against the wall, out of the path of the grim workers as they filed out.

Rifles set aside. Battle's over. He had brought the view too late to witness the battle, but it had to have been recent. It seemed like a small blessing; he wasn't sure how much worse it would have been to witness the slaughter.

Cadmus followed the trail of blood until he saw it. There was a wavering archway in the air down the main tunnel, pressed against the side wall. Through the hole in Tellurak, he could see through into Korr. Standing side by side was a peculiar pair. One was a kuduk who looked to have been half replaced by clockwork parts, the other was an elderly daruu, leaning on a cane.

As the theater refilled with hastily armed Errol Company employees, Cadmus addressed them. "I'm going to count down, and I want a swarm of bullets in the air. Those two you see there, first of all."

There were a dozen questions in the air at once, but Cadmus ignored them. The questioning voices quieted down one by one as Cadmus began his count. "Three..."

Cadmus looked to the dynamo, sputtering along, doing the best it could.

"Two..."

He reached up and gripped the heavy handle of the switch that controlled the world-ripper's eponymous function.

"One..."

Eziel, Lord of War, grant us this chance to attack.

"Now!"

Cadmus threw the switch and the world-ripper shuddered and crackled. The theater erupted with the deafening din of dozens of shots being fired in an enclosed space with wonderful acoustics. The machine went dark as bullets tore into the wire meshwork that crisscrossed the open expanse of the frame.

Kuduk and daruu stood side by side, watching through the world-hole as the mine was cleared of human bodies. For a brief moment, there was a silvery flickering of light across the hall. It was gone as quickly as it had arrived.

"What the bleeding rutting blazes was that?" Draksgollow asked, pointing where the light had been a moment earlier.

"Haven't the muddiest notion," Kezudkan replied. "We can shut the machine down and examine it once the clear-up is done."

Chapter 13

"Lord Eziel, grant us mercy from our enemies. Let us find peace among our fellow man. I am your servant, teach me to persevere."
–Invocation to Eziel, modern phrasing

A spark bulb that was about to burn out had the curious habit of glowing brighter than usual. Rascal was no expert on suns, but the one that hung over Yellowcorn Sky seemed ready to pop any minute. It threw off waves of heat like an open furnace door in the heavens. Sensible folk took refuge in the deep, where the pervasive earthy cool sheltered them from the abuse under the sky. Sensible folk didn't build Yellowcorn, which sat on soil too loose and soft for even a proper basement. The lack of a deep kept most kuduk away though, and that went a long way toward excusing the weather.

Rascal was dressed in the local fashion—or what passed for fashion in the northeastern farmland of Ruttania. He wore a dull white cotton shirt with wooden buttons the size of monocles (he was now the sort of man who could afford wooden buttons), with the top two undone to let out the heat. His trousers were twill, the pale brown of the local hay, and durable but stiff. They were made for field work, but it was all that was sold in Yellowcorn; everyone from plowhands to wheat mill owners wore them. A pair of stiff, calf-high leather boots had taken weeks to break in, but with streets pockmarked with horse and ox dung, low slung footwear was inadvisable.

The one indispensable companion Rascal had met during his stay in Yellowcorn was his hat. It was a paltry thing, made of woven straw and shaped like a deep-dwelling gentleman's hat except for a brim that was as wide as his shoulders. When the noontime sun could boil the sweat from your brow, a portable source of shade was essential.

Rascal took refuge under both the hat and the porch roof of the Blistered Saddle Ale Hall, occupying one of the painted wicker chairs. The Saddle didn't take kindly to loiterers, so Rascal sipped at the cold beer he'd purchased to earn the use of their shade. It was a weak brew, easy on the stomach in the hot hours but not something he'd recommend to a friend. Rascal pressed the glass to his forehead, wiping the condensation across his skin and letting it leech the heat out of him.

Traffic on the street plodded along, mostly wagons and horses led on foot, with a few simple pedestrians mixed in. There was a general cessation of work in the fields each midday, to keep the workers from overheating in the worst of the day's sun, but not everyone worked out in the fields. The couriers, drovers, and deliverymen of Yellowcorn still had jobs to do. They dressed in light fabrics, dyed in pale colors. Most wore hats like Rascal's own, at least ones of similar function if not style. He had lost a bit of his deep-dweller's pallor in his days on the run, but Rascal's skin was still pale by comparison to the sunbaked locals.

If there was a bright spot to Yellowcorn—besides the one cooking them all from above—it was the women. Rascal had grown up in the deeps, where Korr's temperature rarely varied. There were boilers and steam pipes in plenty keeping buildings warm, but out in the tunnels and caverns there was a chill that never went away. Residents wore sturdy cloth and dressed in layers. Sensible humans wore light jackets or coats when out of buildings. In Yellowcorn sweat poured openly and beaded in droplets on the skin, so garments tended to cling. When not fighting with the resistance, Rascal served as a priest of the Church of Eziel; he had avoided establishments where women's forms were on such display as they were daily in streets of Yellowcorn.

A woman in a pale yellow dress caught his attention with a wave. She was blonde and slim, with delicate limbs. Rascal guessed she'd grown up in the city, not among the outlying farms. "Excuse me, sir," she said, briefly grasping the edge of her bonnet between thumb and finger and giving a nod.

"Afternoon, ma'am," said Rascal, lifting his own hat with a fingertip. "Care to join me?" He indicated the empty chair next to him, then took a sip of his beer.

She accepted the offered seat, perching on the edge with her back stiff and straight. "Do they call you Rascal?" she asked. Her voice was slow and soft, with a quaint accent common among sky-dwellers that kuduks considered uncivilized.

"You have the advantage on me, ma'am," replied Rascal, finding himself mimicking her cadence.

"I'm Pella," the woman replied. Rascal tried to guess her age, but the tan of her skin made his assessment difficult. The sun seemed to bake years off the body, but crisp the skin in return. She could have been anywhere from twenty to forty for all he knew. "Your big friend asked me to come find you."

"Did he now?" Rascal asked. "Just to make sure we're talking about the same big friend of mine, how many fingers has he got on his right hand?"

"You're one for tricks, Mr. Rascal," Pella replied. "He's got five, just like you and me. It's his left that's missing two, not that a lady should pay any mind to those sorts of things."

Rascal took a sip of his beer. "You get to be cautious, living around kuduks."

"Mr. Hayfield said—"

"We ain't landowners, and we ain't kuduk," Rascal said. "Me and Hayfield ain't 'misters.' We're just regular folk getting away for a bit of travel."

Pella pursed her lips and gave him the long eye. "You may be, but you're still strangers in these parts, carrying a hearty heap of coin. Seemed only polite. You have my apologies if I offended you, Rascal."

"I don't offend easy," Rascal said, smiling to reassure her. "I think Hayfield likes people puffing him up though. Before the hand, he used to play crashball, and—"

"Oh, I know. He showed me the little clips he kept from the papers, him and his old team. Even had one of him in a flashpop, showing off his uni."

Rascal snickered, and reached up under his hat to scratch his head. "Well, can't blame the old bull for trying, I guess. Sorry if he bothered you, Pella. He's not really a bad sort."

"Oh, I took nothing amiss," said Pella. "He never had a hand wandering when we spoke, and nary a misplaced look. Might not have minded if he did, neither. Been years since I had crashball sweepers fawning over me."

"I'll be sure to mention that to him," Rascal said, punctuating with a wink.

Pella crossed her arms and made an exaggerated pout, "You wouldn't dare, *Mr.* Rascal."

"Naw, I wouldn't," Rascal replied. "If anything, I'd pull him aside and twist his crank a bit, tell him he shouldn't subject a fine lady to flashpops of his rotten old mug on yellowed papers." Pella chuckled and uncrossed her arms. "So what's Hayfield got to say?"

"I've got a couple folks bunked at my family's house. Hayfield says you should meet them."

"I'm sorry, I might have asked this earlier, but aside from your name, who are you?"

"My family owns the railyard maintenance depot. My dad keeps the books. My mum's the head mechanic. My two elder brothers are her assistants, and I work for my dad."

"Nice business," said Rascal. "I'm still getting used to everything being human-owned out here."

"Not everything," Pella said. "Not even most, really. There's still a dozen or so kuduk families in town, owning most of the land and all the slaves. We don't see so many collars as you're probably used to back west and below, but the ones you see are theirs."

"Does your family own their own land?"

"One of the few. That's why your friend wanted you to come meet our guests. We've got 'em holed up safe. Safer than them coming out."

"Who are these 'guests' of yours?" Rascal asked.

Pella looked both ways, as if she were considering crossing the road instead of telling him something. She leaned in close, until her bonnet brushed against the brim of Rascal's hat. "They're with the rebellion."

Rascal and Pella strolled through Yellowcorn arm in arm. It was less suspicious than walking as companions or business associates, since Rascal was new in town and the few who knew him believed him to be traveling for leisure. Pella seemed not to mind the simple deception, nor the fact that his arm was basted in a layer of sweat. Much as he found Pella fetching, he would have preferred a bit of space between them for ventilation's sake.

When they arrived at her family's home, Rascal found it typical of the city, though perhaps less shabby and weatherworn. The paint on the corrugated steel roof and the brick facade were both a dull white to keep the heat away—and blind gawkers like himself with the glare. A path of brick paving stones led from the dirt road to the porch, some hundred paces long. Out beyond the house was a barren field, and across the way there was a larger building adjoining the thunderail tracks.

"Doesn't it get noisy around here, right by the tracks?" Rascal asked as they walked the brick path.

Pella loosened her grip on Rascal's arm so she could turn without her bonnet knocking his hat off. She gave him a curious look. "Only when the cars thunder by," she replied. "Living down in a deep, you must get used to a din, what with no place for all the sound to escape. I can't imagine being boxed in with that many people, not to mention trolleys and steam wagons, and thunderails of your own."

"It's not quite as bad as you make it out. There's always some sort of noise, but it's comforting. The city has a sound, and when it gets quiet, you know something's gunked up. Here? It took me five nights to get a proper sleep, what with all the quiet. I almost bought myself a pocketclock to put under my pillow, just to stop me waking up ten times a night to see what's wrong."

"I always heard kuduks were noisy people," Pella said. "Ain't enough of them around here to get the feel of them, but I figured it'd be nice having the quiet, knowing it means they can't be around."

Rascal kept a watch on the windows, and saw one of the curtains pull back as they approached. The glare from the glass kept him from seeing whoever was keeping watch for them. "I suppose there's that. Say, Pella, are we expected?" Visions of an angry father flashed in Rascal's head. There were some men that liked to keep their families safe even from innocuous strangers, and more than a few of the freeborn humans of Yellowcorn had cast baleful looks at the pale deep-dweller who had slunk in among them with no apparent profession.

"Aw, don't you worry yourself. My dad and mum are good folk, and your friend's waiting inside too."

Rascal offered his hand when they reached the steps, and helped Pella up. The gesture felt silly as soon as he made it, since it was her own home and she probably took the steps a dozen times a day without anyone to help her. To her credit, she didn't say a word, just gave a shy glance and accepted his aid. The door opened as soon as they reached the porch. Pella's assurances blew away like dust before the thunderail when he saw the double-barrel of a scattergun aimed at his chest.

"Step aside, Pella," said the square-jawed man with a salt-and-pepper beard and the weapon trained on Rascal. "You, stranger, what's your name?" The man wore a gentleman's shirt with wooden buttons like Rascal's own, and light grey slacks that brushed the tops of black-polished shoes.

"Pious Henlon," Rascal answered, giving his civic name and title in the church of Eziel. He let his arm go slack as Pella disentangled herself, and put his hands up slowly. "But I go by Rascal among friends. Am I among friends here?"

"Koop, let him alone," a familiar voice boomed from inside the house. "If that ain't the guy I've run jobs with for nine years, he's got a brother he never mentioned." The scattergun lowered and its owner nodded and jerked his head toward the inside of the house.

Rascal pulled off his hat and returned the nod before stepping past Koop and into the house. Pella followed on his heels and Koop shut the door behind them.

"What's the matter with you, Dad?" Pella asked.

"Just being cautious, sweetie. Can't be too cautious with this business," Koop said. "Pardon the lead-slinger, Mr. Rascal, but I'm not used to this business yet." There was no family resemblance between Pella and her father, save for the uniform darkness of their tanned skin. His hair was dark where hers was light. His frame was stocky, almost pudgy, where hers was delicate. By their facial features they could have been different species.

"No shot, no pardon," said Rascal, hoping that the phrase was known out in the skies. His friend Hayfield stepped past Koop and clapped Rascal on the shoulder hard enough to knock him half a step to his right. "What've you got us into here, Hayfield?" Rascal backhanded the big lug in the chest, drawing a grin. It struck him that Hayfield fit in better among the sky-dwellers than he had in Eversall Deep, where his skin was darker than most. Among the locals of Yellowcorn, he blended right in—aside from his towering height and shoulders like the booms of a crane.

"Come on, got some new friends for you to meet," Hayfield replied. "They can do most of the talkin'." He leaned forward and in a low tone, added, "If you can get 'em to clamp up for two runnin' minutes, I got a ten-bill for you."

Koop hung his scattergun on a pair of hooks on the wall and led them into the sitting room, with windows looking out toward the thunderail tracks. Seated in three of the wicker seats scattered around the room were two women and a man, all human. The one in the sleeveless grey coveralls with her blonde hair pulled back and tied in a plume had to be Pella's mum. If she looked nothing like her father, Pella was a cast copy of her mother with the years polished away.

The other two sat right beside one another. The first was a dark-haired man in his late twenties with a fire burning in his eyes. Rascal had seen the sort before; he was being sized up, weighed, and judged, and by someone too young to know caution. No-Boots had that look often, before he got himself hanged. His companion was dark-skinned and haired, like someone who grew up in the skies of the northern climes, dark enough even to stand out among Yellowcorn's locals. She seemed more at ease, with the relaxed features of someone who had just been interrupted from a pleasant conversation.

Hayfield made the introductions. "Rascal, this is Gahwin, our hostess."

"Pleased to meet you," said the older version of Pella.

"And these are Kinmi and Syr." Hayfield indicated first the man, then the woman. He'd have never have guessed by the names alone. Foreigners, both.

"We've heard a lot about you," Kinmi said. He stood and offered Rascal his hand. He had the grip of an innkeeper, or a confidence man. It was just firm enough to not be insultingly gentle.

Rascal cast a glance over at Hayfield, who tried and failed to keep a smirk from his face. "This old leather-head tellin' stories out of hat?"

"Don't look at me," Hayfield said, holding up both hands in mock defense. He nodded to Kinmi. "You go ahead and tell him."

"We've heard about you for years, Rascal. We've been authorized to let you in on a number of confidential matters. Not the least of which—"

"We're friends of General Rynn," said Syr, in a charmingly melodic accent that told him he was right about her heritage; she had to have lived most of her life in Braavland.

"*General* Rynn?" Rascal asked. He reached up and stroked his scruffy little beard. "You can't mean our little Chipmunk?"

"No, not anymore," said Syr. "They finally convinced her to drop her human name, but yes, the same girl. She told us that the two of you used to run the gang she fought with."

Kinmi spoke up. "Her account varied by story as to which of you was in charge."

"Neither of us, really," Rascal said. "I'm a priest, firstmost, so everyone in the lowest layers knew me. Just about everyone knew Hayfield though, top to bottom. Can't hardly be helped playing fourteen years in the pro leagues, getting your flashpop in the paper monthly and your name in there after every game."

"Who'da thunk it'd be Chipmunk climbing over bodies to get to the top," Hayfield said.

"Bodies?" Rascal asked. "This 'general' thing isn't literal, is it?"

Kinmi nodded solemnly. "The war's started. It's scratch and scramble for now, but so far, we're winning."

Rascal blinked. He must have misheard. "Winning? Winning what?"

"You were there, she said. You saw her new guns work," Syr replied. "She's studied the old daruu arts and is using them to arm us, to keep us mobile, to give us the advantage."

"Eziel give us strength," Rascal whispered. "It's coming."

"What's that?" Hayfield asked, cupping a hand behind his ear.

Kinmi burst out laughing. He turned to Syr. "I always wondered if the priests even knew. I guess so."

"Know what?" Hayfield asked, looking from Rascal to Kinmi and back again.

"There were twelve gods that watched over Korr," Rascal said in the voice he used when acting as Pious Henlon. "When the kuduks ground our kind underfoot, we took one as our patron, to keep humanity united as best we could. Our ancestors chose Eziel, and for good reason: Eziel is the god of war."

Hayfield looked at Rascal as if he'd caught fire. "The same Eziel that we pray to for bread in our bellies and a good lock on the door? The Eziel that collects coins for the poor and turns them into soup? The same Eziel that—"

"That kept our numbers strong for thousands of years, until his original purpose was forgotten by all but the ordained?" Rascal asked. "The Eziel that forbids us to harm our own kind, but lets me sneak off after evening prayers to put bullets in kuduk heads? The Eziel that our ancestors prayed to before battle? Yeah, that one."

"Don't worry, Hayfield," Kinmi said. "Rascal's little secret is nothing. I'm going to twist both your heads into candy knots. General Rynn authorized us to tell her old gang *everything*."

"Lord Eziel, grant us vengeance upon our enemies. Let us share our strength as comrades and become fearsome to our foes. I am your servant, teach me to kill in your name."
–Invocation to Eziel, original phrasing

Chapter 14

"Every time some sailor waxes poetic about how big the bloody sea is, I want to punch him." –Avrax Coalic, builder of the first transcontinental thunderail

Life aboard the drifting *Darksmith* was a series of minor annoyances. With the ship listing to starboard, everything slid. Food had to be kept in hand while eating, playing at dice was impossible, and sleeping was done in the lower corners of rooms, with bedding jammed in the crook of walls like hard, cold hammocks.

The limited number of serious injuries was one of the small blessings the crew had been afforded. Most of their casualties in the firefight with the *Fair Trader* had died quickly, if not cleanly, and most of the other injuries were minor beyond mentioning. One gunner had lost an eye, and likely his livelihood. A few others had gashes that took stitches to mend. There was little else for Jamile to do aboard after that but mother after her charges and see that infection didn't set in.

The last thought rankled Madlin, and since rankling was one of the few activities she had available, she did a lot of it. Though she had pencil and paper aboard, drafting on the uneven floors of the *Darksmith* was a chore. Trying to use a desk would have required welding a chair to the floor first, and she had no welding equipment. And so she watched the sea, watched the rest of the crew, and watched Jamile.

If Sosha had been half as attentive to Rynn as Jamile was being to the injured crewmen, she'd still have two good feet—well, Madlin had them, but so would Rynn. Rynn never would have been tackled by a lumbering oaf if she had two working feet to dodge her aside.

Rynn. Rynn. She kept pounding the name into her own head, using it every time she thought of her twin, making an effort of it. Her father had been right, but it had taken Sosha's reasoning to show her why.

There was something to be said for image. When her father entered a room, people stopped what they were doing and paid attention. He wasn't a physically imposing man, but he looked the part of a Mad Tinker, always covered in grease, wearing coveralls to meet princes, peering through multi-lensed spectacles.

Madlin reached down and felt below the knee of her left leg, just to remind herself that it was there. She'd always been close with Rynn, as much as any of the twinborn she'd spoken with. Some felt the connection more keenly, others viewed the twin as more a partner than a second self. Madlin and Rynn had always been among the former. While it made sharing memories and skills more fluid, it came with drawbacks. Rynn had woken on two separate occasions since the loss of her foot only to fall heavily to the floor when she tried to put weight on a foot that she had trod upon only minutes earlier in Madlin's body. For her part, Madlin was wary of standing with nothing to hold onto, constantly worried about losing her balance—though the nagging feeling faded as each day wore on, only to be renewed the next morning.

The injury reminded her troops of the sacrifice she'd made, which was stupid, because it was her own carelessness that had gashed up her foot, not anything the kuduks did to her. Her persistent imprisonment in the murderous collar should have been a far better symbol of her treatment under kuduk ownership. Unfortunately, it was too subtle, too familiar to most of the troops. Most of the Korrish aboard had worn a collar in one form or another. Her inability to escape hers was more a subject of pity than inspiration. The Errol Company troops that were aboard the *Jennai* couldn't grasp the scope of the horror.

Madlin blamed Rynn for her own injury and the repeated tearing of stitches that led to her septic rot, but she blamed Sosha for not noticing soon enough to stop it. Rynn had her own plan in the works to be rid of her crutches, and Madlin—paper or no—was determined to help.

As she stared out to sea, her eyes lost their focus. Within her head, images of steel and leather evolved. Free of the confines of the workshop or even the drafting table, she snipped and stretched, bent and cut, bolted and welded pieces in her mind. She envisioned the workings, saw how they would interact, and made adjustments for defects. While she slept, Madlin would let Rynn put the refined ideas to paper. While she lazed along the railing of the drifting *Darksmith*, she daydreamed of metal feet.

"Land!"

The shout chased away the lethargy that had spread like measles among the crew. Those on deck perked up and took to the port railing, twisting about from the high vantage to better view the horizon. Those who had been sulking below decks boiled up and into the sunlight.

"About bleedin' time," Tanner muttered, edging his way down the deck with a hand to the nearest wall as he took a spot at the starboard railing beside Madlin. "I don't care if it's got jungle cats and snakes and wild boars, so long as it's got flat ground to stand on. Gut me, what am I saying? I hope there's some crazed hungry animals out there waitin' to eat us. It'll make 'em easier to put on a spit if they ain't runnin' away."

"You're not worried about Dan at all?" Madlin asked. She studied his face as he looked along with everyone else to where the lookout with the spyglass had pointed. "Or is that it, you got your fortune, now you're glad to be rid of him?"

"If I were you, I'd be more worried if he was alive," Tanner said. "I saw you push him over. If blowing up a ship didn't set his mood right, he might still be pretty sore with you."

"You don't sound worried."

"Dan's the emperor of mixed blessings," said Tanner. He slouched against the railing and slid down until he was sitting next to Madlin. "He gets us more dark eyes turned our way than I'd like, but he takes heads when it comes time to settle up. He's not really a friend, or a partner, or a boss. Gut me if he thinks he works for *me*. It's more like we're in on the same scams, and it'd piss him off if anyone botched things up on him. I think he'd kill to protect me, same as he would the empress of Kadrin, or a horse he'd taken the time to name. If it's in his garden, he'll be sliced belly to throat before he lets anyone so much as lean on it without his leave."

"Just how cracked is he? Do you think he'd kill me over pushing him overboard? I didn't think. I just sort of did it; it was an accident."

"Want my advice?" Tanner asked. Madlin nodded vigorously. "Tell the little prick he deserved it. If that doesn't work and it looks like he's gonna do you cold, tell him his uncle would never kill a defenseless lady."

"I'm not defenseless!" Madlin protested. She drew her revolver and held it up, careful not to point the barrel in Tanner's direction.

Tanner laid a hand atop the barrel and pushed it back down in the direction of the holster. "You just keep talking like that, and he *might* kill you anyway. He's thirteen and got all the rot that goes along with it. Tell him he can't hurt you and sure as hangin' he'll try. Make him feel like a big man, he won't lower himself to hurt a girl."

Tanner stood once more and squinted at the horizon, shielding his eyes with a hand. "Maybe best if we do find him washed up in pieces though. Kid might've started a war in Veydrus with that stunt of his."

"He better not be dead. I still plan to get him to show me proper magic."

Tanner leaned over the rail and twisted around so his face was just a handsbreadth from Madlin's. "Depending what we find on that little island, I might have an alternate plan."

"What makes you so sure it's a little island?" Madlin asked. "Could be the southern peninsula of Takalia, for all we know."

"We ain't drifted *that* far in a day," Tanner replied. "And tiny, piss pot little islands are all this stretch of Katamic's got."

By noontime, it took no special lens or vantage to spot the grey stretch of rock that jutted from the Katamic in their path. It was the largest of several now visible from the *Darksmith's* deck. For all appearances some ancient god had waded north from Khesh to build Takalia, and his bag of rocky shorelines had torn and spilled in the middle of the sea. The way was dotted with flotsam from the *Fair Trader* like trail signs. Whatever current was dragging them along had made better time with lighter debris than the hulking steel hull of the steamship.

Captain Toller made a few attempts to alter their course, in an effort to put some word in as to where they ran aground. The bait sail was in tatters, but by makeshift rigging the crew had managed to raise it and catch a wind; the Katamic deigned not to notice the effort, and pulled them along in spite of the tiny, ragged bit of cloth that tugged at the ship like a puppy biting at a trouser hem. An attempt at rowing lasted all of perhaps five minutes. A wooden ship the size of the *Darksmith* would take a hundred men or more at the oars. The steamship was far heavier than a wooden ship its size, giving it both more mass to push and a deeper draw to force aside in their path, plus they had no proper oars. Even a crew of landfolk would have soon realized that rifle butts and steel-sheet wreckage from the lower decks were no way to move a vessel.

Thus they waited for the Katamic to be done with them, and see where they ended up.

Madlin kept her vigil at the aft castle, starboard side. "I've been watching the path of the debris field in front of us," Madlin said to Captain Toller when he happened to pass nearby. "We've got a good chance to miss that large island. Only the leftmost part of the swath of wreckage seems to be washing up."

"I've already done all I can think of to move the ship under power—wind, steam, muscle—we've got nothing to do but wait," said Toller. "And pray, I suppose."

"You're missing the obvious one, I think," Madlin said.

"How's that, now?"

"Swim."

Toller's face went slack and his eyes darted off in the direction of the island. "No, we can't just leave the ship adrift. What if someone salvaged it?"

"That one should be even more obvious," Madlin replied.

Toller shook his head. "No. We're better off seeing where the currents take us. We should reach Takalia within a week."

"And we've got two days of food. Four if we ration like misers," said Madlin. "My father had the world-ripper running last night, nearly got it to open a hole. If his flywheel trick works out, we'll tell him where we are and get picked up."

"If we stay on the ship, we get those same four days, except we won't be surrounded by whatever crew of the *Fair Trader* survived. And Cadmus had a dozen dullards with guns blast holes in his machine."

"Just the wire webbing. That's quick to fix."

"Doesn't fill *me* with confidence that he's about to whisk us off to safety," Toller said. He pointed to the island. "We maroon ourselves there, you're betting our lives on your father's tinkering. I'd rather take my chances at sea, and either land starving in Takalia or force Cadmus to pluck us from a moving target."

"Yeah, and what about Dan?" Madlin asked.

Toller bowed his head, revealing the bit of a spreading bald spot Madlin didn't normally have a vantage to view. "Regrettable. He gave his life to save us from those misbegotten rat-kissers."

"And if he didn't, he's probably stranded there, waiting for us."

Toller put a hand over his mouth and rubbed at his stubble. "There's no smoke coming from the island. He seems the type to have laid into them, burning things."

"We owe it to him to look."

"At the cost of a ship?"

"Yes."

"At the cost of *my* ship?" Toller's voice rose.

"My father's ship, and we can start making you airships if we can get Dan to show me better magic." Madlin left out that she was pretty sure she knew enough already, but she wanted more.

Toller's eyes walked a circuit around the derelict *Darksmith*. Madlin gave him a moment free of her badgering to contemplate his decision. She could always start in again if he still disagreed.

When Toller's eyes returned to Madlin, they were somber things, weary after a long farewell. "I have your word? An airship of my own?"

Madlin gave a nod. "My word." She offered Toller her hand and they shook on it. "Besides, how many twinborn can I trust to captain a ship?"

The island had grown huge as they approached. By landmass standards it was still a paltry thing, but it had looked so small on the horizon compared to the wide outcropping of rock that loomed over the *Darksmith* and her crew. There was nothing resembling a beach, just grey granite jutting from the water's depths and continuing on down below them.

"I don't like this," said Jamile, her gaze turned toward the water more than the island.

"You said you knew how to swim," said Madlin. "Seawater even makes you more buoyant. This shouldn't be too hard." She told herself that, at least. She had grown up in an underground labyrinth of tunnels in one world and an icy wasteland in this one. She had gone swimming perhaps five times in her life, on the rare days on Tinker's Island that would be called summer by anyone not born there.

"The pond by the sanctuary had little fish in it, half the length of your hand. Leeches were the worst thing in it. The Katamic has ... well, it has *everything* in it. There's a hundred miles of water beneath us. If you swam straight down, you'd come out the other side of the world."

Madlin scoffed. "Nonsense. The sea doesn't go all the way through Tellurak. And even if it did, the pressure would crush you flatter than a sheet of paper before you ever got there. The Katamic's probably only a few miles deep."

Jamile stared at her, aghast.

"What?" Madlin asked.

"Below us, there's miles and miles of nothing but water, filled with sharks and jellyfish and eels and turtles and spiny little fish that will stop every muscle in your body if you so much as brush up against them."

"Turtles are harmless," Madlin said.

Jamile backed her way up the tilted deck. "Give me a rifle. I'll stay here and guard the *Darksmith* until your father can get the machine working."

"Trouble, ladies?" Tanner asked, sauntering over. Madlin was impressed despite her general annoyance with Tanner that he was still able to act nonchalant walking on the inclined deck.

"Yes, Madlin's mad as her father, wanting us to swim to that island," said Jamile.

"Naw, not from what I've heard," Tanner said with a smirk. "Her dad's a real nutter. Course, most of that stuff they say about him's still brown from the arse it came from. This one though, she took a warlock's tongue to the wrong side of her feelings and heaved him overboard. She's got her old man beat 'til I meet him and see otherwise."

Madlin frowned and made sure Tanner noticed. "Thanks."

"As for me, piss on this swimming business. It's for the fish; you know what I mean? Don't get me wrong, I'm coming, but gut me if I said I was looking forward to the trip."

"Think we'll find Dan there?" Madlin asked.

Tanner sighed and nodded. "Probably made himself a nice little tent out of pirate skins."

"Ew," Jamile and Madlin said in unison. They turned to each other with puzzled looks.

"Yuck," said Madlin.

"Vile," said Jamile. They shared a nod, satisfied that they'd parted ways verbally.

A signal whistle blew, its clear, clean note cutting the air like an arrow piercing everyone's eardrums. After a second it rose, then fell again. Captain Toller lowered the whistle and bellowed. "All hands, abandon ship."

The grim crew stepped over the railing one by one and filed into the water. Some muttered prayers or well-wishes to the doomed vessel. Others just took the meager supplies they were willing to bear as they swam ashore.

Madlin hung toward the back of the group, in no hurry to be in the water. Toller ducked below decks. The plan had been for him to be last off the ship, and for him to personally be the one to open the watertight doors that were keeping several compartments of the ship from flooding. With those open, it would only be a matter of time before the *Darksmith* was claimed by the Katamic Sea.

Minutes passed, and the gentle swells of the Katamic lapped over the deck, soaking Madlin's shoes. The crew was nearly all in the water now, and the remaining handful prepared to plunge in. Tanner was already gone, somewhere near the head of the pack; he was no strong swimmer, but was eager to be done with the ordeal. Jamile hung back with Madlin until they were the last two on deck.

"Go on, get in there," Madlin said, offering a gentle shove with her forearm.

"You first," Jamile replied.

Madlin stared off at the door to the lower decks. "No, I'm waiting for Toller. Captains get some soft-witted ideas in their heads about honor and ships. I'm not going to let him ride this hull down to the bottom."

"I'll wait with you," said Jamile. "You might need help getting him—"

"Just go."

Jamile edged over the *Darksmith's* railing, sitting a moment with her chest heaving and a duffel with the few belongings she could save clutched in one hand. The other hand gripped the railing with white knuckles. Madlin moved behind her and put her hands on Jamile's shoulders, kneading muscles tight as a drive belt. She leaned close and spoke softly in Jamile's ear. "Just relax. Take a few deep breaths. Everything's going to be fine."

Jamile took a long, shuddering breath, then another. Madlin waited for her grip to loosen on the railing. She set a foot firmly behind her, availing herself of the leverage from the deck's tilt, and shoved Jamile off the railing. Jamile hit the water with a splash and came up spluttering.

"Madlin! What were you trying to do, drown me?"

"You can swim. Swim. I'll be along in a minute."

Madlin left Jamile to follow in the wake of the human flotilla stretching out toward the barren chunk of rock that passed for an island. She climbed the ever increasingly angled deck until she reached the door to the hold, which conveniently flopped open downward.

"Toller," she shouted down the flooding stairwell. There was a chorus of waterfalls playing within the ship. "Get your arse up here before you get sucked under with the ship. If you do anything so mush-brained as—"

"Pull the brakes there, General," Toller's voice echoed up from below. Sloshing footsteps were barely audible over the inrush of seawater. "Just making sure this lady makes it all the way to her final resting place. Boil my liver in a pot of rum if I'm taking any chance some pirate gets aboard and floats her."

Madlin let out a relieved sigh. "*Darksmith's* a one-captain girl, Toller. She wouldn't go behind your back like that. Now get up here and get swimming."

Madlin was the last ashore. She emerged from the surf on her hands and knees, dripping saltwater like a soaked washcloth. The small canvas bag she'd left with was somewhere in the vicinity of the sunken *Darksmith* after slipping from her grasp midway to the island. Her spectacles had spotted over with brine that couldn't be cleaned away until her clothes dried enough to wipe them on. One shoe had fallen away as she kicked to propel herself through the water; there was something about left feet that were just ill luck for her. The one true fortune she'd had was that the buckles of her holster and the safety strap that kept her revolver secured within had both held up to the trials of her swim.

When she was past the line where the waves no longer reached, she collapsed and rolled onto her back. The rock was an uncomfortable pillow, but surprisingly smooth against her back. To her hands and her bare foot, it had the texture of a polished tunnel floor like the ones in the nicer parts of Eversall Deep. Madlin closed her eyes against the dizziness of looking up into an infinite sky above, and listened to the sound of her own breathing.

There were other sounds on the island around her. The *Darksmith's* crew milled about, some exploring the terrain, others just basking in the sun to dry, carrying on quiet conversations. The Katamic never quit its assault on her ears. She was growing heartily sick of the sea, and being reminded of it every few seconds by the break of a wave was starting to grate on her nerves. Madlin reached a hand up to her neck to let a trickle of aether into her collar's runes, then remembered that she didn't have one around her neck.

"You all right?" Jamile asked. Though her eyes were closed, the sunlight trying to shine through Madlin's eyelids was blocked by the other woman's presence. "Neck bothering you?" Cool fingers probed the sinews of Madlin's neck where she had reached for it.

It was easier to play along than admit her momentary confusion of worlds. "It's nothing. Everyone accounted for?"

"All the ones who made it to the water with us, at least," Jamile replied. She reached a hand beneath Madlin's head and took her by the arm, helping her to a seated position. "I'll tell you what I told the rest. It's bad for the body to work that hard then stop all at once. Stand up, stretch, walk around a bit. Sit and rest when your heart stops pounding."

Madlin climbed reluctantly to her feet with help from Jamile, wishing she had a pair of crutches to lean on lest her wobbly legs buckle beneath her. She put her hands to her hips and bent forward, wondering if she would vomit up the stray gulps of seawater she'd swallowed as she gasped like a bellows during her swim. She still had the briny taste in her mouth.

"Anyone find Dan?" she asked between breaths, as much to keep her mind from her sour stomach and burning muscles as for any interest in the answer.

Jamile pointed off vaguely over the rise of rock that obscured the inland portion of the island. "Tanner went off looking. Haven't heard anything."

With a long, shaky breath, Madlin straightened and tried to resume breathing normally. "Fine. I'm going to look for both of them." She sat and pulled off her other shoe, lobbing it well clear of the water's edge. When she stood again, she felt the damp, sun-warmed rock beneath her bare feet. It reminded her of playing at the water's edge in Tinker's Island in those fleeting summer days of her childhood.

"I'll stay here, I think," Jamile replied. "Not sure I can be spared here, just yet."

You're not sure you want to see Dan, Madlin corrected in her head.

"It's not a big island, just yell if you need me."

Madlin set off, exchanging a few greetings and inquiries with the crew as she wove her way around the shore to find a way up to the island's interior. It was a climb and a scramble, but there were rocky paths leading up, unintended by nature, but passable by humans nonetheless, strewn with tidal pools filled with mosses and little creatures. The island had appeared utterly barren in a spyglass, but it seemed that anywhere one looked, scraps of life could be found digging in, holding onto whatever they could to survive. If urchins and snails could survive on the island, so could a band of humans for a few days—even if it meant eating urchins and snails.

When Madlin was on higher ground and out of sight of the crew, she drew her revolver. With practiced movements so ingrained as to defy conscious thought, she slid the cylinder release, snapped the cylinder out on its hinge, and pulled the ejector pin. Eight bullets tumbled into her hand, still wet from her extended bath in the Katamic Sea. She didn't stop walking, keeping an eye to the uneven rock as she felt her way along with her feet. She shook the water from the bullets, then blew on them until they were mostly dry. She blew into each chamber of the cylinder and down the barrel as well, for all the good it really did. The gun needed a proper cleaning. It would be crusted with salt and whatever other filth the seawater carried until she got it home to Tinker's Island where she had all the tools she'd need.

She wandered the island, gun in hand. If there were survivors of the *Fair Trader* lurking, she wanted to be ready for them. If she found Dan first ... well, maybe the gun would matter, maybe it wouldn't, but she preferred the feel of it in her hand to traipsing about unarmed. She kept it aimed at the sky as she leaned on her forearm to brace herself against an outcropping as she stepped across a small chasm. The sight lines were poor, with a general upward trend to the mountainous terrain the farther inland she ventured. In her mind she tried to put some familiar shape to the landscape. It was neither a peak breaking through the waterline nor an elongated crashball of land. When Madlin reached one of the higher points, she looked around in all directions. It resembled nothing so much as a ragged cut on the face of the Katamic, puckered and scabbed over with rock, made by a knife—or best yet, a hook—that had caught and dragged along the sea, skipping as it tore, leaving the smaller islands in its wake.

From her vantage, she should have seen everything, but the irregularities in the rock could have hidden half an army—a small one, anyway. She nearly leapt from her skin when something poked her in the back. She whirled with a yelp, bringing her revolver to bear.

She aimed it at the grinning face of the most ragged, bedraggled boy she had seen outside of Korr. Dan giggled with the barrel of Madlin's revolver inches from his forehead as he stood a step below her on the rocks. His face was reddened from sun, his eyes reddened with madness—or at least sleeplessness. The black silks he wore had been shredded. His shirt was reduced to a tattered vest, missing all of one sleeve and most of another. The pants ... Madlin kept her gaze well away from Dan's lower half, which had little left to accord him modesty.

"Got ya," Dan said, and started cackling. He was nonplussed by the aim of Madlin's revolver.

Madlin put her free hand to her chest and held the gun away from Dan's face as she calmed her quickened breathing. "There you are," she said. "Tanner and I have been looking for you."

"Yeah, I followed him around a while, but he's no fun to startle. I might actually get a sword in the gut for my trouble."

"Me and my gun were the safe ones to scare half to death?"

"Halfway there and never the whole, the trick to getting grey and old," Dan replied. "Sorry, the rhyme doesn't work in Kheshi. Besides, you took that gun through half the Katamic to get here; no way it would fire."

Good to know. He thinks these work like flintlocks. Madlin knew better. A wet flintlock, the only sort of gun Tellurak knew before her father's "invention" of the cartridge, was worthless—or rather, the black powder it used was worthless when wet. She'd save the bullet trying it out, but stake her life that her own revolver would fire when she asked it to.

"Are you hungry? We brought what food we could," Madlin said. "The crew's down on the ... well, where there should be a beach."

"I'm fine. I ate three of the pirates before I washed ashore," Dan said. Madlin recoiled with eyes gone wide. Dan laughed. "The look on your face. Winds, I'm starving!" He hopped down the rocks, his own feet as bare as Madlin's. She assumed he was using magic to aid his descent, since he had heretofore shown all the awkward gangliness of a youth not yet grown into his body. She took greater care in following after him.

"So what have you been doing on the island since you got here?" Madlin called ahead, hoping to keep Dan from running ahead by keeping him engaged in conversation.

Dan picked his way along the rocks, but stopped long enough to answer. "I *have* been killing pirates. There's a pile of bodies back there a ways. Until the reinforcements arrived, I'd been playing hide-from-his-lordship with the Zaynes. They're around here somewhere, invisible. They don't dare confront me in the open, so I've been trying to hunt them down before nightfall. I've already lost one night's sleep to them; I wasn't keen to lose another."

"You've been up since the battle?" Madlin asked. She thought back on all the tedium of the past day and a half aboard the *Darksmith* and tried to imagine what Dan was going through during that same time. If he was teetering closer to the brink of madness than usual, she could at least understand why.

"Them or me, and with two of them, they could afford a watch," said Dan. He hopped down and spoke away from her. "I won't trust my sleep to wards with that dead-eyed whoreson around. With you lot around as fodder though, I'll get some sleep and have a bit of warning if he starts killing."

"I feel so much better," Madlin muttered beneath her breath as she followed, falling farther behind by the minute.

Tanner caught the sounds of Dan's triumphant return to the crew of the *Darksmith* as they carried on the wind. The ungrateful brat had avoided him intentionally, he realized. The island simply wasn't large enough for Dan not to have heard his shouts over all the distance he had covered. That was fine; let the boy have his fun. If nothing else it meant he was in good spirits, all things considered. After stumbling on the mutilated corpses of a number of uncouth-looking gentlemen (a couple with familiar faces from when he briefly sailed with Zayne's ship as a twinborn "ambassador"), he hadn't been certain of the pubescent warlock's mood.

With congratulatory shouts fading behind him, Tanner trekked across the barren landscape in the other direction. He kept his hands well away from both pistol and sword, both for balance on the slick, smooth rock and to show that he was, if not unarmed, then at least not carrying any weapon in hand.

"If you can hear me, I want to talk," Tanner said to the emptiness around him, keeping his voice low enough so that keen ears couldn't possibly hear him over the din of his own well-wishers. "I'm your only chance off this island, I think. Best for everyone if you come out and we make a deal."

There was no answer from the empty air, which was more a disappointment than a surprise. He had known the Zaynes years longer than Dan had, and had met both of them face to face, which he was all but certain Dan had not. He knew the contents of Jadon Zayne's bag of tricks better than anyone. The boy and his father could be a pace away, and Tanner might not realize it until he smelled the rum on Denrik's breath.

"If the boy finds you first, you won't get anything like a deal outta him," Tanner said. "You'll get the better end of a deal for sure, since if I duck back there with everyone else, I'm safe as a cloistered princess and you're still hiding from a kid warlock with all the subtle charm of an arsonist."

Around the next jutting tooth of rock, Tanner saw a man of his early fifties, grey hair shot through with streaks of its original black and a beard of patchy stubble to match. Denrik Zayne took his ease on a flat rock shelf just high enough for his toes to reach the next ledge down. The pirate king's uniform was a mocking homage to that of an Acardian commodore, less the Acardian crest and much of the embroidered accents. The uniform had seen better days, the whites stained yellow and smeared with black scorch marks and flecks of blood. The jacket was torn along the seam of one shoulder.

"Mr. Tanner, I am not amused," said Zayne in a tone dry enough to parch Tanner's soggy clothes. "Put down the sword and pistol, and we can talk."

Tanner scratched his head a moment, then shrugged. "I'm sure Jadon could tear my Source out, armed or not. Why not?" He unbuckled both his sword belt and gun belt and laid them on the ground. Backing away from them, he found a suitable rock of his own and sat opposite the pirate.

"That *thing* of yours is a problem," said Zayne. "He's a rabid shark. Any of my crew that didn't make it to the lesser islands is dead. If you help me put him out of his misery, we can deal."

"Heads on platters always your opening bargain?" Tanner asked. "Listen, I got another world to worry about. You do too. To put my cards on the table, if it weren't for Veydrus, I'd have just let the kid hunt you both down and be done with it. But it ain't that simple. I let you kill Dan, he's gonna put my twin's skull in the bottom of his privvy if he even sniffs I was involved. I let him add you to that pile the other side of the ridge, Anzik has himself a tantrum and restarts the war. Sound about right?"

Zayne fixed him with a steady glare, chin resting on his clasped hands. "You have the general concept well in hand, I believe. You'll just have to take care that he doesn't suspect you."

"Back out of that blind alley; I'm not following you in. I've got a way we all walk out of here alive. Well, not *walk* as such, but—"

"Mr. Tanner, you're beginning to babble."

"Right. Well, I'm traveling with the heiress of the Errol Company. We'll get picked up in a few days, I imagine, when another ship comes to look for us. I'll keep Dan from hunting you down—maybe you can even swim to one of the smaller islands to be safe—and get word to Stalyart. I can get word to him through Veydrus, and he can bring the *Merciful* down to rescue you."

"You've still got the ear of that one, do you? I never understood why he kept you around."

"Never hurts to have connections," said Tanner.

"Indeed. But what makes you so certain a ship will be looking for you? You can't have been due in port for days yet, a week or more if you were heading up to that frozen cesspit of the Mad Tinker."

"Twinborn. Mad Tinker and his daughter both. She's together with him on the other side."

Zayne frowned. "What are they, twinborn goblins? Is that where he cooks up those contraptions of his?"

"They ain't from Veydrus. They got some other world, filled with rot like steam ships and fancy guns. He just nicks stuff from there and makes his own. Point being, they got no skin in our brawl, but she's got the connection to get us out of here without waiting a month."

Zayne seethed a breath through his teeth. "What choice have I? Vengeance and likely death? Curse my luck, finally sinking my teeth into an Errol smoke-ship the day it had a demon aboard."

"Speaking of demons," Tanner said, brushing aside the jab at Dan's character. "Where's yours?"

"Close by, Mr. Tanner. Close by."

The whole walk back to the *Darksmith* crew's camp site, Tanner couldn't help feeling that eyes were following him.

Chapter 15

"Only twice in my life have I given a false name. Once was to a tax man, the other to a merchant prince's daughter. On both occasions I was spared a well-deserved reckoning by my foresight."
–Lantham Caige, in The Scoundrel's Lament

The darkened room was quiet, but not silent. A low hum emanated from the wall where cables grew like the hairs of a beard, combed through from the adjacent room. Each cable ran from its own little hole and drooped down to the floor before running across to the world-ripper. The only light in the room came from a few indicators on the control panel, showing coordinates in several axes and the power levels of both the viewfinder and the transport circuits. The latter was dark.

Kezudkan stood in front of the viewing frame with his hands clasped before him, leaning on the butt of his cane. At the controls was the kuduk tinker, Draksgollow, his head turned watching his patron watch the view. The image within the frame was a disused thunderail depot in the Turmon Republic, a few hours travel up the defunct Fairmorn-Tevek line. It was open to the sky in places, an older style of ventilation, simpler than pipes and chimneys for ridding the railyard of smoke, but it allowed in enough light for them to view it without having to turn the machine's main function partway on.

"Looks fine to me," Draksgollow said. "Plenty of space, even some old buildings intact. We could be set up in a few days."

"No, no. Won't do at all," Kezudkan replied, shaking his head. He lifted his cane to point. "You see that? There goes another one."

"Nope, didn't see a human that time either."

Kezudkan twisted around with a sound like a millstone grinding, and fixed Draksgollow with a critical glare. "Might want to look to those optics of yours. I'm five times your age, and I saw it plain enough. The place is infested with humans—probably rats, too."

"Fine. Say there are humans. We can just take care of them the way we did the squatters in your mine."

"Well and good for a bunch of savages from a primitive world, but I want something *secret*, someplace no one knows about. That isn't compatible with exterminating native species that are liable to run off and blather to more of their own kind."

"Then why not look at the primitive world?" Draksgollow asked, frustration slipping into his voice.

Kezudkan turned back to the viewer and shook his head. "I gave it some thought, but it takes more power going between worlds. If anything goes amiss, I'd rather be stranded locally, thank you kindly."

Draksgollow stood, knocking his chair over and stepping aside. He waved a theatrical hand toward the controls. There was a hiss from the compressed air cylinders in his mechanical arm. "By all means then, find someplace your own muddy self."

Kezudkan arched an eyebrow and waddled in Draksgollow's direction. For a moment, Draksgollow's eyes searched for some escape, realizing perhaps too late that he had angered the daruu. Neither of them were athletic, Kezudkan in his elderly third century and Draksgollow gimpy on a powerful but cumbersome steam-piston leg. The prospect of a thrashing at the old daruu's hands wasn't inconceivable. There was strength enough in his mechanical hand to crush the bones of a kuduk, but not a daruu. Infirm as he was, if Kezudkan caught hold of him, he'd be at the eccentric old man's mercy. Draksgollow held his breath as the daruu approached.

When Kezudkan got to within two paces, he snatched up his cane, holding it near the tip, and leveled the handle at Draksgollow's midsection. He held the kuduk tinker's gaze with his own as he lowered the handle, hooked it under the edge of the chair, and righted it. He turned his back on Draksgollow as he eased himself into the tiny seat, which groaned under his bulk but held itself intact.

"Very well," Kezudkan said as he brushed his fingers over the controls, as if reacclimating himself to the feel of the panel and dials. "Go make certain that the parts of the new machine are ready to transport and install once I find us a new home."

"Everything *is* ready," Draksgollow argued to the back of Kezudkan's head. "All the parts, dollies and gantries for hauling it all, kits with every tool we'll need—in triplicate—as well as food and basic furnishings for the new command center, on the assumption that you were going to stick us half up the arse crack of the world in some hovel."

"Excellent suggestion," Kezudkan quipped in reply. "I wasn't considering Korr's anatomy among my criteria. I shall have a look around for a proper crack, then. If you've got nothing better to do, how about finding out why there was a human from the savage world who knew what a kuduk was?"

"I'm no human tamer," said Draksgollow. "I buy mine pre-broken."

"Well, you see where my sculptor's touch has gotten me with mine: brought up on tribunal and my home destroyed."

"Perhaps, but I—"

"Mr. Draksgollow, I really don't give a fornicating pair of rodents what you do with your evening, providing you leave me in peace."

A moment later there was a wash of light from the outside corridor, followed by the hollow slam of an iron door, marking Draksgollow's departure.

"Stones save me from the tinkers' blight that plagues me," Kezudkan muttered as he fiddled the dials and began his search.

Powlo had lived through worse days. They weren't many, but he could fill a count of both hands with them. He had once spent three days trapped behind a cave-in, drinking his own piss and wondering which of his fellow miners would be the first to succumb to cannibalism—or if it would be him. He had been beaten so badly he vomited blood. There was the day that nearly broke him entirely, when his owner had sold off the mother of his children, whom he'd have called a wife if slaves were allowed to marry, a pain he wouldn't admit to his dearest friends. Those memories all came from Korr, from his twin, Chapun. And yet he remembered every one of those events with the clarity of someone who'd been there.

By comparison, the factory lavatory where he found himself chained to a sewage return pipe was a mere inconvenience. To be certain, there was a lingering dread over the whole situation, and he was just a night removed from watching as men he'd worked beside for years were blasted full of holes, bleeding and screaming out their last moments. But nothing bad, nothing truly awful, had happened to *him* yet. He wore a newly riveted collar, but that was more an irritation than anything; he was used to the feeling. There was even enough slack for him to reach both the sink and the toilet, so apart from a rumbling belly, he wasn't in any great distress.

The spark bulb overhead had kept him awake longer than he'd have liked the previous night. The switch for the lights was by the door, which the kuduks who'd taken him seemed keen to keep him from. Powlo's body was unaccustomed to sleeping on smooth rock floors, but Chapun's remembered what it was like. Eventually, with an arm at a contorted angle to ward away the light, he had managed to drift off.

He knew it was a matter of time before someone came to look in on him—and unless they had a spare lavatory, he was surprised no one had done so yet. Powlo kept himself calm and went over what he had rehearsed.

He awoke on the *Jennai*, on the half that used to be the *Cloudsmith*. The lamp in his room was on, and before he had awakened fully and puzzled out why, a voice spoke to him.

"It's me, Chapun," Erefan said. Chapun twisted under his blanket and saw the Mad Tinker's twin sitting at his bedside. "I saw what happened at the mine, but not everything. Did you get away? Are you all right? I tried to mount a rescue, but when I—"

Chapun reached out and put a hand over Erefan's, stopping short the nascent ramble before it got out of hand. "I'm alive. They took me captive."

Erefan's shoulders slumped in visible relief. "Captured." Erefan nodded and his eyes unfocused. "All right, all right ... we can work with that. Somebody brew some tea and round up something to eat."

Chapun looked out the open door of his cabin and saw a silhouetted shape slip away down the corridor. There were more people outside, he realized. A low buzz of conversation rose in the lull after Erefan's order.

Over the course of a pre-dawn breakfast of stale pastry and lemon tea with no sugar or milk (and Erefan's apologies for the shabby state of the rebellion's larder), Chapun described the slaughter.

"When the world-hole opened, I thought it was you, come to check on us and brag that you'd gotten the new one working," Chapun said. "Eziel help me, I had a smile on my face when I saw it—a *smile*. Well that didn't last long; they came through in pairs, armed with rifles. They weren't knockers or regular army, just blank-bearded blokes with twitchy trigger fingers. I screamed out 'kuduks!' but curse me for an idiot, nobody knew what I was talking about except the coal-hearted bastards shooting at us."

"How'd you survive?" Erefan asked.

Chapun shrugged. "Dicers luck? I dunno. Prob'ly one of 'em heard me shouting Korrish and figured I'd make a better prisoner that a corpse. I got slugged upside the head with a rifle butt, woke up chained in a loo. Smelled Korrish; figured they took me through."

"You certain?"

Chapun nodded. "Smelled enough kuduk shit in my day," he said with a sigh.

"I tried to force the world-ripper to work, had a little platoon rounded up for a rescue, ready to fire when I threw the switch."

"I take it you didn't get far with it."

Erefan closed his eyes and hung his head. "No. We had a glimmer; it looked like it might take hold and put a hole through to the mine for us, but the dynamo cut out—didn't have enough power to push through."

Chapun put a hand on Erefan's arm. "I'm alive. I'm breathing. Bolts, I've even got a lavatory all to myself." His shoulders slumped and his voice grew quiet. "Better than the rest of my boys."

Erefan stood. "Eziel grants strange mercies, eh?" He began to pace the small cabin. "We need to figure out what to do with you. Have they questioned you at all yet?"

"A bit, but they didn't get pushy about it. I played dumb, made like I didn't understand them. They knew I was faking. I don't think they're proper army though, cuz they didn't seem like they had anyone on hand who knew what to do with a prisoner. They just left me and threatened to come back in the morning."

"Not much of a threat, leaving you alone all night."

"Well, they didn't feed me. So there's that, I suppose. They might try to starve information outta me."

Erefan rubbed at his chin as he paced. "No. No we can't have you starving. We're going to need you to talk, confess even."

"Erefan, that doesn't sound like a good—"

"Not a true confession, of course," said Erefan. Pieces of a plan were riveting themselves together in his head. "A careful confession, a planned one, one we can use to our advantage."

There was a knock at the wall outside the open door. Chapun and Erefan both turned to see Vaulk poke his head in. Greuder's twin was popular among the rebels for crafting edible food from the increasingly sparse larders, and was known for being an early riser to prepare breakfast. Even for him it was early to be awake. "Can't help the fires of gossip spreading through the ship. I heard you have a bit of a problem with a prisoner."

"Yeah, me," Chapun replied.

"You have my sympathies," Vaulk replied, letting himself in without waiting for an invitation. "But I thought you might want some assistance. This is more my area than yours, tinker."

"I suppose you're right in that regard," Erefan agreed. "But this is hardly Scar Harbor we're talking about. These are kuduks."

"And one daruu you know like an uncle, from what I understand," Vaulk replied. He held up his hands in a gesture of surrender. "No offense, of course. You were in his household under pretense; we all know that. But that means you can help craft a story he'll swallow."

"You think you can write me a twister of a fairy story and get these blighters to let me go?" Chapun asked.

Erefan shook his head and walked between the two men as he resumed his pacing. "No, not go. We can do better than go, I think. Kezudkan thinks humans are all dumb animals, that I was some rare exception. We might be able to set you up as the fool he uses to undo us."

"I presume you mean for him to be mistaken in that regard," said Vaulk.

"I'm not undoing anyone!" Chapun protested. "If I'm a fool, I'm a loyal one at least."

Erefan gritted his teeth and squeezed his eyes shut. "I'm trying to say he'll underestimate you. He doesn't know about the twinborn, and there's no reason for him to learn. We can get you the information you need to feign a betrayal that plays into our hands."

"How do I do that?" Chapun said.

"I have years of experience in smuggling twinborn," Vaulk replied. "I know a thing or two about laying false trails."

"We need to work out the details," Erefan said, "but here's what I think we need to do ..."

"My name is Chapun," Powlo said. "I was a mine foreman for the Genrech family in Bessel Deep."

The kuduk with the mechanical arm and leg smiled, showing teeth in better repair than any other part of him seemed to be. "Glad you decided to stop playing the dumb animal. Now how did you get into that mine we found you in?"

"Blast me if I know," Powlo replied. The words had barely enough space to sneak out of his mouth before the kuduk's metal hand struck his jaw. Spots swam before Powlo's eyes as he pushed himself onto his hands and knees with no clear recollection of arriving on the floor. He worked his jaw back and forth to see if he still could, and felt a pop and a stab of pain as it settled back into its proper place. He covered his mouth to mask his moan (and a muffled curse), and to keep his jaw from wandering away from his skull.

"Chapun, let me level with you," Draksgollow said. "I have neither the experience nor the inclination for questioning humans. But I've got answers I need from you and a whole workshop of tools at my disposal. If I have to muddle through the best I can, I can assure you that you will be the one to suffer for it, not me. I have employees who I can order to clean up the mess I make in here. We clear on that?"

Powlo nodded. It hurt his jaw, but he guessed that talking would have hurt more.

"Now, how does a mine foreman from Bessel Deep end up in another world?"

"Favor for favor," Powlo said slowly, keeping his teeth clenched as best he could. "My freedom in return for running the mine."

"That doesn't answer the question," Draksgollow replied, looming over him.

"His name was Erefan," said Powlo. "He had a machine that made a hole in the world, brought me and a bunch of mine through. Made me an offer I'd've been a fool to refuse."

"Do you know where you were?"

"Never showed us a map, but he said it was off west of the Lumberlands, a place where humans lived free. He needed an expert on mine operation for it though, said I'd keep two percent as my pay."

Draksgollow nodded slowly, seemingly appeased for the moment. He sat—trousers up thankfully—on the seat of the toilet. "And you spoke the language of the locals?"

"Not at first, but Erefan said it was easy to learn. He was right too, only took me a few weeks." Powlo paused to work his jaw up and down. It ached, but the pain had dwindled from "crushed under the wheels of a thunderail" to "hit in the face with a shovel."

Draksgollow didn't wait for him to elaborate. "And where was this machine located? Where is Erefan now?"

Powlo knew this one was important. He tried to imagine that Erefan had betrayed him, had left him to die along with the others. He pictured the carnage in the tunnels and whispered lies to himself that it was all Erefan's fault. His breath quickened and his face grew warm. "I wish I knew. That bastard plucked me away from everything I ever knew and stranded me in that lonesome mine with foreigners I barely understood. He was weeks overdue checking in on us. When your hole appeared, I thought it was him at first. I shoulda known better."

"You're certain you don't know where he might be?" Draksgollow pressed. Powlo tried to look the kuduk in the eye, but the human-like lack of beard revolted him. The chain leashing him to the pipe clattered as he turned away. "You do, don't you?"

"It's an airship," Powlo replied. "He stole himself an airship. Machine's down in the lower shafts of it." He was careful to remember the terms Erefan told him to use. He should be ignorant of how an airship works, sea ships too, for that matter. Chapun would know terms from his own experiences, not a shared set of memories with a Telluraki like Powlo.

"Slag," Draksgollow snarled. The mechanized kuduk slammed his fleshy fist against the door. Powlo ducked low against the sewage pipe, finding its damp comforts preferable to his captor. "Where was the ship? What was its heading? When were you there last?"

"I ... I didn't look out much. I tried, but it gave me the stomach something fierce. Just this great load of nothing out under us, like a bank of steam far as I could see," Powlo said. He placed a hand over his chest. "Take my eyes if I saw a bit that looked like anyplace I'd ever been. It was weeks ago, but I got it stuck in my head like a news flashpop. Still gives me the night frights."

"The heading," Draksgollow said. "Which way was the ship going?"

"Off at the sun, as I recall," Powlo said. "Maybe not straight at it, but close enough."

"The time of day? Was it morning or evening?"

"Can't say I was looking at a clock, sir. Wasn't exactly on shift, so I wasn't worried about the time."

Draksgollow glared down at him, breath hissing through gritted teeth. "So weeks ago, above the clouds, you were on an airship that may have been mostly going east, or west."

"Don't know much about east and west, sir."

"You're useless."

Powlo didn't dare raise his glance above the kuduk's knees, but he had a fine view as those feet spun themselves about and stepped to the door. When the rush of fresh, cool air blew in from the corridor, Powlo spoke up. "Please sir." The kuduk paused mid-step, but didn't turn. "I was stolen. You'd get good coin for me, sending me back to Mr. Genrech. He's in Bessel Deep, like I said. It weren't bad there, really, and I miss home. Just tell him I was stolen and I won't be no trouble."

The door slammed behind the departed kuduk, and Powlo smiled at his side of it. "Well, stuff my hat and call me a banker, he bought that painted-up turd wholesale." He worked his jaw, wondering how long it would be before the ache subsided. However long it took, it was worth the price.

Chapter 16

"For as long as man has dreamed of flight, he has had nightmares of falling. Anyone who would dare build a flying machine must not dream."
–Captain Sebbius Narant, of the sea ship Tamegale

The engines of the *Jennai* hummed, a constant droning which was the only sign that they were in motion. In all directions below them, a bank of clouds stretched out to the horizon, providing a rain-soaked day for the lands below though they basked in the sun. The scale of the clouds was one of the things about air travel that had surprised Rynn. She had never given them much thought, leaving idle musings about the sky to Madlin and her world. But seeing them up close, she realized that they were mountains all their own, tiny white puffs that kept growing and growing as her airship climbed to meet them, until they dwarfed the *Jennai's* little hull.

Rynn's vantage was an eight-seat balcony that had been constructed on the inboard side of the left-front gondola of the combined airship. Her welders had cut a hole in the hull, excising one of the large windows from the starboard dining hall of the original *Jennai* and making a door of it. Rynn sat with her foot up on the railing, sketching on a piece of paper clamped to a portable desk in her lap. She was left to her designing with seven empty chairs for company.

While the *Jennai* and the *Cloudsmith* had been joined side by side and nearly touching, they were only that close by the vacuum tanks. The crashball-shaped monstrosities were several times the width of the gondolas below, and the space between gondolas had been filled with a steel-plate platform that served as a road between ships. Down in that plaza of welded steel, a number of rebel workers milled about, puttering at minor tasks. Rynn watched them walk, concentrating on angles of hips and knees and ankles through all parts of a stride. She watched them bend and crouch and occasionally break into a short jog. All these motions transformed into simplified sketches in pencil line.

Holding tight to the stack of pages with one hand, Rynn unclamped them and reordered them, leaving a blank page at the front. When they were secure again, she resumed her sketchwork with more complex shapes—mechanisms with gears and pistons, or gears and springs, or springs and runes, or belts and chains and gears. Through the light fabric of her trousers, she felt along the muscles and tendons of her one good leg, noting locations of attachment, lever arm distances, rough estimates of dimensions. Rynn had no demarcated calipers to take proper and accurate measurements, but for draftwork her eye was good enough.

A new sound joined the drone of the airship's engines, higher pitched and growing in volume. Rynn reached inside the door and set her desktop on the floor away from the wind's grasp, then tucked her pencil over an ear. The arm of her spectacles got in the way, but she managed to keep the pencil from falling by wedging a lock of hair in with it. She took up a spyglass and looked to the aft end of the ship.

The small liftwing that the *Jennai* carried appeared as a bird in the distance, just a pair of jutting wings silhouetted against the sky. As it grew in size, it was clear to see it was no bird; its wings did not flap, nor did they arc with the graceful curves of nature's animals. It approached from the starboard side of their aft, where the gap in ships was large. From the port side, the gutted hulk of the *Sulfurous* trailed nose-to-tail behind the original *Jennai.* The smaller airship approached gradually, faster than the *Jennai*, and overtook her, but not by any wide margin.

"Taking bets?" a voice from behind startled Rynn. It was Bosley, first of many who were filing in to fill the seats around her.

"This is no betting matter," replied Rynn.

The deck crew scrambled into action. The center of the plaza was cleared in seconds, with roughly half of the workers taking shelter in the shadow of the gondolas on either side. The liftwing wobbled in the air like a child's toy held by the tail and flown with pretend engine noises—an illusion of stillness brought on by the relative speeds of the crafts, large and small. The pilot leveled the wings as the liftwing drew near and eased the vessel up over the plaza, slowing down and eventually matching the speed of the *Jennai* so that it hovered in the air.

Rynn held her tongue and let the crew foreman shout the order to move in. She cringed as two workers from each side scuttled close with grapples and hooked the liftwing by the wing struts and landing gear. One false twitch of the control stick by the pilot could crush any of them in a second. But the grapples caught, and their throwers scrambled out of the way as other workers manned winches, then pulled the lines taut and forced the liftwing down onto the artificial airstrip in the sky. The liftwing's engine spluttered and the propeller spun to a gradual stop.

"Not good enough. Mark the pilot seven of ten. Emergency duty only. I want to see him touch down in half that time, and none of that shaky stick-work on the approach. My guts were in knots watching that. We're going to get people killed if these ships don't dock smooth. Whoever the pilot is, schedule him for another training run tomorrow."

"Her," Bosley corrected. "That's Mayci in there."

"Well, still not good enough, but I'm impressed," said Rynn. "I didn't think any of the one-worlders would take to it. I guess piloting farm tractors isn't so different as I thought."

The crew rotated pilots, and a new candidate climbed into the front seat of the liftwing. Rennon remained in the instructor's seat in back, ready to go again.

"I don't know how he does it," said Bosley. "I'd be heaving my guts out putting my life in a rookie's hands time and again. You'd have to pry my fingernails out of the seat to get me to move again."

Rynn shrugged. "I bet most of you would shy away from filling your body with magic fire to patch the runes back up, too. I'd be surprised if we don't have a few around who'll shit themselves when they first see a gun pointed their way. Takes all kinds."

"Except your dad, huh?" Bosley said a quick chuckle. "All the years I've known him, I've never seen *him* shy from anything."

"You must not have been close enough to see his face when I put a hole in his precious machine."

Bosley smirked, then looked around self-consciously and leaned in close. "How's he doing with the new one?" he asked into her ear. "Last I heard was him blasting holes in it a few days ago."

"He's got some muck-brained idea to give it a jolt by storing up energy in a flywheel. I'm putting runes on the blasted thing the minute I'm home."

"Won't be a moment too soon," said Bosley. "Want me to grab you anything from the kitchen? No matter how much I eat, Toller's stomach is still making me hungry."

"Gut you, bastard," Rynn whispered. "I'd managed to put Madlin out of my head for a few hours. Now I'm starving again. Yeah, bring something meaty, and a mug of coffee or tea or whatever we've got left."

Bosley stood at attention. "Yes, General," Bosley said loudly. He lingered a few moments until the next pilot had taken off from the plaza and departed to the interior of the ship. The rest of the gallery wasn't far behind.

Rynn reached through the door and retrieved her sketchwork.

Twenty three. It was more than Sosha had hoped or dreamed. Twenty three humans who had at least the skill with aether needed to activate a simple levitation construct. She toured the gondolas of all three ships, even the hazardous wreck of the *Sulfurous*, with a detailed diagram in hand. On its pages were the locations of all the installed rune plates, as well as locations of where the rest were planned to go.

She stopped at the middle pylon of the *Sulfurous* and checked her map. Two. She did a circuit of the tank support pylon and confirmed two rune plates had been beaten to match the cylindrical surface and welded into place. Sosha took a deep breath and let her eyes unfocus. The world slipped away from her, and a new world of blue and white whorls took its place. The metal of the ship vanished, but she could see the vague outlines of human forms nearby, brighter than the surrounding ambient mist. The runes stood out as well, though she could no longer see the pylon. They appeared to be aether filled and functioning. She closed her eyes, but her eyelids did nothing to block her vision of the world of aether. A few deep breaths and a bit of concentration, and the world went dark. She opened her eyes, and after a moment's dizziness, she was seeing properly once more.

Sosha made two check marks on her map of the ship's runes.

Navigating the *Sulfurous* was a chore. Anyone who went over to the derelict portion of the ship while in flight wore a rope harness with two long tethers, each ending in a carabineer. One of the tethers was to be secured to something sturdy at all times. Already there had been two incidents of rebels found dangling below the *Sulfurous*, needing to be pulled back up. Only Erefan was both arrogant and stubborn enough to go without. Sosha admitted to herself that Rynn would have refused the tethers as well, had she been sound of body.

"Sosha!" the voice echoed around the corners of bare steel walls, hollow and distant.

"I'm here!" she hollered back. There were no enemies aboard the *Jennai*. It was like Tinker's Island borne aloft, in that respect.

"Ship's rocking," the voice replied. Sosha still couldn't identify whose it was.

"All right. Wrap up for now. Back to the *Jennai*." *We really need a new name for that part of the ship, or a different name for all of it.* Rynn was fond of the name, but practicality told her that the redundancy could not be allowed to last.

Once they balanced the ship with runes, they could let the mechanics bleed a bit more air into the vacuum tanks. When the runes were completely filled, the ship would grow much larger as Rynn's plan to build within them went into effect.

It was hours later and dusk was threatening to steal their sunlight. Rynn had watched another dozen attempts to make a clean landing on the plaza of the *Jennai*, using the downtime in between to draw ever more sophisticated versions of her designs. Some had revealed unforeseen flaws when developed in greater detail and were discarded. Others grew in complexity. A few of the designs branched off and spawned siblings with minor details differentiating them.

"Rynn!" her father's voice shouted from within the ship. She heard his footsteps, quick-paced, impatient, growing louder by the step. With a few quick flips of the clamps and a hasty shuffling of papers, she hid her day's work behind a false front of sketches showing arrangements for the interiors of the vacuum tanks, once they were no longer needed for buoyancy.

The footsteps stopped just outside the door, where the familiar knot of itinerant onlookers was already gathering to come outside with her. "You lot, find something to pass your time. If you haven't seen enough airships land yet, just wait 'til you see a fleet of them buzzing through here."

Erefan lowered himself sideways into a seat with an empty chair separating them. He slung an arm over the back of the middle chair and leaned in to see Rynn's sketchbook. "What's that? Already planning on making us fully rune-dependent?"

"Already are," Rynn replied. "If the runes all went poof, we'd get dragged down like rocks by the *Sulfurous*."

"Rusty, rotted hull...hardly seems worth the trouble toting it along now that your little aerodrome is finished. Maybe we can cut it loose."

Rynn's pencil stopped scratching at a section of vacuum tank that was destined to become a barracks. "Finished? Once you get us a world-ripper on board, I've got plans. We aren't half *started* yet. The *Sulfurous* is going to become a hangar and pilots' quarters."

"The world-ripper's actually what I came here to talk to you about."

"When you didn't stop by first thing this morning, I assumed yesterday was another washout on Tinker's Island."

Erefan shook his head. "I kept it as quiet as I could, so I didn't get hopes up prematurely. I got a hole opened for about three seconds."

Rynn stuck the pencil over her ear, freeing up both hands for her to applaud. "Looks like our work here is done. Victory is as good as ours—daily, in three-second bursts."

"You can be a real prat sometimes. You know that? We added nearly three tons to the flywheel, and the overnight crew is watching as it spins up. I *was* going to ask if you wanted me to pick you off the *Darksmith* as a test, but maybe now—"

Rynn scrambled upright in her seat. "Shit, no! Shit! I'm sorry. Seriously, no, I'll be the test rat."

Erefan raised an eyebrow. "Life at sea so bad you can't put up with another two days or so? You and Jamile still carrying on your little spat? What?"

Rynn sighed. It was time to pry open the engine casing and see how bad the damage was. "We all agreed not to bother you while the machine wasn't running."

"'You all' being who? And what aren't you telling me?"

"Me, Jamile, Toller. We ... we lost the *Darksmith*."

Erefan's eyes shot wide and he took Rynn by the shoulder. "Eziel's mercy! Are you hurt? Where are you?"

"We're fine. Hungry, but fine. We fought off a pirate vessel, but took the worst of it. Lost our engines, took on water. It was only a few levitation runes that kept it from sinking. We swam ashore when we came near some worthless little hunk of rock in the mid-Katamic. Toller scuttled the ship so it couldn't be salvaged."

"You should have told me at once!"

"And what? Have you lose sleep over it? I don't think you'd have gotten the machine running any quicker. You're not known for giving half-arse efforts."

"You said you took the worst of it. Does that mean the pirate vessel escaped?"

"Funny enough, no. That worthless, backstabbing, untrustworthy Veydran wizard I took aboard swam over to their ship and burned it down to the powder room."

Erefan pursed his lips and gave a curt nod. "Sounds like two problems solved each other, then. Did you happen to notice what ship it was? There's—well, me and a few have a pool running over the next one we sink."

"It was the *Fair Trader*."

"Well, bathe me under a sewage drain! We finally got the—"

"And Dan lived."

"Well, at least Zayne and his boy are gone. That ought to throw a rat into their hen house."

"Can't be too sure of that one, either. Dan seems to think they survived. Zayne the Younger is a wizard, he said."

"Bugger."

"Well, it was five days past, and no sign of either of them. Still, we lost most of our food supply in the fight and the swim ashore. I'd be very much interested in getting a one-pace ride back to Tinker's Island."

Erefan nodded. "Of course. I'll set about looking for the island first thing tomorrow."

"Bosley should be able to give you a decent spot to start. I think he knows more or less where we washed up."

Erefan nodded and stood to leave.

"And seriously? A flywheel? Could you just hang a plaque around your neck like some museum relic? I think you set spark back fifty years this past week. I'm runing that thing and showing you how to make a proper battery as soon as I get back."

Erefan grunted a reply, the closest thing he usually gave to an admission of defeat.

When he had gone, she rearranged her papers and resumed her real sketchwork. She was oblivious to the landing of the evening's final craft until the clatter and shouting of a near-fatal mishap startled her. But the plaza crew got things under control, and no one suffered worse than bruising and a good scare. Rynn continued to work until the light failed her, and then a bit longer by the stolen light from the dining hall, leaking through the door and windows.

As she hobbled back to her quarters, she savored the feel of the crutches in her hands. She'd be rid of them soon enough.

Chapter 17

"Spend a day with a quill in hand, and you will write. Spend a day with a sword in hand, and you will kill. Plan your day accordingly."
–Rashan Solaran

Gazing blankly over sundrenched waters, Madlin felt relieved to know that their rescue was imminent, because she suspected that Dan might be trying to decide who to eat first.

"Be real handy if you and yours could keep awake in both worlds," Tanner said. He sat down beside Madlin on the patch of rock that had become her little fiefdom. Everyone had their spot and settled in. They had spread out over a wide swath of the island as they grew weary of one another's company. "Shabby operation, top to bottom, you know."

"My father's been doing this since before you were born. I think he knows what he's doing."

Tanner stretched and reclined, sprawling out on his side facing her. "Like spit he does. He's set up to steal science and build it here. Everything you folks talk about says so. He's got workshops, mines, ore shipments, got himself a bunch of fancy ships."

"Yeah, and?"

"And you're stuck here, and he didn't know where for days," Tanner replied. "Can't say as I like how that went down. Three parrots, no squawk. Makes me wonder who's really in charge. You get on with your old man?"

"Piss off."

"That's a language I understand, little miss. Doesn't change the question though. Am I walkin' into a crossfire between two Errols?"

"Why would you think that?"

"I got nothing to do on this bleedin' island *but* think. And when I overhear you sayin' the Mad Tinker knows we're here, like it's an age-day surprise, well, that got me thinkin' even more. What's your angle? You looking to take over or something?"

"No!" Madlin said. She shoved Tanner and he thumped down onto his back. "My father tries to do everything himself. No man can manage that. We just didn't want to worry him until we knew he had a way to get us out of here."

"What's there to do? He's got other ships. If he's smart—and everyone in this world seems to think he is—he should have his own agents on every ship. Nearest one could have been on the way here the first day we washed up. Gut me, he could have sent one the night after the battle and plucked us off the ship."

"We've got a better way home," said Madlin. Tanner pushed himself up to his elbows and gave her a puzzled look. "You Veydrans aren't the only ones who can get things done with magic."

"Mad Tinker's a sorcerer?"

Madlin snorted. "Not a chance. Built a machine that works magic for him. It'll pluck us from here straight to Tinker's Island, soon as he's ready to fire it up."

Tanner's face darkened. "Thanks. I'll pass." With a grunt he hauled himself to his feet.

"What? Wait!" Madlin scrambled to her feet after him. She wobbled with a moment's vertigo as her empty stomach reminded her that she was out of steam. "You can't just sit here. There's no ship coming. This is the only way off the island."

Tanner twisted around to look over his shoulder. Madlin expected him to say something, to argue, or at least to seek reassurance before agreeing to go. He *had* to agree. Instead, he smiled with one half of his mouth and kept walking.

"I've got to say, this is the most cumbersome contraption I've ever seen," Juliana Hinterdale muttered as she walked around the world-ripper machine. She ran a hand along a copper wire thicker than her finger. It was one of thousands. If she were to trace them all she'd be at it for days.

Don't touch it, a voice in her head snapped. She rolled her eyes elaborately in the direction of the wire spiderweb in the giant frame. Her companion was as invisible as she was, though his eyesight was far better in the aether. She couldn't see him at all.

What? It's not like it can hurt me. She replied in like fashion, speaking mind to mind. *Gutted thing isn't even on.* She couldn't convey the same sense of annoyance muttering so softly that the workers infesting the room couldn't hear her.

That is not the point, the voice of "Erund" replied. He answered to many names, some more his own than others. Erund has started as an alias she'd heaped on him unwillingly, but it had grown on him. Privately she mainly called him Brannis.

Fine. She heaved a mental sigh, long and elaborate, lest any part of her ennui go overlooked or underappreciated. *No touching. No talking.*

No interfering.

Interfering is fun, she replied.

That's not what we're here for.

It could be hours before they're ready to try again, she said. *Are you listening to them chatter? They haven't a clue what this thing is doing.*

I missed it yesterday because I wasn't standing here waiting for them to start it. You don't have to hang around if you don't mind missing it again.

One of the workers walked right toward Juliana as she stood blabbering mentally. She stepped out of the way of a middle-aged and balding mechanic, sticking her tongue out at him as he passed. Unabashed childishness was the privilege of the invisible. She affected a sneeze.

"Yer health," the worker mumbled over his shoulder. A second later, he glanced around to see who was there, then shook his head and went back to his work. It seemed to involve looking at a page of rune-like drawings and comparing them to the bird's nest of wires.

Cut that out, Brannis's voice chided her. *And pay attention, they're about to try again.*

Cadmus savored the unfamiliar thrum in the floor. Despite near-perfect balance, the flywheel was still spinning with enough force to make the whole factory shake. Eight spokes ran from the central hub to the heavy mass concentrated around the rim. All anyone could see of the spokes as it spun was a shimmering translucent surface, blurred together to allow a hazy view to the other side of the workshop where the great shaft ran from the waterfall outside to the gearworks within.

"Helmets and goggles, everyone!" Cadmus shouted over the din of workers and machinery. Rules were for others. Safety was for employees. If the machine exploded, it would be his fault, and his conscience demanded he look after the ones who trusted him. He hunkered down behind a wall of mathematics and science, relying on experience in place of failsafes.

"Enderburt, release the clutch on your side!" Cadmus ordered. Enderburt nodded in acknowledgement and pulled on the lever that disengaged the flywheel from the waterwheel shaft. One of the downsides of the new arrangement was that the dynamo could no longer be run directly from the shaft. It was flywheel or nothing. Even with the new flywheel it would be a hasty retrieval, with the clock ticking from the moment Cadmus's clutch engaged.

"If anyone would like to take a moment to pray, you should have started before now," said Cadmus as he gripped the lever. With no further warning, he pulled and the second clutch engaged, locking the flywheel to the drive shaft of the dynamo. With a shriek of scraping metal, the clutch caught hold and the dynamo flared to life. The control panel of the world-ripper lit at once, and the viewfinder shimmered into focus on a prearranged set of coordinates somewhere in the mid-Katamic.

A cheer rose from the gathered workers. Their task was done for now. They cleared a path for the kitchen staff to wheel in buffet carts for the refreshment of the incoming refugees. The operation ran like clockwork, which was how Cadmus preferred everything to run. Spark was still new to him, and runes a mystery, but good clockwork did exactly what was expected of it.

Cadmus hustled over and slipped into a chair at the controls. There was no sign of the island chain Toller had given as their present location, but it was only a matter of time. The man was operating from sea current charts and gazing up at the stars with the naked eye. A healthy allowance for error was expected. He spun the dial to rotate the view around a full turn, just to make sure the islands weren't standing right behind him. When he was sure they were not, he sent the viewing window roaming the sky over the Katamic Sea.

"Where are they?" he muttered beneath his breath. He finished one pass and swung the view around.

"Wait!" a voice shouted. "Go back the other way. I think I saw something."

Young eyes. Cadmus twisted the dials in reverse and backtracked his latest movements.

"Stop! On the horizon!"

Praise Eziel. Cadmus headed the view off in the direction of a distant speck barely visible at the line where sky met water. The speck grew as the view approached, until it looked like a chain of rocky islands.

The largest of the islands looked newly inhabited. Its natives were a mopey, morose bunch, prone to sitting about avoiding one another's company for long stretches and spreading themselves out an inconvenient distance apart for rescue. Cadmus swooped around until he saw who he was truly looking for and settled the view a few paces from her.

Cadmus uttered a silent prayer, hoping that the god of war had some stray fondness for misbehaving machinery. He threw the switch.

The dynamo crackled, but gave up the spark the machine needed. The view became a hole in the world, letting a warm sea breeze waft into the workshop.

"Madlin!" Cadmus shouted. "Come through! Quickly!"

Madlin scrambled to her feet. "Everyone move!" she shouted. "This is our ride home!" She led by example, and was the first through the hole.

Cadmus sprang from his seat and rushed to greet her. He tried to crush her in his arms, but she disentangled herself after the briefest of embraces.

"Madlin, I was so worried when I heard—"

She took him by the shoulders and steered him out of her way as she pushed past. "Are those turkey legs I see?" Madlin headed straight for the food carts. There was a turkey leg in one hand and a stein of ale in the other before Cadmus caught up with her.

In Madlin's wake, the Tinker's Island welcome crew helped the rest of the *Darksmith's* crew get through the hole. Jamile and Toller had made it through, and the rest of the crew was trickling in from their scattered spots all over the island. Dan stopped in the middle of the archway, looking straight up with an idiot grin on his face.

"*This* is a pretty good trick," said Dan, not budging as other refugees stepped around him.

"Ghet ouffa vere," Madlin shouted through a mouthful of turkey. She swallowed. "Could lose the connection any second, and my guess is it would cut you in half. Besides, there's food over here." She waved her half-eaten turkey leg in the air as bait. That caught Dan's attention.

Juliana watched the scene with bemused wonder. She had seen plenty of magic in her day—magics that were far more powerful. She had worked her share as well, though perhaps not quite so grand. There was still something wondrous and charming about a tropical island opening in the midst of the cold, grim factory in the forsaken northlands, even if it was just a forlorn bit of rock poking above sea level.

Check out the Source on that one, Brannis's voice whispered in her mind.

She envied him his mastery of aether-vision. He could see both aether and light at once. Juliana had to choose. She let the world of light slip from her vision and looked into the aether. The boy gawking at the archway stood out like a bonfire at a torch procession.

A hand clasped Juliana's own, and an arm brushed against hers. It was Brannis's way of letting her know he was by her side without revealing himself in the light. She squeezed the hand and thought back, *forget the boy a moment, what's the machine doing?*

Winds if I know. Somehow I think it's taking lightning and creating its own aether.

How is that possible? Aether comes from a Source; you can't make it.

The invisible hand slipped from her own. She saw a wobbling wake in the aether where Brannis passed near the machine, disrupting the swirling fog. Had she not known he was there, she might never have noticed his passing.

Perhaps lightning is close enough to alive that it has a Source of its own? It's normally so brief, you could hardly take note of it. It could be worth the study sometime when—

Brannis! Juliana shouted into his mind. *Look!*

Two shimmering outlines in the aether slipped through the gate. Both were man-sized, but too indistinct to tell much else about them.

Well, well, Brannis thought to her. *An old friend has brought his son on holiday. Strange place for it, up here in the land that sunlight and warmth forgot. Must be a chore for a pirate to find places he hasn't been.*

Who do you ... Is that Zayne?

Two Zaynes, if I don't miss my guess. The younger one is disguising them both, even in the aether.

Juliana's mind clogged. *What do we do with them?*

Nothing, Brannis replied. *This is actually an excellent opportunity to do a lot of it.*

World would be a better place without his sort, Juliana argued. *What's the point of rules if you can't make exceptions when a need shows itself?*

World would be better without typhoons and plagues, without slavers, without tax men, without petty coin-pickers. It would be better without our kind, too, if we can't keep our noses free of every stray quarrel we stumble onto.

You're not going to become bleeding Tallax just because you swat down a hornet at someone's neck.

There. Right there. Do you hear yourself? You just compared the great Captain Denrik Zayne, Scourge of the Katamic, to an insect. I don't know how Tallax thought, but that sounded like Rashan's words spilling from your mouth.

My brain.

Whatever.

No, not 'whatever.' You're staring out the wrong end of a spyglass, Juliana thought. *Think of it as pruning. You're not tying up braches to a little frame and forcing them to grow to fit your whim. You're just clipping away malignant growths; maybe rotted leaves, infested with weevils.*

You did it again. Insect comparison.

You're sleeping on the floor tonight.

Like an insect? Brannis asked. Through the mental link, she could feel the snicker in his words. *Besides, we haven't pretended to sleep in years.*

Figure of speech, and you know it.

Thanks to efficiencies of mental communication, the exchange passed in seconds. Zayne and his little Zayne had barely passed the gate. The lad with the bonfire Source still stood gaping in the middle of the archway. Juliana was tempted to join him, curious herself what it must look like.

The gateway began to waver. The lightning converters on one side were flickering, sputtering out their aether like a cough, instead of a smooth breeze like the others.

I think the machine might be about to fail.

No fault of its own, Brannis replied. *Zayne's boy is tampering with it.*

Speaking of boys, what happens if the gate closes with that dumb one with the Source standing in the middle of it.

Cut in half or pushed to one side or the other. I have no way of knowing what safeguards are in place. You know, he has a familiar look to him. Winds, I wish I had a memory for faces half as good the one I—

Brannis! It's collapsing! Juliana didn't wait for any response, but leapt for the gate and grabbed the wonderstuck boy as he spun about, looking up at the borderland of the gate. He did not weigh much, but then neither did Juliana. She grabbed his wrist and yanked him forward with a strength that belied her size. The machine sputtered and the gate dispersed, leaving nothing but crisscrossing copper wires in its place.

The boy looked around, bewildered.

"Bloody skulls!" someone shouted.

"The blazes happened? The dynamo's plenty sparked up." "Everyone all right?" "Dog dung it, we left a few back there." "Cut the switch and try it again."

The voices jumbled together, and Juliana let her vision drift back into the light, now that the aether was no longer enlivened by the spectacle of the Mad Tinker's machine. The workshop was fuller than it had been before the machine's activation, buzzing with a dozen conversations and the slop-chow slog of a famished crew gorging themselves after days of deprivation.

I think I saw Tanner. Juliana thought.

Haven't heard that name in a while. Where is he?

On that floating pebble those sailors were stranded on. I caught a glimpse of him when I grabbed the boy. At least, I think it was him. She heard a scratching sound. Brannis always bothered at his scraggly excuse for a beard when pondering.

I can go check, if you'd like. You stay here and keep an eye on those two Zaynes.

But I can't see them!

You're always looking for something fun. Consider it a challenge.

There was quick snap in the aether—a feeling not a sound—akin to the sudden slamming of a drawer. The mental connection broke, and she knew that Brannis was gone.

"What the bloody blades was that?" Dan asked as he sidled up beside Madlin at the buffet. "That thing got the death rattles?"

Madlin swallowed a swig of ale. "Just a little hitch. Oughtta get it sorted soon enough, then I'll get some proper runes on it and he won't need that ludicrous flywheel juried to it." She ripped another bite from her turkey leg.

"There's an amusing picture: you drawing proper runes. Hey, what's good here anyway?" Dan waved a finger around at the rapidly vanishing buffet fare. "Besides, that's not what I meant. It gave a shudder in the aether even after it went dark."

"Couldn't say. Dunno how it works." Madlin set her tankard down and took a huge bite from a warm roll.

"And you plan on runing it? Pardon me while I take my food a mile or two underground and wait until the explosion passes."

"S'not gon bwow up," she insisted. "Juff neeb mo' fpaak."

Dan shook his head. "And I thought Tanner had barbarous manners. The rutting ox piss did you just say?" He grabbed a turkey leg of his own, sniffed at it, and took a bite.

"I said it runs on spark, it just needs more of it."

"This that tamed lightning you were telling me all about?" Dan asked. Madlin nodded as she drank. "Let me have a go at the runes then. I can take that whole twisted wreck of metal out of your way and provide lightning directly from aether."

Madlin shook her head. "I don't see my father letting anyone but me work on it. He's not even happy about that."

"Then don't tell him."

A few of the nearby crewmen from the *Darksmith* gave Dan sideways looks as they pillaged the buffet, but none dared say anything.

"Piss off," Madlin replied. "You want to work on something here, you run it by the Mad Tinker. He owns everything for ten miles in any direction, including the town. I only get leeway cuz I'm right more often than him."

Dan looked over to where Cadmus Errol sprawled on the floor with his head inside the control panel for the machine. A gaggle of mechanics and curious bystanders loomed over him, trying to see what he was up to or offering marginally helpful advice. Without another word to Madlin, Dan set off, turkey leg in hand, to see the Mad Tinker.

"Wait," Madlin said, fumbling with full hands to grab for Dan's arm. He shrugged aside her clumsy attempt to impede him.

"Hey!" Dan hollered over the ambient talk in the workshop. Many heads turned, but Cadmus showed no sign that he had heard. "You Cadmus Error? Because this clumsy contraption just stranded a friend of mine back on that desolate rock."

The room grew quiet. Conversations broke off, and hungry mouths chewed more softly, though no one stopped eating for the first time in days because of a bit of a row brewing. And a row was what everyone expected. Madlin wasn't sure quite what to do. It was too late to call Dan back, and her father had plenty of experience bludgeoning smart-mouths with his tongue. She kept a hand near her revolver and waited.

Cadmus took his time climbing out from under the machine. When he stood, he adjusted his spectacles and looked Dan up and down. "This the wizard you brought me?" he asked past Dan.

Madlin nodded.

"I'm a warlock," Dan replied, crossing his arms. "I don't know how this thing works, but Madlin says it needs lightning to run. I can do better than that eight-legged horse of a contraption over there."

"We've discussed using the daruu arts to power the dynamo," said Cadmus, wiping his hands on a rag tucked into his belt. "Madlin's first job once she's regained herself will be to make the modifications."

"Piss on that," Dan spat back. "Tanner might be a sword-brained lout, but he's *my* sword-brained lout. I'm not going to sit around watching Madlin play clay-block runes like a first-year while he sits there going hungry."

Cadmus rubbed a hand over his mouth and nodded to himself. "Fine. We'll spin the flywheel up again and see if we can reactivate. I can't see anything wrong in the workings. Should be up to speed by morning." Cadmus waved to draw the attention of the workers stationed near the dynamo. "Switch clutches; get it back on the main shaft."

Dan wandered over and watched the process. "These levers connect it back and forth?" he asked across the workshop.

Madlin drifted over and intercepted the question. "Yeah. There's enough friction in the clutch plate to keep them from slipping." As she explained it, the flywheel began to creak and turned at a barely perceptible rate.

"Why not just nail them together?"

"This lets us switch from one to the other. The waterwheel outside gets the flywheel up to speed, then we jam it up to the dynamo and spin it fast enough to make the spark we need."

"So if you want spark, you just need this big bloody wheel spinning fast enough?"

Madlin nodded.

"Gut me if I'm going to wait for a waterfall to move a thing this size. Stand aside."

"Dan, don't—"

Dan flicked a hand and the lever disengaged the clutch from the waterfall shaft. Madlin still hadn't gotten used to seeing things move with no direct agency at work. There was a tingling in the air, a strange feeling of a breeze in a room tucked well indoors. The flywheel turned.

It wasn't the eking inches that the waterwheel had managed; the outer rim was already at a walking pace. Then a jog. Then a sprint. In moments, the floor shook like a weak, but endless earthquake as the flywheel became a thirty-ton tornado of brass and iron.

"Stop!" Madlin shouted. She could barely hear her own voice over the roaring drone of the spokes plowing through the air at cannonball speed. "That's plenty fast!"

Dan turned to gift her with a smug grin and shrugged. "Go ahead." Dan's voice carried through the workshop as if he spoke through a megaphone. "Try it now."

Madlin exchanged a glance with her father, who was watching with his fists on his hips and a glare fit to weld with. He gave a terse nod. Madlin passed the signal to the worker at the dynamo lever, who touched the brim of his helmet before putting his weight to the lever and heaving.

A high-pitched screech of protesting metal pierced the air. Hands went to ears throughout the workshop, including Dan's and Madlin's. The rumbling grew worse as pressure from the clutch transmitted vibrations from the great wheel through the shaft of the dynamo. The increase in rumbling didn't stop, nor did the screeching; the clutch was burning, not catching. Smoke rose from the contact point. Voices shouted, but it was too loud to make out anything.

Madlin retreated to a corner of the workshop; others were pouring out the doors. Cadmus put one of the control cabinets between himself and the dynamo. The worker at the lever abandoned his post. Only Dan stood his ground and watched the dynamo spark to life as the clutch eventually welded itself to the flywheel and spun the dynamo's shaft.

"There you go!" Dan shouted, his magically amplified voice booming through the workshop. "See, nothing a little—"

At that moment, the flywheel exploded. There was no fiery plume, nor a cloud of smoke, but bits of flywheel jettisoned themselves at coil-gun speeds throughout the workshop in a vast vertical circle of destruction roughly in the plane of motion that the flywheel had occupied.

Losing nearly all its mass in the blink of an eye, the flywheel no longer had the momentum to spin the dynamo at phenomenal speeds. It took a few more revolutions and stopped, the largest piece of spoke dangling at the lowest point and rocking the hub back and forth until it settled.

"Is anyone hurt?" Madlin shouted.

Dan spotted Cadmus by the controls. "We get enough lightning before this sewer log of a tinker's toy quit on us?" Dan asked.

Cadmus stalked over. "You bloody, reckless fool! You could have killed someone."

"My specialty," Dan replied flippantly. He let Cadmus step within a half pace of him, never flinching back. "But you're the tinker here, not me. If your bits and pieces couldn't handle it, you shouldn't have turned it on. I could have slowed it. I wanted to make sure it worked better this time."

Madlin had never seen her father cowed. Today was not going to be the first.

Cadmus poked a finger into Dan's chest. "Listen here, warlock. I don't care what you call yourself. I don't care what you can do with your mystical, 'pulled-it-out-me-arse' powers. If you endanger my people again, I will splatter you across two worlds. I don't doubt you could kill me right here, but I have a twin, and he's got most of the resources I have here. I will build another of these machines, and one night you will wake up to a half ton crate of black powder being dumped over you, followed shortly by a lit torch. Then I'll find the coordinates for Veydrus, and I'll scour every foot of it until I find *your* twin, and do the same to him. We clear on that?"

"Sounds like a deal," Dan said. He stuck out his hand. "Set me up with a bed and a bath, and I'll be back in the morning to do the job proper." For all the world, Dan hadn't heard a thing Cadmus had said. It was as if an elaborate string of threats had translated itself in the boy's head to a casual discussion of the device's failings and a contract for repair work.

Cadmus blinked and his eyes darted to Madlin. She put her hands up and shrugged. With no other course of action readily at hand, Cadmus shook on the deal.

Madlin stumbled through the door of her workshop and looked around as if she had been gone a lifetime. Everything had been as she'd left it. Her father hadn't even let the servants in to tidy up; she found herself glad she didn't leave food lying about. After a moment's nostalgia, she closed the door and threw the bolt. Privacy. Oh, how she'd missed having a spot all to herself. She poured herself into the chair at her drafting table and relaxed—truly relaxed, with complete abandon—for the first time in months. She let her father and Dan and Jamile and the stranded crew still on the island all slip away. She took a deep breath and held it a moment. Silence.

Madlin indulged herself for a few minutes of peaceful bliss, doing nothing. When she'd had her fill of nothingness, she got back to work. She took up a pencil and instruments, and set about translating Rynn's eyeballed sketches into drawings she could send down to the machinists. She knew already the design she wanted to try first, and Rynn's head start was enough for her to dive right in.

A few minutes into her draft, a voice startled her. "What is that going to be, I wonder?"

Madlin jumped and twisted in her chair. There was a sword pointed at her, with a grey-haired gentleman in disheveled finery and a week's ragged beard at the other end of it. "No screaming. You'll come to harm only if you cry out." In the man's shadow stood a glassy-eyed boy about Dan's size, with greasy black curls and a peach-fuzz mustache.

Madlin raised her hands—one still holding the pencil—in the most unthreatening manner she could manage. "And you would be ...?" She had a good guess, but a wrong guess before a sword-wielding man seemed worth avoiding.

The intruder dipped his head and lowered his sword briefly. "Captain Denrik Zayne, *formerly* of the *Fair Trader*." He tilted his head at his companion. "And my son, Jadon."

"What are you doing in my house?" Madlin asked.

"I find myself wondering the very same thing," Zayne replied. "I followed you through that gate your father's machine created. It seemed a sensible gamble, since my other lane of escape was tenuous."

Madlin glanced at the boy, who stared at her, not making eye contact. "You're welcome. I guess."

"Jadon, take her gun."

The boy stepped around his father and reached into Madlin's holster. He took the revolver between thumb and forefinger and slipped it out as if it were contagious. There was a delicacy to his touch; he drew it cleanly, neither touching Madlin nor jostling the holster. She only noticed its absence by the lack of the comforting weight on her thigh. Zayne took the weapon with his free hand as Jadon retreated behind him and wiped his fingers on his trousers.

"So what now?" Madlin asked. Something was odd about the boy, more than just a case of shyness. "If you wanted me dead, you'd have killed me already. So obviously—" Jadon kept staring in her direction, but not quite at her. It dawned on her. "Does he ever *blink*?"

The corner of Zayne's mouth twitched. "Not often, that I've noticed. As for my aim here, we may have a common cause."

A single, involuntary guffaw escaped Madlin before she could think better of it. "Sorry, but my father's been at your throat for years. Don't seem likely we've got much in common."

"That boy warlock."

"Dan?"

Zayne's face darkened and twisted into a snarl. "How many Kadrin warlocks have you got stashed around here?" There was an effeminate chuckle from behind Zayne, but when Madlin checked, Jadon had already composed himself again.

"Dan's Veydran, as far as he's told—"

"Khesh. Kadrin is the other world's version of southern Khesh. I don't care to bore you with politics, but suffice it to say that his people have made life miserable for mine over much of the past two centuries, on and off. We are currently in between conflicts, and if I could be rid of that one, it would aid my old heart greatly."

"He's a troubled kid. Not quite bolted together right between the ears. Not sure I'm too eager to try putting a bullet in him. He seems a bit twitchy about burning things that don't meet his approval."

Zayne lowered his sword, and to Madlin's great surprise, sheathed it. "I said I'd not bore you with politics, but I'm afraid I must inflict some historical context upon you. He's told you he's a warlock, but you don't seem to grasp what that means. It's not just a sorcerer, that's what I was, before I was killed. It's what Jadon is, both here and in the other world. A warlock is someone whose blood doesn't race, whose mind is as rigid as ice, and as numb to feeling. A common sorcerer struggles to do battle. Intricate thoughts are dangerous when the mind is harried by fear, made jittery by excitement. Warlocks used to be so rare that generations would forget the horrors they brought. Then another would pop up—an aberration of heredity—and some king or emperor would go on a spree of wars. One such war cost my people their freedom. We were ground under boot by a warlock named Rashan Solaran. He is the great uncle of that thirteen year old madman you have running loose, destroying things."

"So two warlocks a couple generations apart?" Madlin asked, trying to follow along as best she could.

"Two warlocks of the same generation," said Zayne. "His cousin was even more powerful, and only through great fortune did he and Rashan Solaran destroy one another in a struggle for power."

"Yeah, the more I hear about your world, the more it sounds like a worse piss pot than mine."

Zayne smiled in earnest. "This is why I think we may have better cause to ally than find us at one another's throats. The profession your father so loathes really dates back to an old grudge I carry with Acardia. It matters less to me than my son's world, and the fate of the people I died trying to protect."

Madlin shook her head, not in denial, but in disappointment. "I know Acardia warred with Takalia, but that was before I was born. Humans warring with humans ... it just seems ... unbrotherly."

"Ambition. That's the root of most of it. Humans are not the only people of Veydrus, but we dominate it. We'd contest with the goblins if they forced our hands. If the ogres wished to leave their forests and threaten our cities, we'd beat them back. But instead, we scrap amongst ourselves, mostly because the privileged few always want more than they have."

"Your people..." Madlin swallowed. "Did they suffer? What was it like being conquered?"

"They killed our king and replaced him with a series of governors, little puffed up tyrants with all the power and none of the breeding to teach them how to rule. Much as I hate monarchs, they at least knew that much. We were ruled with iron laws, punished whether evidence showed us innocent or guilty. They took our women as their own, even young girls—"

Madlin put up a hand. "Enough. I've got the point." She could picture Korr, with other humans ruling in place of the kuduks. A shiver worked its way up her spine. "These are Dan's people?"

"He's a shining example. Their best and brightest. Once he's matured and fully in command of his powers, I don't know that they'll be able to help but send him off to war. There are certain breeds of dogs that are fit for little else but hunting and killing; it's in their blood. Danilaesis Solaran is most certainly that breed of mongrel."

"And you said warlocks are becoming more common?" Madlin asked. She was doing her best to get a picture of these Kadrins, slanted though it probably was by Zayne's grudge.

A mirthless smile slid onto Zayne's face. "I didn't tell you the best part. They breed their sorcerers like livestock. It's all very formal and proper, but it all comes down to getting the best blood from each generation to rut, and picking the best of that lot to try again with the next."

Madlin felt a bit sick to her stomach. It was possible that she could picture humans treated like livestock only too clearly. It was more likely that she'd eaten too much on a painfully empty stomach. Zayne saw her discomfort, and appeared to assume the former.

"Danilaesis *is* too powerful to simply assault. At his best, Jadon can keep safe and hide from him. We need to arrange an accident for our warlock."

Madlin hugged her arms close around her. "I still don't know. Dan did save us more than once."

With a shake of his head, Zayne dismissed her objection. "You can mourn a rabid dog. You mustn't try to keep it."

"I need time to think," said Madlin. "Take rooms in the city, down by the sailing ship docks. No one here would recognize you except Dan—and Tanner once we get him back." Madlin mentioned the last as an aside to herself.

"Mr. Tanner can be dealt with," Zayne replied. "Very well. I will speak to you again when you are safely alone."

Jadon looked expectantly at his father, who nodded once. The two of them disappeared. A few seconds later, the door unbolted itself, opened, then closed once more. Madlin hustled across the room and bolted it again.

One more complication to my life. Maybe they'll kill each other off and leave me in peace.

Not knowing what else to do with herself, Madlin went back to drawing.

Chapter 18

"Not every puzzle has a solution. Life isn't as tidy as that." -Cadmus Errol

The wind high above the Sea of Kerum whistled among the steel struts and beams of the *Jennai*, adding its own sound even as it stole away the words of conversations that passed among the rebels who milled around the plaza. Rynn imagined that if she closed her eyes she could convince herself that she was alone, standing atop a mountain peak. A crosswind blew, and a metallic groan protested the change. Runes now held the airship immobile, engines idle, and no simple wind would dislodge them. When she learned those runes, she had never pictured them locking something the size of the *Jennai* in place; a coil gun had been the height of her ambition at the time.

It seemed like half the crew was standing around waiting, just as she was. Of course, standing around for Rynn involved sitting herself down on an upturned steel rain-barrel next to the gondola, but her intent was the same as that of the anxious crowd.

"What are we going to do first?" Sosha asked. She had been quiet so long that Rynn had let her fade into the background. Sosha had her arms hugged tight to her chest and her shoulders bunched.

"You should go grab a blanket. It's not worth freezing over."

Sosha shook her head, jittery with shivers. "No, I want to see it for myself. I wasn't watching for it on the island. I just ... I just assumed it would be warmer."

It was true, they were nearing the equatorial region of Korr, but that hadn't meant warm skies. "Air's thin up here, doesn't much matter what it's like down below. Maybe go stand out in the sun." Rynn didn't mind the shadow of the gondola. She had her coat on and her hands in her pockets. The crisp wind kept her face numb and her nose always threatening to drip, but an occasional wipe of her sleeve and it was no worse than home—Madlin's home, anyway.

Sosha huddled close, pressing her shoulder to Rynn's arm. With her perch on the barrel, Rynn was a full head higher. Her first instinct was to pull away, but she decided that she liked the touch of warmth better than she liked having a bit of space. She wished there was someone to lean in from the other side, so the sensation wasn't lopsided.

"Hey," said Sosha. She put a hand to Rynn's barrel. "This thing is warm."

"You try parking your arse on a metal barrel out in this chill. I aethered it up a bit."

"I might have to make one for myself." Sosha shivered, her whole body spasming for a moment.

Rynn disentangled her arm from both her pocket and Sosha's leaning weight, and pulled her tight. "You could always try Dan's trick, you know."

Sosha's teeth chattered as she answered. "Last defense against frostbite, maybe. Rather shiver than become a torch."

"You've got a better feel for the stuff than I do. If Dan makes a sorceress of one of us, it'll be you."

Sosha shook her head. "He's clinical. If he showed up at my patron's office, they'd truss him up in a madman's wrap, haul him off to a sanitarium."

"Might want to keep that to yourself," said Rynn. "He could catch you mid-sentence if the hole opens close by."

"Oh? And then what? He tries to proposition me or leaves dullard's hints about how easily he could kill me? How would that be any different from every time he opens his mouth."

"Dunno," said Rynn. "Seems that he's a bit off. Most boys I've known that age fixate on getting your clothes off, but not so much the killing part. Might be he's just trying to impress you. He gave up on me after I threw him in the Katamic."

"Might have to try that," Sosha muttered.

From the middle of the plaza, there was a stirring in the idle knot of rebels. A flickering of light split the air, spreading silently until it irised into the familiar circular shape of the world-ripper's gates. People scattered to make room, many still unsure just what constituted a safe distance from the phenomenon. Rynn and Sosha didn't have much of a view from their vantage, sitting nearly end-on to the plane of the hole.

Rynn released Sosha from her grasp and retrieved her crutches from the crevice between the barrel and the hull of the gondola. The metallic handles were wrapped for a more comfortable grip, but they still stole the heat from her hands. Images of pouring aether into the walking aids until they melted to slag danced in her imagination. They were constant companions, giving her freedom to get around the ship without anyone's help. Without them, she was reduced to hopping around holding onto walls and railings, or relying on charity for transportation. She could not be rid of them soon enough.

By the time she reached the aperture, workers were already carrying parts and materials through. By prearrangement, rebel crewmen were guiding them to the cargo hold of the *Cloudsmith*, where the new world-ripper was to be assembled. Even growing up there as Madlin, Rynn couldn't help but be impressed with the industrious efficiency of the workshops on Tinker's Island. Even before the first successful test of the world-ripper, they had already plunged ahead with parts for a second. Now, those parts were on their way to give the *Jennai* the weapon they'd need to get the rebellion moving in earnest.

Rynn watched from a safe distance, well clear of the convoy of riggers with wheeled dollies and teams of burly workmen grouped by fours and sixes and eights as they hefted giant sections of machinery and shuffled across the poured-stone floor of Cadmus's workshop, through the world hole, and over the metal deckplates of the *Jennai.* Madlin had studied the plans, so Rynn recognized most of the parts by sight, but their workings remained a mystery. Cadmus played coy when she asked him, but she suspected he understood it little better than did she.

After the machinery was through, there were a number of transfers left to be made in both directions.

"All right," Rynn shouted to be heard over the wind. "There are twenty of you authorized for shore leave. I want to see five by four lined up and ready to call off." She pointed at a space not far in front of the world hole, and a scattering of rebels separated themselves from the crowd and hastily arranged themselves. There was muttering and shoving as they jostled into four rows of five, but it wasn't long before they all stood plumb straight and eyes forward. All of them were Errol Company. All of them were getting a chance to visit home for the first time since Erefan brought them to Korr.

"This is a two-day leave. In two days' time, you're to be ready to come back to the *Jennai*. You're welcome to bring whatever personal effects you like, but bear in mind the size of your quarters. No pets, no livestock. Keep your head about liquor." Rynn didn't need to mention family members, since Cadmus had selected none but bachelors for his invasion force. It was foresight she might not have shown in his position.

A crewman with a list walked down the line, asking each soldier his name, crossing it off with a pencil, and nodding permission to depart. One by one the line of soldiers slipped across into Tellurak. Rynn wondered how many would return in two days, and how many would sneak off on the next non-Errol ship out of port.

Once shore leave was out of the way, more mundane supplies piled aboard: food, water, cookware, furniture, tools, clothing, raw metals, stacks of lumber, panes of glass, welding gasses, keg after keg of ale—good house labels, too, mostly Acardian. The last were an odd collection of personal effects, mainly for twinborn who'd made arrangements for their respective twins. One of them belonged to Rynn. It was packed in a crate that Errol Company used for shipping Errol Horizon Mk-II spyglass rifles six at a time to Takalia.

"Send that straight to my quarters," said Rynn to the pair of workers carrying the crate. One of the *Jennai* crew took over from there and led the way. General Rynn didn't have to deal with such minor details on her own ship.

"What's in there?" Sosha asked. Madlin had kept the contents of the crate secret from all but a few trusted machinists. Even Cadmus didn't know what it was.

Rynn pretended that she didn't hear the question. With the rhythmic thumping of crutches that dogged her everywhere she went, she followed after the workers.

Rynn sat on the floor of her cabin with the curtains drawn, working by lamp light. For privacy's sake, she could have left the curtains wide, and unless anyone cared to rappel down the outside of the ship, she would have worked in peace. But the window opened out on an impossibly large world, too big to feel cozy beneath. Bottled up in the cloying walls of the cabin, it reminded her of the comfortable steel walls of her workshop—not Madlin's, but the little hidden room behind the boiler.

The lid of the crate lay wedged between the bed and the bottom edge of the door, making sure no one could barge in, key or no key. There was straw everywhere from unpacking the crate's contents. A pry bar lay discarded by her foot, useless after she had prised the crate open. There had been a handful of essential tools packed inside, but they were only for adjustments to the real contents.

Rynn felt a strange catch in her throat as she looked over the new leg. It looked like a museum piece from an armory, a discarded piece of a knight's plate armor. Of course, it also looked like a tinker had gotten hold of it, decided that knights and armorers didn't know their arse from their kneebone, and resolved to make a few improvements. The joint was bulky, weighed down by lever arms and reduction gears on the left side, so they wouldn't knock against her good leg. Air pistons acted as cushions against sudden jerks on the joint. Below the knee, there was a cradle for the leftover stump of her leg, with leather straps to hold it in. Rods ran down from the levers above, actuating the ankle joint as the knee bent. The foot was articulated at the ankle, but was meant mainly to keep level with the ground as best as possible. It was fitted with stiff springs to keep it pressed against the ground when walked on. She expected to find a lot in need of adjustment on the lower end.

Above the knee, the mechanical leg was dedicated to keeping the mechanism in place. Two thick, padded leather straps, joined by a pair of flat steel bars rode up her leg nearly to the hip, giving her as much leverage as possible to work the knee joint without anything coming loose. A belt and harness would secure it around her waist, in case friction alone proved insufficient.

The machinists had done good work.

She held the leg close and caught the best light she could from the lamp. Inside the front protective plate, where she ought to have had a shin, there were a number of tiny runes carved into the surface. She inspected them to see how well they were formed. She'd activate as many as it took to keep the bulky collection of shiny steel from tying her down like an anchor, but not so many that she would float away. As she checked them, she smelled nothing but oil and new leather.

Rynn activated the rune structures one by one, until she could heft it as easily as a hammer.

She took a deep breath, then another. With the leg up on the bed, she clawed her way up after it. Lying on the bed, she stripped down to her undergarments and changed into a skirt, which she hiked up around her midsection. Wondering at the oddity of putting on a boot that started just below the knee and went up to her waist, she pulled the leg on. The smooth base of her amputated leg slipped into the cradle. It fit better than she'd hoped. A bit of wiggling around lined up the mechanical knee with her real one, and she pulled the straps tight.

The straps on the leg had no holes; she didn't want to chance the adjustment on anything so crude as the distance between one hole and the next, so Madlin had packed an awl instead. Rynn pulled each strap as tight as she could stand it, knowing the leather would stretch and relax over time, and marked the spot. Once she had marked them all, she took the awl and put a single hole in each, then secured them.

Rynn set her awl down on the bedding and put her hands on the edge. Slowly and carefully, she eased onto her feet. There was a hiss as the piston sucked in air that would slow her if the muscles of her leg gave way and tried to collapse beneath her. In taking her measurements, Rynn knew that her left leg was thinner than the right, probably because she never used it anymore. That was about to change.

There was a teetering moment, a feeling like she was a circus performer, balancing on stilts that no one had taught her how to use. She held her arms out, for balance. It was the oddest sensation. Her left leg was standing in a flower pot, sunk nearly up to her hip. Her right leg compensated; muscles in her toes and the arch of her foot straining to keep her from toppling. Straightening upright was a task nearly a minute in the making, but by the time she stood tall, she felt like a person again. The leg was a proper match in height. Wiggling her hips was difficult, but she was able to judge that they were level. She tried to look down to admire the work, but her collar got in the way. She banged her chin on it—the first time she'd been careless with it in weeks. She trickled a bit of aether into it, same as she did every time she remembered it.

There was nothing to do but try. She held her arms out for balance and lifted the leg from the floor. It handled awkwardly. The levitation runes provided a buoyancy that kept its weight from bolting her to the floor, but it still possessed the same mass. It was like walking through water.

Thunk.

She set her foot down and a squish of springs steadied her. She hopped forward with her good leg, but the walking in water resistance was gone, and she pitched forward, catching herself against the wall. A knurl in the bottom of the mechanical leg kept a grip on the floor, or she'd have fallen in a heap.

"General Rynn," a voice called through the door. A knock followed in belated politeness. "Are you all right in there?"

"You are relieved," she called back. "No guards outside my door." She hesitated a moment. "And yeah, thanks. I'm fine."

She lost track of the time as she paced her tiny cabin. Disused muscles burned in protest, and her skin was rubbed raw. The padding meant to ease the bite of leather on her soft flesh could only do so much. Tight as she could pull the straps, things still moved and shifted. Each pass back and forth across the room, she grew a bit more familiar with her new stride. It was unlike walking of any sort she'd ever done. She limped as the mechanical foot and springs settled with each step, and the unequal weights accentuated it.

There was a rap at the door. "General Rynn?"

She froze in place, suddenly self-conscious of the noise she made clomping around the room. "I thought I said no guards."

"Bit of an odd case here," came the reply. "You've got a visitor from Tinker's Island."

Rynn's mind went to fuzz. She glanced around the room, looking at the wreck of tools and hay and ... and her. "Tell him to come back later. I'm—"

"Piss off, Madlin," Dan's voice echoed through the door. "I'm not one of your little soldiers."

"Sorry, it's just that I'm not quite ... decent ... at the moment."

She heard Dan's laughter through the door. "You got me to look into the aether at least. I half thought there was a fella in there with you. Almost had me jealous."

"I'm not ... it's just ... it's hard to explain. Can you just come back later? Please?"

"Fine. Keep your collar for all I care."

Collar? Shit! Dan had real magic, of course. She'd been pestering him over a month to teach it to her so she could get it off herself. She could skip the learning process and get the result she desired. She lunged for the door.

"Wait, no!" She held the handle for balance and kicked at the crate lid with her metal foot. "Just let me clear the door." She couldn't hear footsteps, but that didn't mean Dan wasn't slinking away soft-footed.

Rynn wrenched the door open, bending at the waist to reach for it rather than stepping into the pull. Backwards would be practice for another day.

Dan gave her a quizzical look when she opened the door. She grabbed him by the wrist and pulled him inside. "You're dismissed," she told the guard who'd first knocked. The door slammed, cutting her off with Dan, alone.

"Bloody black blazes," Dan said, staring at the legs beneath her skirt. Stumbling worries aside, she suddenly wished she'd worn one that went below the knee. Brushing the floor, actually, would have been perfect. "I've known girls who'd take your hand off for putting it up her skirt. Never seen one who might do it by accident. I was wondering when I saw runes below your stump." Dan ran fingers through his unruly hair.

"Eyes up here," Rynn snapped, pointing to her collar. She knew the phrase caught a guilty hook in most men's consciences. "You said something about a collar."

Dan drifted his gaze lecherously up until he looked her in the eye. She knew he did it just to keep his credibility intact as an arrogant little arse. "You asked me about a thousand times how to get it off."

"And you told me a thousand times that you couldn't."

"No, I told you that I couldn't teach you anything to do it. I'm shit as a teacher, and you've got no experience except rune-tending. You'd have killed yourself trying, then Madlin would have gotten pissed at me, like it was my fault."

"So you can?"

"I've thought of about a hundred ways." Dan smirked. "The other nine hundred mighta killed you."

Rynn breathed out a huge sigh of relief. "Thank you!"

Dan held up his hands. "Oh, don't be so quick now. I've got a price." Rynn's eyes narrowed. "I want to see those books I've heard about. The ones your father built the machine from."

"How do you know about those?"

"Please, there are about a dozen people on Tinker's Island who do nothing but gossip over what they think is inside. If the Mad Tinker wanted to keep their existence a secret, he should have started in the dockside taverns and emptied a few revolvers into those loudmouths."

"Why do you want to see them so badly?"

"I don't just want to see them. I want to read them; I want to copy them. I want to open a hole to Veydrus and deliver them. No one here can read them. You're puzzling them out like picture books and recognizing names you can sound out. And just that much got you a machine that can take people from one world to another. Imagine what else is inside."

"And you think that's worth taking a collar off me? My father would never agree to that."

"Gut your father," Dan said, drawing a reflexive scowl from Rynn. "You're in charge here. Make it an order."

"Tinker's Island is his."

Dan cocked his head. "Is it? Stuff in that book might do everyone a lot of good. If I can put it in front of someone who can translate it, I can share the secrets with you. Collar thing's really more of a favor. You should *want* me taking a copy of those books, but in case you don't see it that way, I'll bargain for it."

Madlin looked away, over at the curtains. She wished they had been open, so there was a greater distance to look off into. As it was, her gaze was trapped in the room with Dan. "I don't see my father agreeing to it."

"Confront him or go behind his back. I can deal with it either way. Winds, Madlin, you lost a leg and just up and built yourself a new one. Are you going to let your old man stop you from letting me read some books?"

She could plead incompetence later. She could find a way to help the Zaynes kill him. She could just go along and hope that what he learned was worth sharing, and that he kept his word. What she couldn't do was let her chance to get the killer collar off her neck slip away from her.

"Fine. I'll find a way. Just do it."

Dan put a hand on her shoulder. "Easiest would be for you to lie down on the—"

Rynn slapped his hand away as he tried to push her down to the bed. "What do you think you're doing?"

"I'm going to lean your head out off the end of the bed and—"

"No." Rynn waved her hands between them. "No lying on the bed. That's right out."

Dan lowered his chin to his chest and gaped at her wide-eyed. "You think I'd try to take you? No way I'm rutting anywhere near that rat-trap." He pointed to Rynn's mechanical leg. She felt her face grow hot. "Whatever. Just put your arm over my shoulder and bend forward as far as you can without falling."

Rynn complied with some reluctance. She kept her free hand pinching the neckline of her blouse closed as she reached around Dan's shoulders. He was bony, with less muscle on him than even she possessed. He hadn't reached the point where a man's bulk began filling out a boy's frame. His voice hadn't even deepened much. It was like manhood had begun in his nethers, relocated all thought processes there, and then given up the project.

"What are you—?"

"Just shut up a second. You blab more than Tanner." It was the first she'd heard mention of Tanner since the second rescue attempt had failed to locate him. Dan hadn't seemed worried, but most of Tinker's Island assumed he and the other lost crewman were dead.

Rynn felt a tingling. It started somewhere deep within her and spread throughout her body. It wasn't at all what she had expected, though she couldn't say exactly what she *had* expected to happen. A pervasive tingly feeling certainly was far from it though.

Thunk.

As quick as the sensation came on, it disappeared.

"Done."

Rynn looked down to the floor. There it sat: a simple, ugly, thick ring of iron, decorated with crudely carved runes. She felt for it at her neck, disbelieving that it was really gone, that Dan wasn't playing some cruel trick on her. Her collar was finally off.

"How ... but ... I ... what did you do?"

"I took us incorporeal for a few seconds."

Rynn stared at him, waiting, then raised her eyebrows. "And?"

"Incorporeal: not substantial. You know, like an illusion. Normal material passed right through us."

A moment's panic swept over Rynn. She felt for her blouse, her skirt—she knew by not falling over that the mechanical leg was still there. "How come the rest of what I was wearing didn't fall off? Not that I'm complaining, mind you!" She added hastily.

Dan reached down and scooped up the collar, hefting it in his hand. He held it up in front of her. "Because I am very, very," the blades inside the collar snapped out with a grating clash, "very good at what I do."

As Rynn watched, Dan must have powered the runes again himself. The blades shrank back inside the collar like a cat retracting its claws. As she leaned close to see if she could tell where they had gone, the teeth snapped out again, making her jump and Dan snicker.

"What are you going to do with it?" she asked.

Dan lobbed it to her underhand. "Nothing. It's yours." Rynn bobbled it, but held on. "I'll let you get back to learning to walk on your clock-leg." He pulled open the door.

"Thank you!" Rynn said, belatedly remembering her manners.

"No need to thank me. Just have Madlin ready to get me into wherever your father stores those books." The door clanged shut behind him.

Rynn sat for a long time after Dan left. For one thing, it felt good giving her leg the rest. But mostly she tried to sort her thoughts into the normal, neat little piles in her head. There was getting to be too much clutter; piles spilled into one another, and the pile of friends was the messiest of all.

Sosha was the simplest dilemma. Rynn had played out her anger—unjustly, she realized—and knew that she couldn't keep up the pretense any longer. The red, burning, frustration upon losing her leg needed somewhere to go, and she'd already caused enough damage to herself. She would need to make amends, but somehow she suspected Sosha would forgive her. Being able to stand on her own feet had upgraded her from an invalid to a drunk, which was a marked improvement that would only get better with practice.

Her father kept slipping off of her pile of friends and allies. How anyone could at the same time be so brilliant and so obtuse baffled her. It would be just like him to give her a gift of a finely crafted peg leg, like she was some sort of story-book pirate, or a pauper war hero. At times she got the impression that he wanted her to fail just so he could wrest control back from her. It must have been Eziel's intervention that made him see the same necessity as she had for a duplicate world-ripper aboard the *Jennai.* Denrik Zayne was a puzzle. He ought to have been an enemy, but he could easily have killed her and chose instead to bargain. Was Dan as dangerous as he said? Undoubtedly. Was Dan as unstable as Zayne claimed? That she was less certain of. He seemed to have a disregard for innocents that bordered on psychosis, but he had yet to cause harm to anyone who could be looked upon as an ally. If he was a monster, he was a discerning one, at least. The greater question was Zayne's motive. Rynn knew he could have killed her in her workshop. She couldn't have drawn her pistol before Zayne's sword would have pierced her throat. How much of his story was true?

The crux of his story was the reasoning for putting Dan down like a feral dog. If Zayne was to be believed, Dan was as great a threat to her as was any enemy—kuduk, daruu, or human. If Dan was the champion of a people who were equally bloodthirsty—or frankly, even one tenth so—then she would be handing over invaluable information to a deplorable empire, at least as bad as the kuduks of Korr.

Then there was the collar. Rynn turned it over in her hands, still not quite believing that her imprisonment within its deadly grasp was over. The skin of her neck itched where she could never reach it beneath the iron, and grateful fingers scratched. As she indulged, she studied the interlocking iron teeth inside, like the maw of some snaggletooth monster, and tried to imagine what those would have felt like as they ripped through the flesh of her neck, and cracked through her spine. Not much, she decided; she would have been dead in an instant. Thanks to Dan, she no longer had to worry about finding out. Was that reason enough to entrust him with her father's books?

They're my books, too. Our books. Those books belong to all of us, all the rebels. Haven't we gotten all we're going to get from them until someone translates them?

Of course, Dan might learn all he could from those books, and then use that knowledge against them. To what end?

The questions whirled in Rynn's mind like a cyclone, blowing papers around her piles of friends and enemies faster than she could capture them and return them to their proper places. All the while the questions blew, Rynn asked more of them. Surely there was one question, one answer, one chain of logical thought that would sort everything out. There had to be some way to reconcile her father's paranoia with Zayne's dangled promises and veiled threats, and weigh them against Dan's apparent madness and his brilliance with magic.

None of that even brushed the surface of the mystery of Tanner, who was gone with the rest of the *Darksmith's* crew when the world-ripper was sent for them the next day.

For the first time in months, Rynn was able to engage in the luxury of pacing as her worries swirled.

Chapter 19

"Assume that when you cannot see your enemy, they are moving with great certainty and terrifying swiftness toward your destruction."
–Xizix, demon sorcerer

The tunnels stank of stale seawater. They were too near the surface to be free of it. A string of spark lights dangled from freestanding poles. They hooked up to a portable dynamo to keep the darkness away. Rusted iron supports stood weary guard over the tunnels running in all directions from the central hub, their pitted orange surfaces anything but reassuring to anyone venturing down those shafts. In the entire chamber, only the floor had the sheen of newness. It sat dead level and smooth as fresh poured-stone, but it was just rock that had been worked smooth by hands that knew their trade.

Draksgollow took the place in with his eyes, digested it in his mind, and spat it out again. "You were right, this is the arse crack of the world, sure nuff."

Kezudkan waved away the tinker's complaint. He clopped around on his cane, pointing as if giving a tour. "We'll wall up the outside entrance, get rid of that fetid stink. Vent shafts looked to be in order, though I wouldn't mind one or two of your lads giving them a once-over to be certain. This will be our main control room, where we'll keep the machine. We'll bring equipment through and build workshops down these corridors. There are already worker barracks, and even some nicer suites belonging to the former owners of these mines. It's perfect."

"Perfect shit hole."

Kezudkan raise his hands to the ceiling, twenty feet above. "And it's all ours! No one will think to look for us here. No one will bother crossing the Black Depths just to be thorough. Most importantly, Erefan won't think to look for us here. There is no value to the place except its remoteness, no clue that this might be where we would settle. I never mentioned the Ice Furnace with any wistful longing when Erefan lived within my walls. I have no connection with the place at all. It is absent of anything I would choose for myself—uncivilized, utilitarian, and drab."

"Could have plunked ourselves in the middle of the Lumberlands, if you wanted someplace no one would ever look for you."

Kezudkan graced Draksgollow with a heavy browed glare. "Let's be reasonable. We're not going to live like animals. I wouldn't ask that of you, and I certainly wouldn't volunteer myself for exile. We're hiding away, not turning into vagabonds."

"Fine. I'll get men working on turning this shit hole into a habitable shit hole. I still don't like the other half of this plan."

"First thing's first. We need to get ourselves hidden safely away. Then we'll get rid of Erefan."

"That rat-eater doesn't know nuts from bolts. I don't like losing a machine over him."

"Trust me, if we can be rid of Erefan, we'll be kings."

"He knows we're here," said Jadon. Though sixteen, his voice had not deepened much. He sounded like a woman. "He sleeps lightly for a twinborn."

"He sleeps like a warlock, that's why," Denrik said through gritted teeth. "And you were sloppy."

The Zaynes, father and son, were cooped up in one of the nicer inns on Tinker's Island. The proprietress was under the impression that they were paying well, thanks to Jadon's magic, and settled up through month's end. Everything in the room was white: curtains, bedding, pillows, walls. All was bleached and whitewashed and starched stiff as a mast. It was the sort of place that hung its hat on being a clean inn, the sort of damp praise offered in seedy waterside towns where being free of lice and roaches was a badge of honor.

"He'll tell someone."

Denrik stalked across the room and back. "Who?" he asked at length. "The girl knows, and by all accounts has said nothing. I don't think he gets on with the Mad Tinker at all. They're like kerosene and water."

"We should go."

Denrik fumed, chest heaving at each breath. Such power within their grasp, and that spoiled, sadistic Kadrin boy was standing in their way. His eyes settled on his son, so calm by comparison. Jadon's expression hadn't changed since he arrived back from spying on Dan. Jadon's expression rarely changed, ever. He was the rock in a stormy sea, unbothered by the chaos around him.

Denrik shook his head and blew out a breath to cleanse his anger and settle his thoughts. Heat was bad for the brain, anger bad for judgment, and passion bad for business. "No. No, we can't waste this chance. Too much, too many rely on our success."

"He'll kill us."

"I well bloody expect him to try!" Denrik shouted before remembering that anyone could have been to either side of their room, just the other side of a thin wall of plaster and paint.

"Letters are better."

"What?" Denrik stopped short in his pacing.

"We leave. Send letters. Madlin can find us if you tell her where."

Denrik wagged a finger in the air as he restarted his circuit of the room. "No, that leaves them a perfect chance to set us up for an ambush. As long as we're in their realm, we will be on our guard. If we go back about our business, we'll grow lax and lazy about watching ourselves."

"Madlin won't betray us."

Denrik sniffed. "Lot you know of betrayal."

"Madlin won't betray us."

"You say that like she calls us allies. We've merely dangled the prospect in the water. She's yet to bite or swim off."

Jadon remained silent. The boy's eyes didn't follow Denrik as he paced.

"Why won't she?" Denrik asked.

"In her heart, she is like us."

"'Piss pot of a world,' she called it." Denrik scratched at his beard. He took a decanter from a dainty table by the window and poured himself a glass of brandy. "Think she might join with us? Common cause and all that?"

"The machine can do it. Guns for magic."

"But not if we get killed by that demon child, is that it?"

Jadon didn't answer. The boy always seemed to know when keep his mouth shut. It was what he did best, maybe even better than magic.

"Fine." Denrik swallowed the brandy in a single gulp. "We'll leave a letter before we depart. We need to find Stalyart, so we'll have to find someplace with card halls, whores, and excellent liquor."

Jadon nodded. "Marker's Point."

Denrik smirked. "It always seems to come back to there, doesn't it?"

The Katamic Sea was in a sorry state, licking against the wharfs of Yekina harbor like a dog begging for attention. The tide was as low as it got, but the wharfs were long and sunk deep into waters that would berth an Acardian battleship, if they had any cause to stop in a Takalish harbor. The *Merciful* was a ship that carried no painted name on its side, or rather, it carried many different ones, none its own. Today it was the *Gallant Net*, a sly joke that amused its captain to no end.

The Mad Tinker counted more Takalish among his employees than any other nationality. Of the six who had been stranded from the *Darksmith*, four of them called Takalia home. All six spoke the language. It was a fair sight kinder than dropping them at Marker's Point, which was a day's sail closer to the desolate island where Tanner and the others had been stranded.

"Obliged, as always," Tanner said cheerfully. It was easier to find cheer with a full belly and a head swimming in ale. He leaned precariously over the railing, watching his fellow castaways trudge down the gangplank, the wooden span bouncing beneath each step.

Tanner's companion at the rail looped a protective arm around him. A swordsman has an innate balance that even a sailor could envy, but spirits can fog the optics of the finest spyglass. "Mayhap you stay aboard this time. Word of your survival will trickle back and your little friend can cease worrying over your memory."

Tanner swiveled his head around, pausing a moment to let the sea and ship stop spinning. He looked Captain Stalyart over as if he had never met the man. He was suave, slick-haired, and olive skinned, tanned to a color his parents would never have known him by. He wore a nobleman's garb with a scoundrel's flare, leaving his shirt unbuttoned and his sleeves rolled to the elbow. He wore jewels fit for an heiress at his ears, neck, and fingers. For a moment, Tanner tried to remember whether Stalyart had ever *met* Dan before. Tanner was fairly certain that he had.

"I'm sure ... I'm sure he's all broke up. Pro'bly sacked a city, sacrificed a hundred surgeons in my honor."

"I believe it is virgins that are the preferred offering to the gods," said Stalyart with a twinkle-eyed grin.

Tanner blew through loose lips, making an obscene noise. "Dan's ain't never had no hundred virgins anywhere near him. Sort who'd ... run round 'n orchard wiff a stick. A stick. Knockin' apples off."

"Mr. Tanner, you have misplaced your liver," said Stalyart. "I knew a man who wore your face who drank me out of a case of Cerrian Blue. What have you done with him?"

"Ain't got proper pissed in ages. Rotten little puke. Hav'ta watch him like a block. A ... a hawk. Elsewise he's gonna ... bodiesallovertheplace." Tanner blinked a few times. A moment's fumbling inside his jacket produced a bottle with a splash of amber liquid in the bottom. He pulled at the cork, but his fingers slipped off each time he tried. He held the bottle out to Stalyart.

The pirate captain took the bottle and examined the label up close. "Turning Hills. Acardian, but a good year. I think I paid five hundred eckles for this bottle."

Tanner pointed a wobbly finger Stalyart's way, chuckling. "You don't ... you don't—you stole that!"

Stalyart grinned, showing off sparkling white teeth. "I may have, at that." He drew his cutlass and used the blade to pry up the cork's edge. There was a little *pop* as it came free. Tanner made a grab for it as it sailed over the ship's railing, but came away with only air.

Stalyart raised the bottle to the sun above. "To old friends, returned." He swallowed what seemed like a fair half of the remaining liquor.

"Ole friens," Tanner agreed. He took the bottle and swung it up to his lips in one motion. As he tilted his head back to drain the last of it, he kept on tilting until he fell over, thumping with dead weight against the *Merciful's* deck.

In an ancient part of an ancient building, an ancient man hunched over a bowl of lukewarm stew. There were no sparse rooms in the Kadrin Imperial Palace, nor were any small or plain, or made of anything but polished black marble with green veins. The one Axterion had taken for his own was the one he had best found able to turn cozy, to fill with enough flotsam and detritus from his nearly hundred and fifty summers of life that he could feel like he took up the room. In so much of the palace, the rooms ignored you. A human was a speck of dust or a cobweb, as far as the throne room or the great banquet hall cared. Axterion surrounded himself with books and maps, chests of old clothes, footstools and pillows, anything he could think of to bring comfort to the cold confines.

Axterion was midway through a bite of soggy potato when a knock interrupted his meal. He finished his bite before answering. "Can't a man sup in peace?"

"He can," a young voice called back, "but we're at war." The door opened and Danilaesis poked his face through with an insouciant grin slathered across it.

"Bah, just you." Axterion stuffed another spoonful of soup into his mouth.

"Is that any way to treat your favorite grandson?" Danilaesis asked.

Axterion frowned into his stew. "Remind me again how many I've got besides you."

Danilaesis's face fell. The young warlock slunk into the room and shut the door behind hm. "I didn't mean it like that."

"You ought to try it," said Axterion, sloshing his words around a bite of carrot and broth. "Mean things more often, and you'll make less an ass of yourself. And quit carrying that disinterred bit of dragon about on your back. You're no warlock until I say you are."

"If it flies like a hawk, if it has talons like a hawk, if it can spot its prey from above the clouds and swoop down for a kill, is it not a hawk? Call it a chicken or a sparrow, but it's still a hawk."

Axterion chewed in silence a moment, one brow furrowed. "You've just come from Logic and Rhetoric, is that it? I may need to have a cross word with your Arveron if he keeps filling your head with nonsense about hawks to dump beside my supper."

Danilaesis set his sword down on a table piled with books, balancing it precariously across *Dweomers of the Age of Gehlen* and *Musing on the Conscience of Man.* With a somber mien, he picked up a stack of Imperial Circle reports from the chair across from Axterion and took a seat in their stead. "Grandfather, I didn't come up here to bother you."

"Best news I've heard all day. I've finally cracked completely, and I'm just imagining you." Axterion dug deep in his bowl, giving the watery meal his utmost attention. "Finish a meal in peace," he mumbled.

"Grandfather, I'm serious!" Danilaesis took the old man by his spoon arm. It was enough to draw a glare that would have sent shivers through an army seventy winters ago. "I got hold of some books in Tellurak."

"What sort of books?" Axterion asked slowly. There was something urgent in Danilaesis's manner that piqued the old sorcerer's curiosity, one of the few parts of him not decayed to ruin with extreme age.

"They're written in Arcane."

"Unusual for Tellurak, certainly."

"Exactly! The Korrish twinborn think it's just gibberish written in daruu. They're letting me copy them so I can bring it here for translation."

Axterion set his bowl aside and slumped back in his chair. This sounded like something worth settling in to hear. "I take it, then, that you did not immediately confess to being literate in the dragons' tongue?"

A sly, toothy grin was all the answer he required. "The books are crazy. I don't know who wrote them, but they weren't from Korr, or Veydrus, or Tellurak."

"How can you be sure?"

"Because they're written to help someone who's been stranded. It's like they're manuals for being shipwrecked. They keep calling the reader 'traveler' and refer to a bunch of worlds as the lands of savage children, ours included."

"And this is how they built that machine you told us about."

"Yeah, but that's not the half of what's in there. There's diagrams in there that probably make more sense to the Korrish, but they can't read the text. I'm actually a little impressed that they built a working machine, now that I've seen the books. I couldn't do it. Then again, without reading Arcane, they couldn't have brewed *this*."

Danilaesis reached into his pocket and pulled out a vial the size of his finger. A clear liquid oozed about inside as Danilaesis leaned the vial back and forth, trying to tantalize.

"What is it?"

"What you want most of all."

Axterion snorted. "You young folk. Think you know it all. What I want is a back that doesn't ache no matter whether I stand or sit, a bladder that'll leave me in peace the night through, and enough wind in my lungs to manage the stairs without a stop halfway."

Danilaesis held out the vial. "Then here you go." He wasn't an earnest boy, as a rule. Not one bit. He was a braggart and a bully, a sly prankster and a cruel friend to those few who would even dare call him such. With more than a fair inkling of the budding tyrant he had grandsired tempering his curiosity, Axterion took it.

"What is this?"

"*If your supply of youth elixir should run short during your time among the savages, fear not, traveler! This simple concoction works nearly as well.*" Danilaesis quoted, putting a hand to his chest and enunciating each word like a boy who had just come from his rhetoric class. "And like bloody piss it was simple! I needed Torbur's help to brew it. Half the ingredients need aetherial preparation, and the Academy apothecary barely had enough of a few things to make that much."

"This will make me young again?" Axterion asked, his voice fading to a whisper. He shook his head to clear it. "How much younger? Does the book say?"

"No, and I wasn't about to try it myself. I could end up playing toy soldiers in the gardens with the princes."

"Seems awfully risky."

"Grandfather, be realistic. How much are you risking? A summer, maybe two?"

"I've hung on longer than anyone ever guessed already."

"All the more reason to take your chance while you have it. You could breathe your last any night, just drift to sleep and never wake."

Axterion knit his brow. "Feeling all sentimental today, huh?"

"Me?" Danilaesis asked, pointing to himself. He turned the finger to Axterion. "When I asked you what you wanted most, did your dead children even flicker through your dusty old brain? What about your wife? What about Brannis?"

Axterion gave a cynical chuckle, little more than a pair of snorts at his own expense. "Can't say they did. Guess I'd closed those books; just wanted to twist your ear a bit about the problems I face, dawn to dusk and the night through in between."

"Well, maybe I did think about my father, and Uncle Maruk, and Brannis and Aloisha, Iridan, Juliana, and Uncle Rashan. Gut you crossways, old man, we're all the family we've got left. Drink the stuff and be done with it!"

Axterion felt the cool glass between his fingers, and held it up to the light. "Might be nice to work magic again, not waste my whole Source fighting a slow retreat against age." The wooden cap popped off with a bit of effort; the rim of the vial was tacked with honey. It was the honey he tasted first as he tilted the vial back and poured the contents into his mouth.

The elixir itself tasted like ... sunshine? Axterion had expected something foul and acerbic; he hadn't even dared sniff the stuff, lest he lose his nerve. Instead, warmth oozed through him like spilled syrup, starting at his tongue and spreading through the whole of him.

When he dropped his arm to the side and let the vial slip from his fingers with a sigh more fit for a bordello than an elderly man's lunch table, he found Danilaesis staring him with eyes like coins.

"How do you feel?" Danilaesis asked. His eyes locked onto Axterion's, which drooped under an unaccustomed languor.

Axterion picked up his spoon and bowl. "Famished."

Chapter 20

"If you can't make do, all you'll make is don't." -Cadmus Errol

Rynn paced the cargo hold of the *Cloudsmith*, her mismatched gait coming more naturally now than when she had first hobbled around her own cabin. Rumor had spread about her mechanical leg, of course, but one would hardly guess by looking. She wore baggy trousers and a matched pair of boots. She could have been a war hero come home with a limp, for all an unknowing observer could tell. So what if there was a hiss of air with each step or a faint grinding of metal every time she turned? The smell of lubricating grease hung about her often enough that a bit more was hardly worth noting.

There were many observers there in the hold with her. Every twinborn not on duty had showed up to watch, along with most of the one-worlder crew. The hold was packed with rebel humans, though they gave a bit of respectful (and fearful) space around the world-ripper machine and its attendant equipment. They also kept clear of the dozen rebel soldiers selected for special duty, who stood ready by the aperture.

In the machine's view was Glenwood Sky Aerodrome, a vast expanse of poured-stone littered with stone buildings and parked airships. Kuduk soldiers and workers saw to whatever daily tasks were required of the menial oppressors of humanity. All wore uniforms of one sort or another. The Grangian military favored dull grey for their troops and pale grey for the mechanics and laborers. The base would be quieter at night, but the plan needed light to make it work.

"Get a good look," said Rynn, letting her voice carry well beyond the dozen who required instruction. The hold was quiet save for her voice, the hum of the world-ripper at idle, and the occasional cough or shuffled foot. At a gesture from Rynn, Erefan swept the view down a row of liftwing airships. They were of a different design than the first Ruttanian models the rebellion had stolen, with just a single seat. The Grangian ships were smaller, too, but not small enough for the wingspan to fit through the world-ripper's frame. "I want eight ships off the ground within thirty seconds of the hole opening. Is that understood?"

Eight voices shouted in martial unison. "Yes, ma'am!"

Rynn turned to the four soldiers flanking the machine. "I want cover fire from this side only. None of you are to pass through the hole unless I give the order. If I order the view moved, you are to hold fire until I give the order to resume. I don't want wild shots while the world is swinging around in front of you. Is that understood?"

"Yes, ma'am!"

Letting out a deep breath, Rynn nodded to herself and addressed the waiting eight once again. "Any questions?"

"No, ma'am!"

"Open the hole in five ... four ... three ..."

Sosha's heart hammered in her chest. Sounds from the world around her grew fuzzy. *What am I doing here?* She should never have insisted on flying Rynn to safety when first rescuing her. If Rynn had taken the controls, she could have wiped her hands of piloting and stuck to being a nurse. Through the amber lenses of her goggles, she focused on the airship that would be hers. Her leather pilot's jacket was stifling in the crowded confines of the machine's room, filled with humans radiating heat. It would be different in the air. At her hip was a holster with a coil gun that she and Rynn both knew she wouldn't fire—but all the other pilots had one, and so she had to match.

I'm not like them. It was too late to point that out to anyone.

"Three ... two ... one ..." Rynn pointed to Erefan, her finger shooting out like a bullet.

The switch closed with a clack-thump. The dynamo whined and crackled. The view turned real and beckoned.

Pilots sprinted through the hole, each to their assigned vessel. Sosha hesitated just long enough to be last through, but not long enough to be called a laggard. She blinked at the sudden glare, shuddered at the sudden chill. Clicks from behind, and sizzling whistles through the air signaled the start of cover fire from the *Cloudsmith*. Sosha spared a look over her shoulder and saw the four soldiers each on a knee. One was already reloading.

Her feet pounded the poured-stone as she dodged among the grounded airships and found her own. First thing, she popped the catch and lifted the hood. She slipped a glove off and put a hand to the cool metal of the runed engine. Taking a steady breath, the tingling coolness seeped through her, a sensation no jacket could protect against. Aether flowed into her and out again, directly into the engine. She slammed the hood shut.

There was a three-rung ladder built into the side of the liftwing, but Sosha was in a rush. With a hop, she caught hold of the edge of the cockpit, brought one foot up until it caught one of the rungs, and thrust herself over the edge. It took a few scrambling seconds to reorient herself to a seated position—she could already hear engines firing up in the other airships. The controls were laid out differently, but everything was there. Pulling the knob by her left knee engaged the engine.

There was no time to waste. Sosha heard kuduks shouting as realization dawned on them that they were under attack and being robbed of liftwings. With a quick glance to either side to check for other pilots, she gave the airship some throttle.

The buzz through the seat was strange; a different engine, a different chassis. It lacked the comforting feel of the two-seaters she'd flown previously.

"Come on, you little bucket," she coaxed it, "let's get off this poured-stone and into some nice fresh air. You'd like that, wouldn't you?"

Whether her pep talk had any effect or not, the vessel picked up speed, bouncing along toward the aerodrome take-off strip well behind the rest of the rebel thieves. Once she was well clear of the one-seaters for which the rebellion lacked pilots, coil-gun rounds tore through the rest of the Grangian fleet. None of the other liftwings would be coming after them once they were aloft.

One by one the liftwings took to the air, like birds flying in formation. Sputtering along, Sosha's bird was the one that falls from the nest to be eaten by cats. Each time she gave it more throttle, it seemed to shake more, but not pick up speed. Shots cracked the air, traditional cartridge bullets, not Rynn's coil guns. The kuduks were mounting a ground assault, and she was the only target still on the ground. Answering fire from the world hole was scant comfort when two rounds punched through the liftwing's hull, and another shattered one panel of the windscreen. With gritted teeth, and curses bottled up behind them, Sosha pounded her gloved fist against the control panel. It was a problem solving method ill-reputed among tinkers, but for the non-tinker, it was a fix-all for mechanical problems.

"Eziel, I don't ask you for much, but if you could just help me get this you-damned thing in the air, I'll try to be better about getting to sermons."

Sosha slammed the throttle full forward. The engine rattled like a thunderail careening over rough tracks, then settled into a steady whirr, and the propeller pulled Sosha along with it. The bouncing smoothed out and she raced along the takeoff strip, taking a few more shots to the hull, but none so close as the first few. Pulling back on the control stick, the liftwing did as its name implied and tore itself free of Korr's grasp. The buzzing in the seat died down and the echo of the engines off the poured-stone faded.

With one hand on the stick, Sosha pushed loose glass from the ledge where the windscreen met the control panel. Taking both hands from the stick for just a moment, she squirmed until she got both halves of the safety harness pulled around front and buckled. The liftwing wobbled, but once she regained control, all seemed well. Seven liftwing airships trailed off into the distance in a ragged row, with her taking up the rear guard.

Sosha breathed. It was impossible that she'd held her breath through the whole of her escape, but it felt like it as her lungs unclenched and she settled in to follow the little convoy back to the *Jennai.*

"We ready to cut power?" Erefan asked, shouting to be heard over the cheering and boisterous congratulations being bandied about the hold.

Rynn held up a hand in Erefan's direction while she stared through the hole to Korr. The single-seat liftwings had been reduced to scrap metal, but they weren't the only vessels at the aerodrome. Six vacu-dirges sat idle near a loading platform. Two were chained down, meaning that they were pulling at least some vacuum already.

A nagging bit of geometry tickled Rynn's brain. There were three such airships welded together to form the behemoth *Jennai*: the original by that name, with the former *Cloudsmith* to its right and the *Sulfurous* behind it. It was asymmetrical, ugly, and awkward. She told herself that it was a hazard to liftwings landing in the plaza, that the open structure was weaker without a good way to tie the *Sulfurous* to the *Cloudsmith*. She imagined the extra crew and cargo they could carry with a fourth vessel, once it was runed and hollowed out. All these were true, but drugged with pentothal she'd admit that it was the pattern that bothered her. A piece was missing, and she meant to fill it.

"Close the hole, but leave the view."

Erefan didn't hesitate. His hand was already waiting on the switch.

"Now, bring it around and sweep through that one," said Rynn, pointing to the leftmost of the Grangian vacu-dirges. "I want to see who is aboard, and how many."

"Rynn, what are you thinking?"

Rynn raised her voice for all to hear. She shouted over all their conversations. "I'm thinking we're not done today." She drew her coil gun and pointed it skyward. "We're taking one of the big ones, too."

A cheer rose in the echo of her pronouncement. Erefan shouted something, but the cheering drowned him out and she couldn't read his lips. She pointed to the machine. He shook his head. She waved a finger across the crowd of rebels, then pointed it at the view of Glenwood Sky's aerodrome, then nodded emphatically. Erefan pursed his lips and the muscles in his jaw bulged. Rynn jabbed a finger at the world-ripper's controls, and Erefan broke under her gaze. The view moved.

Kezudkan sat at a table formed from a single slab of stone the size of a trolley car. The surface was strewn with maps and books. At one end, chests of various sizes and descriptions lay open, revealing gold and coins within. His world-ripper gaped, opening into the vault of a bank in some hovel of a human sky.

"Not a single muddy city has so much as a tunnel beneath it," said Kezudkan, "except to wash their filth downstream. Disgusting. They deserve to lose all their gold."

"Pretty simple creatures," Draksgollow said as he watched his workers carrying chests and strongboxes into their hideaway. "Follow any river and it's like a chain of human cities. You'd think they were part fish."

"They're lazy creatures, most of them. Can't work stone, don't like to dig. If they don't live where water delivers itself, they'll dry up and die. Hmm, I suppose they do sound a bit like fish now, don't they?"

"So what now, we just plunder every bank and palace we can find?" Draksgollow didn't sound displeased with the prospect.

"And we'll buy better equipment, hire more troops, build more machines," Kezudkan said. He picked up a map between thumb and first finger. "We'll get better maps from their world, capture locals and learn their tongue, get them to tell us where to find more. Then we'll do the same in Veydrus when we're done. After that, we tackle those strange worlds that don't look like ours."

"When do you plan to hunt down that slave of yours? The sooner we're the only ones with the machines, the better, if you ask me."

"I don't," said Kezudkan. "We're not hunting all over Korr for a human on a stolen airship. We bait the trap and count on his curiosity to spring it."

Draksgollow grunted and went back to supervising the unloading of the bank vault. Kezudkan had lost count of how many times they had trod that path.

The ship had been empty—not so much as a janitor aboard or a mechanic rollicking with his sweetheart in the engine room. Empty. But that was five minutes ago, and now the *Kelleb* swarmed with humans. Five mechanics ascertained that it was air-ready. A rune tender pumped aether into the vacuum pump, whether it needed it or not. A hundred guns fanned out through the ship, taking up positions to fire back at ground forces who tried to stop them.

Rynn took command herself. Stairs still gave her trouble, and her leg ached from the exercise, but it felt good to stand without holding onto anything for balance. She held tight to the ship's wheel because it was hers to steer as she liked, not because it was the only thing keeping her from toppling.

Rynn cupped her hands to her mouth and shouted down the stairs from the bridge. "Cut her loose. Full engines, full pumps."

Something outside the window caught her eye. "STOP! EVERYONE DOWN!" A hangar at the far end of the air strip slid open, four kuduk workers hauling it out of the way. No sooner had they gotten the door clear, than the nose of an enormous liftwing poked out, and the noise of its propellers—four across the wings, each twice the height of a human—roared across the aerodrome. It lumbered free of the hangar's confines, gathering speed as it rolled. Its wings were like a ship's sails, its body nearly the size of the vacu-dirge's gondola, bristling with gun turrets. The liftwing battleship lined itself up with the takeoff strip and gained speed in earnest.

Rynn clomped over to the stairs, gripped the railings on both sides, and swung herself down in two pendulum steps. She raced at a hopping gallop to the spot where Erefan had left the world hole. "Liftwing's after the pilots. Do something!"

Erefan gave a nod in reply. The last thing Rynn saw was his hand gripping the handle of the switch. At his first tug, the image disappeared.

There was nothing more she could do to help. She still had a job to do. "Fire up the engines and pumps! Time to get this turkey off the ground."

Sosha let her craft drift gently off the course of the seven airships ahead of hers. She made corrections with the delicate touch she normally reserved for stitch work on children. Anything more forceful and her ship began shaking again, and each time she feared it would shake itself to pieces. It had its peculiarities, Sosha's liftwing. She hesitated to call it junk, even in her head, while she still needed it to carry her back to the *Jennai.* The last thing she needed was for the poor beast to take offense, and dump her into the Sea of Kerum out of spite. That assumed that she would make it as far as the sea. The aerial convoy was still over land for the next few minutes, at least.

Due to its peculiarities, Sosha had developed a keen ear for the sounds her liftwing made. It was a musical instrument with one note, a sonorous hum like a trumpet, but not as sharp on the ear. When it developed an undertone, Sosha's first thought was that she had reached the end of the liftwing's patience with her. Something was wrong in the engine, and it was humming a new tune. It grew louder, which told her the problem was growing worse.

Unfortunately for Sosha, most of her conclusions were correct, though the causes she imagined missed bullseye and hit hay. Gunfire broke her from her worries over the engine and replaced them with new ones, like getting carved into pieces by rotorifle fire. She was suddenly glad she had found a chamber pot just before leaving.

Twisting in the safety harness, Sosha saw the Grangian liftwing looming up behind her, a great storm cloud trying to roll across and rain bullets onto her. Even under fire, she hesitated to jerk the control stick. Another burst of fire made her duck down in the cockpit. While she was there, she slipped her coil gun from its holster. *Maybe I can disable it.*

Sosha's first shot was the blind lobbing of a cleverly crafted hunk of runed steel and copper over the side of her liftwing. Soon as she brought it up to aim, the terrific wind from her air speed tore the gun from her fingers. A reach and a fruitless grab after it, and she ended up jostling the stick anyway. The liftwing rolled to starboard—Sosha couldn't recall if it was right or starboard when flying a liftwing—and started a gradual climb.

Up was no place to be, with the Grangian liftwing hanging in the sky between her and the sun. The engine was already shuddering like a seizure patient; there was nothing to be done but try flying it despite its protests. Sosha took firm control of the stick and leveled the craft with the horizon, then put it into a dive. The larger liftwing was clearly the faster of the two, so outrunning it seemed hopeless. At least she could get herself away in one direction.

The vibrations from the engine were rattling Sosha's teeth, but with gunfire still crackling in the air from high above, she didn't dare to change her course or slow down. They were missing her, and she bloody well intended for them to keep missing her.

Two cracks, in rapid succession, ended the airborne earthquake. A thump on one wing followed instantly behind. A quiet whirr and the rush of air past her head were the only sounds left—except continued gunfire. The welcome relief was short lived. Something was missing. Though it spun faster than the eye could track, the propeller blurred the air before it, leaving a streak of propeller afterimages that she could see through with little trouble. Now the air at the nose of the liftwing was clearer than glass.

The propeller was gone.

Erefan's hands danced across the world-ripper's controls. He had the viewfinder up and airborne in seconds. It took him just a moment to gain his bearings and head off in the direction of the stolen liftwings and their Grangian pursuers.

"Should have sapped the Ruttanian Air Corps first," Erefan muttered. "Grangians are too proud not to chase."

He brought the airship into range of the viewer. It was shrinking into the distance, but the world-ripper was not bound by conventional locomotion. Erefan switched to a coarser dial and the airship grew by the second as he turned it. The thing was a monster. A hundred feet long with a steel hull and gun turrets protruding from the sides and bottom, it was a skybound battleship.

Tiny dots in the distant sky were his pilots, fleeing in their stolen liftwings. The Grangian craft was gaining on them. Worse, they were leading the way to the *Jennai*.

"Bring guns!" Erefan shouted. "I want that airship turned into a sieve." He kept a steady pace at the dials of the world-ripper. The Grangians were traveling off-axis from the machine's setup, so it took coordination of two dials at different rates to keep it somewhat fixed in view.

Vaulk shouldered his way through the chaos of soldiers and onlookers scrambling to arm themselves. "Your daughter took all the coil guns with her. All we've got are rifles."

Erefan growled, his hands stuck to the controls, lest they lose their quarry. "Fine. We'll fire what we have."

"Want me to get Kandrel?" Vaulk asked. "He can wake as Orris and rouse the boy. Let the little prat earn his keep."

"No!" Erefan snapped. "The boy's a hazard. Get Kandrel, but have him wait. We'll use the boy as a last resort."

Vaulk departed as men arrived back with their rifles. The cheering onlookers who had celebrated the pilots' success turned into a militia to rescue them as they watched it evaporate. They were quick; it hadn't been two minutes since Erefan gave the order to arm. Errol Company men. Worth every fonn he paid them and more.

"Someone get over here and man the switch," said Erefan. One of the soldiers shouldered his rifle and came to the tinker's side. "When I give the word, pull." He raised his voice and shouted for all to hear. "When I give the word, put holes in that thing. Aim for the wings and spinners if you can. If you can't, hit any part of it."

The liftwing fluttered in the viewfinder like a butterfly. Erefan knew it was his own fumbling fingers that couldn't keep a steady rate on two dials at once. A curse of his trade, he found himself thinking how he could rig a device to keep a constant rotation on each dial, and adjust that rate on the fly. Of course, he hadn't the weeks he'd need to fabricate and tweak the design, even if the crude schematic in his head was viable. He got the liftwing centered as best he could.

"Pull ... FIRE!"

The deafening roar of the liftwing's propellers chopping up the air thundered through the cargo hold. A hurricane blew in along with it, spoiling the riflemen's aim. A few recovered enough to get shots off, but nothing had a visible impact. The liftwing lurched and slung itself from the viewer as Erefan failed to keep the dials moving as required to keep on the liftwing's tail.

"Undo the switch!" He repeated the order, but there was neither comprehension nor quiet enough to make his need known. He took a hand from the dials and opened the switch himself. The hurricane subsided, the noise cut short in an instant. A chill that had gone overlooked amid the chaos sent shivers through the crowded hold as it did not depart willingly.

Eyes turned to him, but Erefan was already back to working the dials, catching back up with the Grangian battleship. "Make ready with the switch, and flip it the other way when I call the order."

"Yes, sir," the switch soldier replied.

"Get ready for another try at them," Erefan said. The liftwing disappeared below the view of the world-ripper. Erefan changed tactics and angled the view downward. Soldiers clambered to get away from the view, which showed the Grangian airship a hundred feet below and the ground uncounted thousands below that. A very real, very fatal fall was just a flip of a switch away. The bravest among them took up marksman's positions, kneeling just a few paces from the view frame. "Aim for the pilot's windows at the front."

Erefan guided the view lower, requiring a third hand he didn't have, then caught back up and centered the view on the cockpit. They were looking at it from just a dozen feet away; a novice could pepper it with bullets for hours on end without missing.

"Pull."

The noise of the propellers returned with the opening of the world hole, but not the wind. The wash from the propellers spat out to either side of them and below, but not in the direction of the Errol soldiers crouching aboard the *Jennai*.

Shots cracked from the barrels of rifles, nearly masking the plinking of bullets off steel and glass. The windows of the airship seemed impervious.

"Close." This time the order was heeded. Erefan kept the view over the Grangians as the switch closed.

Vaulk returned with Kandrel in tow, both men puffing for breath. "You need me to get the boy up?" Kandrel asked. He gave a meaningful look at the intact airship taunting them from the other side of the view frame.

"No," said Erefan. Another schematic was piecing itself together in his mind—a much simpler one. It involved: "Rope. Gather it in bunches and bring it here. And we've got rails around here somewhere. I saw piles of the stuff from the thunderail job that got moved out when we brought the machine in. Bring me four good sections." Men looked at him expectantly, as if he had more to say. "GO!"

Soldiers dropped rifles to the floor and ran pell-mell for the other stores aboard the *Jennai*. Erefan let them slip from his mind as he focused on keeping the liftwing in his sights as he readjusted the angle of the view.

By the time the soldiers returned, he was ready for them. "Rope yourselves up. Lash to the ship. Enough slack that you can get to the hole but not put so much as a foot through it." Errol Company men obeyed, sparing worried glances at the gigantic propellers that whirred in silence, taking up the whole of the view screen.

Erefan spared a glance down at the rails. Good, sturdy steel, thick as a fist and about twenty feet by his eye. Perfect. He backed the view off by a wobbling twenty five feet or so, and brought the view a bit higher than the propeller's hub.

"Get as many men on one of those rails as you can. I want a good running start and heave it through." He waited for a crew to arrange themselves and take up one of the rails. There were enough hands that it hefted easily. "Pull." The switch opened and the propeller was less than ten paces away. "Go!"

It was a shuffling run, a threat to no speed record of human, kuduk, or daruu, but the Errol Company soldiers got the rail moving, and as the rope slack caught them, the front most peeled away two at a time. The rail tumbled through the hole.

With a crash that ended sooner than any would have guessed, the propeller was gone, shattered to a thousand steel shards that fluttered back away from the hole, carried by the wind. Erefan gave them no rest. The liftwing lurched from the loss of one engine, but he got out in front of it again and repeated the process three times more. The loss of a single engine wasn't enough to drop a liftwing that size, just slow it. The loss of two was cause for an urgent landing at the nearest practical aerodrome. Losing three was time for prayers and a controlled crash. All four engines out, and those prayers went unanswered.

As they watched the Grangian airship plummet from the sky, Erefan slumped back in his chair. Thoughts of how to build those steady dial-turning devices boiled back to the surface of his brain.

Chapter 21

"Too much." -Cadmus Errol, in response to the question "What have we got to lose?"

Jamile's eyes snapped open in the darkness. Her legs kicked, arms propellered, trying to twist upright before she drowned. There was no scream. Breath was too precious to waste. The tangling of the blankets was her first clue that she was not below the surface of the Sea of Kerum. The linen of the bedding beneath her was wet, but it was her own sweat, not seawater, that soaked it. She gasped and found herself choking with nothing in her throat. Rolling to the edge of the bed, she hung her head over the side and coughed until the sensation passed.

Sosha's last memories were a blur in her head, like someone had smudged fresh ink in a panic before it had a chance to dry. Flying. Falling. Jumping. Blackness. Sheets. She'd heard of the falling dream. Tending little children at the sanctuary had blessed her with a wide vocabulary of nightly visions as she comforted the sleep-wrought terrors away. *The dream can't hurt you. It was all your imagination.* She'd given that lecture a dozen times and now wondered if she had perhaps been comforting twinborn, shocked awake just as their twin had died.

The room was chilly, the stone of the floor a step removed from ice. Jamile slipped bare feet into boots and threw a jacket over her nightshirt. Her hands were trembling. The buttons vexed her, so she clutched the jacket closed in her fist as she ran off through the Errol house and out into the night. The sea wind bit into the exposed flesh at her collarbone and shins, numbed her fingers, nose, and ears. Luckily it was only a few streets over to the world-ripper machine, or she might have frozen on the way.

She shouldered open the door and barged inside. Heads turned, as the machine was manned around the clock. Jamile was known. A hand might have flinched toward a rifle, but no more than a flinch.

"What are you doing out this late, girl?" one of the guards asked. Jamile didn't know his name, but he was thin and slouched in his chair. He leaned forward and squinted her way. "And why ain't you dressed? No night to be out wandering in—"

"I need to get to Korr." There was no time for pleasantries.

Four guards on duty, and none replied. They looked to one another: eyes looking for eyes with answers in them. They all knew her, knew she was friendly with Madlin. It often got Jamile a cut in line at dinnertime or a door held for her by someone who might otherwise have considered himself too busy. It wasn't buying her a ticket to another world.

"Please!"

The oldest among the guards rose. "Miss Jamile," he said in a voice that sounded raw from a lifetime of pipe smoke. "We got one job: keep folk away from the machine 'til morning."

Jamile stabbed a finger toward the viewing frame of the inert world-ripper. "I might be dead!" That was the rub: she didn't know. She had no sense of Sosha—not that she ever did while awake. She knew their waking hours overlapped; both slept less than half the day. But even when both had to be awake, she couldn't see through Sosha's eyes, nor Sosha through hers. She could be unconscious and slipping beneath the Sea of Kerum, awake and treading water, or floating dead with every bone of her body shattered. "I need to get help."

"Even if we could, none of us knows how to work the thing," the older guard said. He didn't meet her eyes, and clutched at his hat in both hands.

Jamile shook with the cold she'd carried in with her. Shivers and nerves forced her to shift from one foot to the other. She needed to act. She strode for the machine. "Just let me try. Maybe they left it on—"

All four guards rose. They didn't bring weapons to bear or anything so unfriendly, but from their reaction she knew she could not lay a hand on it. Jamile froze in place—it was easy, since she was half frozen already—and held her hands out to her sides. Sparing a glance back over her shoulder at the door, she took a step back. "Maybe I'll just go wake Madlin." She nodded, hoping to draw nods of agreement in turn.

The older guard sprang forward, hand out to stop her, despite her being a good twenty paces distant. "No, Miss Jamile. I can't let you go back out to catch your death."

"You don't understand. I've got to—"

"I'll go."

Heads turned to the thin guard who'd spoken up. He slipped on a jacket from the back of his chair and scooped up his rifle and hat as he left his post. Jamile gaped at him. "Thank you. Please hurry."

The thin guard offered a wink for reassurance. "If I survive waking Miss Madlin, I'll have her back here in a whistle." A cutting wind blew through the door as it opened, causing Jamile to shiver even after the door slammed shut behind the guard.

"C'mon over here, Miss Jamile," the older guard offered. He waved her over to the chair her messenger had vacated. "Warmer away from the door." Taking tentative steps, Jamile shuffled over, hugging herself inside her jacket for warmth. One of the other guards helped her into her seat, and the last one poured hot chocolate into a mug and handed it to her. She sipped at the piping hot beverage.

I'm drowning. I'm sitting here drowning and having a nice cup of chocolate. The controls to the world-ripper were two paces away.

She took another sip, eyes fixed on the door, waiting for Madlin.

The *Kelleb* was a smaller vessel than the Ruttanian vacu-dirges, but similar in design. There would be work involved in joining it to the other three airships, but that was a problem for after Rynn was finished stealing it. The kuduks firing rifles at them had not given up their claim to ownership yet, and there was still the matter of the mammoth liftwing that had taken off ahead of them. Rynn still heard the crackling of gunfire from the ground as she steered them clear of Glenwood Sky. She hoped that her coil gunmen were making judicious use of their ammunition. Liftwings the size of the one ahead of them were built solid; rifle bullets weren't liable to do much damage to one. They'd need every bit of firepower they could muster to take it out of the air if it turned on them.

A ship's wheel suited her, Rynn decided. Tinker or no, she'd take her turn as a ship's helmswoman. It was certainly within her purview as General of the Rebellion. It wasn't a formal rank, of course, since there was no authority that grants anything to rebels. That was largely the point of rebellions. Still, a thought nagged in a corner of Rynn's brain as she blotted out the fading gun battle and searched the skies ahead for enemy vessels: *We need a bit of organization.* With work proceeding on turning the *Jennai's* vacuum tanks into crew and cargo space, they'd soon begin gathering up recruits from across Korr, freeing slaves and taking pockets of rebels under their protective wings. She couldn't manage everything with an informal command structure of close associates.

General Rynn. Colonel Erefan. Majors Kandrel and Vaulk. Captain Bosley. Lieutenant Sosha.

She tumbled the ranks around in her head, wondering why the words changed from language to language, but the basic structure was the same for all kuduk nations and half those of Tellurak. The Kheshi knightly class still held military rank as an exception to the rule, and the Feru military was an enigma to Rynn, but the rest all followed the pattern. She wondered if Veydrus was the same. Surely Dan would know.

Miss Madlin!

Rynn's thoughts stuttered like a jostled phonograph. Had someone called her Telluraki name? She looked over each shoulder, and the two soldiers on guard at the door nodded in acknowledgment. No hint that either of them had spoken her name.

Too much going on. It was her imagination. *Everyone wants my time.* Rynn breathed deep, sucking in the cold, thin air that snuck in through gaps in the airship's windows. It was just enough to invigorate without cutting to the bone.

A cloudless sky and an easy course. Father will find a way to shoot down the liftwing and Miss Madlin, please, it's urgent, we can chain this thing behind the Cloudsmith *and tow it along.*

Rynn kept her head still, but checked the corners of both eyes. She had no prickling feeling of someone sneaking up on her. Yet there was something amiss. She knew the sound of her own voice, and the sound of the voice of her own thoughts. Why the two differed she couldn't guess, but they did, and she was well acquainted with both. Someone else was talking in her head, mixing their thoughts in with her own, but the voice of those thoughts was familiar despite her not being able to put a name to it.

"Getting a bit dry up here," Rynn said over her shoulder. "Someone check if there's ale aboard." It was a long shot, since few kuduks had the taste for alcohol and fewer humans the coin to purchase both passage and refreshment. "If not, get me anything wet."

She was developing a pounding headache.

The room was black as tar and quiet as the inside of a drum. Madlin squeezed her eyes shut again when the pounding repeated.

"Miss Madlin, it's urgent."

Gut me, the voice in my head was here. Madlin grunted and rolled herself to the edge of her bed.

"I'm awake," she mumbled toward the door. Fumbling at the bedside table, she found her spectacles and pulled them on. "Coming."

She shuffled across the icy stone floor barefoot, the sudden jolt of cold helping to force her alert. She opened the door and saw a guard in an Errol Company uniform. The sight of them had become so commonplace aboard the *Jennai* that she had to remind herself that she was on Tinker's Island and wasn't Rynn. A few seconds of reflection could have given her the same answer when she noticed two cold feet on the floor instead of one.

"What is it?"

"It's Miss Jamile. She needs your help at the world-ripper. She thinks she might be dead."

That shot a wave of a panic though Madlin's slumber-soaked mind. There were mental contortions required to determine whether she was Rynn or Madlin when she woke in the night, but twinborn logic still made sense to Madlin's thinking. She knew that it had to be Sosha in trouble. "Let's go!"

Madlin owned nightclothes—even wore them on occasion—but commonly slept in her dayclothes. She needed only to pull on her boots and grab her hat and jacket on the way out. Gloves were tucked in the pockets, waiting for her. She pushed past the guard and led the way.

The night outside was polar, winds howling from the north, carrying a winter's chill that cared nothing for calendars. Madlin hunkered down inside her coat and held her hat on with one hand, the collar of her coat closed with the other. It was nights like this that Madlin wondered whether her father should have just gone the whole mile and built the city as a Korrish deep. You couldn't blame the kuduks for having a good idea here or there; he'd copied half a hundred of their designs as it was.

When the door slammed shut behind them in the world-ripper's workshop, Jamile was waiting for them. She hastily set down a mug and ran to meet Madlin halfway as she approached.

"Madlin! My liftwing went down. It was defective. Fell to pieces. There was a big liftwing and it shot at me and when I turned the ship it broke its propeller clean off and then ... and then ... bloody winds, I don't know!" Jamile was panting, having blown the whole story out in one breath. "I'm probably floating in the Sea of Kerum, but it's all gauze in my head."

"You had your floating vest on?"

Jamile nodded, jittery and a few more times than was needed to convey her agreement.

"You activate the runes?"

Jamile opened her mouth, then closed it with a grimace and a shrug. "I don't—"

"Did you jump out?"

Jamile replied with a sheepish smile that carried no reassurance. "I think so?"

Madlin strode over to the control panel of the machine, removing her hat and gloves as she walked, depositing them on the guards' table. "You know I've never used this thing, right?" Madlin flipped switches and the bulbs around the machine's viewing frame lit one by one. When the last of the bulbs lit, the interior of the frame dissolved into a view of the *Jennai's* plaza. "You got lucky."

Taking her seat at the controls, Madlin spun the view to get her bearings. In halting, jerking twists of the machine's dials, she stumbled the view around until she found herself in the cargo hold of the *Cloudsmith*, with the Korrish world-ripper. *Even the machine is twinborn*, she mused. Sitting in a chair identical to her own, Madlin watched her father's hands as they spun dials in lazy circles. He wasn't in a hurry for anything, it seemed. She would change that, soon enough.

With a wince in case she had missing some key step, Madlin yanked the main switch closed. The dynamo's hum, which had been relegated to background noise, climbed to a screeching whine as the view turned real. Her first reaction was relief that the process had worked; her second was the shock of seeing rifle barrels in soldiers' hands, pointed through the hole.

"Get down!" she shouted, and took her own advice, throwing herself from the chair even as Jamile and the guards hesitated. "It's me! It's us! Don't shoot!"

"Madlin?" Erefan's voice called through the hole from Korr. "What in the rusty scrap heap are you doing there? If you're awake, who's commanding that vacu-dirge?"

Madlin peeked out from under the arms she'd flung over her head for protection. The rifles had been lowered. Letting out a shuddering breath she'd been holding, Madlin pushed herself to her feet.

"Sosha's liftwing went down. We needed to get you a message and start a search."

"She still alive?" Erefan asked. Jamile hesitated for a heartbeat, but nodded. "Well, the Grangians had some engine trouble and went down themselves. You can take that vacu-dirge low and look for her."

"I was thinking we could use the world-ripper to look," said Jamile.

"She thinks she activated her float vest," Madlin added. "Runes are on the front, so if she's in the water unconscious, she ought to be flat on her back, floating like a leaf."

Erefan beckoned. "Get through here, both of you. Let's get a course figured for her and find a place to start."

Rynn stood at the helm and yawned. It was the middle of the day, with no excuse for fatigue. Sure, her leg was burning from all the standing and walking she'd been doing of late, but even physical exhaustion shouldn't have played so heavily on her alertness. The intruding voice in her head had stopped, but daydreams plagued her instead. She wanted a world-ripper of her own, and imagined herself at the controls, flitting around the world with the ease her father displayed when he was the one working the machine. She wondered what intersecting two world holes would do, could do: could a straight bar pushed through two worlds come back and touch itself?

She saw an army betray her. Errol Company soldiers knelt with rifles aimed, ready to tear her full of holes, and not the wondrous sort that the world-ripper made, but the red, leaking holes that looked better in kuduks. She fled from them and was saved.

She saw a speck in the sky, floating upward, a trick no bird could manage. It looked human as she drew closer to it, but it was a trick no human could manage, either. Rynn blinked. It wasn't a daydream. She pulled her coil gun and used the sight as a spyglass.

"Shit!" she whispered.

Rynn turned and shouted down the stairs. "MORE VACUUM!" The floating figure was approaching too quickly. Hauling back on the throttle lever, Rynn threw the engines into reverse briefly to slow them, then let them drift forward. The vacuum pumps thumped somewhere below decks, sucking at the dregs of air remaining in the tanks. She hoped it would be enough.

"All hands to the windows. Open the cargo doors. Watch for Sosha. Someone grab her!"

The body in the sky was limp, head lolling back, arms and legs dangling. Sosha looked like a drunk held up by the shirt collar, ready to be tossed into the street. The *Kelleb's* controls were new to Rynn, but made some intuitive sense. She eased the wheel around, feeling the change in course as much as watching it. They could miss Sosha on a pass and try coming around for her, but if they slammed the ship into her it might turn into a recovery rather than a rescue. There was a chance it already had.

The world-ripper's view streaked over the water, backtracking the flight path of the seven liftwings that had escaped Glenwood Sky Aerodrome. Soldiers stared at Madlin, having seen Rynn disappear through the other machine not so long ago, and looking rather less whole than the girl whose eyes fixed on the view frame. Jamile was the same woman they were looking for, but with longer hair. There was nothing to be done about the discomfort of those one-worlders' eyes and the ache it must have caused in their brains.

The Sea of Kerum glittered in the sun, catching the light off every swell and roll. There was always the chance that they'd miss her, sweep right by at breakneck speed without ever realizing. "Eyes sharp, everyone," said Madlin to the crowd of soldiers. She hooked a thumb in Jamile's direction. "We're looking for one of these."

They passed a rocky isle here and there, and to the right, on the horizon, the Grangian coast loomed. The liftwings had trailed alongside it for part of their escape. If Sosha had been over land when her liftwing failed her, the search might well come to an unpleasant end.

While the view skimmed along above the water some twenty or so feet up, the watchers were accorded an expansive view of the sky as well. High above the sea and climbing, they spotted the *Kelleb.* Madlin's gut twisted at the weirdness of knowing that she was aboard it, in the same world. She wondered if Rynn was looking for Sosha as well. If so, the path before them had likely already been covered in the search. They must have missed seeing her.

Unless she floated up.

The thought hit Madlin like a thunderail. Of course Sosha had floated up. She'd seen it with her own eyes. Or with Rynn's. At some level the point was academic, because she had a clear recollection of Sosha's body hanging in midair, drawn skyward as if the sun had hooked her like a fish.

"Bring the view up," said Madlin, her hard tone marking it clearly as an order. "Check by the airship."

"You're not thinking that—" Erefan began.

"She misjudged the runes on her vest. She's lighter than air and going higher."

Erefan swore something beneath his breath and made the adjustments on the control panel. The view angled without warning, drawing an eye-sick groan from the soldiers who hadn't the sense to look away as the world lurched in front of them. Closer and closer, the Grangian airship grew large in the view frame.

"I see me!" Jamile shouted.

Madlin squinted through her spectacles, envying Jamile's eyesight. There it was, growing dangerously close to the stolen Grangian vacu-dirge. Erefan swooped upward and brought them all closer. Having just meat-fingered her way around the Tinker's Island machine, Madlin marveled at his mastery of the dials.

"That's not a good sign," said Jamile, clutching her hands. "My neck shouldn't be at an angle like that."

As they drew close enough to see the runed plate riveted to the front of Sosha's vest, they saw a rescue attempt in progress. The side cargo door of the airship was open and a score of soldiers crowded the gate. One with a rope around his waist edged his way down the loading ramp; he had a second rope in his hand, tied with a loop at the end. With a flick of the wrist, he launched the loop of rope and landed it around Sosha.

"Thank Eziel we took on some ranch hands," said Madlin.

Jamile lunged and threw the switch to open a hole to the scene in front of them. Erefan reached to stop her, but pulled his hand away at the last second. He let her activate the machine.

"STOP!" Jamile shouted through the world hole, rushing right up to the aperture with a thousand foot drop a half step away. "LET GO THE ROPE!"

The startled soldier with the rancher's knack for rope froze in place. He stared with wide eyes at the scene floating in the air not ten paces distant.

Madlin stepped up beside Jamile "Do it!" she ordered.

The soldier dropped his end of the rope and it fell away. The other end hung around Sosha's neck.

"Damned fool," Jamile muttered, backing away from the machine's frame. "If I'm not dead already, that would have killed me."

"We're here, we might as well get her through," Madlin said to her father. "She's still rising. Just bring us around above her and look down. Ropes for anyone who gets near that thing."

Madlin and three of the solders roped themselves in and stood ready at the aperture as Erefan looped around Sosha's limp form to bring the world hole above her. Madlin felt her knees go weak. Just inches away was a shift in gravity that would pull her down to the Sea of Kerum, spread out below them and in front of their faces at the same time.

After chasing airships, Erefan had no difficulty lining up to intercept a young woman floating on the wind and drifting up like a puff of smoke. First through the hole was Sosha's head, which one of the soldiers cradled as the other two gathered in her body. Madlin stayed at the opening, waiting to make sure she was through.

"Cut it!" she ordered.

Erefan switched the machine off and Madlin kept her eyes on the trailing end of the rope as it fell away, snipped cleanly by the closing of the hole. She's suspected it would happen, but it was good to know without anyone getting caught in the middle of it to prove the point.

Jamile was upon her twin the moment Sosha was laid on the floor of the hold. She checked her own breathing and pulse. "Alive." There were gasps of relief from all sides. Madlin watched with a weird detachment. There were differences, but only subtle ones. The hair was obvious, with Sosha shaved bald as recently as two months ago, but there were other changes as well. Jamile was better fed and it showed in the hollows of Sosha's face. As Jamile pulled off the vest while two soldiers held Sosha's body down, Madlin saw the calluses around Sosha's neck and collarbone from years wearing a collar. The vest floated to the ceiling and clung there.

Jamile pushed Sosha's eyelids open and blocked and unblocked the overhead lights. She felt along arms and legs for broken bones, and finally under the neck. Madlin noticed water dripping from the vest down onto the floor near Sosha.

"She must have hit the water and got knocked out," Madlin said. "She's wet."

"But she was falling up," said Jamile.

"Momentum." Everyone turned to hear Erefan weigh in. He had that effect on rooms full of people. "Activated the runes too late, and it took them time to overcome her downward momentum. She probably waited to the last moment to abandon her craft."

"I kept trying to pull up," Jamile said, not looking up from her work. "I thought I could save it, not have to jump out. Maybe land it on the water and swim free."

"You know this now?" Madlin asked. "Cuz before you sure didn't seem to know what went on."

"I do. The memory is clearing up. She probably shouldn't get up for a while, but this is no place to rest. Her neck isn't broken, but she's had a concussion, and most likely whiplash. I'm going to stay here and tend to her."

"Isn't that a little ... awkward?" Madlin asked.

"It's her decision," said Erefan. "She's better suited to it than anyone else."

"I'm not sure I'd want to meet me," Madlin muttered.

"Someone get a stretcher and carry Sosha to her quarters," Jamile ordered. *Lieutenant Jamile?* Maybe doctor could be an honorary rank, strictly for medical orders.

"I can bring some of your clothes in the morning," Madlin offered, feeling like she had nothing else to offer. A whole army at her command, and all she could think to do for an injured soldier was bring a clean dress for her nurse.

Jamile looked up, an impish smile conveying her relief that Sosha's injuries weren't severe. "Thank you, but I should be fine. I think her clothes ought to fit me."

With excitement fading and the rime melting from her face and hair, exhaustion caught up with Madlin as she returned to her own room. How long had she been away? An hour? Two? She hadn't thought to look at a clock the whole while. Pawing around the darkened room, she found the lamp and flicked it on. She tossed her coat on the floor by the coal stove, followed by hat and gloves, then changed into the thickest nightclothes in her wardrobe and threw a cloak over her shoulders.

The room was tepid, not the least unpleasant by any objective account, but Madlin wasn't feeling objective. She was cold and wanted the cold driven from her with a ferocity that would warn it never to return. There were times for being out of doors, and an autumn night on Tinker's Island was not one of them. She pulled open the stove door and dumped half the coal bucket inside. A mechanical sparker rested on top of the stove, with a little pull chain that was sure to get a fire going by the third pull at the worst.

Madlin wasn't having it. She didn't dare try to warm herself with aether, but she wasn't afraid of a blackened lump of inert fire. The refreshing rush of aether spread through her—cold, but an altogether different sort of cold than the one that kept her shivering. One by one each lump caught fire. One would have been enough to set the whole batch burning, but she wanted heat now, not when the coals felt like giving it. Besides, the aether needed to go somewhere.

Madlin huddled herself in a chair and waited for the room to warm. That was when she noticed it—a letter by the door, where it looked to have been slipped beneath the crack. It might have been there when she left, unnoticed in the gloom and rush of her departure. She might even have kicked it aside without realizing.

Bunching the cloak tight around her, Madlin bent to scoop it up. It was a simple sheet of paper, folded this way and that such that a single wax seal could keep it closed against snooping. The impression in the wax was crude, not a seal at all. Someone had taken a quill and used the tip to press tiny letters into it, spacing them well apart to make clear that they weren't meant to form magical runes. They spelled out her name in Korrish phonics: Ma-da-li-n. *Close enough.*

A few wiggles back and forth and the wax snapped. Madlin unfolded the paper and read:

Miss Madlin Errol,

I believe that our continued presence on Tinker's Island is a risk we can no longer afford. All that I have said remains true. All the offers I have made still stand. I still carry the hope that you will see the warlock for what he is before he becomes your doom. Should you wish to contact me, you have the means. Find Anzik, my son's twin in Veydrus. Look for him in the palace in Ghelk, where the Kheshi city of Mabliss lies.

Keep well,

D.Z.

Madlin read it twice, trying to decide if there was a layer beneath the one spelled plainly on the page. It occurred to her to keep it, but she shook the thought aside. Dire havoc would come, should the wrong person read that message.

Before she could second guess herself, Madlin opened the stove and fed the message to the coals.

She set the lamp on the bedside table and climbed beneath the covers. As she blew out the flame, leaving herself in cozy darkness, she had only two words to remember: Anzik and Mabliss. The rest the flames could keep.

Chapter 22

"Friends have always bored me. Enemies are the spice of life."
–Rashan Solaran

Powlo had seen steam wagons before, both through the eyes of Chapun and one that Cadmus had built on a lark. There were no proper roads for one on Tinker's Island—little of it was level or smooth—and bumps and rattles were no friends to the delicate interlacing of machinery that ran one.

The versions Kezudkan and Draksgollow had bought with their ill-gotten gold were a different sort of animal. They still ran on steam, but runes heated the tanks. They weren't open at the top like the front seat of every steam wagon he'd ever seen before, but had a steel canopy and glass windows as thick as the palm of his hand. They rolled on two sets of wide, flat steel belts, each the full length of the vehicle, and seemed not the least bit concerned with the grade or smoothness they traversed.

That all would have been impressive enough, but despite just a two-man crew, the little military steam wagon carried a pair of wide-barreled rotoguns on swivels. One driver, one gunner, and the rust-hearted little monsters fit through the world-holes.

Powlo was part of a crew of sixteen slaves following in the wake of the small squadron of metal beasts. He couldn't say for certain where they were, but it was Khesh by his guess, some noble estate. Repeater gunfire sounded in the distance, down the echoing corridors to meet Powlo and his comrades as they carried plunder back through the hole to Kezudkan's lair. It was his fourth trip, and this latest venture had him carrying off an armload of antique vases, probably getting all scratched up and less valuable by the step.

"Good, good. Excellent," Kezudkan greeted them at the hole from the Korr side. The old daruu glanced at each slave's take as they passed, murmuring little encouragements or comments about the strange wonders that humans of this other world coveted. When Powlo's turn came to pass by, the daruu barred the way with his cane. "Hold there. What's this?" A finger like a sausage carved in stone jabbed at the base of one of Powlo's vases.

Powlo twisted around, careful not to drop anything as he looked under his own loot. "It's blood, sir. The place is swimming in it, some rooms. I doubt there's a rug in the place that will be worth saving."

"We're not here for rugs," Draksgollow said, stomping over with his irregular gait, every other step punctuated by hisses of steam and a metallic thunk against the floor. "And I don't give a glass hammer about flower pots." Draksgollow slapped his mechanical hand at the vases and knocked them from Powlo's grasp. They smashed to the ground and became worthless shards of porcelain. Each had likely been worth more than a slave's freedom price. "Sweep that up before someone gets damaged."

Draksgollow stomped off in pursuit of more slaves to bully, leaving Powlo alone with Kezudkan, the mess, and occasional slaves making the passage through the hole in one direction or the other.

"Don't worry, Chapun," Kezudkan said a conspiratorial undertone, holding the back of his hand to the side of his mouth. "We won't have you much longer. Draksgollow doesn't much care for you, but you're worth more alive than dead."

Powlo was taking off his shirt to use as a broom and stopped with it around his armpits. "You're selling me back home?"

"Indeed. Just got the cable this morning. It's a done deal. It's not your freedom, but at least it will be an owner you've grown accustomed to."

Powlo pulled his shirt back on. "What should I—when should—where—"

Kezudkan patted a hand in the air. "No no, just go ahead and finish that up. I won't let you get left behind. Money is money, even if we can take whatever we want and more. It's principle, you know. Businessmen must maintain a certain sense of themselves. Mustn't be wasteful of coin or goods, just because we're rich as kings."

That evening, Powlo found himself chained in the slave car of a thunderail, heading home. Well, he was heading to the home Chapun had left, but since he had convinced everyone that he *was* Chapun, it was much the same. The accommodations were sparse, to say the least: a double-aisle ran the length of the car, with a pair of steel benches flanking each. The benches were packed with slaves sitting shoulder to shoulder, chains snaking through loops at their collars and loops behind the benches, keeping them all seated for the duration of their trip. There was no meal service in the slave car, no chamber pot to pass around. The doors wouldn't open until the trip was ended, when some poor bastard would have to clean it out with a pump and hose before the next batch were loaded. Powlo's seat was still damp from the last washing.

It was just a matter of time now. Maybe he finished the trip, maybe he didn't. He'd done his job and Cadmus was going to slip him out sooner or later. He liked the tinker, trusted him even. There was just a little matter of pragmatism that told him that maybe he should wait until he was safe and cozy before giving up the location of Kezudkan's headquarters. Sure, Cadmus might be able to tinker it out with whatever black science he used to figure out things a normal man never could dream, but he'd have an easier time rescuing Powlo than puzzling out the route on his own. Cadmus would get nothing from Powlo but the name of a train and its arrival time. Let the Mad Tinker work backward from there—searching a whole city for one workshop—if he was willing to strand Powlo.

"Seemed awful dim, to me," Draksgollow muttered, squirting a bit of grease into one of his joints. It was just the two of them in the room, watching from the Ice Furnace lair in the arse crack of Korr. The view frame showed the workshop they had just launched their assault from, though the steam tanks were all safely ensconced in the not-so-abandoned mines with them, along with much of the loot they had stolen.

"Dim as he needed to seem," Kezudkan replied. "You think he didn't figure it out?"

"Dim enough not to see it for a trap. Maybe too dim to work out where he was, or care."

"And if he was?" Kezudkan turned up his hands. "A few days' holiday before we get back to work. We've earned a good one, I think. We can afford one, certainly."

Draksgollow pushed his chair away from the table. He and Kezudkan were the only patrons of a lounge where the entertainment might not show up for days, if at all. Let the daruu while away his elder years in idle vigils. "I've got work to do."

Kezudkan stared through the view frame. "Of course, of course. You've earned a respite, but I won't force one on you." He flicked a few fingers in Draksgollow's direction.

When the kuduk tinker had departed, taking his whirrs and hisses and grating metallic twitches with him, Kezudkan settled in to relish in the silence. The stone around him was old, welcoming, tied deep to the bones of Korr and little disturbed in decades. He reached into a pocket and pulled out a small figurine, carved from white marble. It was to be part of a set of chess pieces for his grandson, but the rest of the set lay buried in the ruins of his Eversall estate. The human shape of it was bent and weary, pathetic in all ways. Once he had used it as an allegory for Erefan, to warn him to take better care of himself.

Kezudkan crushed it to powder in his fingers.

Chapter 23

"Chess is a game not of gambits, but of patience and preparation. The winner is not the one who moves with most daring, but with more foresight." -On the Stratagems and Underlying Premises of the Game of Chess, Insights of Lord Arvind Kendelaine III

The world-ripper ran from dawn to dark of night, sifting the brave from the cowards across southern Korr from the Turmon Republic to Grangia. Rynn's twinborn agents had been busy, worming their way in among the freeborn locals, sneaking among the slaves, finding out where spirits matched the angry words muttered behind kuduk backs. There were hundreds of them, more than the *Jennai* could handle, but there were barracks in Tinker's Island ready to take the overflow until the expansion of the *Jennai* would let the agglomerated airship hold them all.

Erefan was a great lover of order, of systems, of plans. He took the list of sites where twinborn agents required transport and moved from one to the next, sweeping north to south, nudging the controls east, then sweeping south to north. They had been a day already in scooping up new rebels, shuffling them off to orientation lectures and the beginnings of basic training as soldiers. It would be the rest of the day and beyond before they were finished.

"Yellowcorn's next," Rynn said to Erefan. "Should be like old times here in a bit." She had spent more of her time among the recruits than with the world-ripper, but she had been waiting for this retrieval since they began calling their flock back to the nest.

Erefan spared a glance over his shoulder, making sure she saw just how amused he wasn't. Rynn and her father had settled into a comfortable disagreement over her prior involvement with the rebels; neither budging from their opinions. That didn't usually stop them voicing them. "I've got necks to wring, that's for sure. Maybe you can take over on the controls while I show them around the ship."

Rynn smirked, imagining Erefan giving a tour with particular focus on the edge of the plaza and just how far down it was. Hayfield was twice Erefan's size, but it was never wise to underestimate a man with such an abiding respect for leverage as the tinker.

"You ever play crashball when you were little?" Rynn asked. "Or am I scraping away at the Mad Tinker mystique by asking?"

Erefan let the question hang for a moment as he guided the viewfinder across the Ruttanian landscape. Hills gave way to straw-yellow fields of wheat, stretching on as far as they could see to the horizon. "Not good for a young head, getting knocked around like that. That's what your grandmother said, at least. By the time

I was old enough to think of telling her different, it was already clear I wasn't cut out for that sort of game."

Erefan let the view hang motionless as he turned to fix Rynn with a mild look. She had braced herself for fire in his eyes, but he looked wrung dry. "I should have told you the same thing about running around with rebels when you were still too young to—"

"Don't finish that!"

"—to be running after boys." Rynn didn't know if she had steered him clear of the vulgar, or if she had just gotten too used to the proclivities of soldiers.

"Just go find Yellowcorn and be done with it."

Erefan grunted in reply and returned to the controls. In moments, they had slowed down at the outskirts of Yellowcorn Sky, with its plowed fields surrounding a loose mesh of roads, smaller farms, and houses that spanned miles. Rynn tried to identify landmarks: a courthouse, a tiny aerodrome with one vacu-dirge sitting idle, a scattering of municipal pump stations. They paused in the air as Rynn took stock of the city and Erefan referred to his notes. *I wonder how Bouo would look from above? It's got to be nearly this size.* She filed that note away for when she had an idle moment to play at the controls herself.

Erefan took the view to a small farmhouse by a barren field. Whatever the locals planted there was either out of season or had failed to thrive. *Just like the humans who live here.* It wouldn't be that way much longer. Places like Yellowcorn would become the great cities, places ruled by humans, peopled by humans, defended by humans. The deeps would be the ones to suffer hunger after a poor harvest; Human Season was about to bloom.

On the back porch of a whitewashed farmhouse, Rynn recognized half a dozen familiar faces. Kinmi and Syr were her own agents, newly met in Korr but old acquaintances on Tinker's Island. They were like cousins, infrequently seen but welcome and familiar. The others were her brothers, as much her family as Erefan was. Towering Hayfield, with his deep skin so well suited to the sunlight of Yellowcorn Sky, eased himself against one of the porch supports. He had grown up in a place like this. Buckets shuffled a deck of cards, his twitching glances betraying impatience cooped up in a body too young to contain it. Pick leaned in the shadow of the farmhouse wall, tucked back as far as he could get from the glare of noontime. He looked like a man who needed the deeps. Rascal appeared the most at ease. He sat alone on the porch steps, feet sprawled in front of him, taking shade beneath an oversized hat. The bleach-white clothes on his back made him look gentrified, but he held a scattergun slung over his shoulder, gripping it by the barrel. Though it was cracked open, ready to load and not to fire, it still gave him the impression of a dangerous man—a gentleman outlaw.

"Open it," said Rynn. She stood centering herself in front of the viewing frame, arms crossed and with a smirk set carefully in place.

Rynn didn't look back, but heard the thunk of the switch closing and the whining strain of the dynamo. The figures on the porch stirred and all turned their attention toward the hole as it ripped its way from the *Jennai* to Yellowcorn Sky.

The wafting scent of manure greeted her and wrinkled her nose before anyone said a word.

Rynn waved a hand below her nose; there was no mistaking it for a greeting. "And you fellas thought the sewers smelled bad."

"Chipmunk!" Buckets was first through the hole, all exuberance and no caution, as if he'd been hopping halfway across Korr through hole-ripping machines all his life. He crushed Rynn in his arms like a lost sister and picked her up. "Oof! You're eatin' here, ain't ya?"

As the test subject had survived passage, the rest of Rynn's friends ducked through as well. Hayfield clapped his maimed hand on her back. "Not bad, kid. Ya done good."

Pick slunk in with a nod and kept himself aside. Rascal came through last, after letting Kinmi and Syr pass through to offer perfunctory salutes to their general.

Rascal shook his head, his eyes taking a tour of the cargo hold while a bemused grin kept a place on his mouth and words failed him. "Can't hardly believe it. Father's mercy, this place is beautiful."

Rynn tapped a finger against Rascal's scattergun. "You can toss the pepper shaker. I promised you boys real guns, and you're gonna get 'em." She pulled the coil gun from her holster and pressed it into Rascal's hands.

With eyes ready to well up in tears, Rascal handed his scattergun to Rynn and inspected the weapon. "Don't hardly weigh nothin'. Fancier than your first one, too. *And always arm thyself for war, and take with you the weapon that overmasters that of your foe.* Blessed Father, I think we've finally obeyed you."

A harrumph from the control panel turned everyone's attention to Erefan. "Nice to know someone still remembers."

"Remembers?" Rascal asked. His eyes widened. "You *know*, don't you?"

"All of us do," Rynn said. "Rust and iron, if I'd known *you* knew, I'd have said something years ago. I didn't want to risk smashing your cookie jar if you'd thought Eziel was some shepherd of lost humans."

Hayfield scratched the scruffy new beard making its way down his chin. "Coulda tackled me with a five-year-old when I heard. Always thought our Pious Henlon here was a sham to keep the knockers off his scent. He was too easy with a gun for a holy man, I always thought."

"If you read the scriptures—the real ones—I oughtta really be a swordsman. But they wrote them books a long time ago. Ain't kept up with times. I'm sure if they wrote new ones, they're'd be a whole chapter on pistols and another on long guns."

"I heard you got a proper cook," Buckets said, throwing the switch for a different track.

"Gahwin's cookin' ain't good enough for ya?" Hayfield asked. He cuffed Buckets upside the head.

Rynn headed for the door, leaving Erefan with Kinmi and Syr to scrounge up the less well-connected rebels of Yellowcorn. "Come on, we'll stop by the dining hall on the way. You guys are going to pop a gasket when you see what we've got here."

The torrent of chatter that followed Rynn from the cargo hold died away as she showed her friends around the *Jennai.* None of them had seen an airship up close before, and no one anywhere had seen the likes of the *Jennai.* They all gawked up at the vacuum tanks towering above the plaza, even though only the *Kelleb* was still holding a vacuum. She walked them past the stolen liftwings and let them run their hands over the hulls. Buckets wanted to climb into the cockpit, but Rynn forbade it. By the time they took a meal in the dining hall—with its wide-windowed view of the Sea of Kerum so far below—they had grown somber.

"All this ... yours?" Hayfield asked. They sat crowded around a table with a panoramic view of Korr spread before them. They were high enough that land was visible to the far south, and more water than any of them had imagined possible spread out below.

Rynn shook her head. "I run this asylum. I don't own it. Food was tight for a while, but now that the machine's working, we eat like cooks. Don't be shy about portions; you're not getting special treatment on my account. Everyone eats their fill."

Pick elbowed Hayfield in the ribs. "Be back to playing weight in no time, huh? Maybe the leagues will pick you back up."

Hayfield grunted through a mouthful of pork. "Was muscle back then. Ain't eatin' my way back to muscle."

"So what do we do here?" Rascal asked. He was the only one not struck dumb each time she showed them a new wonder. "Doesn't look like you're short of hands."

Feet maybe, but not hands. Rynn smirked at her own joke. "You might be surprised. You've all killed more kuduks than any of this lot." She shot Buckets a glare. "Except maybe you. The ones from the other world are soldiers, but they don't know kuduks. The freemen are willing, but they've never fought. The former slaves have plenty of want-to, but they need training. We've got a few rabble-rousers we've picked up here and there, but we've got a lot of rabble."

"You want us teachin' 'em to fight?" Hayfield asked. "I ain't much for teachin'."

"You taught me," said Rynn. "You taught Buckets."

"We taught No-Boots, too," Pick observed.

Rynn shrugged. "He knew his business. Hanged is better than collared, but nothing beats free."

"Syr said you'd tell us how you got pinched," Pick said. "She wouldn't give us particulars." Pick's version sounded more like puh-tick-lers.

"No." Rynn shook her head. "I got pinched. I got collared. I got away. That's all anyone needs to know."

There was a hollow thump under the table. "Can you at least tell us how you got the fancy leg?" Buckets asked. Rynn looked under the table and he kicked it again.

"Stop that. Got cut bad escaping, and it took septic. They cut it off just below the knee." *Sosha cut it off.* She didn't see the need to get into blame in her story, but she hadn't quite forgotten, either. "I wasn't going to let a missing leg stop me, so I tinkered one up."

"Can I see it?" Buckets asked. His eyes were lit with a boyish love for the macabre and the weird.

Rynn frowned, the sort that sent her soldiers scurrying off to be elsewhere. It just made Buckets smile. "You always go around asking to see under girls' pants?"

"Yup," Rascal answered.

"He's gettin' worse by the day," Hayfield added.

"Hey!" Buckets looked to his friends, first one then the other. Rynn couldn't tell if his indignity was feigned, but they all laughed at his expense, Rynn included.

Rynn sighed, then ordered another round of drinks. She'd planned to take them all over the ship, brag about all the things the rebellion had been able to do. Instead, she found herself lulled into a comfortable torpor by familiar company.

"So how'd you end up with 'em, Buckets? I thought Tabby had you trussed up in church-day clothes, keeping clear of us ne'er-do-wells."

"Kid's got a sniffer on him, that's how," Pick said. "I taught him too good, and he tracked us down. Can you believe that?"

"How'd Tabby take it?"

"I left her a note," Buckets replied. "Ain't seen her since."

"Think you could send that step-through circle over to get her?" Hayfield asked. "Might not be safe in Eversall, if folk get to puttin' pieces together."

"My father's got a grid laid out, back and forth, up and down across the continent. We were already past Eversall when we picked you boys up. I can see about stealing some time tomorrow to go say 'hi' to her."

"Do I have to be there?" Buckets asked, shrinking down and looking up at Rynn with baleful eyes.

Rynn twisted her mouth up sideways and frowned as she studied Bucket's expression for hints of sincerity. "No. You should be there, but I won't make you. I could use *you* there, though," she said to Hayfield. "You always had a way with Tabby."

Pick snickered. Rascal elbowed him in the ribs.

"What?" Rynn asked, looking from one to the other, then to Hayfield.

Hayfield grimaced and scratched at his head. "Yeah, she's had her way with me, too."

Realization dawned and Rynn's eyes opened wide as her spectacles. "But—but I never—"

Rascal chuckled. "Yeah, you were always a bit dense about that sorta thing, and you were too young for her to talk to you about woman stuff." The rest joined in, leaving Rynn the butt of the joke this time.

"I've missed you guys," Rynn admitted as the laughter at her expense died down.

"Yeah, I saw the way freemen is lookin' at you," said Pick. "You ain't got no one 'round here who knows you for real."

Rynn opened her mouth to object, but nothing came out. *I have Sosha.* Who was as similar to Rynn as a lap cat is to a mouser. *Father. No, not him either.* Rynn and her father were alike—too alike for the comfort of either, yet with enough differences in all the wrong places to make it grate when they argued. The other twinborn were her father's friends, colleagues, underlings. They saw her as General Rynn or Miss Madlin, depending on the time of day and which world they were awake in.

A freeman rebel dropped by with their next round of drinks. On impulse, Rynn hoisted hers toward the ceiling and made a toast. "To having a bunch of low-born tunnel rats around, willing to tell me to piss off when I need it!"

"Piss off!" came the reply in chorus. They raised their mugs and clanged them over the middle of the table, sloshing sudsy ale over the sides.

The engine of the thunderail as seen through the world-ripper had been turned into a ragged mesh, more hole than whole. Kuduks watching from the station platform screamed in horror and fled in all directions as boiler water leaked onto the tracks, tinged with blood. The thunderail wouldn't be leaving while the Errol Company soldiers went to work.

"Search the cars, find the slaves, and get them out here," Erefan ordered. "No human casualties, and that includes you lads. Understood?"

"Yes, sir!"

The Errol soldiers piled through the hole, each carrying a coil pistol at the ready. A team of twenty was overkill, a concept which Erefan appreciated when he was on the proper end of it. Erefan watched them storm into the thunderail, car by car, chasing out kuduk passengers and heaving corpses out doors and windows from the ones that had gotten too involved in the proceedings. Human passengers ducked to keep clear of the gunfire as ball bearings whizzed about at speeds rifle-launched bullets couldn't come close to. They scurried along the tracks and followed the freeborn rebel voices coming from the *Jennai's* side of the world-hole.

Reluctant rebels could be returned later. The priority lay in getting humans aboard the airship before kuduk forces arrived to make things interesting.

Erefan could have spent a bit of time figuring out which was the slave car. He had a good idea just by looking at the outsides, but he could have panned down the length of the thunderail to make certain. But it wasn't about saving one car of slaves, nor was it about the one particular slave that had taken him on this detour from his grid pattern. If they were going to free humans from kuduk rule, there was to be no nibbling the meat from the stew—they would take everyone they could.

After a time, the soldiers found the right car, and a line of unwashed, ragged slaves slogged down the tracks and into the cargo hold with the machine. Among them, Powlo.

"About bleeding time," said Powlo as he separated himself from the herd and stopped by Erefan's chair. "Could you maybe have spared me half a day's ride in that thing?"

"I got the schedule. I knew when you'd be stopped. I wasn't about to attack a moving target when I could take one at rest. Simple physics."

"Bugger your physics. I want a bath."

Erefan nodded. "Next stop is Tinker's Island for you. I want you cleaned up, changed, and ready to help loot Kezudkan's workshop in an hour."

That changed Powlo's demeanor. A tight grin twisted the corners of his mouth, and his eyes hardened. He nodded. "You can count on that."

Erefan took a tinker's eye to Powlo's collar. "Nothing fancy, that. Should come off like a greased fitting. Stop and get one of the machinists to pop it off before you report to Orris. He'll be running the machine from that side."

Everyone had returned through the world-ripper. Erefan opened the switch and turned it back into an observation window. Powlo stood at the ready, waiting. And waiting.

"Any time, tinker."

"Soon as we see that workshop."

Powlo seethed an impatient breath through his nostrils, but relented. He directed Erefan to a workshop in Cavinstraw Deep, and in moments they were staring at a twin of the world-ripper they were using.

"Your word that I get to be there soon as you go."

"Agreed," said Erefan.

The settings for Tinker's Island were so ingrained that Erefan had no cause to look in his notes for the coordinates. They had been nailed to the sky long enough that he'd opened the same hole countless times. Erefan saw Powlo through to Tinker's Island, then slumped back in his chair a moment. When that moment had run its course, he went to see about some dinner. He'd been so long at his work that he hadn't eaten since morning.

Kezudkan reclined with his feet propped on a stool and an elbow leaning on the table. His eyes had a dusty film on them from not having blinked for the past several hours as he stared. The viewing frame in the world-ripper, buried in his abandoned mine lair, showed the same image of Draksgollow's workshop. Without so much as turning his head, he reached for one of the charred pork-on-a-stick delicacies he'd had the cooks prepare. It came on a little wooden spear, just to prove how expensive it was. He dipped it absently in a bowl of tar and crunched down, biting through wood and all.

Patience. Men with patience are rewarded. Men with too much patience ossify in their chairs and need a chisel to rise again. Kezudkan squirmed in his seat, just enough to crack his joints loose before settling in again.

Thus it was with Kezudkan, and when he had waited long enough, a hole from another world-ripper irised open in the middle of the workshop floor. Kezudkan sucked the tar from his fingers and fumbled for his cane. Every joint in his body wanted to make a statue of him, but he lurched to his feet and stood in front of the viewer.

Erefan, you sly rat, you. I've got you now. The slave tinker wore no collar, and might have added a bit of meat to his bones. He was first through the hole, followed by a crew of humans, crawling over the workshop like bipedal insects. When a second hole opened by the side of the first, Kezudkan found himself only mildly surprised. After all, he owned three himself, with a fourth under construction.

The first human through the other hole was Chapun. That wily slave had gotten his collar off as well. These humans were enterprising and organized. *I should have put Erefan in charge of the estate years ago. We could have been a model of efficiency.* Kezudkan was in a generous mood. Why shouldn't he be? He was right once again, and Draksgollow was wrong.

Erefan and Chapun engaged in a brief conversation, then Chapun left the field of vision available in the view frame. Kezudkan could have moved it, of course, but he had set it up so very cleverly and precisely. His view was the reverse angle of the inert viewer in the now human-infested workshop. Patience.

"Camera," said Kezudkan over his shoulder. One of the silent kuduk workers pulled himself from where he was leaning (or napping, perhaps) against the wall and picked up a camera and tripod. "Set up right there, and get me shots that can see into those other two holes there."

Kezudkan's vision was poor by objective standards, though for his age he felt his eyes were better than they had any right to be. He could see the two world-rippers through the holes they created. It was a setup nearly identical to the one they had arranged in Eversall for the prototype. Erefan was nothing if not a creature of habit. It worked, so he kept it.

"Get the guns ready," he ordered.

Two more kuduks stepped out of the chamber's shadows with rotorifles and took up positions flanking the view frame. "Steady with those now. They're the contingency, not the plan."

Erefan was gaping around at the workshop as his minions swarmed around, busy at whatever tasks they'd been given. Kezudkan gave less than a muddy sock about the minions. Erefan was talking to himself, looking up toward the ceiling. He grew more animated by the second, shook his fist at the workshop roof. It was a marvelous show, made all the more special when the flame lit in Kezudkan's mind and he realized Erefan was cursing him from afar. Oh, how delicious! It could only have been more perfect had Kezudkan been able to lip read.

He must think this is his victory speech. I've half a mind to open the hole so he can deliver it in person. Of course, there were good reasons not to do so. For one, he was just as happy not taking the risk that one of those wicked rune-powered guns ended up aimed his way. More importantly, he had worked everything out so perfectly otherwise. It would be a shame to spoil it; a momentary amusement at the cost of a greater pleasure later.

Erefan calmed himself and got down to the business of a more pointed inspection. The idiot Chapun should hopefully have told Erefan that there was only the one machine. He and Draksgollow had talked in front of the human about the progress of the 'second' machine when discussing the fourth one. Erefan had no expectation that he could be watched at that very moment, that there was another machine right there, waiting.

"Yes, that's good. Get curious. You can't help yourself."

Erefan walked to the viewing frame, and despite knowing that Erefan's side was turned off and his own was just a view, Kezudkan felt a rumbling little thrill. A human hand brushed against the webwork of copper in the frame, out of sight just behind the view. It appeared from Kezudkan's view that Erefan's hand pressed against the surface of the hole, a black spot where no light came through.

"Go on. You're curious. Have a seat and find out where I pointed it."

After his inspection of the view frame, Erefan sat at the controls. He ought to have known them, Kezudkan's machine was based on notes and sketches from the original. The book had been vague on details of the controls, so Erefan had filled them in to his liking and Kezudkan copied them wholesale.

One by one, Erefan flipped the switches that lit the bulbs around the frame. As he worked, human workers carried off Kezudkan's stolen valuables: coins, guns, artwork. The daruu ignored them. He saw the pale blue light reflecting from the polished surfaces of the machine's cabinets and the control panel, brighter with each one Erefan activated.

"If you sirs would step aside, well out of sight. Keep the guns handy, but do nothing unless I call for you."

When the last switch was engaged, the world-ripper's view sprang to life. The look on Erefan's face was worth far more than all the plunder his minions carried off. The smartest human Kezudkan had ever met sat in the control chair gaping like a simpleton, eyes like a dead fish. The viewer had been painstakingly calibrated to show the reciprocal view to Kezudkan's view frame—and Draksgollow had tack welded the dials in place to keep it there. The two men, human and daruu, saw each other as if they stood just a few paces apart. Kezudkan waved.

The next part was where Kezudkan was guessing. There was a side to Erefan that he had kept hidden until the very day of his betrayal. Kezudkan had studied the raid, the uprising, all he could find about the rebellion, trying to find out the sort of man he'd fed and clothed all those years. He hoped he had reckoned it properly. One sort of man was a coward, cautious in all things, never acting until he had all contingencies covered. Kezudkan considered himself such; cowards lived longer lives, and there was no shame in taking the wiser path. He had though Erefan to be the same, holed up safe in a workshop that many kuduks would envy, better than anything he could obtain even if he bought his freedom. A coward would have stayed and protected that. But the man who had stormed through Eversall with an army at his back was another sort: a risk-taker, an arrogant bastard who would thrust himself into danger if the payoff was worthwhile. One who trusted to his wits. One who acted. Sometimes rashly.

Impatient.

Erefan drew the gun belted at his hip. Without taking his eyes from the frame, the human tinker reached back for the switch that would open the hole and bring Kezudkan into range of his gun. Kezudkan threw up his hand in feigned terror—or at least how he thought humans did so when terrified. As Erefan closed the switch Kezudkan winked at him.

"Goodbye."

The blast was silent. The view frame was gone in an instant, replaced by a wall of smoke. A few pieces of wrecked metal landed right at the aperture of the viewer

Kezudkan chuckled, to himself at first, but then he let himself loose and guffawed, loud enough that most of the workshop must have heard him. He laughed himself hoarse, and gave in to a fit of coughing. When that passed, he took a few deep breaths and shook his head.

"In the end, you were just a human after all. Smarter than most, but unable to escape your nature. If you'd taken the time to check, you would have found the three hundred pounds of black powder wired to the main switch."

Twisting around to the cameraman, who stood smirking in the shadows, he said, "Go get those flashpops developed. I want to see what the settings were on those world-rippers."

Chapter 24

"In the wrong hands, mathematics is more dangerous than gunpowder."
-Cadmus Errol

Madlin bolted from her bed, clothed, but leaving boots, spectacles, and any sense of decorum behind. She tore down the hall, bare feet slapping on the cold stone. When she reached her father's door, only a quick grab of the handle stopped her momentum. It was no occasion for knocking; she threw the door open.

"Father!"

It was light inside the Mad Tinker's bedchamber. Open curtains let the morning sun add cheer to half the room, while the other half clung to shadows where the sunlight failed to reach. Cadmus sat in those shadows, hunched over his writing desk, pencil scribbling at a frantic pace. He had Madlin's habit of sleeping in his work clothes, and looked to be wearing yesterday's. A grey scruff of prickly fuzz told that he had skipped his morning shave. The jitter of his hand suggested he hadn't eaten.

He glanced sidelong from his work, as if even turning his eyes from it was too large a distraction. Who else called him father? Of course it was Madlin. "What? Don't just stand there, speak."

"I came as soon as I heard. Are you all right? What happened?"

The tip of the pencil snapped against the paper. "What happened? WHAT HAPPENED? I'll tell you what happened. That filthy, coal-hearted bastard rigged his world-ripper to explode." The pencil snapped in half with a crack in Cadmus's fist. Madlin flinched. "I'll get him though. He made a mistake he won't have long to regret. I saw the settings on the dials. I'll work the numbers and find where he's hiding."

Cadmus flung the broken pencil to the floor and took another from a jar filled with sharpened pencils. They were Korrish, fresh through the world-ripper a few days earlier. The Mad Tinker truly looked the moniker as he plunged himself into his mathematics over a scale map of Korr. Madlin edged closer, emboldened at each step by his lack of response. Over his shoulder, she read the number, speaking to her like a third person in the room. They told her that Kezudkan was somewhere in the far north, and was farther underground than the workshop in Cavinstraw Deep. More than that, Cadmus would have to complete finer calculations and make better references to the map.

Or so Madlin thought. "That bastard," Cadmus whispered. He sat back in his chair, letting the pencil fall over his scratchwork.

"What? I'm not seeing it."

"He's somewhere in the Ice Furnace. Years ago—long years ago—there used to by mines all over. All abandoned now. Bastard is under our noses, next world over. Oh, he must be enjoying this."

"Why would he know we're here?" Madlin asked. "If he knew, wouldn't he have done something about it."

Cadmus put a hand over his mouth. "You're right. I forgot. His other mistake. He doesn't know. Thinks I'm dead." Cadmus nodded to himself. "He's not expecting vengeance. That's why we can trust the numbers. You don't false the dials if you think I'm dead, do you?"

"Probably not."

"You leave them as they are. Make sure you got them just right. Check them twice—three times, even."

"Cadmus!" A shout from down the corridor bore a familiar voice. Greuder showed his face in the doorway, leaning against the jamb as he panted for breath.

"What is it now?"

"What do you mean, 'what is it?' What's become of you?" Greuder asked. "I heard the explosion. Some ran for the machine. I came straight this way."

"Get used to this face," Cadmus said, scribbling away at his equations. "It's the only one like it you're going to be seeing."

"Cadmus, I'm so sorry," Greuder said in a voice just above a whisper.

"And I'm busy. Twice as busy, I suppose. If you're here to make me feel better, I'd feel mighty good about an assault team ready to go through that world-ripper in about half an hour."

"You're sure you're—"

"I'm fine," Cadmus snapped. "And you can tell anyone else concerned with my health and well-being that their concerns are both misplaced and belated." When Greuder lingered at the door, Cadmus lit into him again. "Is there a problem, Mr. Greuder?"

Greuder licked his lips. "No, Mr. Errol. No, there's no problem. I'll get right on it."

"He was just worried about you," said Madlin.

"What are you still doing here?" Cadmus asked. "Scoot! Begone! I've got a pile of numbers that aren't killing anyone yet. Go make yourself useful."

Madlin backed toward the door. "Yeah. I'll go help Greuder." She closed the door behind her as softly as she could. Its catch made a gentle click, and Madlin fell back against the wall to let out a breath of relief. Whoever it was inside, she had never met him before. Was it a madness that had lain dormant for years, since before she was old enough to know any better? Had mother's death boiled such rage and mania in him, all those years ago?

Madlin tried to put the conversation with her father to the back of her mind as she joined the crew at the world-ripper. She'd taken the time to dress and arm herself, the familiar old weight of her handmade revolver sitting easy on her hip. If she were going to be heading off on a raid, she'd have liked the feel of a coil gun better, but the only ones on Tinker's Island were in pieces, unfinished. Every coil gun they'd completed had been sent to the *Jennai* to empower and put into service for the rebellion. It was an oversight she'd look to remedy shortly.

The crowd gathered outside the workshop was something she hadn't prepared for. Guards had kept the locals and Errol Company workers from congregating outside her house, and it seemed that the whole town had gathered around the workshop instead.

"Clear a path," she ordered, and the crowd jostled and shoved to make way for her. There was no point stopping to ask for information; if she got one answer she'd get a hundred, most of them hearsay. Answers lay inside, not out in the cold wind amid the press of bodies. She couldn't help overhearing bits and pieces as she wove her way to the entrance, but nothing she hadn't already heard. An explosion. Horrible sight. Tinker's dead. Spray of blood and stone. Madlin found that the cold was making her eyes water and her nose run.

Inside the workshop, it was a worse scene than when the flywheel had shattered. Everyone inside was either twinborn, armed with a rifle, or both. They picked their way among rubble and blood-flecked debris. Madlin had expected a relative calm inside, but the chaos was merely a smaller scale from the scene outside.

"Where's Orris?" she asked. If anyone would know what was going on, it would be him. Orris could also tell them what Kandrel was seeing in Korr. The *Jennai* was suddenly as much a concern as the Tinker's Island, if the explosion had carried through the world-holes.

Greuder elbowed his way through the milling crowd of gossiping twinborn more concerned with figuring out what happened than helping sort it out. "He's in a bad way. They took him up to Tucker's house to get him patched up, since it was the shortest walk."

"How bad?"

"Bad. More red than pink on him. A few pounds heavier for all the metal shards stuck in him. He needs Jamile, and needs her bad."

"What about the *Jennai's* machine. Can they open a hole to send her?"

Greuder shook his head. "Tucker mentioned it before he went off with Orris and the lot of them. Blast took out both machines. No one on the *Jennai* side was hurt because Erefan had gone through and left it unattended."

Madlin shuddered at the fresh reminder that she was short a father. Erefan had sired Rynn, not her, but those waters were muddy enough to walk across. The loss of a leg had left an ache in her beyond the physical wound. There was no way to build a mechanical Erefan to help Cadmus recover.

"What do you want us to do?"

Madlin blinked. Of course they were asking her. She was General Rynn. Cadmus was holed up in his bedroom performing trigonometry at a global scale, unavailable to consult.

Madlin took stock of the workshop. "Get this crowd out of here. The riflemen can stand guard outside and still be ready if there's an assault. Anyone with idle hands, shove a broom in them, give them a wheelbarrow, or get them the bloody furnace of Eziel out of my way."

Despite the grim circumstances, Greuder gave her a weak smile. "New curses?"

"We've got us a preacher of the war god. The true litany's got a bit more spice to it. Now get!"

Madlin waited as Greuder passed her orders along. She remembered when he first moved to Tinker's Island, a chubby, congenial old man with hands that turned dough and sugar into pure decadent pleasure. Cadmus had told her that he used to be a recruiter for the cause, his best agent for sniffing out twinborn and shipping them north. She could see a bit of that in him now, as she watched him wrangle the unruly crowd into obedience. Or it could have just been that years of running a popular bakery had given him a bit of heft in the community—upset the baker and you might be breaking your fast on runny eggs and toast.

When the crowd had thinned and those remaining were the ones who took up the task of clearing debris, Madlin stepped in to assess the damage. It was a task she wished some other tinker could look to. The fragments of steel, copper, brass, and poured-stone were mundane enough, hardly worth a second look. It was the other bits, the bone chips, the shreds of cloth, the red smears and flecks and splotches—some of it might have been Powlo; some of it was almost certainly Erefan. She looked past it as best as she could to the machine beneath it all.

Cadmus had tools everywhere. There was no place in any workshop on Tinker's Island where you could find yourself in need of a simple implement and not have one close at hand. Madlin took one of her father's tool belts and buckled it around the waist, two notches tighter than the well-worn holes her father used. She removed the panels that protected the inner workings, starting from behind the machine where the blast hadn't caught the world-ripper directly.

The insides of the control console were a shambles. Shrapnel had pierced the access panels on the operator's side, causing havoc to the innards. She'd always envisioned the wires as the veins and arteries of any spark-run device. Being twinborn meant never having the dreams that trouble the one-worlders, for which Madlin was glad. Otherwise her nightmares would have been plagued with severed copper wires bleeding red blood. Madlin angled her head so that she wasn't blocking her own light, the better to see how much of the wire would need to be replaced, and how many of the terminals were still intact. Caught up in her inspection, she leaned too close and felt a smear on her cheek as her face rubbed against the edge of a panel. She wiped it with the back of her hand, so used to getting grimy at her tinkering that she hardly gave a thought to a greasy piece of steel. When her hand came away red, she vomited.

Some tinker's instinct got her to turn her head before she lost her prior night's dinner and the acids from her stomach into the controls. Scrambling on hands and knees, she found a rag to clean herself up. The blood was more a worry than the vomit. The workshop was overpowered by the scent of burnt metal and poured-stone dust, but the smell of the blood clinging to her was threatening to turn her stomach out again.

Madlin climbed to her feet and turned her back to the world-ripper. She was done with it for a good long while. Blood could carry spark, so any repairs would have to include a thorough cleaning. It was pointless to get replacement parts covered in blood.

The workshop crowd had thinned down to those willing to stay and work. Workers swept up and carted out debris. They were steering clear of the world-ripper as Madlin checked it over. None of them were eager to break the Mad Tinker's already broken toy. Her eyes caught one, two, *four* mechanics puttering about the room at menial tasks, and summoned them each by name—she knew the name of every one of her father's mechanics.

"You lot, get that machine stripped naked, all panels open. Cut power from the dynamo. I want the insides washed out with clean water—no soap. Get rid of all the blood, the fragments, anything that doesn't belong in there. Any part that's damaged, if it's a spark wire or terminal, take it out and set it aside. If it's structural, make sure it's not going to fall apart or damage anything else and shore it up best you can.

"Any questions?"

"Ain't water bad for spark?" asked a mechanic named Alder.

Madlin shook her head. "Not once we let it dry. Recondensed water is best, but so long as you use pump water and not that Katamic shit, it'll dry fine."

If there was another question, it was swallowed in a hail of rotorifle fire. Madlin spun to see a world-hole open in far corner of the workshop, well clear of most of the wreckage. She'd heard of steam tanks, but never seen one with her own eyes. It was a crawling brick of steel and glass, dragging itself through the world hole on studded steel belts. If certain fascinating details of its construction escaped her, it was because Madlin's attention was drawn to the muzzle flashes of a rotogun spinning too fast for her to even take count of the barrels.

Rynn's instincts took over—no, Chipmunk's. The rebel army could call her what they liked, but it was Chipmunk who had been shot at. Madlin ducked behind the bulk of the control console and saw the cleaning crew torn to pieces. She squeezed her eyes shut to keep any more of the image from burning itself into her mind. There was a distinctive screeching rumble as the steam tank dragged itself into Tellurak, and she guessed that the second such sound wasn't an echo following behind it.

No shot had been fired in her direction. *They want the machine intact.* Well, intact might have been asking too much, but they didn't want to damage it any further. Madlin wasn't about to let that advantage pass without availing herself. There was a small cluster of offices at the side of the workshop, through a door and down a hallway, from when the world-ripper's workshop had been used as a warehouse. A workshop required little in the way of clerical support, but a warehouse needed shippers, accountants, freightmasters, and crew supervisors. Those functionaries had lost their offices in the conversion, but the rooms were still there.

Madlin ducked at the waist and ran, tool belt and holster flapping at her thighs. If she'd been armed with a coil gun, she might have stayed and slugged it out with a single steam tank, hoping to ventilate the crew before they got a bead on her with the rotoguns. With two, the odds of her getting turned into ground meat where she stood was nearly one hundred percent, even if she had a weapon to fight back with. She reached the door handle in seconds, but flinched at every burst of rotogun fire, expecting each to be capped off with a searing pain that never came. On the far side of the door, the hall was dark. She was willing to take the darkness over the invitation of an open door, but when she moved to close it, she saw that two of her mechanics had followed her.

"Come on. Move!" Madlin waved them through the door. No fools, they—the mechanics monkeyed after Madlin's bent-over run and slipped through the door behind her. With both through, she slammed the hall door behind her.

"Alder? Bakersfield?"

"They got got." It was as succinct an answer as she was likely to get. No detail, for which she was thankful.

The hallway ran parallel to the workshop wall. They heard the rotogun fire and shouts from the bass voices of kuduks, all muffled through the stone-block walls, but still too loud for comfort. "Last office on the south side," said Madlin, leading the way without waiting for confirmation. She hustled down the hall, dragging a hand along the left side wall, counting doors. The fourth door was the last; any farther and she would have hit the far wall.

The door opened with a faint click. There was no lock to worry over. A double-window, hung with lavender curtains, was the only thing inside. The desk, the files, the chair, all had been removed. She popped the catch and thrust the window open. She didn't bother to check on the mechanics. They made enough noise that there was no question of whether they'd kept up.

Outside the gunfire sounded distant. Madlin heard it by the echoes from the other buildings, from the mountainsides. Answering fire came in a discordant chorus of single shot rifles. There was no telling how well they'd hold out. Errol Company made the best arms Tellurak had ever seen, but Korrish military hardware was still a cut above. Cadmus had plans drawn up for rotoguns, steam tanks—even the twenty-crew behemoths—but nothing that had made it past vellum. The coil guns were so simple to build by comparison that all production had been diverted to those.

The workshop! Workshops abounded in Tinker's Island, but there was one that came to mind: the one where her coil guns were pieced together. Her first thought, and her first step, was to arm herself. But she stopped. *Father.* She couldn't rush off to play the hero, not until she'd seen that he was safe, or at least on his way to safety. In his current state of mind, there was no telling how he'd respond to the attack. He might slip into despair, he might decide to play general-from-out-front with a rifle in his hand and go out fighting. Madlin was hoping for something along the lines of slipping away quietly into the mountains.

"You two are with me."

The mechanics nodded and followed Madlin on her looping route to her house. There was a straight avenue from the Errol home to the world-ripper, but the population of airborne bullets in the area made it a bit too crowded for her tastes. She and her escorts slipped down side streets and alleys. The echoes of the gun battle caught her ears weirdly, coming from all directions, sounding at times like they were chasing the battle, at other times rightly that they were fleeing it.

The door to her house hadn't arrived soon enough for her liking, but they got to it intact.

"I want the two of you to get down to the docks. The *Treforge* is in port, and her deck guns ought to be able to handle a steam tank, if you can hit one."

"Miss Madlin, I ain't never fired one of them guns." His companion nodded agreement.

"Stop at Captain Tucker's on the way. If you can grab him, do it. If you can't, you smart fellas are going to do some quick learning."

Madlin sped them on their way and went inside.

In the foyer of the house, Cadmus stood with a scattergun in hand, jamming cartridges into the breech. Thankfully the Mad Tinker had the presence of mind to dress himself before heading off for his assault. "Madlin!" He gave a single laugh. "I got it figured out. Ten minutes from now, I'll have my foot on that daruu bastard's corpse. He's in the iron mines a little over a mile from here, except in Korr. Great minds, eh? Hah!" Cadmus snatched up a pile of papers covered in pencil scratches—equations, diagrams, coordinates.

"Father, what are you doing?" Madlin asked. "We're under attack. Great minds, my arse! You got out-mathed. They found us first."

Cadmus's face went slack, eyes gaping. "No. We can't be. He couldn't have guessed. He saw through our world-holes. Must have seen our dials. BLOODY BASTARD! I'LL KILL HIM."

"That's a nice thought, but they brought steam tanks, and we're getting pushed—"

"Is this a festival day?"

Madlin's head snapped toward the hall, where a bed-haired Dan was yawning as he walked toward them.

"Winds, you people make a racket. I was up late studying those—"

"Dan!" Madlin's trip to the workshop for half-assembled coil guns suddenly seemed a like a fool's errand. "We're under attack."

Dan stopped mid-stretch. "You'd better not be dangling apples over my head."

"We're. Under. Attack. Full scale assault from a Korrish force coming through their own world-hole. We're being overrun."

She wasn't sure what she expected. Dan had never shown cowardice, or shyness to fight. But the prospect seemed daunting. The rational part of her considered a soldier's response, a grim acceptance of duty with a clenched jaw and a nod. The worrier in her thought he might toy with her, let the daruu's force take the city and help them escape by the slimmest margin. His actual response sent a shiver through her.

His eyes widened and a little smile grew into a toothy grin. "Happy age-day to me." Dan strode past Madlin and snapped his fingers. The nightshirt he wore transformed, turning into a costume of black silk and matching leather boots, with a long cloak, draped in lacquered chain at the shoulders. She felt the aether swirl around her, rushing in the direction of the departing boy. Though there was no physical force, she found herself leaning against the current of it.

The doors to the Errol mansion were thick timber, bound in brightsteel. Madlin had to lean whenever she pushed them open. Dan threw them from the hinges and stepped through the gaping passage that they left.

Madlin and Cadmus looked to one another in the wake of Dan's departure. "You still want to run out there with a scattergun?"

With the doors burst open, the sounds of the battle carried clearly into the foyer. Cadmus looked down at the scattergun clenched in his hand. What thoughts ran through that mind of his—that twisted conglomeration of gears and levers, all powered on steam, not spark—Madlin was sure she couldn't imagine. It went on too long for her liking.

"Go down to the docks. I sent a couple mechanics to see about using the guns on the *Treforge*. It'd be nice to know someone there knew the workings, if they can't snag Tucker on their way."

Cadmus nodded, blinked a few times, shook his head, and nodded again. "Right. Of course." He set his pages of calculations down on a side table and jogged out the door.

Let him set his mind to a task—anything that kept him from realizing that Dan might be able to clear a path to the invading world-ripper and to Kezudkan beyond. In his current state, he was not fit for vengeance.

Madlin set off in the young warlock's wake. With some hope of fighting back, it was time to act the part of a general.

The exchange with Cadmus had taken mere moments. If Madlin had known how far she had fallen behind, she would have run.

The streets of Tinker's Island still cracked with gunfire. Rotoguns must have numbered in the dozens, and between bursts, the hum and scrape of the steam tanks could be heard plodding along, clearing out opposition. There was nothing shoddy about the construction of the local buildings. No wood or plaster walls stood readily shredded by bullets, but thick stone blocks, piled and mortared. The defenders took up positions in houses and shops, making miniature fortresses of them. They had been built against the harsh weather, but met their new challenge well.

Dan's path through the battlefield was easy to follow. Kuduk ground troops had joined the fight, packed up inside suits of steel-plated leather, with glass-faced helms, each with a filter canister protruding to either side of the mouth. Madlin got a good, close look at them, inside as well as out. The bodies lay scorched and torn in the middle of the road, leaking blood over the cobbles. The suits looked well guarded against bullets, but no bullet had felled any of the kuduks Madlin saw. She could imagine a fairy-story dragon had descended and taken umbrage with the invading force, such were the great gashes and burns covering their bodies.

From a block away, judging by the sound, she heard the thunderous crash and metallic clatter that could only have been one of the steam tanks running into misfortune. A tinkling of falling parts followed, then another great crash like the first. Madlin rounded the back corner of Joskin's Fine Jackets to see one of the steam tanks flipped like a turtle, studded belts drifting to a halt, with the driver's cabin smashed flat. Miraculously, someone was stirring inside.

Dan strode toward the wreck, showing confidence but no sign of hurry. He leaned to peer in through the glassless frame of the side window. "What are you rutting monsters made of?" he asked offhandedly. He stuck a hand into the opening and unleashed a gout of flame. A riot of gunfire answered as the ammunition overheated and fired wherever it lay within. Madlin ducked back around the corner until the bullets stopped. When she dared peek, Dan was already moving, keeping to the sides of buildings but showing no other precaution.

Madlin muttered to herself as she set off in pursuit. "I'm crazy. He needs my help like—" She cut off abruptly, not that anyone was around to listen. Up in one of the upper floor windows of a multi-apartment worker barracks, she saw a glass-masked kuduk taking aim at Dan with a tri-barrel rotogun.

The call of warning died in her throat. Madlin couldn't risk drawing the kuduk's attention. She drew her revolver and took careful aim through the site, lining up the kuduk in the crosshairs much as the kuduk looked to be sizing Dan up for a barrage. She put a bullet through the center of the mask, shattering the glass. The rotogunner fell out of sight away from the window. She had no time to waste. Dan was continuing away from her, not fast, but not stopping, either.

The boy warlock kept his path erratic. He turned down side streets and doubled back after clusters of troops, but always kept a general course toward the world-ripper. It took all Madlin's efforts to keep up with him without stumbling into an ambush. Twice more she fired on and struck kuduk soldiers too preoccupied with Dan to notice her in time.

Peering around the corner onto the main thoroughfare of Tinker's Island, she saw Dan standing off against two steam tanks and half a dozen soldiers on foot, bunched toward the rear of the steam tanks for cover. Dan shimmered in the air, and a moment later there were eight of him standing abreast across the road. Rotogun fire tore through the images, but from Madlin's vantage she could see where Dan had slipped across to cover on the far side of the street. Two kuduk soldiers unclipped twist-top canisters from their belts and lobbed them into the mass of illusory Dans. Yellowish smoke hissed from under the lids, and the gentle on-shore wind blew the noxious fumes up the road in Madlin's direction.

Though she could feel the tug of aether in her, she saw nothing to make sense of how Dan lifted one of the steam tanks off the ground and flung it into the other.

"Dan, the smoke!" Madlin shouted across the way. Stealth be gutted, she didn't want to chance outrunning the wind. She didn't have to. Seconds later, the wind reversed, and gusted with vigor back in the masked faces of the kuduks. By dint of Dan's twisted sense of humor, the masks of the soldiers shattered one by one. As the smoke poured over them like a bank of fog, they fell screaming and clutching at their faces.

"Thanks," Dan called over to her, grinning like a demon. "Great idea." Without pause for respite, the warlock ducked out from behind cover and swaggered down the street. Madlin's heart was hammering to get out of her chest, yet Dan looked like someone playing crashball against a team of younger children, relishing the chance to dish out a thumping with hardly an effort.

Kthooom.

Madlin was several blocks inland, but the deck guns of a steam ship still sent shockwaves through the air and ground, which hit her ears and feet a fraction of a second apart. At close range, the blast was even louder, another split of the same second later. She didn't see where it hit.

As they got closer to the world-ripper's workshop, Madlin heard human shouts, drawing her attention to warehouse roofs and the upper floor windows of the inns just inland of the harbor.

"General. We're holding out. What's going on down there?"

"We've got us a Veydran, and they don't." That summed it up as well as she could explain it. If Madlin had half an hour, she couldn't wrap the turn of the battle in prettier words.

Hired gunners show loyalty in precise proportion to the pay they get, and when that pay begins to look as if it's destined for their next of kin, the value of loyalty plummets. Soldiers fighting for their country might sometimes stay and fight until dead or captured because they believed in the cause, but by the sight of several abandoned steam tanks along the road, Madlin suspected Dan had reached the financial tolerance of this particular band.

Growing bolder as she found dropped rotorifles with no signs of an owner, more abandoned steam tanks, and a lack of kuduk bodies, Madlin picked up her pace. If only the road had been clear of human bodies as well, she might have found some cheer as she rushed after the warlock, but Dan had merely turned the battle, not undone its beginnings. She strode past red puddles and broken friends, faces she'd known since she was a little girl, turned grotesque.

However it ended, Madlin had to see it herself. Cadmus might have been pushed away as if docile while he emerged from his lethargy, but Madlin wasn't going to safe ground while Dan took her vengeance out from beneath her. If the daruu was to die by the boy's hands instead of one of her guns, she at least had to be there. If she could get her own bullets into him first, all the better. Madlin made it to the workshop and skidded to a halt, thumping shoulder-first into the door before twisting around to peer inside. Dan stood with a pile of the kuduks' gas canisters at his feet. As she watched, he lobbed one through the open portal, hissing smoke the whole way. From the entrance, Madlin felt a sucking wind at her back—not aether, but the breathable sort, carrying the scent of the Katamic into Korr along with Dan's toxic farewell. The warlock picked up another, gave it a twist, and heaved it through as well.

She could have kissed him. Not only had he driven the kuduks back, but he had chased them away from their world-ripper's controls. Madlin scanned the room, trying to ignore the human bodies while her eyes moved from corpse to kuduk corpse. There! She found what she was looking for: one of the fallen soldiers still wore an intact mask.

The stench inside the workshop was not so bad as when she'd left it. The Katamic breeze was stronger than the slow-wafting odors of the newly dead. Madlin kept her eyes from the charred hole through the kuduk torso as she unbuckled the mask and put it on her own head. It felt ludicrously large on her, though it fit easily over her spectacles, which was conducive to her plans. It smelled of stale kuduk breath, but luckily for her kuduks didn't sweat like humans. She strapped it as tight as it would go and breathed deep. The hissing echo of the filtered air had the ominous sound of steamworks with a leak, but she could fill her lungs through the filter and that was all that mattered.

"Keep throwing those," Madlin said, her voice reverberating in the enclosed space behind the mask. "Just don't hit me."

She saw the manic grin on Dan's face as he winked and nodded. "And don't blow the controls while I'm on the other side," she added.

Without further introspection or argument, Madlin rushed through the hole and into Kezudkan's lair. She searched the tables, the console, anyplace where there might have been notes. She grabbed every scrap, every bit of documentation she could find. She didn't know how long she had before someone might be brave enough to come back and look. Seconds? Minutes? When she'd taken all her hands could carry, she ducked back through.

"Blow it."

"I don't do this often, so watch close. This is *real* magic. *Halatu ... dunaxi ... tukaso ... xatagotagi ...*" Dan's hands twisted, forming incomprehensible shapes and patterns in the air as he continued his chant. Madlin noticed that his left hand was a bloody ruin, missing two fingers and a chunk of flesh. If it had any bearing on his conjuring, it didn't show.

As Dan finished his spell, the entire room beyond the world-hole caught fire. For an instant, she saw metal panels boiling before the machine failed and the hole closed.

Madlin tore the kuduk mask from her face. "Are you all right?"

Dan furrowed his brow a moment, before checking his hand. "Oh, this? Hurts like I stuck it in a hornets' nest. It'll be fine though. Fingers grow back."

Madlin stood there watching Dan, unable to form words to continue a conversation from that point.

The conjured garb faded back into a nightshirt and slippers. Dan yawned and finished the stretch he had started back in the Errol mansion's foyer. "It's still too bloody early to be up after a night in those books. Don't let anyone wake me unless it's a line of pretty girls come to congratulate me."

Madlin's feet were bolted to the poured-stone as she watched him go. *Rabid dog or perfect weapon? Where can I get a dozen more like him?*

Chapter 25

"War is like chess, except that in war, you can lose your king and keep fighting." –Rashan Solaran

"What was that hollow-eyed monster?" Kezudkan asked. He knocked aside a fragment of metal with his cane. It was an unrecognizable lump that had once been a part of his world-ripper machine. The piece was warped and the surface ran like candle drippings, freshly cooled.

"You're the expert on this other-world rat dung," Draksgollow replied, his voice echoing behind one of the glass masks. There were still lingering fumes in the air from the fogdeath canisters, and the kuduk tinker was taking no chances with his lungs. His steamworks hissed and ground as he bent to inspect the debris for himself. "Never seen nothing like this before. It'd take days to get a smelter up and running to the kind of temperatures to do this to steel."

"Undoubtedly," Kezudkan replied. "But not if you drew runes over them all."

"That little shit didn't cross through and rune this junk."

"Indeed not. I think we've seen unbound runes flying about." Kezudkan flicked a cracked and blackened bit of stone out of his way. It looked like part of the stool he'd fashioned for himself. "I think it's high time we made an investigation of the far world."

"What?" Draksgollow stood with a clatter of gears. "I think it's time we stopped this world-jumping nonsense entirely. Take what we want right here in Korr."

"It's amazing your people ever took over Korr. You lose a fight and you curl up like a beaten animal. They think they've won. We just need a way to deal with that young rune-thrower the humans found."

"You're off your rails."

"What's that? Speak up," Kezudkan said. He lifted his cane and held it close to the glass of Draksgollow's mask. How much effort would it take for those stony muscles to flick and smash the tip into the mask? The old daruu seemed unbothered by the remnants of toxin in the air, but daruu weren't kuduk. Draksgollow had read the pamphlets that came with the canisters they'd bought. It was all couched in military regulation-speak, but it told without softened words what would happen if anyone breathed it, kuduk or human. The only recommended treatment was sedation—a quiet moment of peace before death.

"What do you think we should do?"

Kezudkan smiled and lowered his cane. He walked over and looked at the frame of the former world-ripper. The bulbs around the outside rim had shattered in the heat, and the shape had drooped from circular to a valley between two hills. "We build another. We find a new hideaway. We find new allies."

"Allies? Where?"

"What does it matter where? We have gold, and gold puts loyalty in places it would never grow otherwise. If there are rune-throwers out there, we'll find some of our own. Even if we have to pay humans."

"Humans don't fight their own."

Kezudkan snorted. "Your kind wrote a bunch of nonsense into history a long time ago. I've seen my people's records. Before you stomped the fire from them, humans fought each other with a ferocity and a barbarism that your kind couldn't dream of. They fought over money, over land, over honor and respect and women. Us? We just need the ones who'll fight for money."

Draksgollow kept silent. He had no argument to refute Kezudkan's ancient history, and didn't know that it would even have been worth trying.

"How long before your workers at Machine Two decide to come looking for us?" Kezudkan asked.

"Can't say," Draksgollow replied. "They didn't have orders to come get us, so it could be a while. Then again, they're pulling about five hundred pounds of gold out of that Telluraki mine every day. Dunno if they're the kind who'd fight for money, but if they're the kind who might do nothing and hope to inherit it, we might be in for a long, long wait."

Waves broke against the docks of Tinker's Island. The off-shore wind carried the Katamic's brine with a low howl. The city was otherwise silent.

A hole opened, torn from the deck of the *Jennai*, where the repaired world-ripper was back in operation. Men poured through, armed with coil guns, and set up a defensive perimeter. Workers scurried out in their wake, entering warehouses and workshops, carrying through all that wasn't bolted down, then unbolting those that were, and carrying them off as well. After a few minutes of frantic activity, the workers and soldiers slipped back into Korr and the hole vanished.

The city was silent once more.

"I can't believe I didn't recognize him." A tall, slim figure in comfortable trousers and a loose brown tunic lounged on the rooftop of the Errol mansion.

"Come on, Brannis, it's been six years," said Juliana, sprawled out beside him, their heads just a handspan apart. "You couldn't expect to recognize a young man by the boy he was. They get taller, thinner in the face—"

"And turn into bloodthirsty madmen?" he finished for her. "Face it, Danilaesis turned into a young Rashan while we were absent. Maybe you should stick to calling me Kyrus while we're here. Brannis is dead; he would have stopped this."

"While *we* were absent? You mean Kyrus and Brannis, right? I never had any say with the boy. Besides, it's not like you knew how to get back to Veydrus." Juliana thumped a hand on one of the mysterious books. "Now that we do, maybe you can go back and set him straight. Knock him around a bit; he'd understand that sort of language."

"This is the world I get by standing idle," Kyrus swept his hand over the city. "Piles of dead men and women. Invaders from across the deep aether. A demon-hearted boy made a savior because he's better at savagery than the rest. The question is what could I have done that would have been any better?"

"You could have saved those people."

Kyrus glowered at her. "You were the one who first warned me of the easy trap of power. Tallax must have thought the same thing once: 'I can do better.' And look where it got everyone."

"Over six hundred years of peace."

"Oxen are at peace," Kyrus countered. "You've heard their stories, these Korrish twinborn. They'd just trade one master for another if I got involved."

Juliana reached over and ran a finger through a lock of Kyrus's hair. "You could do better. Maybe seeing the trap is enough."

Kyrus swatted her hand away. "Now you're just teasing me. I'll keep my promise and stay clear. Although ... if they start mucking about with Veydrus, I might see that others keep clear as well."

Juliana's grin was infectious. "I can imagine all sorts of unhappy demons if you do."

"Their problem."

Juliana stood, heedless of the thirty foot drop beside her on the tiled roof. "Come on, cheer up. We've got a whole city empty to play about in. Let's go see what they've left."

She stepped over the edge to plummet, absorbing the impact on the street below with no sign of difficulty. Kyrus winked out of existence and appeared beside her. "Let's."

Other Books by J.S. Morin

If you enjoyed Rebel Skyforce, why not go back to the beginning, and experience the journey of mundane scribe Kyrus Hinterdale who discovers what it means to be Twinborn—and the dangers of getting caught using magic in a world that thinks it exists only in childrens' stories.

The **Twinborn Trilogy** is available for sale on Amazon

War-Bringer
Prequel

Firehurler
Book 1

Aethersmith
Book 2

Sourcethief
Book 3

About the Author

Born in New Hampshire in 1977, J.S. Morin found himself captivated by the wonders of fantasy novels at a young age. He was introduced to the genre via the works of R.A. Salvatore, Ed Greenwood, and Margaret Weiss and Tracy Hickman. He loved exploring other people's worlds, from Shadowdale to Hyrule. He also quickly found Dungeons and Dragons to be a creative outlet for stories, characters, and new worlds of his own creation.

His other passion was for building and designing things, and when it came time to choose a career, he went down that road. A Mechanical Engineer by day, he spends his evenings with his wife in their New Hampshire home, enjoying the simplicity of life in a quiet state.

By night he dreams elaborate dreams of visiting fanciful worlds, performing acts of heroism, and solving intriguing puzzles, which inspire him to craft stories that he hopes will help shape the lives of the next generation of fantasy readers. He hopes to avoid finishing growing up.

17966971R00130

Made in the USA
Middletown, DE
17 February 2015